The Newspaper Man

David Belcher

into books

The Newspaper Man by David Belcher

First published in the United Kingdom in 2023 by
Into Books (an imprint of Into Creative)

ISBN 978-1-7385149-1-5

Cover design and typesetting by Stephen Cameron.

Typeset in Garamond.
Printed and bound in Europe.

For sales and distribution, please contact:
stephen@intocreative.co.uk

DEDICATION

For Janette, Lauren and Nathalie Belcher.

ACKNOWLEDGEMENTS

Special thanks: John Comerford.

Thanks: G. E. Armitage, Dorothy Bell, Robert Bell, Ruby Bell, Ruth Bell, Charles Boon, Mary Brennan, Captain Ian Bruce, Paul Buchanan, Sergio Casci, Francesca Casci, Wattie Cheung, Michael Harry Cole, Stuart Cosgrove, Don Coutts, James Grant, Roger Hart, Eddie Harrison, Keane, Kevin McCardle, Morag McIntosh, Sandy McLean, Neil McLeod, James McShane, Frank Miller, Gerald Rusgrove Mills, Keith Moore, PJ Moore, Frank Murphy, Patrick Nevin, Ross Noble, Anne-Janine Nugent, Kat Orr, Tom Rafferty, David Sheppard, Paul Smith, Alison Stroak, John Swadel, Sally Swadel, David Walsh. *E - in particolare!* - Paolo Zemauno.

Additional thanks: Stephen Cameron and Jan Kilmurry. They told me what I needed to hear, which wasn't what I wanted to hear, thus making me do the job properly.

Extra thanks to the eagle-eyed, empathic, enthusiastic editor: Paul Marsh.

Sing when you're writing: Sir Hugh Keevins, Kennyth MacDonald, Ewing Grahame/ Graham Hume.

RIP: Hélène Milligan Anderson, Doug Baillie, Ian Bruce, Ted McKenna, Joseph Ottolini, Robert Rainey, Eddie Rodger, Bill Sutherland.

Dedicated to Refuweegee - www.refuweegee.co.uk - because we're all fae somewhere, and to hell's antidote: Highwater House, 104 Westwick Street, Norwich (www.stmartinshousing.org.uk).

David Belcher

Giovedì/ Thursday
Chapter 1

"What's my job?" Tony Moscardini said when anyone asked. "Journalism, once upon a time. Thirty years. Print... I was a newspaperman. Had to give it up, though - I couldn't go outdoors... every time it rained, I fell apart."

As jokes go, it wasn't the funniest, but it let Tony use his favoured stand-up comedy voice. The hard-bitten 60-smokes-a-day Stateside growl of a seen-it-all late-night clubland jade.

The same kind of rasp you'd hear in old Hollywood gangster movies, some hard-nosed news hound barking "Hold the front page!" to trumpet reports of the latest Mob shoot-out in Capone's Chicago.

Which was the kind of newspaperman Tony had never been, in Scotland - a country that wasn't America but often wished it was. What kind of newspaperman? He'd written about the arts in Glasgow: A city that wasn't Hollywood or Chicago or New York, yet was convinced it could be, if only Glasgow's gangland bosses were as murderously ambitious as its artists.

Tony had left Scotland, but not for America. For the past two years he'd lived in Italy, the land of his ancestors, wherein he'd spent all his childhood summers, in a mountain backwater so small - population 7,435 - most Italians had never heard of it. A tiny town in a tourist-free corner of Tuscany: Castel di Colonia, in reality castle-free Colonia, its 1400-year-old fort long ago crumbled to nothing.

Here, he'd try out comedy routines addressing his complicity in the senseless slaughter of a million trees ("Innocent forests slain in my name") amid denials he'd ever used a typewriter - "It was a tripewriter - I typed tripe." It amused his best friends, bearded Ken Moody and bespectacled Ted Bartolomei, Glaswegian same as him.

The two 60-something retirees, each 10 years Tony's senior, enjoyed forming his pretend-crowd. For as all three of them agreed, everyday truth was better served by a little creative embellishment: craft with which to fashion art.

Indeed, hadn't they spent much of the preceding six months embellishing and crafting in truth's name, filming their own small and unlikely piece of cinematic art on the little town's narrow, twisting streets: making a movie in secret. An undercover movie that was only 10 minutes and 53 seconds long and wholly without dialogue, but a movie nevertheless, one which served to advance an odd kind of love story, complete with a beginning, a middle and an end.

Why the secrecy? Their film-making mission had been conducted covertly because the trio knew some of their small-town neighbours would grow resentful, voicing objections.

Colonia sceptics wondered aloud what those old Glasgow fools were playing at. Moody, Bartolomei, Moscardini - MBM Studios they'd been heard calling themselves. Self-imported and self-important. Self-styled big shots. Taking to the streets with cameras, taking over the town. Had they sought permission? Who did they think they were? How dare they use Colonia as a mere backdrop! How dare they!

Tony knew he was daring to risk more tangible perils on a

day such as today, a hot and sunny Italian Thursday morning in mid-July: he was embarking on a three-day return to Glasgow, settling up old Moscardini family affairs, signing legal papers. An extended Glasgow weekend - all of Friday, all of Saturday, plus Sunday morning. Big-city excitements. Big-city threats.

Tony was a fearful pessimist, so he envisioned the many dangers posed by a long weekend in the city of his birth. Historic failures. Former temptations. Faces you didn't want to see again. Distractions. Trip wires. Booby traps.

In a city where there was so much going on, Tony might slip into his old journalistic role as a passive spectator, letting events unfold… a Glasgow newspaperman likely to be caught out when the rain began.

His dank and chilly Glasgow past was ever likely to scuttle his summery Colonia present, thereby jeopardising his safe return for MBM Studios' motion picture premiere on Sunday night.

He would need to be on his guard. He must survive Glasgow's impositions and obligations - its diverting thrills - if he hoped to savour his film's first public screening in Colonia. For his film was more than simply a film, it was now an event that seemed certain to attract most of the town as an audience.

He'd written about film as a features writer for Scotland's grandest national broadsheet newspaper, *The Daily Chronicle*. All the arts: film and music, books, TV and theatre. Stand-up comedy, too, of course. And so as much as he loved jokes, he loved film quotes.

But his joy in quoting movie dialogue had soon made even Ken and Ted, fellow-cineastes, groan and roll their eyes. So he confined himself to jokes. Devising new ones that resembled old ones.

He'd seen so many mediocre jokers on stages, he knew that he could pass for one well enough to aerate heat-deadened Italian July afternoons. And if his two pals couldn't laugh with him, he'd always assure them, they could laugh at him.

"Who can object to a guy's generosity in trying to make his comrades laugh?" he'd once asked.

"Any comrade with functioning ears," Ken had said.

Ted - a former maths teacher once nicknamed *il Professore* but now addressed simply as Prof - might then wonder aloud whether Tony had finished being funny yet. To which Ken would shrug and inquire as to when did Tony ever start.

Lately, though, Ken had more often looked up from the communal laptop that he and Prof were staring into on Tony's kitchen table to say: "Shut up and get on with what we're supposed to be doing - making a gosh-darned movie."

****

Did Tony abandon journalism, or did journalism abandon him? He'd grown less sure during the two years he'd spent clear of the trade, free of Glasgow.

Maybe Tuscany's unpolluted mountain air aided the process of forgetting. Colonia: altitude 440 metres, tucked away in the hills 35 kilometres north of the nearest city, Lucca, a place less than a tenth the size of Glasgow.

"Ah, the relentless rural splendour of Italy's Apennine range," he remarked out loud at least once a week like some smarmy Florida time-share-holiday salesman. Ken and Prof shook their heads and tutted, but there was never any stopping him.

"Colonia! Narrow winding streets. Textbook Tuscany. Honey-coloured mediaeval stonework. Terracotta-tiled rooflines, clear blue skies. Sunshine… olive groves, vineyard terraces… walnuts… ancient chestnut trees at every crossroads.

"A window-box on every sill – lemon-scented geraniums.

Pure mountain air fragrant with acacia blossom, the idyllic aroma of *la bella Toscana* - it would fair sicken you, pal, so it would, so it would."

Glasgow comic vernacular delivered in a bogus American accent - never as funny as it thought it was. Which was ironic, he sometimes felt, given that unfunny people with genuine American accents had eased him out of newspapers, propelling him from Scotland.

Two years earlier, the *Chronicle's* US-based owners had decided that his segment of the commentariat was over-paid, over the hill, and over in some far-off Scottish place that didn't matter. He was officially old - 55 - and in the way of optimised shareholder dividends.

So he took what he enjoyed describing as *involuntary redundancy.* "I took the bucks and got to fuck. I arrived at the paper by bus aged 24… I figured I'd exit 41 years later in… well, if not a solid-gold Maserati, maybe a coffin with a go-faster stripe."

"Instead, I'm binned 10 years ahead of retirement age… handed barely enough change for a cab while some dweeb from Human Resources spouts corporate horseshit: 'It's not you that's redundant, Mr Moscardini, it's the job.' Aye, right, mate… slip a jobbie in my jacket pocket, tell me it's a Mars bar."

Ken and Prof had heard it all before. They sported dutiful half-smiles, eyebrows raised, humouring him. "Not that you're bitter," Ken always deadpanned.

Tony's bitterness was played for laughs, of course. Who could be bitter about sentencing himself to a warm, pretty place where lavender grew waist high and contented bees buzzed? If Glasgow had any bees, they'd be coughing and spitting phlegm, cursing and trampling the lavender into the dust, headbutting each other.

Who could complain about listening to well-adjusted Italian bees make honey? What kind of ingrate could tire of lavender's scent?

A Glaswegian ingrate like Tony. As hard as he tried to convince himself otherwise, he'd grown to feel life in Colonia was dull, no match for wintry Glasgow's all-action hustle and bustle. Nothing happened in Colonia, very slowly.

Italy offered stability, few surprises. Stable relationships with his two local film-making buddies. An anchored, grown-up romantic relationship with a level-headed local woman, a business-like businesswoman.

"Gabriella Sarti - Sarti Estate Agency... *Sarti Agenzia Immobiliare*," he sometimes muttered to himself, marvelling at the literal beauty of the Italian language. *Immobiliare:* real estate was immovable, rooted. Just like Gabriella.

How he'd wished for such a grounded, scare-free love in Glasgow, instead of his miserable failed marriage and a lurching series of fevered fixations upon unsuitable female targets.

One stupid man failing over and over again with a series of smarter women, he thought: such an agonised approximation of a love story. There was something to be said for being bored in Colonia after all.

And at least he didn't have to work every day. "Freed from the cruel and malicious indignity of full-time employment, liberated from wage-slavery's yoke," he liked announcing, movie-trailer style. Whenever he did, Ken would tell him to stop saying how free he felt, and just concentrate on feeling free to help make their film.

If he had any real bitterness or anger about his newspaper career's conclusion, it concerned those bright-eyed young hopefuls who had planned to follow in his ink-smudged footsteps. One sunny morning early in his new Italian life, he'd begun working up some fresh piece of stand-up about the old business's expiry, pacing back and forth in his hall, setting up a performing rhythm, declaiming aloud.

"When I see young latter-day dead-tree jockeys consigned

to extinction beside the sievewright... the costermonger... the arrowsmith, the haberdasher and indeed the dodo, I am... I..."

It had caught in his throat. Stopped him pacing. He'd run out of comedy, his eyes tearing with rage and sorrow.

A new generation of journalists denied the chance to do what he'd done... earn a comfortable living by not working too hard, all in the name of informing, alerting and entertaining 100,000 Scottish newspaper-buyers six days a week.

He'd taken a deep breath and stared at his reflection in his shadowy hallway's full-length mirror: jowled, shaven-headed to mask his baldness, mottled, crepe-skinned at the neck, bulging at the waist. He saw himself for what he'd been: a vulture, culpable in the death of the daily newspaper.

He'd drunk deep at the well of journalistic plenty, helped drain it. Sure, he'd only sipped tea while his fellows glugged beer and whisky, but with the same result: drought, oblivion.

He knew there was nothing he could have done to prevent the industry's financial collapse - one man alone in a blizzard of shredded profit forecasts - but he still felt guilt at having spent three decades sleepwalking through the last days of its golden age.

Lazy, semi-educated guys like him had had the best of it without noticing. An era when your average effort-averse journalist was well enough paid to buy a decent house, and in his case, fill it with music and books - largely obtained gratis.

Free stuff: almost reason enough to become a journalist. Review-copy novels and albums: TC Boyle, Kem Nunn, James Lee Burke, Seth Morgan, James Crumley; Pixies, Sonic Youth, the Blue Nile, REM, Cardiacs, the Cramps, Trashcan Sinatras, Suicide, Primal Scream, the Pastels... the Smiths when Morrissey's songs were sensitive hymns to otherness.

He had a gag about Morrissey's reactionary decline, of course.

Ken and Prof droned it in lifeless unison at any mention of the Smiths: "The sweet youth who mined camp becomes a bitter old troll channelling *Mein Kampf.*"

It was this kind of sharp-seeming stuff that he had toiled to get into the *Chronicle's* pages, most often failing to smuggle anything the tiniest bit outrageous-looking past the paper's sub-editors. Under their forbidding stewardship, the paper presented as an elderly Presbyterian lay-preacher who had heard of the Beatles and disapproved of their gimmicky adolescent noise-making, finding solace in knowing it couldn't last.

The *Chronicle's* focus was on the immutables of grown-up Glasgow life. Dreary lists, turgid numbers. Stocks and shares, suburban semi-detached house prices, scores from golf clubs where the semi-detached swung their mashie-niblicks and spoke of how their annuity was faring.

Young Tony had seen the *Chronicle* as a vessel of journalistic laziness, complacency and tiny-minded self-satisfaction, making it his purpose to torture the paper with his wild crusading enthusiasms. To flay mainstream taste and jolt its staid, out-of-touch columns with peculiar coinages and arresting turns of phrase.

"And if you didn't like those, my most deeply-held journalistic ideals, then I had others," he would tell his two-man Colonia audience in a pay-off stolen from Groucho Marx. He'd had one or two governing journalistic principles in his time at the *Chronicle.* The basics: who, when, where.

But he'd been keener to make life hard for himself, forever trying to snare the why-oh-why of it all, aware his attempts to divine the meaning of human existence were doomed to fail.

Because he'd never decided in advance what a story was. He'd never teased quotes into shape, massaged facts to fit some sensational pre-ordained yarn.

His working life would have been so much easier if he had. In his view, the story was what the story turned out to be, having spoken to each reliable witness, as many informed parties as he could find.

Simplify and exaggerate? Never one of his newspaper principles. His all-time favourite journalistic rule was both simpler and much more complicated: start every day by asking yourself what do *we* know that *they* don't want us to know?

****

It was a simple journalistic equation, but one that entailed so much work. Devising the right questions to trigger the right answers. Cultivating the right sources. Drinking productively in the right pubs.

So he gave in after three decades of fitful endeavour and took what the *Chronicle's* overseers had offered for his early exit, embracing a change of direction, a different location, a slower pace: the little settlement in which he'd never truly lived, despite having spent all his youthful summers there.

He had pitched up in Colonia not knowing anyone, the Moscardini line being extinct. A few second cousins he could nod at, the odd Casci or Palumbo. But in the same way as his recreational inner life of old film scenes and comedy routines, Colonia provided comfort in familiarity.

That was not how the town had been during his childhood, though. Back then he'd been scared by the ancient settlement's age. By night, its centuries lived on in the walls of its buildings. Ghosts to torment a small boy's bedtime.

Yet he'd still retreated there from present-day, big-time Glasgow, fleeing the city, although he tried not to admit such a thing. What was he escaping?

The consequences of Thursday, September 18, 2014, although

he'd never admit that, either. Scotland's independence referendum, the vote to reject self-government, had happened two years before his departure from the *Chronicle*.

He had never been a deep political thinker, but he did view himself as a rational Scot, not the fevered 90-minute football supporter type. So he found the referendum decision shameful, uninformed, craven. Immoral. Wrong.

What kind of feeble, backwards-looking land chooses to remain in thrall to its far-away ruling neighbour?

A self-certified weak-kneed Scotland was no home for a Moscardini. He'd always had an Italian passport, courtesy of his grandparents and the principle of *jure sanguinis:* Italian citizenship through right of blood. He would go.

His views hardened the day after the referendum when he fell into conversation with the *Chronicle's* two football reporters, Brendan Gallagher and Jim Powrie, amenable-seeming men who had roamed the world covering the Scotland national team as well as reporting on Glasgow's so-called Old Firm.

One lot draped in Union Jack red-white-and-blue, bellowing their pride at being British. Their green-shirted opponents proclaiming themselves Irish. Both based in Scotland, denying they were Scottish.

Such self-loathing. Tragic. Inexplicable. And now this latest act of self-obliteration - Scotland votes no.

Gallagher and Powrie, he was sure - funny guys who'd made careers as overseas Scottish witness-bearers - must both be saddened by their country having gone to the polls to snatch electoral defeat from the jaws of constitutional victory: the same suicidal process they'd lamented in print so many times whenever the Scotland football team did it.

"Delighted to stay British, sick of hearing about independence," Powrie had said, staring into his desktop monitor. Dogged. Grim.

Cold. Tight-lipped. Angry. Unwilling to engage.

Tony was sure he must have been joking. He'd turned to Gallagher. "But anybody who's Scottish…" he began.

"I'm not Scottish - I'm Irish," Gallagher said, spitting the words. "Where my grandparents came from - Ireland. Scotland under the SNP is all shouting… strident. It's a cult. A one-party state. Unhealthy. Nationalists. No dissent tolerated. I'm getting an Irish passport."

Neither man was joking. Tony knew the pair's basic trade was in unsubstantiated rumour - which football player was or wasn't going to whichever club, which player's broken leg/ strained groin/ depleted confidence might recover most quickly - but he was still surprised and depressed by their lack of insight, their willingness not to think.

He'd been shocked by their lack of belief in Scotland. Scared by it. Saddened by their rage.

"But Ireland's independent," he had said in a soft, reasonable tone, "so if you say you're Irish, why wouldn't you want the same for Scotland?"

Gallagher swivelled from his keyboard, stabbing a finger at Tony, his face reddening. "What's Scotland got to keep it going… to keep this dump afloat?" he said. "Industry? Resources? There's nothing.

"It's all about money - you'll be complaining when there is none… when you can't blame England for everything." In the background, Powrie the Brit mumbled in support of Gallagher the Celt.

Tony fought back. "Scotland's got resources," he said. "It contributes more than it takes out - it's got water…"

"Aye, that'll make up for Scotland's oil running out," sneered Powrie.

"Hydro-electric power," Tony said. "Sustainable energy… wave-power, wind-power…"

"Plenty of wind-power at Holyrood," Gallagher sneered.

Tony ignored him. "Seafood - exports worth millions," he continued. "Shellfish that restaurants in France and Spain go mad for, the best in the world... tweed, whisky, tourism, our universities - Scots themselves... the people. Clever folk - *us*."

Powrie and Gallagher snorted in loud disdain. United. The Old Firm.

"Nobody gave Ireland independence," Tony pressed on. "You complain about Scottish nationalists shouting. Ireland did more than shout - they started a war, armed struggle on the streets, an uprising... guns, shooting at the British army - killing soldiers, getting shot.

"Not a good look in 1916, treacherous Irish nationalists stabbing Great Britain in the back while it fights a world war. And they carried on fighting for independence for years, even when this other terror starts up... a global pandemic, the Spanish flu."

Gallagher scowled. It was plain he couldn't think what to say. He battered his keyboard harder, more words about some twinkle-toed hod-carrier's strained calves.

Neither he nor Powrie had an answer. So Tony had chosen to walk away from folk like them, a Scotland filled with self-hating Scots. A dependent Scotland was a dying Scotland.

This was not, of course, the answer he gave when people asked him why he'd set up home in Italy. Accord himself the status of a political exile? Over-dramatic. Plus it might make it look like he'd abandoned Scotland in its hour of need. He knew he hadn't.

So if anybody asked him, he'd put an extra glum look on his face and say he left Glasgow to elude some of his past choices in life, along with his own worst present-day elements: "My overwhelming optimism, my relentlessly sunny disposition." Sometimes he got the laugh he'd been seeking.

Chapter 2

His relocation to Colonia didn't mean Glasgow was ever very far away, though. For whereas many Italian towns and villages were emptying and dying, Colonia was kept alive by droves of Caledonian incomers. It was a bona fide phenomenon, with each new media report prompting Tony to vent disgust.

Because it had inspired a phrase that appeared in every single British newspaper travel profile: Colonia was Italy's most Scottish town.

"Italy's most Scottish town, my arse!" he always bellowed. "Lazy cliché-ridden newspaper travel writer bastards!" Whenever he began denouncing newspaper travel pieces about Colonia, Ken and Prof knew the trio's work was finished for the day.

They'd close Ken's laptop and sit back arms folded, watching Tony's face turn red, awaiting entertainment.

"OK, in numbers, Colonia *is* Italy's most Scottish town," he'd shout. "But that's not all it is - lazy bloody modern-day fucking journalists in lazy bloody modern-day fucking newspapers never get anything right about anywhere."

"So you keep telling us," Ken would say, which led Prof to add how much they enjoyed seeing Tony get so worked up about fucking lazy bloody fucking modern-day journalists in lazy fucking bloody modern-day fucking newspapers, although they did both fear for his coronary health when he did it.

Then the two of them would grin at him. A calm and agreeable duo. Good friends to a man as intense and downbeat as Tony knew he sometimes could be.

If he was going to mount a familiar hobby horse, at least he knew that Ken and Prof would both have their hands on its reins, ensuring he didn't ride it in circles for hours, or off a cliff.

Their kindly concern half-explained why the two of them had got together with him to become film-makers. Although when it came to knowing why the three of them were making a film, none of them was absolutely certain.

Tony tried not to think about life's why's anymore. Plain facts were enough. Facts about Colonia? The facts that made it remarkable?

As scores of small Italian towns withered and shrank, Colonia's increasing tally of Italo-Scots kept it growing. Newcomers drawn by old family ties. At least 50% of Colonia's inhabitants were Scottish by birth, descent or marriage, from Glasgow and its surrounds.

His own relocation had been facilitated by his pension and a cash lump sum sufficient to fund a fresh start by providing him with a reliable German car (Mercedes) and efficient German photographic equipment (Leica).

A camera, not a laptop?

Si, si, si. Because in the very moment his old career died, he determined that an uncaring world would pay a price for his abrupt ejection from daily newspaper writing.

Because while he might not understand himself entirely, he knew enough to know he was a life member of the Contraryite Tendency. He would show folk what they were missing - by not giving it to them.

On the day his post-*Chronicle* life began, he took an oath of *omertà* - a silent vow which he couldn't help but tell everyone all about, of course: he would never write again.

He had called upon the world - Ken and Prof - to witness his proud and public secret pledge never to type another fucking word, form a sodding written sentence, put pen to bastard paper, kill another cunting tree.

"In addition to hanging up my tripewriter, I have blunted my nib and pissed in my inkwell," he'd said. "My copybook will remain unblotted. And no, I won't give you that in writing."

His two chums, not having known him long at this stage, had nodded in vague agreement, as though pacifying an eccentric old relative who'd announced they were giving up gardening for heroin. He could imagine a different reaction from his former *Chronicle* colleagues: "Moscardini's given up writing? Too bad he didn't stop 30 years sooner!"

Tony and his fellow scribes: no love lost there. The antipathy had been mutual. He'd been aloof, a snob, superior, haughty - his newsroom detractors had deserved it, hadn't they?

They hadn't, but he justified his dismissiveness each time he recollected having once overheard his writing's merits judged by workmates - two old *Chronicle* newsdesk eejits, in his opinion. Eejits: an uncharitable term. He liked to think that he'd grown less ready to spot the difference, more willing to embrace his fellow man's shared humanity. But back then folk who weren't lucky enough to be Tony Moscardini had been eejits.

Especially never-was *Chronicle* eejits who wouldn't know a well-turned sentence if one reared up and bit them on the bahookey.

He'd overheard the pair one Friday morning, after the publication of his weekly album review column. As ever, he had tried to frame each 90-word summary with memorable concision, deploying what he hoped was inventive wit. But no.

"Written in riddles - he always has to try and be funny," he'd heard one begrudger sneer to the other. If only he'd made more effort to hide the effort he took to make his stuff look effortless. So there would be no more writing bylined Tony Moscardini.

There was of course another reason why he chose not to write, the real reason. It was because in his long experience, writing that wasn't driven by deadlines and guided by word-count and that didn't take concrete printed form could be injurious to its author's mental health.

A 400-word book review by next Tuesday. A gig review, 240 words max inside the next 40 minutes. That kind of writing was useful, do-able.

Writing without time constraint and any definite prospect of being read by anyone else? That malarkey would lead the author into lonely reflection, unhealthy introspection, disturbing self-analysis.

For at one stage, when he was at his most love-lorn and troubled, post-divorce, he'd sat down and tried to compose some kind of journal that would make sense of his life.

The end-product? Maudlin free-form poetry and maundering autobiographical self-pity. Writing as a plotless act of self-harm: he didn't need to do any more of that, thank you very much. He might manage a shopping list, but nothing more.

****

He had chosen to become a photographer in Italy, using the craftsman's traditional tools of hand and eye, because he was convinced it was a practice that was closer to doing and acting, rather than writing about actors who did, the stuff of journalism. He chose to live in the moment, not to look back, rarely looking too far ahead.

Every photograph was there in front of you, if only you saw it.

You didn't have to dress it up on a page in words. Look at it. See it. Frame it. Capture it. Try not to let your hand shake as you do it.

He photographed Colonia's irregular ancient streets, a pleasing architectural patchwork evolving by accident over centuries, in accord with human need, free of pre-planned interference.

Narrow stone-paved thoroughfares where 400-year-old houses leaned on each other as if returning from a night of drunken revelry, a study in harmony between pale yellow granite and earthen-shaded plasterwork - umber, ochre, terracotta, russet.

But this close proximity - shoulder to shoulder, cheek by jowl - likewise fostered in Colonia's inhabitants the neighbourly arts of eavesdropping and malicious gossip. He wasn't blind to the mediaeval town's shortcomings.

You just had to look at his other photographs, his record of mediaeval Colonia's mediaeval-looking old folk, altogether less picturesque. Their lined faces bespoke decades of neighbourly wisdom, affection and patience alongside equal measures of small-town distrust, bitterness, accumulated enmity and suspicion.

For small towns breed pettiness, incubate resentment. Colonia had its begrudgers, too, he knew, having encountered a variety of objectors, obstructionists and outright chancers during the course of his photographic endeavours ("Any fee for my front door being in these photos of yours?").

More happily, his photographs had soon created their own online market. They sold - and sold well, at wondrous prices he always found staggering - in the form of handsome big prints via a gallery in Glasgow.

Which meant that his few writing chores were done in moments. Raising invoices, addressing envelopes, titling photographs.

Old Colonia Couple. Il Duomo by Moonlight. Piazzale de Torre. Porta Antica. Porta Reale. A photo of a milky-eyed old Coloniesi and his battered Piaggio Vespa: *Original Scooter Boy*. He hoped the locals might one day refer to him by his new title - *il fotografo artigianale* - the artisan photographer.

But that would be way too middle-class, as well as way too Italian. Which is to say that semi-Scottish Colonia's less-than-wholly-Italian attitude had the right measure of non-deferential working-class Glaswegian to it.

Few residents were dazzled by professional status. The pawky outwitted the grand. He had thus grown accustomed to being described as "The boy that used to be with the *Chronicle*" and "That guy from the papers who takes photos now."

He took a perverse comfort from the fact that he'd never heard anyone in Colonia call him by his old trade, *il giornalista*.

His great-grandfather, Giovanni Moscardini, had taken a distinguished- sounding job - *commesso viaggiatore* - when he'd arrived in Glasgow in 1883. A door-to-door salesman.

Along with four of his seven brothers, Gio' became a pedlar, little more than a beggar, before eventually working his way up to a grander-sounding position: *proprietario del negozio di pesce e patate* - the owner of a fish and chip shop.

For whereas educated Lucca had nourished the world with the gift of opera courtesy of Giacomo Puccini, its most famous son, neighbouring Colonia's nameless offspring sustained the West of Scotland with deep-fried fast food. Haddock. Chips. Scotch pies. Gammon with a slice of pineapple on top. Pizza, too.

And yes, with great reluctance - and only if you're visiting the chip shop as a know-nothing tourist and you insist, having read all the online reviews posted by all the other know-nothing tourists, the gullible fools, and despite the mess it makes of the fryer - the occasional deep-fried Mars bar.

At least deep-fried Mars bars only pose a risk to the health of the folk eating them, and not that of their vendor. For Gio' got into food as soon as he realised his first Scottish job posed a unique workplace hazard.

Pity the *commesso viaggiatore* selling door-to-door in certain tenemental areas of Glasgow, as Gio' did, pitching up speaking sing-song English that was suspiciously Latin-sounding, selling plaster casts of Catholic saints.

He'd find himself liable to swift and angry readings from the unforgiving Protestant Gospel of St Phuxache You Papist Bastard, accompanied by the instant laying-on of fists.

If you can't beat an angry Scottish mob on your own, his great-grandfather had worked out, join your fellow aliens in seducing them. Work out what their appetites are. Satisfy their basic needs. Food.

He'd first joined some of his fellow Italian incomers, selling ice cream from a cart. Sweet-tasting gelato often in frivolous shades of pink and green. Outlandish-looking self-indulgent luxury food that earned denunciation from Presbyterian pulpits for leading its Glaswegian devotees along the primrose path to hell, away from the kind of decent stodge-grey, gruel-brown fare that it was a punishment to eat.

And so was founded one generation of Italo-Scots entrepreneurs after another. Gio' and his ilk were so successful in their cafe businesses that they reversed the course of international trade.

Italy had spent a century exporting its poor. From the 1960s onwards, their well-to-do descendants self-imported back from Scotland. *Il Rimpatriati*, the repatriated, they called themselves. Tony opted to annoy them with a different title: the *fishandchipocraci*.

Worse still, some life-long Coloniesi were less welcoming, referring to the incomers - behind their backs - as *oriundi*: immigrants, of Italian origin but somehow lesser, forever foreign.

The *oriundis'* forefathers had turned their backs on their homeland in time of national woe, thrived for a time in foreign soil and had plainly now been found out. Why else would they return?

They should be slinking back, grateful that Colonia still chose to give them houseroom, but no: here they were, strutting with a superior air, flaunting their ill-deserved gains, their big new un-Italian homes. There was much muttering about "exiles who think they're at home here straight away, instant overnight locals... *one of us* - no way!"

He couldn't help training his satirical wit on the issue, of course, enraging some of his fellow Scots-Italian returnees by calling them economic migrants, asylum-seekers, refugees from Glasgow... *RefuWeegees*! How his intemperate father, Guido Moscardini, would have hated the term.

Because Guido's annual summertime visit to his ancestral homeland was less a family holiday, more an opportunity for him to parade about, gesticulating and shouting in a brand of Italian that he was unaware betrayed a vaudeville comedy Glaswegian twang.

He thought he was displaying his status as a buccaneering business mogul, an all-conquering global magnate of the deep-fat-fryer, renowned from one end of Maryhill Road to the other, dazzling Colonia's stay-at-homes, "the frightened stick-in-the-mud old fossils."

For their part, Colonia's old-timers looked Guido over, shrugged and assured themselves that there was something to be said for being an obdurate Italian fossil, as opposed to a preening buffoon who had built his life on hot fat and cold Glasgow rain.

In truth, there was something flinty about Colonia's life-long natives; they seemed almost as impervious to change as the rocky outcrop upon which their town was founded.

Change was a nuisance. It was to be denied, ignored, resisted, accommodated slowly at best. If possible, change should be circumvented altogether.

Chapter 3

It was easy to accuse Colonia of living in the past - not that it was a charge Tony brought. After all, he'd failed for most of his working life to live in the moment himself.

Why? He reckoned it owed something to his strongest recollection of his annual six-week-long Italian childhood summers in his grandfather's increasingly ramshackle farmhouse. The painful ritual of the unlearnt history lesson.

Each visit had begun with his father lecturing him about some long-gone aspect of backwards wee Colonia, keen that his lad should know the place's history and accept that Glasgow was better, an escape route.

The sombre rite inevitably ended with a question that his boyhood self could never answer. The town's very name became a recurring test.

"It's Castel di Colonia - *Castel*," his father said in a monotone, his annoyance on a low simmer, like the fat in his chip-shop frier. He had reverted to what he was in Glasgow, an undemonstrative anti-Italian, no arm-waving theatrics.

And what happened to the castle? Guido demanded to know. If Tony was lucky, his mother might appear from the kitchen and rescue him with a gentle prompt. "The old castle fell into disuse so long ago, no one knows where it stood," she'd say. "The local people took the old granite stones and re-used them in the walls of every building in Colonia."

"So that old, old castle is still around us today, its past lives in the fabric of every house, in their very walls." And in trying to help him, she managed to frighten him. Ghosts in the walls!

On one occasion, she went further, daring to chide her husband. "Don't be so hard on the boy, Guido, he is sensitive," she said. But only once.

And on the sole occasion of his mother's attempt at protection, unforgivable Guido noticed Tony's reddened face and quivering lips, and called him a little burst-balloon boy, a cry-baby, adopting an effeminate high-pitched fluting voice to mock his wife and his son: "Tony is so sen-si-tiii-ive!"

Humiliated and speechless, Tony had fled to the darkening bedroom at the top of his great-great-grandfather's old, semi-abandoned farmhouse, which only ever saw summertime occupancy as a patched-up holiday home.

There, menaced on the brink of sleep by the room's looming shadows, he would be overtaken by a range of supernatural childhood terrors.

For in this ramshackle house of dust and collapse, its water supply erratic and a tree rooted in the larder, growing through the kitchen roof, a frightened little boy pondered his father's rage and his mother's words about the house's crumbling walls.

The ancient masonry was surely haunted by the castle's long-dead occupants: spectral robber barons protecting fortunes amassed by fear, skeleton monks shaded in sinister cowls, the dungeon-bound ghosts of vanquished mediaeval knights tortured in clanking chains for all eternity.

His seven-year-old self had been much less alarmed by a large hole in the bedroom floor, through which he could peer from his bed all the way down to the farmhouse's front door. In later life, he'd marvelled at how a man as unimaginative as his father and as ineffectual and downtrodden as his mother had between them conjured up the stuff of nightmares so effectively.

His parents had both been dead for 30 years. He owed them his ability to blank out background noise - his father's ceaseless ranting (at his mother, at him, at the world) and his mother's passive bleats - and submerge in his own thoughts.

For his mother, cowed by his father's roaring presence, he felt pity. Towards his father, whose visits to Colonia were intended to underline how much better life was in sun-starved and lavender-free Maryhill, he felt anger.

He hoped his own quieter, more considered presence in Colonia constituted amends for the crimes of his father's odd one-man Scots-Italian War of Disunification. Guido's boastfulness. His casual Italophobia. The sneers and condescension.

He inhaled a deep breath of today's fresh Colonia air. What was the worst thing that locals might say about him when he was dead? That he'd always had to try and be funny.

But they'd surely allow that every so often he succeeded.

****

His flat adjoined one of Colonia's surviving gateway forts, the Porta Reale. He'd slept well, long having outgrown menacing childhood dreams inspired by half-millennia-old chunks of the town's dismantled castle.

He sat at his kitchen table and sipped a morning coffee, staring out of the window, idly focusing on the unchanging and far-distant Alpi Apuane, registering green forests of chestnut, oak, walnut, grape vines.

Stepped terraces of olive groves rose from the rich rust-coloured soil of the mountain range's foothills, cut and tilled by hands centuries dead and planted for all eternity in the same red-brown earth of Colonia's cemetery.

Such a panoramic testimony to permanence contrasted with the anonymous bungalows which had latterly laid siege to those sections of wall still girdling Colonia's historic town centre, the *centro storico*. Every retired Scottish chip-shop proprietor had imported his ideal dwelling with him, imposing Glasgow's suburban deadzones on the Tuscan landscape.

Not Tony. Scotland was behind him. A windowbox was all the garden he needed. He didn't seek isolation. He'd always relished the throb and babble of inner-city tenement life, its ready amiability and occasional thrilling conflict, scores settled via Glasgow's traditional duel: the late-night stairhead rambunction.

His old-town Italian abode was one of the six flats in a three-storey block, erected by coincidence around the same time his great-grandfather had left for Scotland. His attic apartment was part of a short terrace that began at the old town walls, lining about a third of Via di Mezzo's length, the widest thoroughfare in Colonia's close-clustered old town centre.

The online estate agency had described his attic flat - in the fanciful estate agent manner - as "a residence of Art Nouveau intent." Despite being no expert, he was sure there was nothing intentionally Art Nouveau about his building.

Perhaps each flat's curved wrought-iron street-front balcony hinted at it. Maybe there was a touch of sensuous Art Nouveau swirl to the curlicues engraved in the opaque glass panels of the heavy old wooden doors at the building's main entrance.

But there was no artistic subtlety in the building's stained pale lemon stucco exterior or its heavy Alpine window shutters. Nor in the brown wood-panelling that engloomed the building's common areas, its entrance hall, landings, stairs.

There was certainly nothing at all Art Nouveau about his aged neighbours, a collection of stooped and arthritic gnomes far removed from the willowy, rich-hued sirens depicted by the only Art Nouveau artists he could think of: Alphonse Mucha, Klimt, Aubrey Beardsley.

He nevertheless liked to think that in one regard the estate agency had rightly played up his flat's tenuous link to Art Nouveau decadence. First-time visitors were always startled when he invited them to "sample the wanton flamboyance of my Art Nouveau Oscar Wilde memorial *en suite* lavvy with unique non-modesty protector.

"What do you make of this funny-looking partition dividing the bathroom in two, straight down the middle, waist-high - no privacy guaranteed."

It was indeed an unusual feature, around 1.5m in height, separating the side of the bathroom housing the lavatory from the other, containing a sink, bathtub and shower.

Less alarmingly, the front of his flat overlooked a small gravel-surfaced car park, empty but for the occasional (non-Scottish) tourist. Sure, like every other hilltop settlement in Tuscany, the town's old centre had an imposing *duomo*, a cathedral, along with scenic views, but as Tony knew, no one ever holidayed there unless forced by the bonds of family.

Beyond that, his living room window overlooked the not-especially busy road that skirted Colonia's centre and led to the next town of any size, Barga, eight kilometres distant.

Across the road stood a grey three-storey concrete block of governmental buildings, an unlovely structure erected in the nineteen-twenties to house Mussolini's improving armies of administrators and clerks, along with his less-benevolent National Fascist Party informants and enforcers.

Latterly, the building sheltered every office of municipal regulation. Tax collectors. Social service providers. The Italian postal service's mail-delivery vans, plus telephone engineers, roadmenders, workmen who tended underground water pipes and electrical pylons, each essential overseer of civilised everyday life.

The structure couldn't help looking ugly, but as he reminded himself: don't look *at it*, look *beyond it* to the full Alpine splendour of the *Apuane*, a vista unavailable in Glasgow. The windows at his house's rear afforded views of other far-distant blue-green Apennine hillsides.

Closer, seemingly within touching distance, sprawled the orange-red terracotta-tiled roofs of his nearest neighbours' properties, a centuries-old kaleidoscope of angles and sweeping organic curves that seemed to hypnotise print-buyers in Scotland whenever he photographed it.

The ancient tiles formed a work of art compared to Glasgow's grim steel-grey Victorian roof-slates. They looked beautiful, kept out Colonia's infrequent wintertime rain and rarely blew loose in its minor gales. To those who already have everything, he sometimes lamented, God gives more.

His Colonia flat still delighted him two years on, and not only because he'd bought it for half the amount raised by his Partick single-end, at half the size and minus all *la dolce vita Toscana's* natural benefits (sunshine 300 days a year, clean sweet-scented air, recognisable seasons).

A long, wide-windowed hallway led into a large living room with a fully-functioning fireplace to dispel the occasional light winter evening chill. A well-planned new kitchen completed this wing of the house, which was easy to keep clean - especially as he limited his chef's repertoire to dishes capable of being cooked with a minimum of worktop spatter: minestrone, mince'n'tatties, lamb chops'n'mash with cavolo nero, spaghetti marinara, spaghetti bolognese, steak'n'chips, bacon and eggs, risotto alle vongole cremoso.

Scottish stodge 4, fine Italian cuisine 4. A draw.

Three small bedrooms completed his apartment, perfect for his occasional Scottish guests: his ex-sister-in-law, Susan; her daughter, Anna, his teenage niece, and sometimes Susan's partner, Dorothy.

"Just because I'm in love with a woman, don't call me a lesbian," was how Susan had announced her unexpected new relationship five or six years earlier.

"But now I can mean it when I tell folk I'm a friend of Dorothy," he'd said. Susan had thumped his upper arm hard enough to make him cry out, grinning as she did so.

Glasgow: the city that will punch you in easeful friendship. The city that will never stab you in the back, Tony often mused, when it can stab you in the front with a matey smile.

Susan and Anna were the one part of his trip to the city he was looking forward to. Otherwise, he visited Glasgow only when he had to. Five years after the death of his brother, Armando, the due demands of the legal process were dragging him back against his will.

Yet more documents to sign. Typical Armando, he thought: my brother drinks himself to death, almost ruining a long-established business and leaving everyone else in the family to clean up a needless mess.

****

Fifteen months apart in age, he and Armando had been distant as continents. Different flaws. Different strengths. They had squabbled. They had fought.

Armando had left school at the first opportunity, aged 15, for the grown-up world of work. Tony had stayed on. To learn. Read books. Use his mind. Study. Play. Stay boyish. Grow more thoughtful. And speak as little as necessary to Armando.

Which seemed fair, given that Armando spoke to few people apart from pub barmen and off-licence sales assistants throughout the last 30 years of his life, adrift and semi-submerged in a sea of drink.

In its final decade, Armando's illogical UK tour of towns and cities was charted by late-night phone calls - mostly to Susan, sometimes to Tony - from hospital A&E staff and homeless-shelter workers: Blackpool, Brighton, Manchester, Hull, Norwich, Bristol, Newcastle, Liverpool.

From whisky via no-brand vodka into super-strength lager and tonic wine before the ultimate descent: cider. Drinking the family business, Café Moscardini, to the verge of fiscal collapse.

Tony granted his brother was methodical, stoic, dedicated: one distillery, one vodka factory, one cider orchard after another. Norwich, Sunderland, Leeds, Plymouth, Ipswich. And back to Glasgow to die.

At least Armando didn't drink himself to death without leaving something good behind: his clever daughter, Anna. He'd drifted away soon after she'd been born.

Men. Fathers. Male biology. Necessary, Tony knew, but not essential.

Could he have done anything to stop Armando? Could he have helped his brother? He could have. But he hadn't.

He sometimes wondered what his last words to Armando must have been, snarled during their far-off teenage years, ignoring one another in the old parental home in Maryhill. Something callous, off-hand.

At least he'd done something by stopping Armando's drinking harming its blameless victims, Susan and Anna. He'd funded costly legal measures that ensured Susan kept the business functioning in her name alone, free of Armando's pillaging impulses.

Otherwise, he'd looked on from a distance as Armando's doomed spiral accelerated. He'd lacked brotherly tolerance, understanding, love. He'd hardened his heart. Washed his hands.

In all this, he knew he was avoiding those actions to which he'd attended as a journalist. He'd asked no questions, sought no answers.

Sure, he'd read up on alcoholism, noted the terminology of modern-day care. And then dismissed it. He'd staged no intervention. He'd avoided reaching out. Shunned the notion of going on a journey.

He'd let his brother float away, half-alive for longer than seemed possible before sinking from sight. Most of the time he succeeded in convincing himself he didn't regret it.

****

He'd jettisoned his brother in the same way he'd given up writing and taken up a camera, he realised whenever real regret sneaked up on him. Taking photographs, looking at scenes without looking for any one thing in particular, finding accidental order amid organic disarray, capturing things as they are without explanation, turning your back on a drowning man: staying semi-focused, distant. It was easier.

It was how he'd learnt to cope with his life's other regrets, too. Ignore them, focus on the small stuff. New shoes that hurt your feet, novels you'd never get to the end of, minor behavioural failures it might be feasible to avoid repeating.

A mislaid wife, lost girlfriends. All of his big regrets concerned failed relationships, principally his marriage. These were the most pained regrets that had arisen in Glasgow. So he'd left them behind in Glasgow.

By comparison, his initial everyday Colonia annoyances had been few and small, concerning his apartment. His chief regret about the place was the fact that he'd speeded up the moving process by adding a small sum to 27 Via di Mezzo's purchase price so as to buy it complete with all the depressing brown furniture it contained.

He should have pressed for a discount, such was his daily anger at every item's oppressive bulk and darkness, every drawer and cupboard's refusal to operate.

Each obstacle had belonged to the flat's long-deceased previous owner, an elderly widow who had moved in with all the damned stuff 60 years previously and then made it her life's work to fashion it into her own mahogany mausoleum.

It was surely no accident that some of her mid-sized side-cabinets had the look of coffins while smaller ones evoked tombstones. Funeral chic, he thought: the joy-slaying look that died in most Glasgow homes with the onset of the swinging sixties. Not in Italy.

This stuff had to go, but how?

He had often daydreamed about hefting his hideous furniture out into the street direct from his living room window, all the while knowing that such an act of impulsive and grievous impropriety would ruin his emergent social standing among his nearest home-grown Colonia neighbours.

For he had swiftly risen to become a man at whom locals might nod when encountered on the stairs, or favour with a shrug in nearby shops. So for his first few weeks, he'd let the hulking cherry-wood monstrosities sulk in the shadows they cast.

Chapter 4

He had sought to accommodate the furniture - live his life around it, sidestep it - as much as it obstructed him at every turn. He'd had to take action about the rodent infestation, though.

His bedroom abutted what was originally the Porta Reale's guardroom, now garrisoned by mice, many of whom had mounted determined raids on his kitchen during his first few months' residence. Ah, those pestilential mice - their droppings on his otherwise pristine kitchen surfaces.

He poisoned them. Dying, they dragged themselves to their lairs leaving trails of blood across the floor. Then new offspring returned to chew the packets in his larder.

The sporadic success of his war on Topolino and family left the apartment with only two enduring downsides, both minor: ancient radiators which failed to radiate sufficient heat in the sunny cold of a Colonia winter, and the original tiled floors which imposed an air of shabby misery on every room all year round.

In morose shades of brown, grey-beige and black, cobwebbed with dirt-filled cracks and grimy grouting, the hexagonal tiles depressed him every time he walked in.

But given the mess and prolonged disruption that their removal and replacement would generate, he let them stay. His more pressing domestic heating issues were remedied with brisk efficiency by the brisk and efficient woman who had become Tony's brisk and efficient love interest: Gabriella Sarti.

She'd swiftly despatched a team of heating engineers. She'd likewise masterminded ultimate victory over his armies of mice and squadrons of moths, defeating them with legions of pest-control contractors and other assorted tradesmen.

A cadre of carpenters stopped up holes in the flat's walls, skirting-boards and flooring so the mice could no longer enter from their medieval redoubt next door. Platoons of plumbers, painters, plasterers and electricians followed, all thanks to Gabriella Sarti.

"Gab-ri-ell-a," he enjoyed saying aloud, savouring the name, lingering over its exotic syllables - but only when dark and brooding Gabriella wasn't there to hear such foolishness. She didn't welcome open displays of affection.

She especially hadn't welcomed it over the next two years when, as they settled into a low-key romantic routine, he sometimes tried to signal his affection for her via some obvious show of overplayed public comedy. He once sang her name out loud to her in the street as though he was an operatic tenor, earning a scowl so bleak and reprimanding it chilled his soul.

Who was Gabriella Sarti? A residential property expert, the owner of Sarti Immobiliare, Colonia's longest-established real estate agency, founded by her great-grandfather in 1910. Had she been the realtor tasked with marketing his flat, there would have been no mis-directional wordplay about "Art Nouveau intent."

They'd been introduced to one another by a sense of outraged professional displeasure: Gabriella's. She was irked that he had bought his Via di Mezzo apartment through a faceless internet agency and not the local expert - her.

She had half-hidden her annoyance during that first meeting after having appeared at his door not long after he'd moved in. Gabriella Sarti - Sr Moscardini must have seen her estate agency shopfront in the town. She was wondering whether he needed her informed advice on improvements, as it seemed that - three months in, was it? - he had yet to empty the flat of its oppressive old furniture.

Furniture that she'd noted when the property's inheritors, the former inhabitant's children, had invited her appraisal, the cheapskates, choosing the false economy of the online sales route, failing to invest even a little to maximise profits.

Staring through severe black-rimmed spectacles, she had re-surveyed his flat that first time they'd met, prowling room by room, her heels clicking on the tiles, a consummate performer in her chosen arena, summarising the property's overall worth with outspoken accuracy and bluff legal exactitude. The precise import of its official energy performance certificate, its facilities, utilities, operating costs, its dimensions and cadastral parameters.

As Tony had half-absorbed her dry realtor's expertise, he had focused on her lips, full and pink and somehow rose-like, and he had marvelled, daydreaming about her own cadastral parameters, her certificated energy performance. A thirsty man gazing at a waterfall could not have marvelled more. She was entrancing.

Those lips continued to form words that were poised, measured, designed to initiate action. He continued to half-listen, rapt, even as she outlined her frank strategy with regard to selling a problematic property which, like his, was not in an ideal location.

Such a truth would be left unsaid - she wasn't a fool - but her estate agency would not be accused of duplicity: she was a diplomat, pragmatic, a realist. But she would have no truck with baseless assertion. Nor would she fall back on lies of omission.

Her clientele were advised to fix their homes' drawbacks prior to engaging her aid in the sales process. If they didn't, such foolhardy folk would have to set a lower asking price. Or hope to meet a gullible client such as Tony.

He had overpaid for 27 Via di Mezzo, she flatly stated. He had wondered whether he'd received this verdict with his mouth gaping open, so awed by her did he feel. She had smiled at him. He thought he might swoon.

Her regal progress round his apartment concluded with a list of its most obvious flaws: those ghastly tiles, skirting-board gaps, exposed wiring, shabby decor - the obvious rodent infestation.

She did manage a grudging compliment on his kitchen's cleanliness, before uttering a casual aside - pointed, so not casual at all - which held that in Italy real cooking was about making real food, which entailed making a real mess.

She made real food, she went on. She would make some in her kitchen - which was properly messy - and bring it to him. Soon. On Saturday. She looked him up and down, not completely underwhelmed by what she saw.

And so in the middle of the afternoon two days later, she appeared at his door carrying two picnic hampers filled with aromatic food, warm and part-cooked. "You will enjoy cleaning up the mess after we have eaten," she said, bustling past him down the hall and into the kitchen, switching on his oven and slamming assorted pots and dishes inside it, tutting and shaking her head as she did.

Over the next hour she presented him with five courses, in the process spattering his pans, tiles and worktops with soup, red wine, sun-dried tomato. *Ribolita. Torta de ceci. Involtini. Lampredotto. Peposo. Castagnaccio.*

Traditional Tuscan ways with left-over bread, chick peas, cabbage, tripe, chestnut flour, cheap cuts of meat - all of it emphasising his ignorance about his new home, despite his upbringing and his many, many visits to Colonia.

Her meals became regular occurrences. After eating - but not immediately after - she would always return home to her village high above Colonia, Faggio Basso, leaving him to clean up the mess she'd left behind. He enjoyed it.

But such hard work to strip his bed of tangled sheets, scented with what he could only call *Profumo di Gabriella*. Because after he had enjoyed tasting her food, the two of them had enjoyed tasting each other.

And so the cycle of improvement had been set in motion. Domestic. Professional. Personal. Romantic. His betterment was her alloted task, as his task in her wake was to clean his kitchen surfaces. And re-make his bed.

What was she to him now, two years on? Lover was too crude and impolite a word. He thought again. She was his... well, obviously, in crass ownership terms, she was not *his* anything.

Gabriella belonged to Gabriella. A study in self-possession. Confident. Sure of her own worth, where she belonged. She seemed happy to have him around. That was as much as it was safe for him to think.

****

He loved her, he was sure. She seemed to love him, and yet...his relationships with women had ended in his unanimous rejection. Why would this be any different? How could it be?

Fatalism had never let him down. Failure in love had been his one constant triumph. He'd had great success in making women feel that he'd failed them. Failed himself. Failed to change and grow and develop his strengths, whatever his strengths might be - he wasn't sure he knew - according to almost all the women he'd been involved with.

Some women felt he'd failed to curb the growth of his flaws, which included being preoccupied, not listening to women listing his flaws and snoring. He kept falling in love with women, that was his real flaw.

His rejections had all been conducted without explanation, no exit interview. Tony Must-be-a-dumpee. Annoying, surplus to requirements, not required on voyage.

He'd been binned by his wife. On top of that, years before back in Glasgow, he'd been binned by his wife *and*, within the same week, he'd been binned by the woman he'd been almost cheating on his wife with.

Craven Two-Time Love-Rat's Double Dumping. If he'd known little else at the time, he'd known he'd deserved both women's scornful rejection.

He'd been too comfortable and too cowardly to leave his wife. At the same time, he'd enjoyed being courted by a woman who wasn't his wife, as well as too lazy and complacent to ask her whether she wanted to be more than an almost-but-not-quite mistress, kept in limbo. Accessed at moments convenient to him, not her.

Any karmic credit he might have accrued for almost-but-not-actually cheating on his wife he'd squandered by blaming the woman he'd almost cheated on his wife with for his own near-treachery.

It wasn't his fault. She'd ensnared him. He was vulnerable. He'd done his best to resist. And mostly had resisted. Only he knew he hadn't.

If Tony had flaws - and he knew he manifestly did, over and above the snoring and the not listening to women listing his flaws - this non-admission of self-awareness was the worst.

What had gone wrong that he could be so calamitously dumped twice over by two different people inside 24 hours? He'd wasted years thinking it over.

In its 15-year span, his bloodless marriage had ossified into a list of querulous questions no wife wants to hear herself saying out loud, and that no husband wants to answer. Have you put the bins out? Did you lock the garage door? Are you sure you turned the oven off? You're not almost having an affair with a younger woman you've met at work, are you?

His marriage's end was simultaneous with his almost-but-not-actual-mistress assuring him that "it was just as well you never told your wife you were leaving her for me... because I don't want you."

What did Gabriella want from him, though?

He was aware he hadn't been accorded official perceived-partner status despite the fact that he and Gabriella featured regularly as a couple in Colonia public life, at arts and crafts events, openings, receptions, promotional events relating to her working life.

But not once in the past two years had they spent an entire night together in the same bed, and never a single moment together in hers, despite enjoying many shared afternoons in his. For after a tender hour or two, she would make a determined exit, bustling back to her own home in a village four kilometres away, 200 metres or so higher up the *Alpi Apuane*.

****

Gabriella Sarti had employed her trademark professional insight to make her own home part of a second successful property business: holiday accommodation contained within an extensively-converted grouping of former farm buildings.

She occupied a large and ancient stone-built farmhouse, once the focus of a high-walled farmyard. Her home formed one complete side of a rough square delineated by seven renovated former agricultural buildings, now well-appointed cottages centred on a new swimming pool: a lavish *agriturismo*.

She was aided by her forbidding brother, Piero, a jackbooted officer of the Carabiniere whom Tony, praying his face didn't betray his emotions, had found alarming on those few occasions they'd met, along with Piero's twittering wife, Daria, whose placatory nerviness around her husband he quite understood.

As well as worrying how frightened he might look in Piero's company, he couldn't help fretting about his status with Gabriella, despite strenuous efforts to suppress it. Emotional fretting was a pastime he'd promised himself he'd given up, on health grounds.

He had recovered from the failure of his marriage, but the nature of that marital failure - without real warning, and with Tony the party adjudged lacking - had led him to grieve painfully and for far too long, thinking himself to a standstill: endlessly subjecting himself to the same pointless question - what had he done wrong? - until he had fallen into a bleak depressive spiral that felt inescapable.

A black pit of worry and fear. His family had form in this respect.

As a teenager, he had witnessed his mother's repeated hospitalisation with what, in medical parlance at the time, were deemed nervous breakdowns. He'd ferried her to and from sessions of electro-convulsive-shock treatment.

He had seen his mother enter such treatment sessions querulous, hunched, pitiable, trapped in a cycle of unanswerable questions. He'd noted her return, accompanied by a slight but unmistakable singed aroma, stunned into better health by ECT's fiery destruction of the concerns that plagued her.

He'd imagined such front-line exposure to his mother's illness had inoculated him against any form of mental distress, depression, anxiety, panic. His own collapse after the end of his marriage had then taught him he was not immune.

So he strove hard not to submit to uncertainty about his role in Gabriella's life. Nevertheless, the question sometimes composed itself unbidden: what was his future with her? His lasting prospects of love and happiness?

She was not a part of his everyday life in the same way that Ken and Prof were. Did he want her to be? Yes, he did. In her presence, he felt calm, comforted. But did she want to be part of his everyday life? He couldn't be sure.

What might Gabriella go on to become to him in the days, weeks, years ahead? How much time did they have together? He dared not ask directly, worried she'd state her terms precisely - maybe present him with a written notice of legal severance.

She could not be referred to as a girlfriend - a *girl*, Gabriella? He found it impossible to imagine her as ever having been anything less than an elegant, fully-formed woman - a woman-in-waiting earlier in her life.

If the two of them had met as much younger people - an odd thought, not least because he guessed she was 15 or so years younger than he was, maybe more. Their exact age-difference? He daren't enquire. Like so much else, he left it unaddressed, a question unasked.

She was always formal. Cold, might it be said? No, not cold: responsible, an overseer. Less a marble statue in a gallery, Tony allegorised, unable to silence his ever-present comic impulse, more the gallery's most hawk-eyed attendant - a natural enforcer of behavioural standards.

There were so many such laws in Italian daily life, small national rules of social conduct, most of them unwritten. Gabriella was his dutiful teacher, expanding his knowledge, offering deft nudges; guiding, informing and reminding him.

Yes, Gabriella. No, Gabriella. Thank you, I was unaware of my grievous impropriety in addressing a stranger with "Ciao" and am mortified at having been caught in public at 11.01am drinking cappuccino, like a child...

When he knew she wasn't looking, he would still shake his head each autumn over how, no matter Tuscany's temperature on, say, October 8 - even if it stood at a sweltering 33C - wintertime's official start on October 1 meant compulsory scarves, gloves and coats all day, every day until the following March, over-ruling all non-sanctioned periods of inconvenient torrid heat.

She delivered her lessons in a soft voice, but with firmness. Italy and the Italian language: poetic-sounding while being prosaic. Plain-spoken prose was her medium. In her business dealings, in her personal life. Definite. Definitive.

Letters of interest. Written contracts. Depositions. Deposit instructions.

Oddly, though, whenever she employed the elaborate grandeur of Italian contractual law, listing her day's workplace toil over *contratto di provvigione, il prenotazione, il compromesso*, her business sounded to him like love-song lyrics, gourmet meal components, a lover's sigh that caressed his ears.

She always dressed formally of course: prepared for battle, business-like, ever-ready for the signing of legal documents. Not for her a weekend casual look, no dressing down in jeans or t-shirt.

She presented at all times sharply-creased, buttoned-down, suited, armoured, her clothing without evidence of disarray, whether creases or stains, dust or crumbs. Indeed, she chewed every mouthful of food with minute deliberation.

She never spoke as she ate, often holding a dainty hand over her mouth to disguise the mechanical process of digestion. He was disarmed, charmed, captivated.

She wasn't spontaneous, that was a fact. It might have worried him, triggered doubt, but he deemed it a plus - a major reassurance, in fact, given that he had in his past been dazzled in an instant and then discarded by various spontaneous women, any sense of exhilaration they provided soon swamped by misery.

Did he perceive any of her traits as flaws? No. They were virtues that had been un-apparent to him in other women.

Yet it had latterly dawned on him that she never held his hand in public, nor kissed him within sight of anyone in Colonia. Rigid Italian etiquette forbid!

When he raised the issue with her outside her office one day in what he meant to be a casual manner, as if a fleeting summary of some half-heard news concerning minor developments in a far-flung land, she smiled a thin half-smile and wagged a reproachful finger.

"I have chosen you, Signor Scotsman," was all she said, turning her back and starting to walk away, halting after a few strides and beckoning him to follow her to his flat. Plainly, she felt their exact relationship was of no concern to anyone else, the wider world.

Her behaviour perplexed him. She conducted so many other routine registrative public functions, why not some small outward act of recognition that they were in a relationship?

It must be against some rule he'd not yet mastered, he supposed.

So he didn't ask about it again, rarely venturing one step further, not even slipping his hand into hers as they exited Immobiliare Sarti's office together into Via Pascoli en route to some post-work ceremonial event at which they would jointly and severally be apart together.

In truth, she was an indisputable old-school Italian matriarch, whose cast-iron will and primacy were not to be contradicted; whose commandments of social behaviour were chiselled in stone. *Mamma mia…* He'd often heard her waxing volcanic over the phone at hapless clients.

At such times, bits of word-play formed in his head - "I'm your hot lover, share your hot lava with me!" - which he knew were best left unsaid. To become the subject of her quiet, unsmiling gaze was to grow very uncomfortable.

Chapter 5

Gabriella knew that she could seem forbidding, cold, walled-off, a fortress, but these defences had felt necessary in her youth. She was glad that Tony persisted in loving her despite them, and she was sure that, given time, she could lower the draw-bridge, look less stern, grant him full admission to her life. She might even be able to find joy in his puerile sense of humour…

But she had been forced to grow up so very quickly, taking over the family firm when she was barely 20, at the same time being forced into the role of her young brother's guardian.

Their parents' death in a plane crash had been devastating, so she had steeled herself inside her black business suit and coped, become self-reliant, got on with the job. The task would not defeat her. She needed no help.

For Sarti Estate Agency had naturally been besieged by solicitous-seeming competitors offering assistance - all men, middle-aged and avuncular, but all of them out to relieve this girl of the burden of being a realtor by assuming her firm into theirs.

She would not let them. She had worked in the business from the age of 14. She loved her work in matching homes to buyers, finding value, fixing Colonia's fabric in its many different forms. She knew she was good at assessing property; knew her somber, dependable manner reassured vendors and purchasers alike.

And then out of the blue at the age of 23 she had fallen pregnant, a single unwed mother, the head of a complete family, raising an infant son alongside her 12-year-old brother.

Her child's father? He was of no lasting consequence. A young estate agent, of course. Thankfully from a town far away from Colonia. A brief fling. Virtually a one-night stand. An outlet for her physical needs.

She had gritted her teeth and conducted her pregnancy without any thought of what gossip-riddled Colonia might be saying about it. Likewise, over the next two decades her son and her brother had been the only men she needed.

She was the redoubtable Gabriella Sarti, after all, armoured against all foes - but she had been startled, bemused and ultimately pleased to realise that, in the presence of Tony Moscardini, she felt somewhere closer to being amused by life, softened and enriched. She began to feel herself relax. To bloom.

Tony ought to have been surprised by her announcement that she was the mother of a grown-up child. But no. Another area of her well-managed adult life to which she was only now granting him partial admittance. Were there many more other things she had still to tell him? Who knew, not him.

She'd announced it one Sunday afternoon during one of his brief, ultra-rare visits to her *agriturismo* home. She hadn't had much choice.

Tony had driven up the steep, winding four-kilometre road through a forest of tall pines to Faggio Basso, feeling dismayed to see her addressing a fierce-looking young man aged around 20 dressed in black motorcycle leathers, stalking with purpose around a flame-red Moto Guzzi Daytona, stooping to adjust some lever here, tighten some cable there.

When Tony had stepped from his car, Gabriella had simply introduced the youth as her law student son, Paolo, racing back to university in Bologna with mama's stolen cooking.

Paolo looked embarrassed but narrowed his eyes to shake Tony's hand, a sniper staring down a gunsight. *Impress me, old Scottish goat.*

He sought to deflect Paolo's glare by stooping to examine the motorbike. It was familiar. By chance, decades before, Armando had owned the exact same model for a year or so before the thing suddenly vanished, traded in to cover some debt, Tony assumed, maybe for a case of vodka.

Typical Armando. He'd coveted the bike for months, Tony growing weary of his brother's praise for the machine's revolutionary something-or-other, its endless hymning as a big burly beast - a racing motorbike in road-going form, for guys who really knew what they were doing.

"Moto Guzzi Daytona," said Tony. "A racer in road-going form - a big beast. A guy has to know what he's doing, riding that. We had one in my family back when they were new. Revolutionary in its time, I guess."

Paolo raised his eyebrows, nodded, mumbled something that sounded like "Sure, not for everyone." For a second, Tony considered faking more biker banter, but thought better of it.

Paolo turned back to his mother, kissed her on the cheek, hoisted a leather satchel on to his back and affixed his motorcycle crash helmet. He nodded at Tony before roaring off in what seemed a dismissive dust-cloud.

"Just like his mother, good-looking… accomplished," he'd said - longing to ask who Paolo's father had been and where he was now. She'd raised an eyebrow and given him a look to which he'd grown accustomed: *can the cheek and don't say another flatterer's word, Glasgow joker-man.*

She'd raised Paolo as a single mother in her early twenties, she'd said at last, after a worrying pause. Paolo's father had entered history before Paolo was born, no further discussion necessary.

There had been a harsh edge to her voice as she'd skirted around the precise detail of her son's birth. Tony realised he'd been holding his breath as her tone rose, edging towards shrill and aggressive. Such a relief that it didn't get there.

He exhaled and murmured something indistinct, jolly, thankful. As an Italian mother, she could never be wrong, was never wrong. A woman of unshakeable certainty. Her opinions were the only logical ones.

She had never been wrong about anything in their time together, he had to admit.

He'd spotted recent signs that she was formulating some sort of decision which concerned him. What cool conclusion might she reach in the wake of him leaving Colonia for his short Glasgow stay later that day?

He'd become aware she was evaluating him with the kind of detachment she employed in everyday business. As if he was a run-down apartment which had lingered unsold on her firm's books for too long.

Her gaze was stern, lingering. Once or twice, when she seemed to think he wasn't looking, she had lowered her spectacles, staring over them at some aspect of him as if seeking confirmation of.... what? He refused to think.

Was he an older property with decor in need of light refreshing, or did he require costly total refurbishment? What meagre long-term prospect of profit did he he offer?

Did he comprise a desirable family residence, all modern amenities, panoramic views? Unlikely, he felt, at his advanced age, 56. Safer to be realistic and reckon that she'd perceived him to be suffering from irreversible structural decline. Subsidence.

Dry rot. Woodworm.

Maybe he was a flood risk. Old men and their worn-out plumbing. A questionable piece of real estate, to be disposed of cheaply: the best he could expect.

He framed the threat to his future happiness in hackneyed newspaper terminology: a ticking time bomb lay in his path - no, it was worse: he was riding a rollercoaster knowing that around the next bend lurked a busted rail.

He recognised the signs of an impending goodbye. He braced for a tender farewell caress delivered with the force of a slap to his face.

He couldn't bring himself to ask her directly, of course. Not asking about things was his defence against all emotional wounds incurred during hand-to-hand combat in love's warring trenches.

Likewise, he speculated about Gabriella's past but kept his mouth shut, while looking away from what might lie ahead. Was it her habit to avoid commitment? Had he done well to last as long as he had, these past two years?

Paolo's father, whoever he'd been… whatever he'd been. Her first serious love? A youthful indiscretion? A regrettable fling?

He knew his thoughts could turn maze-like, hedged by confounding sub-clauses and dead-ended with qualifying footnotes. Stifling them was an unequal struggle.

A defiant comedy routine nagged itself to life inside his head, a crazy scene set in a wood-panelled court of law in which he was a Groucho Marx shyster attorney, some blustering deadbeat lawyer advocating on behalf of another deadbeat, a loser by the name of Tony Moscardini: "My esteemed client Signor Moscardini, the first party of the last part - the worst part of the second party - wonders whether Signorina Sarti sees him as an appreciating asset or a ruinous liability?

"All he knows for sure is ever since they met, she's been trying to sweep him off her shoes." His inner stand-up comedian was always trying to get him into trouble.

****

Men and women, locked in a life-long siege-state of mutual incomprehension, it seemed. Yet he'd been so grateful to Gabriella's all-female workforce one morning when they'd provided accidental evidence that he had some form of relationship status with their boss - that he was her male... *something-or-other*. Definitely. Kind of.

He'd walked in on the quartet in the *immobiliare*, her secretary and three saleswomen, the boss away, and as soon as he did, they'd begun giggling and looking embarrassed. They were glad *la capo donna* at long last had a man in her life, they'd spluttered, instantly growing worried and asking him not to repeat it.

For the next few moments he had stood taller, light-headed with relief, his chest swelling. But knowing Gabriella as well as he did, his shoulders soon slumped to their default setting, resignation.

She would not confide her personal life to her staff. They were confirming he was the only man they'd seen her with at work-related evening events. He was merely an item of office gossip.

As much as he worried about Gabriella ending their relationship, he was just as troubled that his arsenal of hilarious re-purposed old jokes lacked all power to amuse her.

His Italian had grown more fluent, but his sense of humour resisted translation. She laughed at him, but never with him. Perhaps their mis-aligned sense of comedy had something to do with her being 100% Italian, unlike him, the tempered Scots-Italian.

Whatever the reason, it was disturbing. He had never before

had so much as a five-minute relationship with any woman from whom he couldn't tease laughter, or amuse into bed, joke into a better mood.

It was frightening, but it was exhilarating, too. Was he a ski-jumper tensed on the ramp before a controlled free-fall, or was he a hot-air balloonist ready for flight, he asked himself, pondering the subtle difference.

He must not be downcast. He would continue to court laughter. As had once been observed, he always had to try and be funny. It was his destiny.

And with each proud new dart of comic invention, she would fix him with the most sober of her sober gazes, weighing him for the foolish non-Italian schoolboy he so evidently was.

He had never had an argument with her, and hoped he never would - in losing, he'd be eviscerated! And if ever they did argue, he would be forced to mention her inability to enjoy his jokes.

He'd have to do it with tact and delicacy - as a comic announcement: "Your scornful rejection of my comedy is killing our relationship - laugh now or we die!"

How ridiculous could he make it sound? Enough to make her laugh? He hoped so. Maybe he should try it soon. No, he shouldn't. It was not a gamble worth taking.

From time to time, he was minded of an old gag he'd once heard, told by some veteran comedian. He polished it inside his head.

"In our marriage, I handle all the major decisions - politics, world events, the economy," the routine began. "It's me who outlines our official position on the big issues of the day… our response to the Government's handling of the newest Balkans crisis… trade tariffs with China, whether TV news favours the political party of the hated ruling elite over the glorious workers' revolutionary caucus, and so on and so forth.

"To my wife, I leave all life's smaller issues… the little things in a marriage: what'll we eat for dinner, which town or country we'll live in, which house to buy… how many children we'll have, when we'll have them."

So much he dare not say within her hearing.

He felt on firmer social ground in his relationship with the town of Colonia. He'd become a ratified Scots-Italian inhabitant of an Italian colony of transplanted Scots.

It was almost home. He knew it. He knew the people. Or so he tried to believe.

Like a large percentage of Colonia, he had grown up in two countries simultaneously, sustained by an intertwined network of grandparents, aunts, uncles, cousins, nephews, nieces, in-laws - most of them in his case now deceased and lying in perpetual rest side by side in Colonia's cemetery.

The roll call of the Scots-Italian departed. Anderson, Botti, Cardosi, Casci, Franci, Giusti, Hendry, Macdonald, McDonald, McGinn, McGurn, Moscardini, Nutini, Ottolani, Ottolini, Palumbo, Pardini, Paterson, Pieraccini, Robb, Stewart, Stuart, Zavaroni.

Colonia's constant incoming residential tide flowing forth, ebbing back and flowing again from Scotland's west central belt, primarily Glaswegian, but including the post-industrial rotten-tooth zones of Ayrshire, Lanarkshire, Renfrewshire, Stirlingshire.

Airdrie, Alloa, Ardeer, Ardrossan, Beith, Campbeltown, Coatbridge, Denny, Falkirk, Girvan, Greenock, Irvine, Johnstone, Kilbirnie, Kilwinning, Lochwinnoch, Motherwell, Paisley, Prestwick, Rothesay, Saltcoats, Shotts, Stevenston, Stirling, Troon, Wishaw.

What united all these one-time steel towns, played-out coalmining villages, tatty seaside resorts and erstwhile lace capitals?

They were all peopled by Scots who welcomed being rendered overweight and prone to coronary thrombosis by comforting deep-fried pizzas fashioned in chip shops run by Colonia exports prepared to betray their healthy Tuscan gourmet heritage in the name of commerce.

Clogging arteries. Shrinking the world. Small is best.

Tony witnessed such international harmony every time he was in Colonia's main supermarket, Conad - Consorzio Nazionale Dettaglianti Società Cooperativa, the Co-Op - marvelling at the effortless bi-lingual colloquialism of check-out staff and customers, the cosmopolitan array of goods. Irn Bru side by side on the shelves with Aperol: two disparate drinks united by their lurid and inorganic orange hue.

In Conad's aisles, he might be asked to help an archetypal stooped Italian *nonna* accompanied by a Scottish grandchild, the old woman switching non-stop between fluent Italian and demotic Glaswegian: "Shush, Stacey this'll be us since Tuesday if you keep asking for *grissini*… gonna give us the Coco Pops down, big man, I'm too wee - and the *aglio e olio* and all while you're there." Shopping as universal communion, a hint of theatre.

And what could be more Italian and yet even more Glaswegian than Colonia's established Thursday-evening summertime spectacle, conducted *al fresco* in its central car park: 44 women in garish luminescent peek-a-boo nylon athleisurewear enjoying a vigorous spin class on ranks of static bicycles.

To a vaulting techno soundtrack, the weekly assembly whooped to a questionably healthy finale, self-lubricating with discreet glugs of Lambrusco from water-bottles. Complementing this tableau vivant, a feckless crew of punters milled around outside the adjoining bookies, old men checking out female contours in form-fitting Lycra with no attempt at subtlety.

The perfect blend of Italo-Scots culture, he reckoned. Loud! Life-affirming! Gallus! Less dedicated to fitness, keener still on making a common racket in public. And thankfully no bloody rain…

On adjacent Colonia streets, permanently in session on oak benches, groups of men conducted the business of *la nostra vecchia parlamento*, the talking-shop of the old-timers, as they'd doubtless done for millennia, ever since Julius Caesar copped a chibbing in the Roman forum.

Colonia's wizened senators watched the world go by and *checked the nick of that galoot, yon saucy besom, those cheeky ragazzi.* In other Italian townships, Tony was sure the local sages would be clicking rosary beads. In Colonia, they stared with deeper religious fervour at mobile phones, forever seeking fresh football news from Glasgow.

No elderly women were ever visible engaging in such open displays of idleness, of course. Too much work to do at home. Dinner to make while spouses waste each other's time beneath the sheltering branches of *il quercione* - Colonia's most useful landmark, its oak - in impassioned discourse about footballers' strained limbs and mis-timed kicks.

He studied the huge tree, 500 years old at least, he supposed, standing on Via Roma's crossroads, at the boundary between old and new Colonia: a site sufficiently timeless to inspire deathless newspaper prose from endless squads of bad travel writers.

He smiled. He could rhyme off such a gushing article, all clichés and unconsidered platitudes tripping over one another, jostling for attention. "As well as spanning past and present, *il quercione* stands on Colonia's eternal border between modern Scotland and traditional Italy.

"The venerable tree - an observer, a guardian, a talisman - is a place of age-old Tuscan magic where dreams maybe come true. It's a time-travel portal… a passport to a slower way of life, timeless bonds of family, lost ideals."

Maybe one day if he stood at *il quercione* long enough, he thought, it might work its spell on him. Make him feel more like he was enjoying belonging here... make Colonia seem less dull - prevent him pining now and again for Glasgow's big city excitement.

"Aye, right," he muttered, "as if that's going to happen."

He reminded himself of local lore which insisted that it was on this very spot in Colonia a century earlier, beneath the oak's leaves, that the author of Pinocchio, Carlo Collodi, had lain one day with pen and notebook, crafting his famous children's tale of the boy whose nose grew ever longer with each new lie he told. Hence the nearby Bar Nasone: Big Nose Bar, capitalising on the story's birthplace. Or supposed birthplace.

One evening he'd stood beneath *il quercione* with Gabriella and mentioned Colonia's role in Pinocchio's nativity. She'd looked at him with concern and amusement, as if he'd been out in the sun too long without a hat and she was unsure whether to slap him for his stupidity or take his temperature.

"Pinocchio? Born under Colonia's oak tree?" she'd said, her voice more disbelieving than scornful. Didn't he know the exact same claim to fame was made throughout the whole province by every single village that had an oak tree?

"Pinocchio came from Colonia?" she said again. "Oak trees are very common round here - it might explain why so many locals have big long noses. And loud mouths."

She'd overheard plenty more Coloniesi assuring so many other gullible visitors that not only was the town's oak tree the birthplace of Pinocchio. Why, it was home to dozens more storybook characters.

"Listen to some folk and this old tree helped conceive the Daughter of the Sun, the Dragon and the Enchanted Horse, the Fearless Fool and the Milkmaid Queen," she said, baffling him with old Italian fairytale characters he didn't know. She saw his confusion.

"Just be assured Colonia's the place whenever it's foolish parents receiving lessons from their wiser children, cunning villains duping naive villagers, or folk discovering that love is blind and a glossy wrapper can hide shoddy goods," she said. "All first written down on this very spot."

"So many folktales dreamt up here, by so many writers. There can hardly have been room under the branches for them all. They must have sat on each other's knees, juggling pens and notebooks, a circus act."

"*Il quercione* - the ideal place to meet and chatter, and waste time… and fashion nonsense to entertain unsuspecting crowds." She said it with such sweetness, the patient schoolteacher, the wise mother guiding a child, with the slightest of sighs.

He put his arms round her waist, drew her to him and kissed her in public for the first time, with a sudden tenderness she could not resist. She took her time before pushing him away, and as she did, she was smiling and blushing - and, he was pleased to note, not fuming with rage.

Beneath Via Roma's old oak tree: the ideal place in which to fashion nonsense to entertain a crowd, she'd said. To stage surprises, too, perhaps. Maybe *il quercione* was the ideal witness to something as ridiculous and surprising as true love, too.

****

It was hard to avoid walking past the oak tree in a town as small as Colonia, of course. On a mid-morning stroll not long after making his home there, he'd spotted a solitary, frail-seeming old man slumped on a leaf-shaded bench, half-smiling and nodding as Tony passed.

Should he engage? His path to spoken fluency had been slower than he'd hoped, and he was grateful his flawed Italian hadn't halted his equally tardy climb to a place in the multi-lingual Gabriella's heart.

Having grown up in Maryhill in a dual-language home - grating Scots curses, softer Latinate imprecations - he'd been disappointed when locals had adjudged his initial approaches as halting, awkward, those of an outsider.

But that morning he'd risked revealing himself as an obvious non-Coloniesi - maybe the elderly native was unwell.

He addressed the ancient bloke in Italian with slow-paced textbook clarity. The fellow was likely deaf, and probably the oldest, most Italian-looking old Italian man in all Italy, his skin tanned by an eternity of Tuscan sunshine and consumption of olive oil.

The old-timer's Latin antiquity was further underlined by an aquiline profile which gave him the look of a serving centurion in Rome's legions back when Julius Caesar had been a boy. *Are you feeling OK, signor… pardon me asking…*

The old man opened his mouth to assert that he was just waiting for the bloody bus to bloody Barga and it was late again, the bloody bus to bloody Barga, your arse in parsley. He'd be fucked if he was going to sit here all fucking day. A Scot.

The old man went on to reveal - using Scotland's lexicon of undeleted expletives to its full - that he'd lived his adult life far from the sun-ripened vines of Tuscany, amid the redundant miners, laid-off chemical factory workers and displaced cabinet-makers of Dalry in Ayrshire's perennially chilly, rain-soaked and unromantic-sounding Garnock Valley, and the fucking buses there were just as fucking bad.

"You'll surely prefer it here to Dalry, though, eh?" said Tony, abandoning Italian and admitting defeat.

"Aye, well… the weather's better here," the old man agreed, "but have you not watched Italian telly? Pure shite! You couldn't call it entertainment - late-night discussions about Italian politics with wrinkly old skeezers like me and the missus.

"And when they try and make you laugh - give us a break. Italian comedy? My grandchildren acting daft falling off their trampolines is less stupid. Thank fuck for my Sky subscription.

"And nothing ever happens round here. Nothing. But nothing happens anywhere except what folk make happen. And most folk round here don't want anything to happen. Folk. World's full of them. Makes you sick. Useless bastards mostly."

And with that, the old man hobbled off towards the bookies.

He'd run a chip shop, of course: Dalry's finest, he'd also admitted. Colonia had become home to so many retired Scots fish-and-chip fryers that the town's grand-sounding Office of Municipal Economic Development - in reality one man, Paisley's retired erstwhile town clerk - had figured their culinary skills must be capitalised upon.

In this, the Office of Municipal Economic Development was both right and wrong. Colonia's annual *Sagra del Pesce e Patate* - the only Fish and Chip Festival in all Italy! - continued to salute the town's prominent role in Caledonian culinary history while raising funds for local charities. Staged on the town's playing fields over three summer weekends, the event offered al fresco ballroom dancing, a beer tent, fish and of course chips - the latter items cooked without the participation of any of the town's many skilled veteran Scots fried-food experts.

The retired *chipshoperati* had taken a unanimous vow: none of them had any inclination to sweat over hot bubbling fryers ever again - "Especially not in the fucking 35C heat of an Italian summer, what do they fucking take us for - mental?"

Nor would they peel potatoes. Or use lesser Italian piscine

staples - seabream, swordfish, cod - in place of Scotland's one true silvery chip shop monarch, the North Sea haddock.

Thus the fish and chips on offer at the festival were - whisper it - from Conad's frozen section. It was only know-nothing tourists who ate the stuff, anyway, so who got hurt?

This year's Fish and Chip Festival would feature a genuine Scots-generated innovation: a world film premiere, *sotto le stelle* - beneath the stars, same as the ballroom dancing. Under the old oak tree on Via Roma. Indeed, Sunday's opening night festivities would begin with the first public screening of the short work co-created by Tony Moscardini, former journalist.

****

Ex-journalist. Working photographer. Budding film maker. Sporadic comedian. "Enough already with the self-deprecating Scotsman act," he'd told Ken and Prof more than once. "Two years in Colonia and I'm helping you two build Hollywood on the banks of the river Serchio!"

His first cinema project owed a little to his everyday photographic work, but wouldn't have existed without his two closest male friends in Colonia.

Retired BBC Scotland film editor Kenneth James Paolozzi Moody, widower, once of Paisley. Eduardo Luigi Bartolomei, latterly a maths teacher at Milngavie Academy; re-named the Professor during his swotty teens less due to his studiousness and more to the fact that his name was so Italian that post-war Glasgow found it unpronounceable. Moody-Bartolomei-Moscardini: MBM Studios, cop a load of these guys!

Ken and Prof were not only Tony's most responsive comedy audience; they were his wisest and most informed counsel on all matters - practical or philosophical, from Mars bars to marscapone, chips to chianti.

Ken in particular was widely-read and thoughtful; sage in all matters pertaining to Colonia's history, cinema history, films and filming, cameras, lenses, shots, framing devices, photographic lore. A man to whom there were no insoluble problems, only challenges capable of being surmounted.

Ken certainly had words of balm whenever Tony chafed against some ingrained aspect of Colonia social custom, its insular tendency to resist admitting any place that had the ill fortune not to be Colonia.

During one mid-morning chat in the trio's favoured caffé, for instance, Tony revealed how much he missed Glasgow's favourite imported dish. More than pizza, Glasgow was crazy for curry.

"Not that curry is something you can pine out loud for in Italy," he'd said, recollecting his mistake in having praised Indian food to young locals he'd judged as "open-minded…rational… left-wing, liberal - the good guys."

He'd been shocked when his innocent appreciation of pakora, peshwari naan and aloo saag led to a denunciation of Indian food as foul and poisonous muck, scarcely fit for any civilised European.

"Buzzing bees amid lavender scents… and still the wee stink of racism to taint Italy's pride in all things Italian," Tony sighed. His two-man audience nodded.

Ken sat back while clasping his hands tightly together over his late-middle-aged-man's paunch. It was a pose Tony had christened - with admiration - the Ken Moody Paisley Buddy Buddha.

Italian regional pride should not be mistaken for fascism, Ken quietly stated. "We all spout shite from time to time," he went on, "but it doesn't make us hang the man next door from a lamp post because he doesn't look the same as us."

"And never mind your delicate sensibilities being offended by folk in Colonia - folk from *here* had a worse time of it over *there* in Scotland at first. There'll be examples from your own family history - and let me tell you, the first Moodys had it bad in Paisley.

"The name-calling... the mockery... Moody's not the original family name - we're *Lunaticis*, temperamental, governed by the moon, erratic, unstable, moody. 'You eye-tie loon!' You can see why my great-grandfather took a Paisley pal's advice and changed it."

The un-temperamental Ken had a more recent tale of Scottish anti-Italian sentiment, too. His grandfather had set up a successful Italian-import leather goods business in Paisley in 1920, giving it a partly Italian name, Pelli Leathers.

It was a title with a price. When Mussolini declared war on Britain in 1940, Pelli Leather's owners had marked themselves as a problem - potential Italian sympathisers, in hiding.

Maybe the Moody family remained traitorous *Lunaticis* at heart, some whispered. If the Moody adult males hadn't changed their names, they'd be joining Paisley's obvious Italians in being barred from travelling three miles from their homes, ordered to report daily to the police. For a time, Pelli Leather's showroom windows kept getting smashed in the night.

Worse followed in the early post-war years when Pelli Leather's warehouse burglar alarm went off one night. Ken's grandad arrived in time to disrupt the robbers as they made off with his old metal safe, delighted to see them drop the heavy monstrosity yards from the splintered front door.

With the police's arrival, his good fortune ran out, though. The unopened safe was confiscated as evidence. At the police station, Ken's grandad unlocked it.

The large sum of cash inside was untouched. Sadly, its owner had no documented proof as to how he'd acquired it. Ken's grandfather was charged with tax evasion, found guilty and sentenced to six months in jail.

"They never found the safe-robbers," Ken said. "I'm sure the police never looked. They already had their guilty man, the bloody Tally in front of them."

At this point, Tony couldn't help but ask what all this had to do with his initial complaint about Colonia sometimes failing to extend a ready welcome to exiled Scots.

Chapter 6

Ken expelled air out of his nostrils, sat back and laced his fingers across his stomach. Time for another expert lecture, its lessons gleaned from stories he'd grown up listening to his mother tell. This one was about the first time the rest of the world made its way to Castel di Colonia.

It had been at the end of Italy's involvement in the second world war, late in 1944. Military forces entrenched in their thousands amid the town's forests. Roads were blocked. Heavy machinery droned and rattled through the night.

There was fighting in the mountains. Explosions. The thud and whine of heavy artillery. Machine gun fire. For a brief spell the town's streets were filled with death and horror. Alarm, chaos. Armed figures lurking in doorways.

Terror. Blood. Screams. Uniformed corpses lay where they fell. German soldiers. Italian soldiers.

And of course American soldiers - most of whom were black African-American soldiers. And British troops who were mostly Indian. The one-time enemy forces loomed dark and hostile, posited now as Italy's rescuers, new allies against the Germans, but looking alien.

Always wary of outsiders, Colonia felt itself besieged by a lethal and strange variety of obvious non-Italians. "Some of the old locals' wartime memories I've heard… the ones you don't want to quiz on their views about *Il Duce*," said Ken.

"Stories that as children, they'd been warned away from the black monsters - away from the vile stink of the Indian soldiers' food, camped nearby in tents. Maybe it's not so surprising to hear some modern-day Italians say they don't like curry…"

Ken and his two-man audience had grown aware the café's usual volume of ambient chatter had dropped. They were being listened to. That's what a casual mention of Mussolini will do in some public spaces in modern-day Italy.

As a result, the trio took two important decisions. They changed their meeting place to a bar with a higher background noise-level. They resolved to keep their public discussions to a no less impassioned but less dangerous and controversial topic: film. And that was how the three of them came to make their own movie.

****

While the physical process of filming and editing their motion picture project was soon done, the entire business had been a long one. Very long. Three lifetimes long, Ken had remarked.

The three of them had each loved movies from childhood. Tony's focus was English-language film, ie Hollywood. Ditto his two associate Colonia cineastes, but with an added natural inclination towards Italian-made cinema and all its genres: *Futurista, Cinecittà, Neorealismo, commedia all'Italiana, Spaghetti Western, giallo*.

Ken and Prof were further united by a love of two very different directors, Federico Fellini and Mario Monicelli.

Tony had submitted to DVD screenings of the former's *La Strada* and *Amarcord*, before giving up on both with great relief well before their finales. In contrast, Monicelli's black and white 1950s comedy-heist caper movies made him chuckle.

And so it was on this sunny Thursday late morning in July that, as he began his long-anticipated exit from Colonia, he had pictured himself strolling along its stone-flagged streets as though in a classic monochrome scene from Monicelli's most enduring comic gem, *Guardie e Ladri (Cops And Robbers)*.

His model as a leading man was naturally the film's star, Italy's droll Prince of Laughter, Antonio Griffo Focas Flavio Angelo Ducas Comneno Porfirogenito Gagliardi de Curtis di Bisanzio, more readily known as Totò.

Tony imagined his film-star progress down Via di Mezzo attracting an admiring audience of transplanted old Glasgow *Coloniesi* hanging above him from their wrought-iron-balustraded windows and cascading down cheeky quips, irreverent requests and last-minute reminders.

In reality, those were the types of comment he'd heard the previous night in his favourite bar, Zio Beppo, from various exiled Scots topers. "Why do you keep taking photos of us old ruins - take photos of young women with no clothes on!" one elderly man had shouted.

"Young women won't let me take their photos when I've no clothes on," Tony had replied, prompting catarrhal cackles and earning the initial speaker a swift clout round the head with a rolled-up newspaper wielded by his wife.

Another old Scot had reminded Tony to be sure and bring her back the latest Denise Mina novel ("I think she's maybes Italian - sultry-looking enough to be, but not from round here - not with a monicker like Mina, mind… her folk must have come from further south, Naples or someplace").

"Back on Sunday? Bring us *The Grubber*," yet another voice had urged, a dagger-like request into Tony's wilting old journalist's heart, derailing his Hollywood day-dream stroll down Via di Mezzo. *The Grubber* was a lurid fanzine, 24 shoddy A5 pages commemorating the nasty doings and tawdry times of Glasgow's real-life crime dynasties.

To his dismay and disgust, it sold in skiploads for 50p, thriving in direct proportion to the decline of dinosaur daily newspapers hung up on tedious bygones like grammar, spelling and the laws of libel. *"The Grubber,"* he complained *sotto voce.*

He'd received other requests in Zio Beppo, some communicated more discreetly by winks and nods. Health bulletins best not shared aloud.

Because most of Colonia's elderly Scots needed their free NHS prescriptions collected. He often mused about what might happen if he was ever stopped at Pisa airport by customs officers on the homeward leg of a Glasgow journey, his backpack crammed with pills.

Might he be detained as a drugs smuggler? He trusted that his illicit stash of narco-contraband would be identified for what it was: prostate medicines to ensure the efficient flow of urine from old men's bladders, rheumatoid arthritis treatments to prevent aged joints seizing up.

In this role, as a bearer of gratis healing, he knew he was of more daily use to more Scots than he'd ever been as a journalist.

He went back to savouring inside his head the cinematic possibilities of his short walk down the street, re-running its imagined soundtrack of good-natured verbal back-and-forth.

Praise be to film-comedy deity Totò that Tony's own film hadn't required him to pen a single word of dialogue.

****

It was ironic that the trio's film owed its genesis, in a roundabout way, to a subject about which Tony knew almost nothing: football.

A man from Glasgow who didn't like football? It was impossible. Peculiar. It made him a figure of suspicion, derision and sometimes outright scorn ("You don't *get* football? What's wrong with you, Tony Mustbeafanny!").

He was sure his newspaper career had been damaged by his lack of engagement with football, most Scottish males' single topic of conversation, the closest they ever came to admitting an inner life.

It marked him as an outsider, rendered him dubious, unmanly. It was especially galling - shameful, even - given his family links to a famous Scots-Italian football figure from the two countries' shared sporting history.

Back in the 1920s, Giovanni "Johnny" Moscardini, a one-time lodger in nearby Barga, had been among the first few non-native-born Italians to play for the national football team: one of the first of the *oriundi*.

That sneering term - not entirely without racist import, Tony knew - was applied to those footballers of Italian parentage who had allowed themselves to be born overseas, the willful fools. Skilled enough to represent the country thanks to mere ancestry, not birthplace.

In Johnny Moscardini's long-ago era, football garnered him acclaim, but no money. So after a few sporting seasons, Johnny had returned to his old job in his old life, working in the family cafeteria in his birthplace, Falkirk.

These few facts about his distant relative amounted to the sum total of Tony's football knowledge. His zero football knowledge was still more than Ken and Prof could muster between them, though. This communal ignorance of garish polyester football costumes and tribal chants only strengthened the trio's friendship, he supposed.

But how was it relevant to their becoming film-makers?

It had been a cold February evening when the stellar principles of old Hollywood aligned in cosmic harmony with Colonia. The three of them had been in Zio Beppo, as usual.

Around them, as usual, 40 or so cursing, bellowing men were gesturing violently at multiple outsized TV screens showing some football match involving their favourite team.

As ever, the three film buffs were the only men in Zio Beppo utterly uninterested in football. Which was why they'd chosen to be there.

Why? Such was the room's hideous background level of sport-derived blare that the three could safely analyse any number of topics likely to incur them physical harm in other public spaces in Colonia: the post-war defeat of Italian fascism, its modern resurgence under Berlusconi, why Mussolini calendars are on open sale beside the glossy gossip magazines in some newsagent's shops, no longer hidden under the counter.

But not that night. Film was the sole item on their agenda.

They had wearied of observing a roomful of grown men raging, bawling and shrieking like over-tired toddlers on the verge of tearful collapse, and began considering exactly how they themselves might create a screen entertainment that would grip a mass audience far beyond the feeble, contrived and repetitive 90-minute TV narrative of a football game.

Glasses of chianti were involved as a philosophical lubricant, so some details had become blurred. As the drink flowed, however, it became clear that they were in complete agreement: to create a gripping film was to fashion a sense of excitement that grew and grew, a relentless increase of tension and meaningful spectacle.

Technical craft was paramount, one of the three men suggested. On-screen performing artistry, too, of course, said another. And then the nascent film collective spoke with a single voice: "A car chase!"

As they roared the next fateful word in unison - *"Bullitt!"* - their affirmation of celluloid certainty over-rode Zio Beppo's football hubbub.

In that instant, they had committed to filming a shot-by-shot recreation of a celluloid car chase they adored. Steve McQueen's most compelling 10 minute, 53-second-long movie sequence right there in Colonia!

As Ken had stated, it was the most crazy, beautiful, pointless and organic notion that three sane men could ever devote months of their lives to, for no fiscal profit and with cumbersome physical and emotional demands.

A few moments more and the film's title was magically on their lips. *Bullitt da Colonia! Bullitt From Colonia* would be done because it could, should and indeed must be done! Practicality was a petty matter for another day. More chianti!

****

The next day dawned too quickly, as the sore-headed, hungover trio went about nailing down those few insignificant details they'd overlooked - minor things like cast, crew, equipment, location - during Zio Beppo's glorious eruption of intoxicating unity.

"If we were genuine Italians, we'd have paced our drinking, stuck to chianti and we wouldn't feel so awful today," said Tony.

"But we're Scots-Italians," said Ken, "so we know life is a thing of exquisite doom, a game that's lost from the start - so you might as well give in and kick off with an Aperol spritz, a few glasses of chianti, then a couple of G&T's and wind up on the grappa."

Prof winced, removing his glasses to massage his temples. "Can you both speak more quietly," he said.

In the same way that the film's title had presented itself immediately, so other aspects of *Bullitt da Colonia's* production soon emerged... in the form of obvious major hurdles.

As they sat at Ken's kitchen table watching *Bullitt's* original car chase on YouTube, Ken outlined some of them.

"I've identified three big problems - but there'll be more," Ken said, with a jauntiness that relaxed his two partners, who didn't know enough about film-making to be as alarmed as they should have been.

Ken had made Scottish TV news and current affairs programmes for 40 years. He knew everything. More or less...

"Our first problem is that we're making a film in Colonia starring Steve McQueen, and we have no Steve McQueen," Ken said. Prof frowned. Tony belched chianti fumes.

"Second, we're recreating a car chase that took place on San Francisco's steep, hilly streets - many of them wide and long. We're shooting on Colonia's short, less steep, and very narrow streets.

"Third, we've got no growling muscle cars. No green metallic V8 Dodge Charger. No black V8 Ford Mustang GT Fastback.

"No four-wheeled stars. No speed. No Steve McQueen. No big hills."

"Isn't that four problems, not three," said Prof.

Ken ignored him. "On top of that," he went on, "we have no urgent, propellent musical soundtrack like Lalo Schfrin's - it's as much a character in *Bullitt* as the two cars and the three actors: good guy Steve McQueen plus two baddies."

"We can't just steal it, it's too American," said Tony.

Ken nodded. "So that's one more major problem on top of the three I thought we had," he continued. "In short, what we truly have is... Gentlemen, what advantage do we have?"

Ken sat back, raising expectant eyebrows, looking back and forth from one partner to the other. Tony stared at Ken. Prof stared at Tony staring at Ken, then stared at Ken himself.

Time halted. A trapped fly buzzed at the kitchen window above Ken's sink.

Tony gulped, stared, his mind empty. How witless and irresolute he must look. They were as stuck as the trapped fly.

****

"I'll tell you what we *do* have, though," Ken said with a mild emphasis that still made Prof jump and spill his macchiato.

"What we have is our diligence, our doggedness, our expert knowledge of what makes a compelling film, the unique complementary nature of our individual strengths and talents - as well as our willingness to make the best of what we have, to bend those few natural resources around us - no matter how lowly or ill-suited - to serve the nobility of our common purpose!"

Tony felt like cheering, but on the edge of his vision, he saw Prof tentatively raise his hand, a quailing schoolboy seeking permission to go to the lavatory.

A question was shaping up in the old mathematician's mind. Ken nodded, bidding his ancient cohort to speak.

"What is it we have again?" Prof asked.

Ken looked irked, forbidding. Then he began laughing, and kept laughing till he started wheezing, then coughing and Tony had to slap him on the back and fetch a glass of water.

Whereupon, after draining the glass, Ken listed those few actual resources they had, and explained how their littleness would trounce the mightier amounts of stuff they lacked.

So the three of them did not possess a pair of snarling all-American automotive icons. But Colonia did have two vehicles that were every bit as emblematic - emblematic of all Italy!

The Piaggio Motor Company's 395cc three-wheeled Ape delivery wagon, an uglier mutant cousin to that nippy, stylish two-wheeled embodiment of all-Italian transport, the Vespa scooter.

As Vespa is Italian for wasp, so Ape - pronounced *Ah-peh* - is, in English, Bee. "We'll be busy bees," said Tony.

Ken conceded that neither of their Bees had the low macho internal combustion engine growl of a V8 monster. Instead, each Bee whined and buzzed and sputtered like an angry apian swarm trapped in a tin can.

However, Ken insisted, the Bee's relentless clattering parp was a characteristic Tuscan voice capable of transmitting fearsome rising tension in the same manner that Detroit's iron thunder embodied menace and impending violence.

In addition, Bees did not squander fuel like an old-time American car, 10 gallons to every mile. Their car chase would be an eco-conscious car chase! A world first!

Prof began to look unsure again, raising his hand, but Ken ignored him, his words an unstoppable tide of artistic certainty. So they didn't have Lalo Schifrin to create them a brand-new ominous soundtrack - but they did have Signor Schifrin's original creation for the film's soundtrack.

A musical theme called *Twistin' Gears*. It could be improvised around, re-worked, re-imagined and translated - and Colonia had the very musician, another Glasgow self-import like them, to do it.

A dedicated, hard-working musician. OK, on some afternoons he could be found lying beneath the spreading branches of *il quercione*, fast asleep, spooning his guitar.

A musician with scuffed shoes and blonde hair that stood up on end as if electrified. A tattered musician, not the fastest-moving man in Italy, crumpled but unbowed, with a shy smile and pockets full of ancient harmonicas.

Tony and Prof glanced at one another, hoping no look of renewed doubt clouded their faces. Ken chose not to notice.

"Cometh the hour, cometh Davide Pastori!" Ken stated. Sure, the fly-blown eccentric - another thwarted RefuWeegee in retreat from his birthplace - would be using assorted battered and dust-coated instruments instead of a Hollywood sound-stage and full orchestra.

The Davide Pastori Quintet, ancient local musicians and their even more ancient accordions, fiddles, guitars, trumpets and clarinets, would get the job done, Ken knew. "The guy's diseased with the rhythm," he said, "plus he's got a recording studio in his house. Brought it with him from Glasgow - me and him worked with it years ago on a TV job.

"I've already got him listening to *Twistin' Gears* and made him watch the whole *Bullitt* chase sequence on YouTube," said Ken. "We'll have his version within six weeks. Because I told him we needed it in a fortnight.

"We're already well ahead, see? Music in the pipeline. We know our 11-minute film segment back to front... not to mention another thing we haven't got - our biggest positive of all."

Tony and Prof composed their least-puzzled expressions and avoided looking at one another, while thinking the same thing: how could such a lack of something be a positive? They knew Ken ignored all obstacles, but this was too much.

"We don't have a screenplay, no scripted dialogue," said Ken, "and neither does our sequence in *Bullitt* - no need to write a single word!"

Another heaven-sent bonus, Ken continued. For hadn't Tony disavowed pen, paper and keyboard?

The more Ken spoke, the easier everything became. Did they have the latest in digital shape-shifting green-screen film technology? No. Perfect. Neither had *Bullitt*.

Not one hokey faked second, which was why the car chase looked so great because it looked so real, because it was real - Ken was declaiming his words now, a holy roller at the pulpit - as real as their Bee-chase movie though Colonia's streets!

At points in Ken's ceaseless sermon, Prof's hand had almost fluttered aloft, never quite catching Ken's eye, which was in any case trained elsewhere, on a celestial prize: *Bullitt da Colonia!*

Ken was on a cinema crusade. His voice grew hushed. Some sort of verbal climax was on the horizon.

"I'm sure you'll recall me beginning with our huge casting problem - our crucial lack of a magnetic Steve McQueen in a film sequence which lives and dies by the magnetic presence of Steve McQueen."

Tony had of course forgotten all about it, such had been the rollercoaster exhilaration of Ken's monologue, paused while its speaker drew breath. Momentarily.

"I announce that I have our Steve McQueen!" Ken exclaimed, punching the air with a clenched fist in sudden triumph, forcefully enough to make Prof gasp. "Magnetic! Compelling! Colonia's *very own* Steve McQueen - we have him!"

"We do?" Prof asked in a feeble voice.

"Yes!" said Ken. "I've asked him to do it - and he's agreed. He's delighted … especially as he's got no lines to learn. Our own Steve McQueen - the one man in this town with genuine screen-acting experience! Lorenzo Ottolini!"

Chapter 7

Tony and Prof blinked and looked at one another in shock. Lorenzo Ottolini had arrived in Colonia from Glasgow as a retiree 20 years previously. Lorenzo Ottolini was a slow-moving, stooped old man in his 80s.

Lorenzo Ottolini had grown up in Glasgow where few people had noticed Lorenzo Ottolini until he changed his name and became very, very famous. Lorenzo Ottolini was an actor: Lorenzo Ottolini was the one and only Larry McMillan. Larry McMillan, star of worldwide Scottish hit TV cop show *Lochhead!*

Stunned into silence, Tony and Prof's disbelief was plain to Ken's all-seeing eye. They were rattled. They were perplexed. The pair's obvious unease - which Tony tried in vain to mask by grinning at Ken and giving a thumbs-up - had two components.

The least of their concerns was the derision which had hobbled *Lochhead!* throughout its 20-plus years of production. *Lochhead!* A terrible show!

Lochhead! An implausible police procedural so dull, so wooden it had been nicknamed *Blockhead!* Why, its multiple detractors had smirked, the exclamation mark in its title was the one exciting thing about it.

Tony and Prof were way more bothered by its star's professional reputation. His millions of worldwide TV devotees hadn't known

Larry McMillan had been a fabled alcoholic, routinely drunk on-set. Unreliable. Unpredictable. Unprofessional.

True, since his transmigration to Colonia, Larry had been a model of public sobriety. And a figure of tonsorial marvel.

By some uncanny means, Larry retained the thick, lustrous, wiry and highly un-Italian curly copper-blonde hair that 40 years earlier had been his screen trademark - a close match for the thick, lustrous, wiry copper-blonde curls of Steve McQueen.

It was a wig, of course. Although a wig like no other in the whole of Colonia. All Tuscany, all Italy. A charismatic wig. Convincing. Real hair. Just not Larry's.

The Wig became the actor. The actor was the Wig. And throughout the week or so that Larry and the Wig were involved in filming *Bullitt da Colonia*, they had acted in impeccable union.

The Wig performed every task required of it. Ditto Larry, turning this way and that on cue whenever directed, accepting take after take, phlegmatic, captivating - a star… like Steve McQueen. Not exactly like Steve McQueen. But more than close enough.

At that first meeting, though, none of them had known any of this for sure.

At this early stage of not-knowing, Prof had again raised his arm, voicing the question that had tormented him since Ken's address began.

"You say we have two Bees. *We have two Bees?*" he queried, earning a puzzled nod from Ken and a baffled grimace from Tony.

"The town certainly has two Bees, one red, one yellow," Prof went on, "belonging to the wine shop… the wine shop run by the most ill-tempered twins in Colonia, Renzo and Sergio Botti. Enoteca Botti's much-polished and barely-used Bees.

"So are we to assume that these prize possessions will be loaned to us by the terrible Botti twins to be driven by other people - us?

Other actors? Feeble Larry McMillan?

"Or - dear God! - will this quarrelsome pair, these human volcanoes... will they themselves need to occupy the Bees' driving seats, subjecting us to their hourly bursts of murderous rage, and if so, this is surely not the best..."

"Yes, and yes. But we are getting ahead of ourselves," said Ken. "For now, let's study the blueprint." He began re-running *Bullitt's* car chase once again on his laptop on the kitchen table.

"Trust me," he added. "Nothing is beyond your Ken."

Tony and Prof shrugged like genuine Italians, joining Ken at the laptop, staring at their religious text, the *Bullitt* bible. Over the next few days, they paused, rewound and took notes all the way through its 10 minutes and 53 seconds of pulse-quickening motorised cat-and-mouse.

****

"Let us never forget our mission statement," Ken said one afternoon following their first intense week of video dissection. They were tired, slumped at the kitchen table. "Our mission statement?" Tony and Prof both thought.

Ken had been studying Steve McQueen's freeze-framed air of watchful cool, alarming himself with a belated doubt: maybe Larry McMillan had nothing to match it after all. He looked up from the laptop and spotted Tony and Prof trying to compose purposeful expressions, succeeding only in looking blank and shifty.

Ken smiled. "You've forgotten the mission statement already," he said, tut-tutting. "My big speech - our expert knowledge of what makes a compelling film, blah blah blah... unique and complementary nature blah blah... individual strengths and talents, willing and quixotic - did I use the word quixotic? Don't think I did. Should've done.

"Words - too forgettable. It's as well we're not using any in this film," said Ken, rolling his eyes. "Thank god Professor Bartolomei and his rigorous maths are keeping us afloat."

It was true. Prof had demonstrated a supreme fluency in logic, numbers, timings. To him had fallen the chores of scene-by-scene analysis, the meticulous creation of a storyboard, a shooting script.

He had a priceless charm, too. Of the three of them, Prof was longest resident in Colonia, as well as being the most patient and diplomatic. Faced with his geniality, tact and diffidence, no one in the town could be annoyed.

So whenever the need arose - which was almost daily for the length of the filming process - he was on hand to mollify, divert and placate their film's most implacable on-screen talent: its principle stunt-drivers, the almost-identical Botti twins. Splenetic Renzo. Foul-tempered Sergio.

Prof it was who regulated the double-spouted Botti volcano. He also monitored the details of their physical appearance as they alternated between one seat and the other, in accordance with the logistical dictates of that day's filming and how fiercely they were arguing about whose turn it was to sit at the Bee's wheel. Which of them would be Bad Guy Driver (black suit, white shirt, spectacles) and which Bad Guy Passenger (cream raincoat).

Behavioural scientist. Wardrobe master. Continuity supervisor. Acting coach. Lion tamer. Prof: master of 1000 roles.

Tony's strengths? Basic camera skills, plus he was a young and vigorous stripling of 56 compared to his partners, both pushing 70. His relative youth suited him best for the hard physical labour that filming entailed.

And hard physical labour it had been. Week in, week out, early

March into mid-May. Long hours, most days. In a confined space. Exceedingly confined.

The only human suited to fit a Bee's back-seat area - without room for an actual seat - was a small child. For a small child, travelling by Bee was a rare treat.

For Tony, larger than a small child, the vehicle's cramped confines were a torment, a rack. A contortionist's nightmare. A chiropractor's bonanza.

But for all the aches, pains and twinges he developed, his skills as a movie cameraman improved. He got the right shots quicker.

Bullitt's hilly San Francisco street sequences took countless lavishly-equipped Hollywood film technicians five weeks to shoot. He was one man operating with a hand-held camera, often crammed behind the driver of one Bee or the other, and he amassed their film's entire footage - precisely timed, shot-by-shot from Prof's meticulous story-board - within 12 weeks, sometimes filming five hours a day.

Ken brought everything else the film required: the technical expertise, confidence, experience and not least the equipment. *Bullitt da Colonia* would never have been remotely possible without practical Ken's decades-long hands-on motion-picture industry experience and his connections.

Take, for example, the small matter of Ken's unofficial retirement gift from his BBC Scotland chums. Storeroom-savvy pals had commemorated his departure by awarding him sundry non-management-sanctioned gifts: top-quality, low-mileage, one-owner professional digital film cameras and associated editing gear.

Filming had been Ken's job. It remained his life, undiminished by retirement.

With Ken's aid, Tony soon became an authority on the hand-held merits of a Sony Z1 over the Sony F55 or the Canon C300;

the pros and cons of the Sony FS7 versus the Sony A7S Mark II, the possibilities offered by a GoPro MAX.

In addition, three months of intensive movie-making provided him with a working knowledge of craft terms ranging from depth of field to big close-up.

He knew the difference between looking-room and head-room; mastered a lexicon of shots running from high-angle wide to medium long. He grew acquainted with sundry lenses and mounts, gimbles and grips, extension poles and at one point a drone - all of it quality equipment that elevated *Bullitt da Colonia* multiple leagues above home-movie level.

More vitally still, the film could never have happened without Ken building Tony's confidence by assuring him that, despite his lack of movie experience, he was "the cameraman who can... the chap with an eye for a snap and the ability to get it before it's gone - you're the very dab!"

Because Ken was a natural director - a guide, a teacher, an enabler - who educated his charge with words of fond encouragement, offering practical tips that were memorably expressed, endless insights kindly shared.

Tony was never berated for doing something wrong. Instead, Ken took time to inform him of some small, readily-attainable old pro's measure that might improve upon whatever over-cautious/reckless beginner's method he'd used before.

Tony had grown accustomed to Ken's patient sigh of mock-exasperation followed by a rueful half-smile and some jocular reprimand. Phrases such as "Ach, what are you like, son?" or "Do you think I button up the back?" Then there was "Yep, you've done the work of two men today, laddie - Laurel and Hardy" and "I wouldn't trust you to put nuts in a monkey's mouth, you gorgeous quarter-wit."

Above all, as time went on, Tony knew that Ken was ever-ready to overcome any problem himself. By filming it himself. Or by piloting a scooter from which Tony could film the Bees behind him.

By re-imagining the problem, transforming it into a life-affirming dare.

****

Everything had of necessity begun with repeated viewings of *Bullitt's* car-chase archetype. Each time they watched it, the trio's schoolboy enjoyment of the 10 minute 53 second segment grew as they became more and more engrossed in its creators' skill and ingenuity.

Hours of dissection and re-dissection. Days spent in frame-by-frame analysis and relentless annotation. The harder they pored, the more they realised that no amount of study made the film less of a spectacle, deadened its thrill, diluted its power to quicken the pulse.

It could have been a dreary task, but never was. Nevertheless Tony was relieved to be spared most of this early YouTube hack-work, as it would have meant him writing again, penning notes and observations, timings, and so he deferred to Ken and Prof.

Likewise, he'd deferred to Ken for a film-making masterclass. True, he couldn't now remember much of it now in detail, as he'd soon worked out that he didn't need to be a master film-maker himself. He just had to point the camera where the real master film-maker, Ken, told him to.

What did he need to know? The terms Ken would use to guide him. What kind of shot Ken was aiming for. How the shot would look on screen. Ken's tutorial had begun with the range of shots they'd use.

"Perspective shots showing one Bee in relation to the other," Ken had said.

"Reaction shots - the looks on our three actors' faces... shots from their point of view as if we're in their place."

Doubtless Ken had listed other types of shot. Tony hadn't been listening.

There were plenty of potential sticking points, Tony was all too aware. Need they seek official permission to close Colonia's streets to film in, he mused aloud, answering his own question with an instant "No." As they all knew, it was best never to volunteer any information to any official Italian authority about anything.

Plus they could depend on Colonia's oldest central streets never being very busy even at their busiest, in addition to which they'd be filming in springtime, well before any summertime influx of visitors. Between 11am and 3pm most days, Colonia was as good as deserted, with few pedestrians - and no other vehicles of any kind, the Bees alone being sanctioned to make deliveries within the old town centre.

"Who can object to one guy with a camera filming two Bees doing under 15kph while a couple of other old guys hang about nearby?" asked Ken.

In the weeks to come, they would all be surprised by the complex answer to this simple question. But back then Ken's powers of positive thinking had rolled them onwards, seemingly unstoppable, identifying streams in need of fording, mountains begging to be climbed, rainbows which led to dreams.

"Shame Colonia's not as steep as San Francisco - can't get much speed up," he said, speaking more to himself than either of his novice sidekicks. "Then again, a bit of camera shake, a hint of a blur - and there's our speed.

"Timing's what matters. How close the Bees are to one another

- will we get the right shot? Easy to ruin it if the second Bee gains too quickly on the first or the first Bee pulls too far ahead.

"On the plus side, it looks to me like *Bullitt's* shots weren't all planned, so it gives us some leeway. Although they did have the world's best camera operators… and we've just got Colonia's most willing trainee camera operator.'

For the first time, Tony felt worried. Ken had fallen silent.

"Yep, that's where it gets tricky," he went on at last. "*Bullitt's* cameramen had the skills, years of experience. They could make the split-second decisions - whether to pan or to zoom when one vehicle or the other makes a move… always in focus.

"Difficult. Very difficult… extremely difficult," said Ken. "So my advice, Tony, is just point the camera in the right kind of direction and I'll take care of anything complicated.

"We can't go too wrong. It's not like we're starting with a blank canvas. We don't need to be geniuses. *Bullitt's* geniuses did all the hard work - they put everything right in front of us. We just need to copy it." Tony exhaled in relief.

Chapter 8

Of course, there were some things that *Bullitt da Colonia* couldn't copy - in particular, the original chase's ending: one vehicle upside down inside a ball of deadly flame in an exploding gas station.

The operators of Colonia's sole fuel-vendor were unlikely to sanction such a spectacular and risky film recreation, everyone knew. As for the Botti twins… their on-screen participation had been swiftly agreed (within five seconds of being invited), but neither wanted one of their Bees set ablaze, or upended.

So the film climaxed without fire and smoke, instead a thick dust-cloud into which a fully-upright, non-blazing Bee disappeared amid thick roadside pines on the fastest, straightest section of the chase, apparently crashing on the twisting drive up out of Colonia to Faggio Basso. In reality, the Bee's dusty cinematic entry into automotive Valhalla was facilitated by Prof - in a single take - using two leaf-blowers.

"There'll be a disclaimer in the end-credits," said Ken: "No Piaggio Bees were harmed during the filming process."

There were two further daunting problems of screen mechanics. One was simple to fix, the other less so: 1) *Bullitt's* non-vanishing VW, 2) its crashing motorcyclist.

It was easy to recreate the original *Bullitt's* infamous continuity flaw, a recurrent green Volkswagen Beetle that keeps popping up at illogical stages of the chase, having already been overtaken by both pursuit vehicles. They borrowed a neighbour's elderly green Fiat 500 and parked it in all the wrong places, correctly mimicking all the incorrect sightings.

But how to find a skilled two-wheeled stunt driver able to topple a moped and then slide it across a road onto a verge when menaced out of the blue by onrushing Bees?

Tony had shared this worry with Gabriella. Her solution was straightforward, although it required him to swallow his wariness about close first-hand exposure to her taciturn cop brother, the hulking Piero.

She would simply ask Piero to stage the violent, dangerous stunt for them. Her brother knew all about falls and upended vehicles, she said in an airy manner which Tony found unsettling.

As she'd gone on to explain, Piero - a fan of daredevil stunt TV shows in his youth - had devoted his teens to riding a moped over logs, off roofs, and up mountainsides without fear or major injury.

Which was how he had ended up looming over Tony in his police uniform the following sunny morning, casting a frightening shadow over Gabriella's lawn in Faggio Basso, where Tony knelt oiling her lawn mower's blades.

"I can slide a moped better than anyone," Piero growled, making Tony catch his breath. "Tomorrow afternoon, be ready with your camera."

As Piero strode away, Tony had shouted *"Molto grazie"* with as much baritone bravado as he could counterfeit, hoping his voice didn't betray fear.

Piero had showed up as promised with his moped on the film's designated section of mountain road. He was given an old jacket and jeans to disguise his tight-fitting Kevlar biker leathers, thereafter toppling and sliding his moped with masterful ease.

He'd shredded three sets of jeans and jackets in the process - prompting rare mutters of annoyance from the film's otherwise placid Head of Costume, Prof - but had avoided damaging himself, the moped, any trees, the road surface or either Bee.

Nor had he inflicted harm, physical or verbal, on Tony, who'd thus begun congratulating himself that his two-year romantic entanglement with Piero's sister had earned police approval.

But whenever life pats you on the back and ushers you two steps forward, it's guaranteed in that moment to grab you by the scruff of the neck and haul you three steps back.

And so it transpired, the two worst types of agonising setback began plaguing Colonia's MBM Studios. People! Events!

****

Problematic people? Dozens had emerged, not least the Botti twins. The camera's presence seemed to dampen the siblings' impulses to bicker, which was better than good - it was incredible.

But whenever Tony tried framing them in his lens, Renzo and Sergio became cinema's two most self-conscious men, Bad Guy Bottis stealing every scene with their bad acting.

Rigid and unnatural poses. Pained half-grins and uncertain stares. Awkward twitches. Yet all the duo were required to do was sit at a steering wheel and drive, or sit next to a steering wheel and be driven. Look ahead. Look left a little. Look right.

And each time they faced the lens, one inflexible brother would start pouting and frowning while the other bared his teeth in a dead-fish grimace. They lolled their tongues. Narrowed their eyes. Closed their eyes. Chewed their lips.

To display concentration? Fear, brutality, psychosis, dyspepsia, ecstasy? All of these feelings at once it often looked.

It didn't help that the only films the Bottis had ever watched all the way through were Sergio Leone's three Spaghetti Western classics starring the brothers' hero, Clint Eastwood.

A Fistful of Dollars. For A Few Dollars More. The Good, The Bad and The Ugly - The Bad, The Worse and The Botti Twins.

The project would have been sunk without Prof's adroit and tender ministrations. "Cigar, cigar… grit your teeth - do nothing, Clint Eastwood," Ken and Tony sometimes heard him murmur during takes, reminding Renzo and Sergio to focus on clenching an imaginary cigar tight between their lips in honour of Clint whenever either felt tempted to try any other facial expression.

Prof was likewise on hand to check the brothers were correctly-costumed Bad Guys. Driver: dark suit, specs. Passenger: off-white raincoat, shotgun.

He it was, too, who reminded the pair to keep their eyes on their Bee's direction of travel when needed; to look in its driving mirror when instructed, cooing "Right" or "Left" or "Straight ahead" whenever the pair's faces veered off course.

Thank the gods of cinema that it had worked, aided by a tangible daily end-product: footage of the twins' activity that, to everyone's surprise, looked convincing.

So convincing that it silenced Renzo and Sergio's recurrent complaint: that this whole movie enterprise should not imitate Steve McQueen, it should recreate Clint's scenes from his Dollar trilogy. Prof silenced them by handing them each a cigar.

If the twins were satisfied with their toil, so was Ken. "Wrong guys, right movie!" he asserted each evening after having presented everyone with that day's filmic output, banking each second into the final 10min 53sec pay-off.

****

One Friday night, having totted up their weekly tally of screen-worthy minutes and seconds, Ken insisted on drinks for all in Zio Beppo. Celebrations were due. "Wrong guys, right movie!" he said once more.

Working frame by frame to assemble their movie, they'd reached the six-minute mark, Ken reckoned. More than half-way there.

Tony had a question. Ken's mantra: *Wrong guys, right movie!* Who did it apply to - the Bottis?

"It applies to all of us," said Ken. "We're the wrong guys to be doing a movie as good-looking as this, a film that works as well as it does, on no budget.

"We're too old. We're not yesterday's men - we're the day-before-yesterday's men re-making last century's greatest movie car chase - *a car chase*, in this day and age, when cars are Mother Earth's enemy... how out of time can we be?"

"But no... because we've engaged in the timeless act of making art. And we've created something bigger than all of us... bigger than the Bottis' foul tempers.

"Us oldsters... giving what little time we have left to art, using our fading stamina and ingenuity. And our accoomer-lated... accu-lated..." Ken had stumbled over the word, five glasses of chianti deep into the evening.

"The acc-rumbulated wisdom of the crumblies. The pissed wisdom of old boys with nothing else to do but try and make art - record time's wingèd chariot running over our bunions before it kills us.

"Old guys with stiff legs, sore arms, sore backs and full bladders - there I go. Shift yourself, Ace Lensman, I'm away for an old man's piss."

"I'm sure the old man will give you some, no need to ask him," Prof said.

Tony had awoken at noon that Saturday morning felled by the first hangover of his time in Italy. Pubs and drinking: he'd never been a man for either.

He smiled as he pondered Ken's drunken movie-making declaration. For an on-the-spot, made-up-in-the-pub theory of artistic intent and old age, it had some truth to it. Sure, *Bullitt da Colonia* had been an amateur pastime. Yet their efforts and their will had given it concrete form, brought it to life.

So what if they'd set out to copy someone else's masterpiece.

In succeeding, they'd created something that was theirs alone - which could be enjoyed by anyone, regardless of whether or not they knew the source of its inspiration.

Better still, the film process had asked things of them that no task had asked before. Tony, Prof, the Botti twins: all of them had been required to use talents they hadn't known they'd possessed, new skills. They'd been freed from being passive by-standers - mere consumers. In becoming artists, they'd gained control.

In particular, no one could overlook Prof's practical wisdom, his miraculous directorial alchemy with the Botti twins. He had transformed the life-long behaviour of the squabbling duo, making them realise that the two of them being their best filmed selves was more fun - and easier - than the two of them being their usual worst everyday real-life selves.

The Bottis had bickered because they had nothing better to do, nowhere better to be. The pair had been given a place, a role, a use, a purpose.

They all had.

In the Bottis' case, immortality had beckoned them to sit in their Bees same as usual, but now looking to the far distance with coiled intent, avoiding unwise impulses to smile while clamping their jaws on an imaginary cheroot. Cigar, cigar - Clint Eastwood!

"If this is acting in the movies, we've both been Hollywood stars for 75 years," Sergio said.

"They'll put our names up in lights - Clint Eastwood, Steve McQueen, Larry McMillan... the Botti twins," said Renzo.

Renzo looked at Sergio. Sergio looked back. Then they began laughing. Together. Colonia's old granite walls had never echoed to such uproarious fraternal harmony.

People and events will always trip you up, of course. So it was now in this time of unprecedented communal rejoicing among all peoples, that an event clubbed the cast and crew of *Bullitt da Colonia* round the head. It was a setback that was both unexpected and calamitous, more saddening than shocking, a terrible event: death claimed their Steve McQueen.

****

Larry McMillan's death came as a grievous shock to Colonia's film-makers, but it had often been anticipated during his long-ago TV star peak - no, death had been willed upon him by one ghoulish Glasgow tabloid story after another, snatched paparazzi shots hymning his stark physical decline on a near-weekly basis throughout the eighties and early nineties.

Larry's bleary, waxen-faced exits from showbiz parties. Bouts of drink-induced raging incoherence at awards dinners. Numbed late-night falls in and out of taxis.

His alcoholism had caused black-outs, black eyes, seizures, frequent absences from *Lochhead!* shoots, prolonged spells of hospitalisation and rehab. His liver was permanently damaged.

His eyes had latterly been a more clouded blue than in the

long-lost days of Detective Chief Inspector Lochhead, but Larry's Colonia life had been one of untroubled sobriety. Years of drink had damaged his short-term memory, though. Hence his pleasure in a movie role with no lines.

Larry's decline had been obvious during the first day's filming, his pained old man's struggle to climb into the Bee and sit at its steering wheel. It wasn't enough to pretend not to notice, the three of them knew. Better to pitch in and be helpful each morning.

Set down a small box to ease his uncertain step up into the vehicle's cabin, and provide steadying hands and shoulders for Larry to brace himself against.

What had Larry given them in return in his 10 days of filming? None of them knew how to put it, how to measure the touching seriousness with which he'd taken their little project.

"He was gracious... courteous... a presence - a star," Tony said as they'd sat forlorn in Zio Beppo on the day of the news of his death. "He was too quick agreeing to help us - he shouldn't have, for his health's sake. And he stuck with it for a fortnight, gave us a respect our work didn't merit right away.

"Him, the veteran actor, and us amateurs, enthusiasts - a bunch of pests. But he treated us as equals. No condescension.

"Larry donated his professionalism," he said, surprised by his own oratory. This was no comedy routine. "He stuck at it when it wasn't easy. Two or three hours every day for 10 days. He showed us tolerance, patience, generosity, humility.

"He was an actor, but the way he treated us was no act. Dignified. Serene. Regal - no, that's not it. Larry was statesmanlike - no, he was Presidential, in the best old-time sense of the word.

"Larry carried us along with him, a leader making sure his troops got somewhere. Bloody shame he never got to see the finished article, how good he'd made it... to see how good he looked on film to the very end."

Ken nodded at the impromptu eulogy. "President Larry McMillan, hail to the chief," he said. "Now you've mentioned it, that face of his wouldn't look out of place chiselled up there on Mount Whatsit - Mount Rushmore.

"Lincoln, Washington… those two other guys - and our Larry McMillan. Never thought I'd hear myself say that out loud."

"And it's not how my wife would put it," said Prof. "She'd seen Larry about the town the past few months - reckoned he had the look of a poor soul who knew his time was up. Mind you, she didn't get to see the old trouper at close quarters like we did."

"This is no boast, but I reckon we gave Larry something in advance for what he gave us," Ken said. "That thing he said between takes, remember?

"I could weep thinking about it: 'Nobody in TV wrote me a line worth saying - and you give me a big role worth acting.' No showbiz guff, no self-pity. He meant it.

"His gift to us. Our gift to him. It's good we didn't know it was his last scene - we'd've cried all the way through. We let him sign off as the King of Cool."

Ken ducked his head and fumbled for a hankie. Prof removed his spectacles, mumbling about something in his eye. All three raised a glass, saluting Larry's memory.

As they did, there was small consolation in knowing that every single one of their star's most identifiably Steve McQueen-esque shots had already been filmed.

****

Those few few unfilmed post-Larry sequences had been the active uptempo ones, fortunately. The ones that evoked the car chase's

101

tension, amounting to three minutes or so of screen-time, all shot looking straight-ahead through the Bee's windscreen, its driver's magnificent blonde locks glimpsed in passing, on the periphery.

So in the days after their star's demise, *Bullitt da Colonia's* makers were well served by a secret last-minute stand-in Larry, equipped not with The Wig, but its acrylic cousin: a passable trimmed-down, wavy-blonde hairpiece.

To avoid demeaning Larry, they'd always kept his stand-in and his stunt-double wig secret from him.

Larry's replacement was younger than Larry. More physically able than their three creaking selves. As well as being the most skilled and daring driver with whom Tony had ever had the terrifying misfortune to share a car journey.

Gabriella. "Gabriella Ferrari," Tony called her. She owned every boy racer's dream car, a Fiat Abarth 595, and drove it flat-out, always. Very fast.

"How else to drive, I am Italian," she said whenever Tony asked her to slow down, dizzied by her high-speed ascent of the tight hairpin bends between Colonia and Faggio Basso, always on the wrong side of the 5km road, steep falls and treetops flashing past in a noisy blur, shadow and sunlight alternating non-stop.

So she hadn't enjoyed the stop-start nature of filming during her week's work, restrained from getting the Bee anywhere near its claimed top speed of 60kph. Still, when she'd seen the on-screen results of her work, there was grudging acceptance of the film-making process. It worked, it looked good, she was forced to agree.

"But who apart from stupid men would enjoy doing this same little routine so many times, the endless repetition of it - and so slow! - the same one damned thing over and over again," she'd said early on, not noticing Tony's stifled laughter, his hand clamped over his mouth, "but I suppose there's satisfaction in making the stupid business look right."

He'd laughed aloud at this, going on to repeat the phrase to her after their more intimate bedroom moments - "Did you find eventual satisfaction in our endless repetition of this slow little routine, over and over?" - to her annoyance and exasperation. Which made him laugh all the more. And her, too, eventually, sometimes.

Within the week, MBM Studios had ceased needing to keep on doing the same damned thing over and over again. They had the shots, the right amount of digital footage to absorb Ken in weeks of productive final-editing.

****

Eleven months after they'd begun, two weeks before the deadline for submitting their film as an event at the coming summer's Fish and Chip Festival, MBM Studios' three heads had clustered around Ken's kitchen table and watched their finished product for the umpteenth time.

It worked. It was good. And it had survived the latest obstacles placed in its path.

People and events are omnipresent threats to any enterprise, of course, but they can be joined by another monstrous tyrant: needless over-thinking. That's the horror that truly saps the will and blights ambition.

It had reared up without warning in a scary late-night phone call from Ken Moody - a call with the potential to sink the project by removing its greatest facilitator: Signor Moody himself.

Ken had sounded most un-Ken-like over the phone, rattled and annoyed, shaky, breathless, speaking in an odd high-pitched voice. "I've just realised what it looks like we're doing," Ken had said. "We'll look idiots copying a bad TV show. I don't think I can go on… I really don't."

I can't go on… was Ken serious? He sounded it. "Wrong guys, right movie" was one thing: a cheeky hair-ruffle, a nonchalant gesture of support. Hearing Ken say he didn't think he could go on was a knife in the guts.

If Ken wasn't there, putting his heart and soul into his film, their film…

Tony tried to keep a panicked whine from his voice as he asked Ken to explain.

Ken took a shaky intake of breath. "Imagine the headlines when the tabloids back in Glasgow find out - and they will find out because we've got the actual Lochhead from the actual *Lochhead!*" he said.

"It makes us news. We'll be all over the papers - mocked, patronised, derided. 'Old Italian Jokers' Italian Job Joke - The *Lochhead!* Blockhead's Back And He's Brought His Pasta-It Chums With Him!' We'll be accused of re-making *Lochhead!*"

Ken had a point. Old fools playing at recreating Lochhead! To be accused of copying nonsense. It was the opposite of what MBM Studios were doing.

But if you had a mind to make the link, to be a lazy tabloid reporter and join the dots and present the outline of a baboon instead of what the artist intended - a mighty lion…

There was a moment of doubt, but then Tony inhaled, inflating his lungs with ease - and he knew 100% that he could talk Ken out of this impasse.

Chapter 9

Their film would not be halted - not when it was so close to completion. For theirs was a noble quest. An admirable feat of technical ability. Undertaken with bravado, not self-deluding stupidity. He told Ken so.

Ken, however, remained in existential crisis mode, his confidence undermined. "You were a TV critic - you must have slated *Lochhead!*" Ken was saying.

"They'll dig out old *Chronicle* columns and call you a hypocrite for doing what you used to say was rubbish - or they'll call you a thief, stealing ideas. A thief *and* a hypocrite."

Tony spoke with kind insistence. "They can say whatever they want, Ken, but not a word of it can harm your reputation as a film-maker, or put anyone off *Bullitt da Colonia.*

"If it was just me making a home video, some clueless old fool kidding himself, claiming he's Martin Scorsese - that would be sad and stupid. But our film's got Ken Moody. An auteur creating a cinematic homage… conducting an exercise in conceptual movie-making… employing your craft, your expertise - Bafta winner Ken Moody!"

There was a long pause. Then Ken spoke. "Only a wee Scottish Bafta, hardly worth mentioning, but still…" he said. The battle had been won. Ken was back on board.

"We can't worry about being in the papers," said Tony. "We will be in the papers because we owe it to Larry to tell the world how great he was in his last role. So we'll be in the papers on our terms.

"We stress your technical skills and our knowledge, the thought that's gone into everything - 'We're big fans of Steve McQueen, sure. But we didn't ask Larry to do an impression of him. And we were more inspired by Bullit's director Peter Yates - he laid down such a massive technical challenge, we couldn't resist.'

"We admit our limitations - we're not claiming to be the next blockbuster... We stress what we're doing is a passion. It started as a labour of love and somehow became a job we'll never get paid for... no, it's our calling, our destiny - a work of art!"

Ken was chuckling now, Tony sensing he'd laid the hyperbole on too thick. He kept talking anyway: "We know why we're doing what we're doing, that's all anyone else needs to know."

"And why are we doing what we're doing?" asked Ken, his everyday perkiness restored.

"Because it's fun... because we can... because we can't do anything else - because we might as well, because we must!"

"Some folk might focus on *Lochhead!'s* flaws - but all TV shows have flaws. And 40 years later folk all over the world are still enjoying Lochhead! The character Larry McMillan created is still enjoyed... still believed in. And we were so lucky that he gave us a final gift with his last performance in *Bullitt da Colonia* - not just his last performance but one of his best...' Imagine the headline: Poignant Movie Farewell of TV's Top Scots 'Tec."

Ken growled a response: "Let me at the bastards - I've got a film to finish editing and be proud of!"

Tony's reply - "Death to too much thinking!" - fizzed and crackled through the telephonic ether. Unseen by one another, they both punched the air.

That night's big crisis had been talked into submission. The next big crisis wasn't slow in over-thinking itself to life, though.

It was a lot more public, too, and more troublesome: in reaction to their film, a vicious hand-to-hand guerrilla conflict of cultural opinion had started raging on Colonia's streets - and more than once it had gone beyond angry talk and taken physical expression.

****

They'd begun referring to it as *Colonia's War of the Opposing Schools of Thought on Film* as if it was a little joke, a small nuisance. But it became alarming.

In part, the debate reflected the depth of the movie-mad town's engagement with cinema. There had been initial succour in the thought - at last, an art-form that locals care about! The townspeople certainly had little time for any other form of cultural activity.

Theatre? A yearly one-off: the children's Christmas Nativity pageant at the duomo. Painting? Sculpture? Tourists came in little groups for a week to learn how to do such things on expensive holidays held in a couple of Colonia's grander villas, taught by Scots-Italian art-school graduates.

Music? You rarely heard it drifting from peoples' homes, no pop hits, no concertos, no arias, no practicing piano players. Occasionally, you might be assailed by a child violinist's tortured sawings.

Live public music performances were confined to the summertime disfigurement of the Piazza Antica - shrill and earnest Puccini opera recitals by shrill and earnest American college choirs on exchange visits.

There was no book shop, so no one ever read or discussed

literature. Newspapers? In truth, no one in Colonia needed to read a newspaper because everyone knew everyone else's business - often before they themselves did.

Tony recalled starting one of his frequent stand-up lectures by saying, to murmurs of recognition, that you could take it as read that no self-respecting Italian reads anything.

The town's sole print media audience was, as Tony knew, Scottish, exiles wanting him to import trashy Glasgow crime and football gossip sheets, a special treat from home, like deep-fried pizza but less healthy.

But Colonia sure liked going to the movies. The town's sole arts venue, Cinema Italia on Via Roma, sold out its 400 seats most days, most weeks. "In Italy, all roads lead to Rome - in Colonia, all feet tread roads leading to the picture house on Via Roma," he'd said into another laughter vacuum.

Daily since 1933, Cinema Italia had shown every type of film. Newsreels. Mainstream native-made hits. Cartoons. Overdubbed modern-day Hollywood blockbusters. Art house imports with subtitles, although these - since they needed to be read - incurred resistance.

Cinema Italia was where young and old met. Glasgow returnees and Colonia never-leaves alike. Deviant devotees of Dario Argento. Star Wars buffs. Gloomy dogme addicts. Folk who laughed fit to bust at Italy's biggest modern comedy, *Quo Vado?* Because films were the one cultural form to set local tongues a-wagging.

Those wagging tongues had started producing huge volumes of outraged noise the previous summer when the town's populace registered Tony's camera on Colonia's streets and its three-wheeled focus.

The Bee-propelled hell-driving of the menacing, devil-may-care Botti twins! Such a peril, such an affront, such a hideous din! For some kind of film...

According to these locals, filming had threatened public safety by inciting shameless, reckless high-speed antics in the town centre. It was madness, a blight on all that civilised Colonia society held dear.

According to other observers, such pitiful play-acting was the slowest spectacle they'd ever half-watched for two minutes before losing interest - and by the way, they knew what uncivilised Colonia society held most dear: gossiping and holding itself better than its neighbours, so those types of folk could *vai a cacare*, go take a dump.

Every single resident of the town had an opinion on some aspect of their film, it seemed, and the more tangential their feelings were, the louder and more frequently they voiced them. *Fuck yourself, Hollywood old men! Welcome, new Colonia cinema pioneers!*

There were those who thought the film was A Good Thing because it might increase tourism, and thus boost local business. There were those who thought the film was A Bad Thing because it might boost tourism, and thus destroy Colonia's self-reliant pre-capitalist identity, formed over centuries, while also boosting local businesses for a brief spell, making them dependent on tourism - and what about afterwards, when the unsustainable tourism boom was over?

Another faction feared that the film might not boost their business, but it could easily boost that of their rivals. There were yet more Colonia business owners who feared that this damned film would somehow ruin their rivals, driving them into penury, and if that were to happen, what enjoyment would they have in their lives if they could no longer day-dream about their rivals' penniless downfall?

Even worse, in looking down their noses at their broken old commercial foes, they might grow conscience-stricken and end up taking pity on the poverty-stricken bastards whom they'd enjoyed hating for so long. They might end up helping them! And then what would be their life's daily purpose - what?

Chapter 10

Colonia's committed cinephiles were the ones who most irked Tony, Ken and Prof. The ones with pithy expert opinions, based on decades of movie-going, expressed with searing cogency. Others were happy being contrary for contrariness's sake. Denunciation was rife in both camps.

Some proclaimed MBM's filmic monster the wrong kind of film, whatever kind of film it was... and OK, maybe they didn't know for sure what kind of film it was because, like everyone else, they hadn't seen it, but they knew enough to judge a film by its title - and a cousin they'd bumped into at Cinema Italia assured them it would be called *Sex And Lies in Tuscany!*

Bullitt da Colonia's unseen status proved no barrier to impassioned disparagement. Why wasn't it a Sergio Leone-style Spaghetti Western? Or a satirical sci-fi sexploitation giallo? An old-time Busby Berkeley musical extravaganza? A modern variant on *The Bicycle Thieves?*

Tony of course devised a comedy routine with which to disarm all detractors: "Folk slagging off our film for not being this, not being that... you might as well decry my Auntie Annie for having a fanny and not having a knob - how dare she never be my Uncle Bob!"

Ken was the only person who got to hear Tony say it, though, flicking a rictus grin on and off before telling him not to be transphobic.

Spokespersons representing Colonia's many and varied political claques and schisms added further layers of dissonant racket. Just the thought of their ceaseless braying made Ken wring his hands and raise his eyes heavenwards in mute supplication to the all-knowing God of Cinema whom he, Tony and Prof were agreed resembled John Waters.

Still their critics' barbs fizzed and crackled. Some left-wing idealogues *entirely* understood what such an appalling film was truly about - if only their fellow Coloniesi could open their eyes to its indigestible underlying message of paternalist hegemony ("It propounds the evil doctrine of American corporate capitalist cultural imperialism and must be resisted!").

They were in marked contrast to those avant-rightists who misunderstood exactly what the film was about, it was as plain as the jutting lower jaw on Mussolini's face ("It concerns the innate superiority of American corporate capitalist free will, the embrace of which only fools can spurn!").

Some mumbling grumblers hung about on street corners, grumbling and mumbling whenever Tony passed by, muttering that they couldn't see much harm in this stupid film idea, so long as the damned thing wasn't shot outside their front door. Worse still were those who with 100% certainty *did* want it shot right outside their front door: such commercial possibilities - the scope for self-advertisement!

The arrival of a Bee, a Botti or a camera needed only be rumoured and garish posters appeared in windows in some streets advertising their occupiers' services as gardeners or vendors of home-grown produce.

There had been one benefit, though. To the trio's relief, Colonia's residents had displayed less than the customary amount of antipathy to each other during the social insurrection inspired by their film.

Sure, there remained low-level disputes over mis-sorted domestic refuse being placed in recycling bins. Perennial arguments about Sgr P parking his car in Sgr G's space saw the routine deployment of homicidal throat-cutting gestures.

Otherwise, boiling local wrath enveloped the trio's movie-making, reaching alarming intensity with the appearance in chalk, scrawled by unknown hands, of pro- and anti-film slogans on paving stones.

The absolute peak of written hostility was attained when, under cover of darkness, some anonymous Italian-speaker took a thick black marker pen to the red UK pillarbox in Piazza Antica. A gift from Glasgow's Lord Provost, now it announced *"Nessun nuovo film Scozzese!"* - No new Scottish film!

Did such graffito signal the emergence of a terrifying division between native Coloniesi and Glasgow-born incomers, some residents wondered. The town's weathered walls, evolved over slow centuries, so photogenic: would they be disfigured by modern spray-painted expressions of bigotry and international discrimination?

Would the quiet old streets soon resound to ugly curses in a sectarian Italo-Scots turf war? Barricades? Fist fights?

Happily, fears of war proved momentary, dissolved into laughter overnight when *"Nessun nuovo film Scozzese!"* was amended to state *"Nessun uovo film Scozzese!"* - No Scottish egg film!

Over the course of the next month, Colonia's appetite for internecine strife shrank, failing to take violent physical shape. Instead, strange and tortuous philosophical alliances arose between unlikely partners.

The Loose Alliance of Elderly Chip Shop Migrants and Ironic Local Hipster Skateboard Kids took up a pro-*Bullitt da*

Colonia stance against The Shifting League of Established Native Academics, Grocers and Young Incoming Professionals.

Other campaigning groups emerged - a self-spawning amoebic cluster of sub-divisional mutant factions, cadres, splinter groups and cliques. Thankfully, each new movement defused and diluted Colonia's fury. Five-minute-long verbal jousts between opposing groups on Via di Mezzo subsided into sporadic conversational sniping in Zio Beppo.

****

The war of words was abating, but now and again its three main frontline troops found themselves subjected to fusillades of ill will..

"I'm going to impersonate you telling one of your terrible bits of jokey wordplay - give you a pain same as the one I've just suffered," Ken told Tony one morning. "This flame of controversy we lit - it's hanging over Colonia like the sword of Damocles!

"That wheezing fraud Pardini, the butcher, in his shop. He detonated a social embarrassment grenade on me at close quarters. Nobody but me and him in the place - and he keeps me waiting for 10 minutes, deliberately ignores me, the blood-stained old rogue, shuffling around, hiding behind the salami-slicer."

Prof reckoned any delay was more likely coincidental, on account of the myopic, slow-moving veteran butcher, who had to be over 90, simply not seeing Ken.

Ken remained peeved. Enough was enough, he declared. "So many hours of public outrage over a film less than 11 minutes long," he said. "Time to piss on every begrudgeful fucker's *tagliatelle* by keeping our heads down and just getting on with it."

So they did.

It also helped that what Colonia's angry swarms of protestors, counter-protestors and blowhards failed to spot was that Tony had completed all the action-sequence filming during the preceding first weeks of May.

None of them noticed he'd gone back to his old stills camera, taking his usual portraits. The two competing Bees had ceased their buzzing, long eclipsed by locals' howls of peeved controversy.

Tony spent three hours one morning filming head-shots of the cast inside a Bee parked inside Ken's garden, each member of the trio nudged, calmed and/or supported by Prof. Most importantly, Ken finessed *Bullitt da Colonia* into life, second by painstaking second, in Hollywood-on-the-Serchio's edit-suite: the laptop in his kitchen.

They had sidestepped the storm by outpacing it, hiding from it, and then ignoring it.

****

Shouldering a backpack, Tony locked his front door and walked towards his car for the hour's drive to Pisa airport and his three-day Glasgow stay. Returning to the city always made him anxious, jittery.

His stomach clenched and his jaws tightened. His temples grew taut, his head aching with his life's current big question: *Gabriella - has she decided to finish it... us... me?*

More questions barged in. He'd disappointed another woman, must have done - how had he done so this time? By repeating old mistakes? Or committing new crimes? How sad would he be without Gabriella? Events. People. Men. Women.

He shook his head as if that might disperse its flock of questions.

Ken had sat him down to watch *A Night To Remember*, a famed

British black-and-white film from the fifties depicting the sinking of the *Titanic*. The era's special effects hadn't aged well.

An obvious papier-mâché iceberg. An oncoming model *Titanic* afloat in a studio water-tank. "And now you're going to see something - what film students learn to call 'crossing the line'," Ken had said in one of his many lectures, with an insistence that made Tony feel deflated, depressed.

To be confronted with something he didn't know, new information to comprehend. Forced to learn yet another new lesson. At his late age. At 56, he knew all he needed to.

Facing the unknown was for kids. Education was exhausting, forcing you to acknowledge you didn't know everything already. What grown-up wanted to peer into the void of their own ignorance? He hoped he wouldn't be required to learn anything new in Glasgow; wouldn't be compelled to make the effort to become educated.

He'd stared at Ken's laptop, the monochrome film paused before the big impact. Port and starboard, left and right, Ken had said: "Left-hand point-of-view, right-hand point-of-view - watch for the error."

He regarded an unconvincing depiction of Arctic seas: a bogus *Titanic*, a fake iceberg. Each drawn to the other. Cameras mounted on both. Left-side. Right-side.

Suddenly the film-maker's error became plain. The fake iceberg was floating on the model ship's left - moments later, it gouged the vessel's right flank. It didn't make sense. An illogical cinema mistake.

"Take heart," Ken had said. "You've seen the *Titanic* look all wrong as it hits a wrong-looking iceberg. But the mistake didn't stop you watching it. As in making a film, so in making your way through life. Mistakes happen. Few folk notice.

"So what I'm saying is we're going to be OK with our film - because it's got no mistakes in it."

Philosopher Ken, dispensing food for thought. He'd made Tony wonder whether in all his mostly-failed relationships with women, he'd been the *Titanic* or the iceberg. Was he Gabriella's iceberg? Or she his? Starboard can become port, left somehow become right. Illogic reigns. Stupid men, smarter women.

Was it logical to wonder whether there was a comedy routine in all this? He began devising one. His mood brightened.

My grandfather was there when the Titanic sank... three times he shouts out a warning to the crowd, louder each time - "It's gonna sink!" What thanks does he get? They kick him out of the cinema!

Whether the iceberg hits the Titanic or the Titanic hits the iceberg... one side of the ship or the other, it makes no difference - there's still a collision, the ship sinks, the iceberg floats on regardless and everybody's feet get wet.

One more task remained before he left Colonia for Glasgow: a fond farewell to the woman he loved, he feared - and feared he would lose. He stood in Via Pascoli outside Gabriella's estate agency, watching through its large window as she spoke on the office landline. She cradled the phone on her shoulder, pressed to one ear, intent, both hands switched to 100% maximum gesticulate mode, unaware he was outside.

She was frowning, absorbed in some property deal, a piece of commerce she'd doubtless conducted a thousand times. He smiled to himself: professional expertise marked everything she did, including her dealings with him.

Her voice grew louder, with a scolding edge to it, a harshness of pitch. She could be abrasive, as well as elegant. The maternal force who would not be brooked. Who was not always easy to be around.

Her eyes narrowed and grew more severe beneath her dark brows as she paced her office floor, with its large, tasteful and modern dove-grey tiles - unlike those in his flat. She stepped with fastidious purpose and precision, pointing her toes so as to avoid the lines between each tile.

She'd told him why she avoided the lines during a moment in which he'd glimpsed a different Gabriella, playful, adolescent - a moment she'd allowed him, a moment he'd never forget.

For if she stood on any line between the tiles, she confided that afternoon when not only had she tip-toe'd barefoot but also wandered naked throughout his whole apartment, bad luck would ensue. Then she'd giggled and stuck out her tongue.

As he re-ran that moment, she half-registered him through the window pane at last, her eyes looking a little beyond him, an idle gaze, seeming to appraise him as a less desirable part of her roster of properties. The hard-to-shift backstreet structure in need of renovation. Whose viability was moot.

Despite Colonia's 30C heat, he felt himself shiver under her unfocused look - until that second when she truly saw him. Her face brightened and without breaking off her phone conversation, she widened her eyes, lifting eyebrows, the hint of a smile on her lips.

And then she turned her back, slowly stepping away, twirling the phone's cable with one hand. Was he being dismissed? Banished to Glasgow? Then she faced him again, offering a real smile... still preoccupied, but her eyes engaged on his. He pantomimed wiping away a tear, and waved.

She raised her chin in reply, her eyes locking on his in a wistful way he hadn't seen before. Still smiling, she half-turned to look at her office's wall-clock before facing him again, pointing over his shoulder into the far distance, regal, gesturing for him to flee.

He must catch a plane! Shoo!

He bowed low in an elaborate comic curtsey, earning himself a half-smile. She pointed into the distance, bidding his departure.

As he obeyed, turning away, he felt a stab of sadness. She might not miss him, but he would miss her. He would miss Colonia, too, he realised, as dull and soporific as it was in its unchanging sun and heat.

As usual, he was returning to Glasgow because he had to, out of duty. The city would be grey, rain-soaked, chilling, windy. There was perhaps the possibility of unforeseen excitement, but big-city pitfalls, too.

And yet his visit didn't prompt the usual overwhelming sense of foreboding. He'd been making an effort to defer to Gabriella, to accommodate her. He'd likewise been working to make himself overlook Colonia's lack of excitement.

So for the first time his pulse quickened with mild anticipation about his three-day absence in Glasgow. Stuff happening. A wee jaunt. A change. A holiday in the big city…

Was it wrong to look forward to a break from the woman he told himself he loved? Maybe it confirmed their relationship was too sedate, lacking vitality, lacking passion.

He reminded himself, too, how Gabriella had been even more self-contained over the previous few weeks, more withdrawn. He imagined his return. Heard her deliver the deadly phrase meant to soften the blow of a romance's ending: *It's not you, Tony, it's me.*

But how could he truly be looking forward to even one day in Glasgow, let alone three. A drab, cold place in which to ponder a drab, cold Gabriella-free future.

His past six months of film-making had been a fool's distraction, he saw now: a sideshow. Just like the strangely enjoyable month-long uproar around *Bullitt da Colonia*. He'd indulged himself with the whole process, grown lazy, stopped himself answering questions about what kind of man he was, what kind of place Colonia was, whether he should be there.

He could no longer work out whether the town was a deadly-dull backwater or a haven of restorative calm. He was also unsure whether he was a by-stander in life or a participant, a perpetual outsider on purpose or by default.

Where did he belong? Who was he?

Whoever he was, his old critics said he always had to try and be funny, slipping into his familiar comedy persona, the seen-it-all stand-up cynic. Being simply serious was simply beyond him.

Concentrate on the serious blazing promise of a Glasgow summer, Tony: the city's streets were guaranteed to be flooded, gale-scoured, Siberian. A test for his near-year-round Colonia outfit of shorts and polo shirt, linen suit.

So at least he'd return with a new Italian winter wardrobe, assembled in response to Glasgow's emergency summertime climate: raincoats, sweaters, tweed.

He could buy a kilt, too.

Tony Wearzakilty: Gabriella would be amused - no, appalled. And a woollen kilt would be too hot and sweaty for everyday wear in Colonia, although it would look good on Sunday night's red carpet. Not that Colonia had a red carpet. *No kilt, Tony.*

Three days until a world premiere in a town that found it hard to admit the world. He wondered what could go wrong in those three days in Glasgow.

Historic errors resurrected? Monstrous unbidden distractions? The slow evaporation of Gabriella's love? He set off from the town which half-fitted him for the city he was still shrugging off.

Friday morning
Chapter 11

He'd congratulated himself on his weather forecasting skills when his flight had landed in Glasgow on the Thursday evening. A typical peak west of Scotland summertime, mid-July: skies a wintry grey. Runway puddled with rainwater.

During the short walk from plane to terminal, he'd been soaked by a steady downpour and chilled by a temperature less than half that of sun-baked Pisa. The airport building's interior was of course over-warm, sweaty, damp, bacteria-laden.

Three seasons in five minutes. Too cold. Too damp. Too hot. "Welcome to Glasgow, city of summer rainstorms and year-round bronchitis," he'd told his hotel's stone-faced young receptionist on arrival.

She'd briefly flickered her too-white-to-be-true teeth, sliding him a room-key, sidestepping a workplace hazard: the cheesy old Glasgow joker. You're welcome, funnyman.

It was still raining the next morning when he arrived at his sister-in-law's house in suburban Shawlands. Susan lazed in an armchair, sipping coffee, grinning as she absorbed Tony's evident unhappiness at being back in Glasgow.

First up, his well-worn rant about the weather - "You can never dress right, it's impossible!" - followed by a new one lamenting

Glasgow Airport at its summer holiday peak: "Back from Benidorm, snottery sunburnt screaming kids getting slapped. Trackie'd-up noodle-heads with high-pitched whiny voices, squawking and squeaking - you'd hear tougher-sounding seagulls fighting over dropped chips."

She picked up the bulky envelope containing the legal forms he was in Glasgow to sign, shaking it in his face until he took it, placed it in the leather backpack at his feet.

"Snob," Susan chided. "You're just annoyed Glasgow isn't Italy at its most…"

"Civilised? Non-Glaswegian?" he said.

Susan flung a cushion at him. "Colonia wins on sun," she continued, "but Glasgow's your place for low-life spectacle."

"Oh aye," he said. "You'd have more fun at a Glasgow knife-fight than a month in Colonia - or at a wedding in Edinburgh."

She laughed, reminding him she was coming to stay with him soon. "Next month," she said. "Me and your niece. Sorry you can't stay here - bedroom redecoration, you have to take Glasgow tradesmen when they deign to turn up."

She nodded towards the packed plastic carrier bag standing upright on the coffee table. "I'm glad I won't need to bring you the usual ton of pills and potions - Colonia's NHS stash, assembled as requested," she said.

"You should charge the locals for being their drugs mule. I've got two more prescriptions still to collect, promised for tomorrow, so best leave this pile till the whole lot's ready. Come round as early as you like on Sunday. You're on the midday flight back?"

He nodded.

"Wake me up. Hammer the door. Not a problem. I'll combat sleep-deprivation in Colonia. Although it always feels wrong lying around doing nothing in a place where there's nothing to do but lie around doing nothing. There's more satisfaction in finding work to dodge.

"Three days in Colonia and I see why your forefathers needed to escape. 'Mamma mia, give us 18-hour days in chip shops in rain-lashed Glasgow - anything's better than sitting about in this relentless boring sunshine!' "

Tony pictured his brother. "Not enough excitement for Armando in Colonia, no chance of being led astray - he never went back past his 14th birthday," he said.

"Anna's 14, she'll not be an eager visitor much longer," Susan said. "We never thought you'd last two years there. Colonia's not exactly Las Vegas, is it? Good for you, turning the place into Hollywood."

"Movie moguls, that's us," he said. Susan told him to quit being self-sabotaging, it was the most annoying thing about him.

"Stuff's happening in Colonia thanks to you and your pals," she said. "Better than hanging about moaning, waiting for something. Get up and do it - life, colour, art. Your photography, now your mad film. All obstacles overcome. Wish I could be there on Sunday. A movie premiere beneath the twinkling night sky - no bloody rain."

"Pah!" he said. "I dismiss your praise with a contemptuous snort. Lots of stuff happens in Colonia. Week past Tuesday… window of Giusti ironmonger's, a new dead wasp. When you're over, pay your respects… it'll still be there.

"Ach, it's not that nothing ever happens in Colonia. It's just… slow… predictable. The patterns repeat. Colonia's not the place if you want surprises. Surprises are over-rated anyway.

"Cities are all random zoomers staggering about, being random zoomers, making a racket. Like Glasgow airport. Shouting. Mad folk. *Zoomers.* There's rules in Colonia, what's acceptable, what's not. Maybe too many rules, but folk know the limits, where other folk start and finish. Folk give each other room, respect.

"I get why Armando stopped going to Colonia - locals didn't take to him, barging in straightaway, super matey. They didn't like it. He'd get really pally with folk for 20 minutes, trying to get something off them. All smiles. Too close.

"Then he'd get bored when he got what he wanted, or get annoyed after folk got wise to him. He'd drop them and move on to the next thrill, the next mug.

"It was all a big long party, till it suddenly stopped after 20 years and he'd practically drunk away a chip shop and two restaurants. And a marriage. And a daughter. You're saying I've done well to stay in Colonia so long. You did better staying married to my brother for as long as you did - seven years?"

"Plus six years divorced - 13 years of being.... disappointed... unlucky 13," said Susan.

"Unlucky for nobody but Armando," he said. "You got the best of it eventually, you ended up with what you deserved: with Anna, and the deli. And you've got Dorothy, a proper partner."

"Armando was... difficult," said Susan. "He was still your brother, though - and I hate brothers and sisters falling out, losing touch. Me an only child - desperate for a wee sister, a wee brother."

"I got a big brother who acted like a wee brat," he said. "But at least it led you to get me for a big ex-brother-in-law. Me and my humdrum Italian sunshine and my boring fresh mountain air, my predictable good wine and dull holiday accommodation."

Susan flipped a coaster at him. "All those shared childhood experiences," she said. "There must have been happy times when you and Armando were kids... to lose that..."

He feigned a look of intense thoughtfulness. "Happy times - oh, so many of them. That one time Armando gave me a pound... oh, no - he borrowed a pound... then a fiver. More than once.

"Until I said no, I wasn't lending him anything till he'd paid me back, so he started stealing money off me. *Him* - a working man from the age of 15 - stealing money off me, a schoolboy, so he can go to bars because he looked old enough, even though he was just 12 months or so older than me.

"He's drinking in the bars I can't get in because I'm too young-looking - plus I've no money because Armando's taken it. Yeah, wonderful brotherly memories.

"All the records, CDs of mine Armando borrowed and lost. Clothes he borrowed... stole really, to lend to his mates - no, he gave my clothes to his mates. I never saw them again. Well, I did see my brown leather jacket again - the school tough nut was wearing it.

"So yes, I envy other brothers being pals - I wish it had been that way for me and Armando. But it wasn't. Couldn't be. The drink was his only pal, as you know.

"A real pal. It never let him down. Never spoilt his fun, the drink. A better pal than everyone who tried to talk him out of drinking. And that didn't include me - great guy, I am - because I'd given up on Armando years before."

Susan sipped her coffee. "There must be some funny memories," she said, "ones I can tell Anna - come on, King of Comedy."

He puffed out his lips. "There's one, but even now I'm anxious thinking about it.

"Every Saturday night, mum and dad are working in the ristorante, me and him are left in front of the telly. Off go mum and dad, that's the signal for Armando. Flee the house, catch the bus to some youth club, some teenage disco. Some pub with lots of girls.

"And Armando knows almost to the exact minute when our parents will be back - the ristorante ran like clockwork. So every

Saturday I'm in on my own, the responsible wee square watching some cop show on the telly, getting more and more worried the closer it gets to half past 10, stomach ache, scared.

"No sign of Armando, only a minute till mum and dad are back - the clock ticking, seconds left, how am I going to explain why Armando isn't there?

"I'm up and down every 30 seconds at the window, looking out for the last bus, the only one Armando can possibly be on if he's going to be back in time. Will he be on the bus?

"Maybe the bus will be late. I'm terrified. Thank God - the bus! I see him getting off, running up the path!

"Relief! In the door, chucks his good going-out clothes on his bed, pyjamas on, into the living room, leaps on the sofa, and I've got just enough time to tell him that week's plot from Kojak, The Sweeney, *Lochhead!* or whatever show it is.

"Seconds later, mum and dad are back, dad's asking Armando what's been on the telly, which murder case had Lochhead solved - which guest actor is the murder victim or the obvious killer.

"Armando sounds bored. A dull Saturday night, same as ever. Same sofa, telly, same shows, and he's reeling off every detail I'd told him about the plot, inventing a few extra touches of his own: 'You were meant to think the guy with the beard did it - but naaaw.'

"And by now our dad is looking at me, this silent kid who always looks worried - because he always is. The responsible kid who's older than his older brother.

"Dad's happy, one drink to celebrate a Saturday night, the ristorante full. He's looking at me and he makes the same joke he always makes: 'And what about you, Tony? You're not saying anything - you been out gallivantin'?' "

Susan laughed. "But that's not all," he went on, "because every week, my face bright red after the same big laugh at my expense - me, the little stay-at-home who's never out gallivantin'.... and after that, what does Armando always say?

"He puts on an American accent and gets an even bigger laugh from my dad: 'Tony, never forget you have the right to remain silent.' Every week!"

Susan laughed again.

"It's maybe how I got interested in stand-up comedy - me getting laughs, not being the butt of the joke. And did big brother Armando ever thank me for being his weekly stooge, his straight man, his Saturday night alibi? No.

"And I never thought to ask. It was the start of us not speaking to each other. The beginning of the end of the Moscardini brothers.

"Not that this ancient fraternal trauma left me scarred, twisted. Much. Leather jacket gone, responsible behaviour unrewarded... I think I turned out pretty well - only one failed marriage."

"He was good at failing," Susan said. "He failed at loads of things. Marriage, business, fatherhood. I can't regret being married to him, though. Like you say, it did give us Anna."

"There's one thing I regret about Armando," he said, "well, envy more than regret - Armando got a proper Italian name, not like me. I get a name Italians can't pronounce."

"Yes, they can, I've heard them. Tony - *Antonio!*"

"It's not my real name. My full name. I'm Hugh - Hugh Antonio Moscardini, it's on my passport. My mother gives me the one bloody name nobody in Italy can say. They see 'Hugh' written down, the closest they get is 'Eh-Oog.'

"Folk in Scotland say Hugh wrong, too - by choice. Drove my mother nuts. 'Orrite, wee Shooey. Shuggy. Shug. Shooglemeister.' Lucky I had Antonio for a middle name."

Susan looked pensive. "What name do you get called by your

most special Colonia friend… la bella Gabriella… Signorina Sarti. How's your *re-la-tion-ship?"*

Susan elongated the word, almost sang it. "You've been seeing Gabriella Sarti the whole time you've been in Italy, two years. *Che romantico."*

He grimaced as though having difficulty remembering any such *re-la-tion-ship,* any such person. "She lives in a farmhouse far away from Colonia," he said.

"Hard to remember how far… five kilometres? Up a steep hill… very steep. Mountainside, really.

"Difficult drive, single-track road… twists and turns - at one point, glance right, all these branches… tree-tops, 100 metres tall! Keep your eyes on the road, don't look down."

Susan pretended to be impatient, mock-exasperated, drumming her finger nails on her coffee mug.

He sat forward in the sofa, pantomimed earnest conspiracy. "Would you believe it, there's actually folk down in Colonia - lifelong residents, they say they don't know where Faggio Basso is, they've never been.

"It's an hour's walk! Only seven minutes by car! Five kilometres I say - six max. But it's true - most Colonia folk haven't trekked up to the far-distant alien village, the lofty peak.

"Astounding! I never get up there in summer, mind you - it's the Sarti family's *agriturismo* business as well as their home. Very busy. Loads of folk.

"Self-contained guest apartments. French and German tourists paying top dollar for a swimming pool, exclusive panoramic views, hideaway setting - they don't want shifty old locals like me lurking about. I'm not invited."

His joke non-answer was growing unfunny; Susan was looking around for a missile. He ploughed on. "Walking up there in summer would kill you, mind, the heat, I don't blame the Coloniesi for not going. I did walk down once… shaded by the giant pine trees, much cooler… the Alpine scent… pleasant stroll. Forty minutes downhill."

"I'm going to throw this bowl of fruit at your annoying fat head," said Susan.

"Arance! Limoni!" he sang. "The Sartis grow them. Grapes, too, obviously, in a little vineyard, for a wine co-operative. Honey from their beehives, an olive grove - bottles of their own olive oil."

He fixed Susan with his most annoyingly sincere look, knowing he was skating on very thin ice. On he pirouetted.

"Most of Faggio Basso is second homes, very sad - the folk in the house next door drive over from Edinburgh every summer. You travel a thousand miles to get away from people from Auld Dreichie - and they follow you!

"Faggio Basso's not much - 200 folk. A little piazza, one deli, Bar Lampone - never open… have you noticed I'm doing what magicians call distraction - nothing up my sleeve.

"I'm making you look one way while the magic happens somewhere else… which is obviously annoying for you, the audience, but… look closely as I fail to produce a rabbit from a hat - *molto, molto prodigioso!"*

"Work clairvoyance into this bloody magic act and you'll see a coffee table rattling off your shins," Susan said.

"Just tell me how things are with Gabriella. I ask because I care, Anna's favourite Uncle Shuggy, you sack of shite. Is it love, Ell Yew Vee? Is everything OK?"

Chapter 12

He sat back. "I'm not answering your question… because I don't really know exactly what's going on, and I'm feeling a bit down about it, but heigh-ho, that's life. I'm a big boy, I can handle rejection - I've had enough practice.

"I know how I feel about *la bella Gabriella*. I know how I'd like her to feel about me. But I'm so old… she might… she maybe feels it's time I'm put out with the recycling."

Susan shushed him and told him to stop being ridiculous, always so pessimistic. "I'm not being pessimistic," he said. "Her family are suspicious of me.

"Understandable. She's the head of a family empire. Wealthy. What's my game? Some old chiseller, gold-digger. They don't know me very well. There's no welcome banners with my name on in Faggio Basso.

"When I met her son up there, a student… he didn't actually punch me in the face, but it looked like he was thinking about it.

"He's protecting his mother, I get it. I'm some pretend-Italian Scottish artsy-fartsy waster alongside all Colonia's other pretend-Italian Scottish artsy-fartsy wasters. Another chancer reckoning he's just what sleepy old Colonia needs… some prodigal Glasgow kiddy-on Italian, maybe after Gabriella's money, a leech.

"Wait till I tell you, though! There's been a major thaw in relations with Gabriella's frosty brother, Piero the Paramilitary Polis.

"The lumbering fascist in the jackboots," said Susan. "Struts about ready to shoot folk for parking on double yellows? You're pals with *him?*" She looked shocked.

"Piero's our movie stuntman," he explained. "Didn't take much convincing. He's your man for a good moped crash." He almost laughed aloud to see how shock had been joined by puzzlement on Susan's face.

"Moped crash? Stuntman? Piero?" she said, suddenly sitting upright. "One minute, the neighbourhood agent of state repression hates you for dating his sister, the next he's falling off a motorbike for you?"

"A moped," he corrected. "And he didn't look happy... hard to tell with a crash helmet on, mind - but he was very good at it. Tootling along one minute - the next, whump, down goes the bike, Piero takes a slide. One take, essentially.

"Gabriella got him to volunteer - he spent his teens watching those daredevil TV shows, half-wits setting their pubic hair on fire and jumping off roofs in Arkansas. I wonder if Piero would set his pubic hair on fire?

"I won't ask him to, mind - delicate diplomacy: I leave that to Prof and Ken. No one in Colonia says no to them - oh, right on time, a text from the man himself."

Tony squinted at his mobile phone - another potential crisis averted by Ken's persuasive powers of organisation. The Fish and Chip Festival's PA system did not now need to be in two places at once.

"I'll send you the film on a memory stick," he told Susan, tucking his phone away. "It's how us movie moguls work these days - digital technology."

"Never mind the film, back to Gabriella," said Susan. "Your flat was like an old folks' home when you moved in. Left to you, it would've stayed that way."

"I'm an old folk," he protested. "I live in an old folk's home."

"Maybe that's why she's reconsidering your future, *if* she's reconsidering your future," said Susan. "You'll not be giving off the right signals. It's not a *house* renovation project she's doing, you're the renovation project! Idiot man. See men, see signals - men never do."

"She's never stayed a single night in Colonia with me, in my house," he replied. "What signal does that send?"

Susan sighed. "What sane woman would stay in a single man's grotty flat - tatty film posters for decoration - when she's got a perfect home of her own 10 minutes away?"

"You might have a point," he said. "Female logic: never my strong point. When I met her, she'd not long lost her father. I wonder whether she's thinking 'This old goat's got 15 years on me... I don't fancy nursing another old fossil into the grave.'

"I feel I'm being surveyed... dry-rot, woodworm, subsidence, rising damp. I've a good location - handy for official public display purposes round town of an evening. But investment potential? Long-term profitability? I'm just a quick flip - as some women have complained the morning after..."

"I'm not going to get any sense out of you about Gabriella," Susan said. "You do remember Anna and I are coming to stay with you in the school summer holidays? Not long now. Me for four days. Anna at her cousin's for a week, then with you till she gets bored."

"Has Anna grown out of what you said was last year's passing teenage phase?"

"Which passing teenage phase was that?" Susan asked. "The passing phases blur into one that never ends. The current one is make-up, sparkly tops and gossip about boys. It's lasted months."

"Last year's phase - when I was last in Glasgow, last summer," he said. Susan looked blank. "When she was this wary Glaswegian city kid, afraid to leave the house, putting limits on her life, fearful… obsessed with what other kids might think, not wanting to seem different."

Susan still looked blank.

"We overheard Anna lecturing her Colonia cousin about what she mustn't do when the two of them were together on the bus into town," he went on. "I'm sure kids in Italy don't lead such straitened lives. Anna's cousin looked terrified… I was terrified, listening.

"Anna's teenage restrictions - one mad 'Don't' after another. 'Don't talk to me in Italian when we're out, folk'll know you're not from Glasgow and they'll beat you up. Don't talk to me in English, you don't sound Scottish so they'll think you're English and they'll beat you up.

" 'Don't say anything to me or sit next to me on the bus - if you talk to me and sit next to me, they'll think we're gay and they'll beat us both up. Sit in the seat in front of me and stare out the window, don't turn round… pretend to be, like, mentally-disabled… Glasgow's soft on retards.' "

"I remember now - what Dorothy called the 10 Teenage Commandments," said Susan, "only there were 100 of them."

"You don't have teenagers, so you don't know the one thing that matters to teenagers, all teenagers, everywhere - here, in Italy, on Mars, wherever - is what other teenagers think about them.

"Yes, it's sad and barmy, but I suppose they're working out where they fit among their peers. They know nothing, they're uncertain about everything, but they know they have to look tough.

"I'll bet Italian adolescents invent exactly the same daft scary rules. But the weather's better so young folk are out of the house all day and us grown-ups don't have to listen to them."

"Did you never wish you had children? They are at all times a boon. Never a problem. Until they are. Always smiling. Except when they aren't. Children…"

"My ex-wife didn't want children. I'd never thought about children, still haven't," he said. "My photographs and my film are my children, all of them beautiful. My art is my lasting gift to the world!"

Susan tutted. "What's your hotel like? Full of nasty Glaswegians? Like that dummy from the *Chronicle*, the grinning ginger fool in the glasses, crude big eejit - McCrindle. Claims to have just one stupid name. McCrindle…"

"That's his name, Susan, try not to wear it out," Tony said, making Susan bare her teeth. "Yes - McCrindle's in the hotel, and a crude big eejit's the least of the things he is."

Susan tutted again. "I'll bet bloody McCrindle's slagged your film off without even seeing it - jealous," she said. "Stupid man… stupid men - clowns, the lot of you."

He thought about it. "McCrindle's seen some footage, same bits I've sent you, and you're right, he's not been ah, *emotionally supportive*. I didn't expect him to be. It's not what McCrindle does. Insult your mates, spur them on - banter, that's him.

"He's a persuasive eejit, though. He's trying to talk me into a *Chronicle* retirement do tonight in Glasgow's dreariest pub. A pub filled with all the *Chronicle* folk I hated - and they hated me back."

"There must have been some you liked - some who only found you a little objectionable?" said Susan.

He pondered. There were one or two *Chronicle* folk he'd liked - one woman in particular. Meeting her again would prove worse than meeting the folk he'd hated, though. He changed the subject.

"Why do you hate McCrindle?" he asked. "You've only met

him once. Hating him before you get to know him saves time, sure, but…"

Susan sighed. "A mother knows a bad influence soon as she sees one. And there's plainly something wrong with a grown man who claims to have just the one name - 'Call me *McCrindle.*' Honestly…"

"Can't fault your logic," he said. "Right. I'll away to do the jobs you've given me. Sign legal papers, solicitors in Bath Street. Collect Armando's stuff. Tarry me awhiles with McCripple. McCrapstickle. McCunticle - McCRINDLE!"

Susan glared at him. "Promise me," she said, "you'll never invite McCrindle to Colonia when I'm there… do *not* bring him here with you on Sunday morning!"

****

Where to start with McCrindle, Tony thought as he awaited the city-centre bus. A Features writer, same as him, but for the *Chronicle's* Saturday magazine: travel, food reviews, design, architecture.

"I write the same soft shite you do - only harder," as McCrindle had once said. And then said again. Throughout the 15 years they'd worked together. "Fluff… colour pieces - mine are BLACK and yours are fucking hot pink, poof-boy."

But whereas Tony had taken his *Chronicle* redundo dosh and renounced Glasgow and renounced journalism, McCrindle had pocketed his pay-off but stayed in the game, heading overseas to those few places where English-language newsprint still retained a foothold.

Dubai first, then Hong Kong, becoming some sort of on-line production editor for a paper that had found the secret of modern-day alchemy: monetising an internet readership.

The pair's semi-regular video calls took place at the end of their respective working days: 6pm Colonia time, 1am Hong King time. HK's temperature was always a humid 35C judging by McCrindle's flushed, sweaty face and woozy demeanour.

There he'd be in his non-air-conditioned living room, greasy red hair standing on end, an idiot grin on his lips, lying on a sofa in a grey-white singlet, a living homage to Glasgow's greatest perambulatory street philosopher, Rab C Nesbitt.

Their most recent call had been meant to establish the details of their coincidental joint trip to Glasgow, McCrindle visiting his ageing mother. Few concrete facts emerged during the chat, naturally, apart from their shared hotel's address.

Instead, McCrindle did what McCrindle inevitably did, via video-call as in life: adopt some crazed persona. It was a drug-amended WC Fields this time, spiralling off on a frazzled word-association game, beginning with a claim to have parachuted out of a plane he'd hi-jacked: "I done got me a sack of dollar bills! Hoo-di-hoo, I am the DB Cooper of my generation and I just robbed me a flying frikken bank!"

He was holding aloft a glass of what, to McCrindle's delight, Tony mis-identified as urine.

"It will be urine once it passes my luscious pouting lips," McCrindle said, "but for now this impending urine remains the finest Scotch malt I can buy here in Honkers for what would to you be one hundred and twenty-two of your increasingly worthless and puny Scottish sterling pounds... to me, half a renminbi, or two US cents!"

Tony had noticed McCrindle's growing keenness to point out how poor Scotland was. To jeer. To gloat. To say how much better off he was now, abroad, than he'd ever been in Scotland, such a dump. Tony had begun to find McCrindle's chat grating.

He'd started figuring out why. Like McCrindle, Tony had left Scotland because it held no job for him. But unlike McCrindle, he didn't feel Scotland had failed him. He didn't feel spurned, thwarted.

He'd outgrown any feeling of having run away. True, staying in Scotland might provide unhelpful reminders of some of his mistakes. Of feats unachieved; feats unachievable. It was also where he was likely to encounter those he'd failed. People he didn't want to see; who no longer wanted to see him.

But he'd left Scotland because it was too wet, not warm enough, grey. Not because it was too wee, too poor, too stupid. Italy: lazy but productive buzzing bees. Lavender scent. Warmth. Glasgow in summer: annoying flies, dirt, draughts.

Unlike Tony, some Scots emigrants - McCrindle, sad to say - could only display how successful their new life was by decrying the old one. It wasn't a game Tony felt a need to play.

Sure, Glasgow held bad memories. But he'd always let the good memories outshine them. Or tried to. His move to Italy certainly wasn't a decision that required justification - unlike McCrindle's, it seemed.

But at least staying in touch with McCrindle ensured Tony didn't forget how to read. Because McCrindle was a master of the entertaining written crudity, firing off endless text messages, a 55-year-old schoolboy passing obscene notes in class.

Most mornings, Tony awoke to some foul but amusing McCrindleism: "I hope you find assistance through prayer that your living corpse's stenchful fishiness might abate, may the blessings of Satin be upon you."

Too often he found himself staring at his mobile phone, scrolling back for old gems. He did so now, sheltering from the rain.

He found his favourite, in which McCrindle depicted himself

"in masturbatory reverie, my tiny penis in one hand, a magnifying glass in the other, standing one bright HK afternoon at my tenth-storey living room window.

"At climax, I shower my seed upon unsuspecting fishermen mending their nets on the quayside far below, while amplifying and focusing the sun's rays by accident - igniting my scrawny orange pubes at the very moment of triumphant ejaculatory release.

"As the fishermen savour my salty issue on their tongue, they are able to laugh at my flaming genital agony."

"Now *that's* funny," Tony muttered to himself at the bus stop.

****

He climbed to the bus's upper deck, reminding himself to keep his phone in his pocket and avoid savage Glaswegian teen gangs keen on punishing the crime of a public display of mirth.

Two youths, aged 14 or so, sat at the front of the bus, wearing matching blue football shirts - Rangers fans, he knew. They jerked around, giggling. He puzzled for a moment, watching them flick a cigarette lighter on and off, waving it in front of them at the window-pane. They were incinerating flies.

Beneath leaden Glasgow skies, he thought, *my bus-borne odyssey in the company of under-age sadists loyal to the UK monarchy.* Midsummer was a week away. Would the rain be continuous till then? Probably.

He cleared condensation from the window with his sleeve, staring out at sodden figures plodding a puddled cityscape. The bus's filthy floor was part-covered with discarded free-sheet newspapers. Best use for them. Soak up pish.

He'd forgotten the unique acrid tang of Glasgow's public

transport. He mused how it might be bottled and sold as an authentic scent of the city. *Aqua di Sant' Mungo d'Urinale? Vita Vomito Scozzesi Disperata?*

He'd managed to buy a Lyle and Scott woollen crewneck jumper and a waterproof Barbour jacket from a golfing store en route to Susan's home. On foot on Glasgow's wet streets, the outfit kept him dry. On the bus, it made him too warm. He should have known.

His law-office signing session took all of three minutes and exposed him to the repulsive catarrhal sniffing of an abrupt, angry-faced woman of his own age whose all-black ensemble was offset by a yellow-hooped waistcoat.

Zany fashion statement? No mirrors in your house when you got dressed this morning, hen? Sideline as a wasp tribute act? He considered asking all these questions, but decided against.

Instead, he thanked her, got up, shouldered his backpack and exited mouthing a wisecrack at a volume low enough that she wouldn't hear: "That's me buzzing off."

No such comic opportunity arose during his visit to Armando's final residence - a place called Highwater House - to collect those few possessions amassed in his brother's lifetime. A lifetime for the most part wasted, he held.

He apologised to Highwater House's harassed director for the length of time - years of postponed visits - it had taken him to retrieve Armando's stuff, managing not to observe out loud that the young man's grey tracksuit gave him the look of a care-home resident, not its manager.

If only he hadn't enjoyed dismissing his brother as an annoying alcoholic nuisance for most of the previous four decades, he might have got here sooner, Tony thought, mumbling some self-serving excuse about living abroad, travel difficulties.

Highwater House's director handed over Armando's effects - one pitiful crumpled carrier bag - and began outlining the home's policy. Tony half-listened - peering inside the plastic bag at its contents, a dozen or so CDs - figuring the man's address for a reprimand or a sales pitch, some bid to play on his conscience, tug his heartstrings, loosen his wallet.

He'd always assumed the place was the usual grim council-run institution, a hostel for the homeless, the feckless, the unlovable and the unloved; a waste bin for the problematic and the pestilential.

To his surprise, he learnt Armando's final year or so had been spent in a place of genuine care and respite; a secure long-term residence for people with substance abuse and mental health problems, run by a charity.

"Residents stay with us for as long as they need to stay - it's their home," the director told him. "They're the ones who named it Highwater House. 'Everybody here's been to hell already,' one of them said.

"We differ from some care institutions… we try to be forgiving, accept that folk will fail, suffer relapses. Whatever harm they do to themselves, they're still welcome."

The man made no plea for a donation. Tony made a mental note: send Highwater House money. And judge not that ye be not judged.

He apologised again and left. Now that he understood Highwater House's purpose and its policy, the place seemed less gloomy - more hopeful, brighter.

A resident sat in an armchair in reception. An old guy, smiling. He nodded at Tony. "OK, mate - finding your way?" he said, baring a gumsy pink grin.

Tony nodded back, half-smiling, keen not to engage, striding towards the door - and seeing another armchair, another man. There was something familiar about him. Older, unshaven, with a bloated face, a waxen pallor and watery, bulging eyes. Unfocused. Unmoving.

He realised he'd known the man's face in better, more buoyant times, 20-odd years earlier before its full submersion in an ocean of drink. It had been a *Chronicle* by-line photograph.

The face then had been supercilious as well as drunk, the trademarks of the newspaper generation preceding Tony's. It had been displayed atop a well-written twice-weekly statement of languid outrage decrying all things and all people less sparkling than the column's author: George McHattie.

McHattie had drunk pricey malts back then. Cheap cider now, more likely. Tony remembered George once saying a wee drink got him jacked up, made him think on his feet, made more sense of the everyday horror that was the news.

Maybe it had, Tony thought. Now, though, years of alcohol only explained why the one-time star wordsmith no longer resembled his old patrician byline portrait but a yellowed photo-copy of a yellowed photo-copy, a member of the living dead.

Tony was shocked but not surprised by McHattie's decline. Nor was he saddened. The guy had been more vicious and offensive around the *Chronicle's* offices than he had been in print. Vain and waspish, cruel and cutting. A saint would struggle to show pity for him.

So this was the Olympian peak from which George had always wanted to look down on the rest of the world. His heroic drinking had paid off. Who knew how little George McHattie saw these days as he stared into the middle distance.

Outside in the street again, Tony was for once glad of a brisk Glasgow summertime breeze. Fresh air. Fresh enough to blow away his own rank sanctimony in judging another man wanting, his pleasure in someone else's decline.

He winced to admit his own lack of compassion. As he walked slowly to the bus stop, he opened the carrier bag.

Every battered plastic CD case was coated in a tarry film of what he assumed, given Armando's history, must be nicotine and assorted alco-spillages. He delved deeper, parting the clump of stuck-together CDs with a little finger, tutting with disgust.

Dross, mostly. Unlistenable. Albums by T'Pau, Simple Minds, Runrig, Phil Collins, Deacon Blue. Three of the discs had been Tony's, though. Trashcan Sinatras, *A Happy Pocket*. Michael Marra's *Gaels Blue*. *A Walk Across The Rooftops* by the Blue Nile. His favourite Scottish albums.

He'd long ago re-purchased all three, resigned to their non-return by Armando. He prised the Blue Nile disc from its case. Scratched and stained. Ruined. Unplayable.

As he waited at the bus stop, a ragged figure began working the queue, begging for loose change, repeating the two words over and over. He puzzled over the meaning of what sounded like "Loose chains."

Tighten your own chains first, mate, he thought as the man now stood before him, a grimy hand extended. Lost in thought, Tony proffered the bag of CDs - worthless, dirty, sticky to the touch.

The beggar took the bag, looking puzzled, and moved on, leaving Tony puzzled, too, but with a growing sense of shame. For the next few moments he sought to excuse what he'd done.

He'd misunderstood the man's request, he told himself. But he hadn't, and he knew it. He'd palmed off a pauper with a bag of rubbish on purpose, to save himself the hassle of carrying it. Or maybe as a cruel instinctive joke.

The bus drew up. He boarded, climbing the stairs, taking a seat, turning to look back. The homeless man trudged through the rain, carrying what Tony had dumped on him, the plastic bag with an unplayable Blue Nile CD in it. An inaccessible masterpiece.

Tinseltown in the rain, he thought: *Here we are, caught up in this big rhythm… one day this love will all blow over.* Easy come, easier go.

****

McCrindle was loitering in the hotel foyer, sprawled on a sofa. "Phoney Tony Marscarpone! I prescribe a dose of Doctor McCrutchcrippler's non-PC comedy," he said.

"I'll manage without," Tony said, sitting beside him, "but that won't stop you cracking your offensive jokes anyway. You've been back in Glasgow a day longer than me… any charitable thoughts about the beggars on our home town's streets?

"There's loads more than there used to be, poor sods. And what have I just done? Some homeless guy asks me for loose change and I hand him a bag of scratched-to-buggery crap CDs. Gone before I could apologise and find a pound coin - I'm a monster." McCrindle hooted with laughter.

"He caught me off-guard, I wasn't thinking," Tony said. "I insult a desperate vagrant in his hour of need - 'Fifty pee for a cup of tea? Sorry, mate, have this bag of shite.' "

McCrindle dabbed away imaginary tears of mirth. "You've updated the parable of the Good Samaritan for the cruel and barbarous age we live in," he scoffed.

"Passing by on the other side would've been bad enough. But, oh no. St Tony actively wanders over *from* the other side for a closer inspection of the bloodied, battered wayfarer lying mugged in the gutter, before whipping off his beshitened old scants and chucking them in the fella's face.

"But I forgive you, my son - you've only done what I'd do. World's a tough place. Tottering piss-weasels, who needs 'em? Scrofulent scum-sucking Glasgow scrotes begging on every corner... no gangs of verminous vagrants littering Hong Kong's spotless streets. The Party won't allow it, Tony, because the Party cares - so the Party shoots the filthy sods.

"Ya gots ta trust the Party! Get yo' bad self on the good foot, good God y'all - the Party won't stand for it when me and James Brown touches ourselves!

"Git on up! Git on up-aaaah! The Party gittin' on up like a killin' machine! The Party shoots! The Party teargasses! The Party accuses! In that order!

"The Party provides what the people need... a warm, wise guiding hand... night and day... mostly at night when folk least expect it... the Party's helping hand warmly grasping the people's throat.

"Folk who won't work. Folk who get a bit lippy... a bit westernised and democratic. The Part-aaaaaaay!"

Tony was glad the hotel's foyer was empty. Once set in motion, McCrindle's runaway Transgressive Satire Express was hard to stop.

What did it say about him that he found McCrindle so funny? What inhumanity did it uncover at the heart of Tony Moscardini?

"Maybe Hong Kong could do with more septic scrotes on its streets - extra colour," McCrindle was saying. "Glasgow's vagrants add to the pavement palette with their generously-voided sputum and assorted body-fluids.

"Plus all their vogging, vomming and pissing stops them agitating for human rights, liberal democracy, socialism, self-determinism, political freedom and other such regressive western fol-de-rols."

McCrindle's pause for breath allowed Tony to derail him.

"Colonia's only got one beggar," he said. "A poor soul, hangs about outside the supermarket hoping for the odd euro from your shopping trolley's coin-slot.

"Nobody in Colonia actually gives her anything - they know she's fed and sheltered by the church - but none of them would do to a beggar what I've just done in Glasgow. Tony Moscardini: spurning the helpless, the hapless, the hopeless.

"That reminds me - I saw George McHattie this afternoon, in the same sheltered living place Armando ended up. More dead than alive. Alcohol is not a preservative."

"The self-pickling George McHattie, a legend-in-everybody-else's-lunchtime," said McCrindle. "Nasty, nasty man.

"Two bottles of whisky a day, every day for 30 years - but mind he always went on the wagon for three weeks over Christmas and New Year? Sneered. '*Office party season* - I'm not drinking with amateurs.'

"Then he'd drink lemonade and tut at folk - if he wasn't making noises… very loud… cars, jet engines, speedboats… you'd hear a vacuum cleaner, turn round and it's George piloting an invisible Hoover up to the bar to order a pineapple juice.

"Remember yon time he was introduced to Calum Ronald's widow?"

No one who'd been present would ever forget. Calum Ronald: Scotland's late world land-speed record holder. Killed on live TV in a smash everyone had seen a million times and wished they hadn't. His grieving wife the butt of McHattie's bad taste comedy.

"Classic McHattie," said McCrindle. " 'You're married to Calum Ronald?' A long impression of a high-speed car crash, squeal of brakes, crunch of metal, car in a fatal barrel-roll - '*That* Calum Ronald?'

"Poor woman complained to the paper. No sense of humour, some folk.

"Late-stage George McHattie, not long before the *Chronicle* binned him... subs spent all their time devising titles for his autobiography - my favourite was *Never Knowingly Sober*. A towering genius of the Scottish scribbling trade, of course.

"What was it George said when he got his official medical diagnosis as an alkie? 'The doctors have told me I can't drink anymore, my body can't take it, I'll die... so I'm just on the brandy.' "

McCrindle and Tony shook with laughter. The halcyon days of Scottish journalism.

"And somehow he's still alive," McCrindle said. "Some drink-sodden *Chronicle* giants must have succeeded in killing themselves recently - for sheer entertainment, you can't beat the news of an alcoholic former colleague's extinction.

"Tell me who's deaded himself - give me some good news."

Chapter 13

"Edward Penney's dead," said Tony. "A profound loss to Scottish drinks industry profits."

"Hello, honey-bunny!" McCrindle warbled in a phlegmy, fluting, semi-strangled sing-song. Edward Penney's regular greeting, three parts Lady Windermere to two parts Bryan Ferry, with a hint of Noel Coward.

"The bad Penney spent - he'll turn up no more... he once asked me to get him drugs... me!" McCrindle said. He was indignant. "And not *good sensible drugs*... he asked me to get him heroin! *Heroin!*

"I told him: 'I don't mainline no loser shit, man - I gets high on The Truth. And a bit of weed sometimes. Maybe the odd bit of coke, one or two eccies like anybody rational.'

"*Heroin!* I was cut to the quick. Too stunned to reprimand him. 'My good fellow, we are not in Auld Dreichie - I fear you're confusing me with the frightful Edbro low-life novellas of Irving Walsh.'

"Edward Penney, dead. Terrific writer - head and shoulders above a hack like you, Tony. But too drunk even for the *Chronicle*. Not for public display.

"For his own safety, and the paper's, they make him a sub-editor, chain him to the office's nocturnal routine, making lesser writers' words fit their allotted space. Improving them.

"It's that as much as the drink that killed him, you'd reckon. Beautifying other peoples' ugliness - it rots the soul. The drink rotting his liver must've helped, mind.

"Aye, an era of heroic Scottish drunkenness come to an end. At the going down of the sun, by which time Edward Penney was bouncing off the walls and scarcely able to stand up, and in the morning - when he was lying in George Square in a puddle of his own urine and someone else's vomit - we shall remember him. The pitiful sot."

****

There had been one other recent *Chronicle* departee: Frank Auld. McCrindle's face lit up at the news.

"Frank fucking Auld!" he said with glee. "Frank Auld's deid and I'm alive to revile his name… my ship has come in and this time, baby, I'm not waiting at an airport.

"Sanctimonious old shitebag…. Frank Auld. Never frank. Always auld. Pawky but pish. Pompous prick. Never met a millionaire or a celebrity he couldn't fawn over.

"And Frank Auld met them all. Tycoons, tyrants, tie-less showbiz celebs! And they took Frank Auld to their hearts. They all had a good word for him - cunt. Grovelling Scotch cunt to be exact.

"That's what the Beatles called him. Same as Adolf Hitler. And many more. But you've only given me two dead crap Glasgow journalists - I need another for the full set. The Three Roasters, the Three Unwise Monkeys, the Three Pished Dead Scotch Hacks - it's got to be George McHattie… yass, god, yass! Take him now!"

"Long may our boyish japes halt our mortal decline into responsible adulthood," said Tony.

There was a long silence before McCrindle spoke in a flat tone Tony had never heard. "I wish I'd had a child," he said.

Tony studied him out of the corner of an eye, waiting for the inevitable bad taste punchline. But McCrindle's face had reddened and he seemed about to cry. Neither man could speak to fill what was becoming a very odd silence.

McCrindle spoke at last: "I wish I hadn't thrown my wife away, the wife I made so miserable. Doing it made me miserable, too. I'd like a wife again. A wife for having children with, the babbins.

"A younger wife. Of child-bearing age and propensity. A saucy one - juicy." Tony could see the old McCrindle reasserting himself. "But I'll never get another wife. Do I want another wife?

"No, I don't. How long ago was it you got married - 30 years? If you'd-a had kids, female issue - I could-a married your daughter! Especially if she looked like you…"

Tony sighed. "Tell me why I should go with you tonight to this *Chronicle* retirement party you've harassed me about for months - whose party is it?" he said. "I hardly knew anybody, didn't like anybody…"

McCrindle grew animated. "It's that guy, the features sub - features legend," he said.

"The Ninja Sub. Crept about in tartan slippers. 'He's behind you!' Never said a word. Same clothes for 20 years. Nicotine-stained stonewash jeans. Brownish-yellowish-looking cardigan. Capstan Full Strength - Captain Fag Smoke. Worked nights.

"He'll be much missed… strange, given folk hardly knew he was there. The Ninja Sub floats… the Ninja Sub looms… the Ninj!" McCrindle saw recognition in Tony's eyes.

"See, you *do* remember him! He floated. He hovered. Might have been roller skates, now I think of it. Or levitation. Electro-magnetic. Everybody liked him… well, nobody disliked him.

"The Ninj - he never said anything to upset anybody - never said anything. Not that I heard. Considerate, diplomatic? Or brain-dead, mealy-mouthed - a right sniveller? A man after your own heart, Tony, either way, you gutless turd.

"It's him we'll salute. The unknown *Chronicle* sub. Top bloke. The Ninj. Whoever he was. Did he have a real name? I never knew. They broke the mould before they made him. And now he's gone... the useless fuckwit." They both giggled.

"Frank and fearless, that's how I wanted to leave newspapers - the big kiss-off," Tony said. "Open contempt... noble self-sacrifice - Captain Oates meets Johnny Rotten.

"A mix of dug-shite and cat-piss jetted all over the office frontage. Brown-out the big perspex *Chronicle* sign at the top. Oh, and the stink - magnificent." He pictured three filth-spattered plate-glass storeys.

"I missed my dream farewell - too elaborate, too many choices," said McCrindle. "Take a flame-thrower to Human Resources? Or drive a combine harvester through them?

"Into the Editor's office, wheech his chair through a window? Overturn his desk. Spray-paint a single word on the wall - red capitals, two metres tall.

"My proud declaration of personal responsibility. Mine alone. Heroic. Angry. Honest. I'd only have done it after folk had gone home, mind..."

Tony stopped him. "Your one-word signature protest, giant letters..."

"Moscardini!" McCrindle shouted. "I'd have made you a hero. Instead, us two mouse-men creep away in the paper's first big cull, before big culls became monthly. Maybe I'll have belated vengeance tonight, in a shower of glass and blood - I'll throw you *into* the *Chronicle's* reception from the place next door... your favourite Glasgow pub."

"Vic's," groaned Tony. "Vic's is where you're making me go? That dump. Those same clowns."

"Everybody who's nobody will be there," McCrindle said. "Big names from the halcyon days. Guys you wouldn't piss on even if they were on fire. Jerks, tossers, arseholes. Every one a *Chronicle* great.

"And maybe… just maybe… a very special lay-deh. Some bird or other from way back. There must have been one. A saucy old piece of danger-minge from the past… thrills rekindled."

There had been a woman, but Tony had never told McCrindle about her. It wouldn't have been wise. She'd been his secret, not to be shared with blabbermouth McCrindle, for whom nothing was sacred, nothing was serious.

Some saucy old thrill rekindled. Danger. Maybe that was what his life lacked. Vic's might be fun for once.

Friday evening
Chapter 14

Vic's unspoken formal name was the Victory Bar, home day and night to the *Chronicle's* dwindling tribes of hacks and subs, scribblers and snappers, busy evading work in the building next door.

None of them would admit to shirking, of course. The career idlers were oiling the cogs of the newspaper process; developing leads; cementing ties with valued contacts; conducting first-person research into Vic's suitability as a venue for their retirement parties.

"God bless the *Chronicle* and all who fail in her," Tony murmured under his breath as he entered from rain-lashed Britton Street, tangling his feet as ever in Vic's man-trap double doors, cursing. No sign of McCrindle.

McCrindle was an accredited Vic's hero; Tony loathed the place. Its regulars had loathed him back. Now here he was, alone, chin-deep in allegating alligators, history an ambush-in-the-making.

His inky past was ready to grasp the new improved Tony-over-the-water warmly by the throat, reminding him he'd been seen as a prissy no-mark by his newspaper peers. Nowhere to hide. He might even have to speak to people.

One person in particular. McCrindle had been right. Way back, there had been some woman. *A saucy bird.* A bit of danger. A woman he'd worked hard to forget in the 20-odd years since.

A sudden burst of machine-gun cackling jolted him back into the moment.

He concentrated on easing through a packed Vic's chortling Friday-night mob, fearful of being spotted. As he did so, an oblivious toper lurched a pace back from some conversational scrimmage, treading on Tony's toe, half-turning to anoint his jacket with a swill of lager. The place had provided worse welcomes, Tony reasoned.

Unlike most journos, he'd never felt at home in a pub - especially one as oppressive and male as Vic's. Whisky-smelling, fluorescent-lit, a shoebox of a place packed with gruff Glasgow newspapermen barking and grunting at each other about other gruff, barking, grunting Glasgow newspapermen.

He wagered that every *Chronicle* regular felt more at ease with their fellow drinkers in Vic's, with the bar staff, than they did at home with their families.

Home was where they went to sleep it off. Semi-detached villas. Semi-attached *Chronicle* journalists. From Milngavie to Cathcart, wives and children posed daily questions that demanded every journalist's mortal enemies: thought and effort.

Family homes: terrifying places scarred by natural light and fresh air. And without a solid, comforting bar for a fellow to prop himself on.

At home, you were meant to work out how folk felt. Tell them how you felt, who you were. Impossible demands.

In Vic's, there was no question more complex than "Fancy another drink?" Lazy men half-motivated by impending deadlines could shrug their shoulders and excuse any failure with their workplace credo: "We did the best we could in the short time available. It's all chip wrappers. Another pint?"

He could never relax in the beery, blokey bonhomie of the

boozer. A pub's din and heat was hellish, infernal torture. He was a shy fretter-and-worrier, an innate internal monologuist, not a bluff outgoing networker, and alcohol made the act of lessening his reserve more fraught.

Drink might loosen tongues and dissolve most folks' bonds, but it made Tony feel tense, uncontrolled, liable to calamitous spillage. Especially so in Vic's. Too many folk who reckoned they had his measure. Too many folk who resented him for having weighed them in the balance and found them wanting.

Time spent drinking there was time wasted, he had believed. Time better invested at the workplace - just metres away… at his desk, at his computer, on his phone.

Vic's close proximity to his *Chronicle* desk had been a taunt throughout his 30 working years. Not so much a pub, more a midge bite that made his skin crawl and itch.

Casual mentions of its name - "Fancy nipping down to Vic's?" - almost induced an allergic reddening, had Tony clawing at his scalp or neck, feeling it chafe on him as he sought excuses to body-swerve the place.

On his rare visits to Vic's, he'd felt his jaws tighten, his mouth clamp shut. Speaking became an effort. Stone-Face Moscardini. Tony Tight Lips. His voice feathered and failed, catching in his throat and faltering against Vic's constant din. Whoever he was talking to was forced to lean in to hear whatever it was he was trying to say, undermining his confidence that his words were worth saying in the first place.

And so it proved amid the retirement party crowd's rising heat and conversational volume. He became more withdrawn, shrunken, diffident and - to his great annoyance - deferential-seeming to those cheerier, more seasoned booze-hounds around him, the drink-enabled, the alco-expanded. In Vic's, he could manage no smile better than a rictus grin.

"Cheer up" he'd often been told by one regular after another - so often that it inspired one of his first comedy routines. A satire addressing his own unwavering commitment to pessimism. An outspoken routine. Which had always gone unsaid in Vic's, of course.

How had it gone? He retreated into his imagination, deafened, sipping warm beer as he ran the old lines through his head.

"I'm not one of your glass-half-full optimists," he saw himself deadpanning on a packed comedy club's stage. "Not a glass-half-empty pessimist, either. I'm more the kind of guy who walks into a pub and says: 'This half-glass you've given me - it's got a crack in it... there's lipstick on the rim - and this drink... It's not what I ordered.' "

His phone vibrated in his jacket pocket. A text from Ken Moody, assuring him that *Bullitt da Colonia* was on course for Sunday-night's premiere. "Ongoing low-level gibber re hired PA. All rite on nite. New challenge - outdoor big screen? Too small. Made our own. 12 white-enough white bed sheets. No obvious stains - stitched together. Problem solved. Await further problems."

He slipped his mobile phone back into his pocket and became conscious of a louder, more raucous cheer diluting the Vic's usual hubbub. Braying, hooting, somebody in the mix making bugle noises, too. McCrindle had arrived.

****

McCrindle stepped through Vic's doors, smiling his trademark mile-wide dazzle of a smile, a bobbing cork aloft on a frothing human tide of welcome, greeting every happy face, bellowing assorted surnames - most of them unknown to Tony, despite his 30 years at the *Chronicle* - and bear-hugging a delighted succession of glassy-eyed drunks.

McCrindle's back! The Drinkmeister! Hail the conquering hero back from… how long is it? Where the fuck is it he's been? Somewhere! Everywhere! Saudi? Oz? Hong Kong! The long-lost brother… the returning prodigal… fatten up a calf… take a drink…

McCrindle's appearance was a relief, the latter's popularity letting Tony skulk, mope and loiter more enjoyably in his chosen age-old *Chronicle* metier, the background. Yet his arrival bore a potential cost, too.

McCrindle offended some folk as easily as he charmed most. Tony would need to monitor the evening for sudden spikes of potential outraged violence.

Unnoticed and inaudible, he slipped into his role as a shadowy walk-on mumbler, forever part-clearing his throat. He spotted someone with whom to engage in dutiful small talk. A guy who looked as though he'd rather be elsewhere, same as him: the event's retiring star, the Ninja Sub.

He checked Old Ninj's clothes and footwear, hoping Old Ninj wouldn't notice. A brown suit tonight. To hide the tar and nicotine. Good choice.

Proper shoes for once, too, laces and everything. After tonight, in what remained of Old Ninj's post-work life, Tony reckoned, the guy would pad about silently at home in his slippers each day, denied a communal arena through which to glide, unseen and unheard.

Previously, he'd gone unnoticed. Now there'd be no one not to notice him. A subtle difference. A profoundly sad one. Tony felt he might cry.

The Ninja Sub couldn't have bagged a wife, could he? Impossible. How would he engage with any potential marital partner, given that he almost never spoke? A displaced, disengaged sub-standard sub-human Sub padding around at home. Invisible. Alone.

Maybe he'd end up the same, Tony thought.

He recalled seeing old video footage of himself years ago at some wedding, one of his wife's workmates. He'd been a reluctant attendee, of course. On film, a stand-offish figure, a wisp; a preoccupied half-smile, fluttering on the periphery of every conversation, not listening, unconsciously wringing his hands, looking around him for some better place to be. And not finding one.

The accidentally-recorded Tony Moscardini. He wondered whether his *Chronicle* colleagues had viewed him in the same way he viewed the Ninja Sub... looked down on him.

In that instant, he felt the crushing weight of more unexpected sadness. Poor solitary silent Ninja Sub. Poor Tony.

"The man of the hour - the retiring hero!" he said, extending the jovial hand of human kinship, wearing what he hoped was a matey air. "A departing *Chronicle* employee of long-standing - even longer sitting, probably!" He joked, grinning hard. "Employee of long-standing - *even longer sitting,*" he repeated.

The Ninja Sub stared at him. "What?" he said.

Tony swallowed his grin, admitted his lame gag's defeat. "You'll be looking forward to retirement... time to, er... be your own boss... you know - freedom," he ventured.

"No," said Old Ninj, swivelling and turning away.

He had made the effort, done his duty, acted as a diplomatic envoy for polite social engagement, and been rebuffed. The Ninja Sub had no idea who he was. After all, Tony had never spoken to the guy before in all their hours together on the *Chronicle*.

He knew how he must have appeared in his working-life. Superior. Disengaged. Never knowingly soiled by workplace amity. Forever holding himself aloof from those he perceived to be the common *Chronicle* herd.

He retreated into himself. The honking racket of Vic's. Newspaper journalists. Flushed red-grey faces, oystery eyes, lager-legged old drunks jigging about, the piss-head shuffle. Bad breath, stale beer, sweat.

It was six o'clock on a Glasgow Friday night. Vic's noxious blare raged on.

In Zio Beppo right now, he was sure, folk would be drinking moderately while talking *with* one another, not *at* one another. Seriously. Rationally. With relative rationality, anyway. More so than in Vic's. The overall volume of Zio Beppo's two-way communication would have a natural ebb and flow, rising and falling as people listened to one another, exchanged sentiments, experiences, ideas.

In Vic's, folk with closed minds opened their mouths to bellow and quaff, flinging themselves headfirst into their drinks with desperation, competing to be noisiest, jolliest. Scoring points. Settling scores.

So it had always seemed to him. He surveyed the roistering mob over the rim of his glass of Vic's trademark warm lager-style drink, hoping he didn't look as disdainful as he felt.

It was as though the good old, bad old days of the *Chronicle* at its alcohol-soaked finest had never ended. He began shaping a stand-up routine in his head. It had always been evident to him that drinking eagerly, often and to excess didn't constitute a barrier to success in the newspaper game. Quite the opposite.

Drink and roar yourself along the employment fast-track the *Chronicle* booze-bag way! If only he'd mastered the craft of getting and staying professionally gassed, he might have had more career success. Instead, he told himself, he'd hobbled his career by remaining coherent while not falling over or vomiting into his coat-pocket... or anyone else's.

Never a promotion. Never a merit pay-rise. Always out-beered. Always out-ginned. Failing to be a professional pishy-pants is one thing. But oh, Signor Most-Condescendi, the ignominy of never having tried.

****

He noticed Vic's had fallen quieter. The main bar was emptying, the quacking throng subsiding as folk exited in ones and twos through a doorway in the corner. The retirement party was adjourning to its formal arena, Vic's dowdy, ill-lit first-floor function suite.

He followed the invitees up the stairs into a windowless room that featured at its centre a small rectangular wooden floor, sticky underfoot, looming walls panelled in brown Formica. Brown leather banquette seating on three sides, with a scattering of small tables. Coffin-esque, he supposed, quieter than downstairs, thankfully.

A small bar lurked in the corner to your left as you came in, complementary opening drinks. Two trestle tables at the room's far end were spread with the *Chronicle's* broadsheet pages, a thoughtful touch which failed to redeem an underwhelming retiral buffet: grey, grease-sheened sausage rolls, bowls of crisps, a plate of Scotch eggs and three or four silver foil platters of curling white-sliced sandwiches (none of your Fancy-Dan brown stuff).

He half-recognised seven or eight desiccated old men in uniform beige. Placid sub-editing backroom boys, not high-rolling reporters. They milled about variously testing the tepidness of the sausage rolls with a forefinger, or hugging piled plates of chow close to their buttoned-up cardigans, others having seated themselves, clutching glasses of white wine between bony knees. Subby Normal and His Big Night Out Band.

He'd been relieved that his own exit from the newspaper industry two years previously had gone unlauded. No ceremony. No flags flown at half-mast above the *Chronicle's* roof. No leggy strippers - male or female - showing up disguised as traffic wardens. No 21-gun salute. For an 11-stone galoot.

Fifty-plus redundancies had been enacted at once, necessitating two farewell drinks sessions in two different nearby bars - neither of which he'd visited more than half-a-dozen times in his 30 years at the *Chronicle*. Tony's glasses had steamed up as soon as he'd entered the redundo send-off in Vic's, which he'd seized upon as a sign to turn on his heel and flee. He hadn't recognised anyone in the other two-thirds-empty pub. He'd let himself melt away unseen, as was his wont.

In the same way he planned to melt away tonight, snubbing everyone he didn't like, sidestepping the headache-inducing strain of enforced joviality.

He stood at a remove, same as normal. Watched. Waited. Glugged a bit more tepid lager. Took a condescending view of the rest of the world, chiding himself for his arrogance as he did so, recognising his unwillingness to join in.

What he saw - and despised, he had to admit - was a room filled with greyer, fatter, balder, jowlier versions of himself. A set of thwarted overweight bulldogs sculpted from ham. The Lard of the Shite Brigade.

He turned cutting similes over in his head, weighing their stand-up potential. Guy with a face like an ancient dowager duchess's burst handbag retrieved from a builders' skip after three years. Face like a peeled tumour. Face like a half-chewed caramel stuck to a cat's boil-encrusted bumhole.

A roomful of folk for whom life had ended, he sneered. Everything good and funny and meaningful had already happened. Fresh pastures would go unsought. New memories unforged.

Each conversation he'd half-overheard downstairs in Vic's

had been a tale of better times long lost, never to be equalled. Magnificent folly, former glory, hilarious ruin, terminal ascent.

Why did so many people choose to live in the past, he wondered. Sure, reach your fifties and you'll discover you're looking to a bright future that entails mortal illness, pained decrepitude, crumbling ignominy, redundancy, fungal toenails, grim death.

Bu he and McCrindle remained different, better, sharper, more youthful, he liked to believe.

"Me and you, Tony!" the latter had roared years earlier in a taxi queue following some monumental gig at Barrowland (the Cramps, had it been?). "Wild-eyed freebooters racing towards the golden promise of the now-a-go-go, me and you, forever... grasp the moment!

"Life's fleeting pleasures will ripple through the soft curves of our lithe young bodies into all eternity!"

McCrindle had of course been drinking, which had been why he'd stumbled, and fallen to the pavement. "Ah fuck, I've broken my soft curves," the prone McCrindle had groaned, laughing and wincing.

Tony smiled at the recollection, aware the crowd around him in Vic's might wonder why he'd suddenly begun grinning to himself for no apparent reason. He and McCrindle had always found hilarity where few others did - and on cue, McCrindle appeared in the middle of the function room's centre, surrounded by ex-workmate admirers.

"Which one of you propped-up corpses thinks you're not dead yet?" he shouted.

****

Why was death something Tony and McCrindle found hilarious? It must have stemmed from their day-to-day exposure to the gallows humour of the journalism business, death as a routine tool of the trade.

Late-night groups of newsroom sub-editors painstakingly examining that day's road crash-site photographs – Family of Five Perish At Holiday Accident Blackspot, Wrong-Way Bridge Smash Claims Newly-Wed - to determine the makes of car involved.

The jokes. Terrible jokes. Q: What was the last thing to cross High-Speed Celebrity Death-Victim X's mind when his car hit a tree? A: His testicles.

He scanned the elderly crowd. None of the oldsters at the Ninja Sub's sign-off was likely to find death amusing anymore. It was too close now, too real a prospect.

His focus softened. The beer was starting to do his thinking for him. He tried to convince himself he wasn't doing what he was doing, which was scanning the party's attendees for one particular face. A female face.

McCrindle suddenly startled him with an act of apparent mind-reading, up close, growling in his ear. "Tony's slow expert glance gauged the heft of every pair of heavy-melon mahumbas on display… seeking out one special set of well-kent norks.

"Don't deny it, Tony. Me, though, I'd sooner shag those dried-out sandwiches on that table than any of these dried-up old tarts." He said it under his breath but still loud enough to offend somebody. *He's dangerous*, Tony reminded himself, *same as you*.

McCrindle drifted away, joining a loud cluster of ex-Chroniclers engaged in cataloguing recently-deceased ex-workmates. Within seconds, McCrindle - master of the inappropriate gesture - had uttered a gleeful shout of "Three-nil!" underscored with a victorious punch of the air, as though celebrating a last-minute Scotland World Cup-winning goal.

He was hailing the death of a much-loathed *Chronicle* assistant editor, the boastful and preening Malcolm McMurdo - aka Turdo. Open joy at Turdo's demise was unlikely to provoke violent wrath, but you never knew...

For how badly received had been McCrindle's infamous joke about Turdo when he'd voiced it one news-deficient springtime Sunday afternoon? Very badly.

Turdo had been out and about seeking material for his *Chronicle* columnist role. For he was the paper's couthily-comic Man on a Mid-Life Crisis Motorcycle, riding a Harley Davidson around Lanarkshire.

He'd ridden it into a wall. Not comic. Not couthy. The *Chronicle's* news desk had gathered in silence to ponder the list of his injuries, supplied by a local freelance who expected a bonus payment for it (he didn't get one). A 50/50 survival chance. Strong likelihood of paralysis or brain damage. Possible leg amputation.

In a move denoting the deepest concern, no *Chronicle* news photographer was despatched to the scene. No point, McCrindle had whispered to Tony, as the subs already knew what bike McMurdo was riding, so no winning bets to be placed on name-the-death-marque.

The respectful silence persisted, proof of an accord: never mind that McMurdo was a bullying borderline sociopath, the chap was a fellow human being, a comrade, mortally wounded. His colleagues furrowed their brows.

And into this pool of silent compassion, McCrindle had pitched a tiny question that almost resulted in him being punched in the face: "But how's the bike?"

This was his most abiding memory of Glasgow. Cruel and shameful comic exchanges at someone else's expense that you forced yourself to laugh at before they claimed you as their victim.

Chapter 15

Tonight's news of Turdo McMurdo's death was evidently making McCrindle feel more alive - so much so that he began eulogising the deceased aloud, using the oily, consonant-smoothing quasi-American voice of every fifth-rate Scottish TV newsreader. Which, when Tony thought about it, was pretty much every Scottish TV newsreader.

McCrindle's bulletin was delivered at maximum volume, with maximum sententiousness, aimed to cause maximum outrage.

"Dear old Turdo," he slurred. "An udderly delideful combinayzzhun of Mother Deresa, Jesus Chryzzd, Osgar Pizdoriuzz and that tramp with lice in his beard who played the spoons on Saddurday nights outside the Gregg's on Argyle Streed. Now Turdo's probbing his elbow on God'z bar - fiddling with a heavenly choir of angeligg schoolboys."

McCrindle's audience shifted uneasily. "Fellow's scarcely in his grave... time and place... show some respect," someone muttered.

A new voice chipped in: "Fuckin' arsehole!" It was Terence Keenan, a short-fused news reporter whom *Chronicle* colleagues knew as the kind of guy to start a fight in an empty room.

Keenan's movie-star profile - chiselled jawline, blue eyes, a hint of Paul Newman - contrasted with his ugly big knuckles, which were almost always bloody, grazed, scabbed and/or swollen from punching people who'd offended him for being less drunk than he was.

He'd been drinking at the party, of course. Oh dear, thought Tony. This did not bode well.

Luckily, a quick-thinking group of retirement-party peacekeepers averted the threat of war by starting a discussion about the optimum death awaiting every ex-Chronicler. The most merciful exit was the one which concluded a short illness, at home, loved ones in bedside attendance.

There was no saving McCrindle from himself, of course. "At home, loved ones by your bedside?" he shouted. "Loved ones? Mistress, barmaids, bookie, pawnbroker - how many guys here can afford a house with a bedroom that size?"

The selfless defusers of unexploded ordinance ignored him, sticking to their task. Better still, one of them chuntered, was a death the week after a terminal diagnosis, an agonised life sentence commuted.

"Deathly sentences!" McCrindle said: "What *Chronicle* news chimps hammer out on a keyboard." Keenan made an angry, scornful sound from the corner. He'd put his glass down, a sign he wasn't going to throw it imminently. *Set portents for ominous anyway*, Tony told himself.

Violence was deferred when one of the Ninj's sub-editor colleagues stepped up to give a speech. It turned out that the Ninja Sub had an actual name, Gavin Donaldson. His subbing career had moreover, according to his colleague's speech, been rendered uproarious by sundry perilous tight spots from which Gavin always effected last-minute extrications.

Inopportune coffee spillages. Grievous software glitches. Missing 200-word articles replaced in the nick of time with ones Gavin kept on file for just such occasions.

Gavin's colleagues had clubbed together to buy him a retirement gift to further his full-time enjoyment of his favourite pastime, snooker. There ensued the presentation of a folding cue ("Plus new tartan slippers!").

Applause broke out. Tony joined in, saddened by the smallness of another man's ambitions - and by his own inner flush of superiority. For once, McCrindle refrained from voicing offensive thoughts.

****

"A right good sesh on the electric mouth-wash - you can't whack it," said McCrindle, handing Tony a pint. "The swally. The bevvy. A wee wet. The dear auld Glesca banter - it'll have you in stitches... *under the doctor.*" He moved off for further sport.

Every other Friday-night tippler in Vic's had a head start on Tony. Despite not being a drinker, he had succumbed to the event's week-ending alco-holiday mood, downing his maximum three pints of lager already.

The party's limited supply of free drink had run out, thinning the crowd. So when Tony glanced around, he saw the face he'd half-longed to see, half-feared seeing ever again. Rachel Ballantyne.

Twenty years on from the scene of the crime, he was looking at the woman for whom he'd as-good-as-betrayed his wife. Undermined his wedding-day vows. Failed at being a husband. Lacked sufficient willpower to become an adulterer. Lost all sense of who and what he was.

She still looked the way he remembered her. She hadn't aged, or put on weight - hey, Tony, why not go over and tell her she's not as wrinkled and fat as she could be, you silver-tongued Lothario. Best not.

She'd grown to look different over the past two decades in small ways he couldn't define. The same way he knew he looked different, too. She was none the worse looking, though. That familiar twine-toed walk. Shy. Hesitant.

Perhaps a little more stooped, rounder-shouldered. Odd how flaws can make someone more attractive.

Her hair, not cut into any recognisable style, same as before - tomboyish, he supposed. Hair as shiny as back then, but darker. What was the old gag? A suicide brunette - dyed by her own hand. Rich coming from him: the man with no hair, yellow teeth, a thickened waist, neck like an old crepe bandage.

A ready but shy-seeming smile, a familiar face that was up for engagement, social warmth. A fuller face? Deeper frown lines. Flushed-looking. Shinier skin, redder cheeks. Menopausal?

He tried to fathom her exact age, factoring in what little operational knowledge he had of womanhood's hormonal seas, tides, currents. Darker shades beneath the eyes. Eyes that he knew held danger; eyes best avoided.

Dark-brown eyes extending equal measures of comfort and challenge, certainty and cheekiness. Forgiving eyes. Inviting. Maternal and reassuring, yet exciting, too. A face to feel at home with.

A face to swoon into bed with. He was staring at her face, couldn't help himself. He tried to be subtle, avoid being caught in a lingering gaze. After all this time…

Two decades since his career had lost all forward motion, then gone into reverse. Two decades since his marriage had withered and died - and there she was, Rachel Ballantyne, the woman whose wholesome-seeming, unremarkable features he'd been unable to stop himself fixating on for years as the root of his life's two most wounding failures, the professional and the personal.

As he wondered how to pretend he hadn't seen Rachel, four men he'd never wanted to see again spotted him. A tubby quartet of *Chronicle* tormentors, ex-workmates. The Four Lame Horsemen With the One Poke of Chips, as McCrindle once called them. Over they trundled.

MacConnachie: coarse ginger broom-bristle moustache. Chisholm: swinging an imaginary golf club, he'd wandered the newsroom driving invisible golf balls. Grieve: unwanted advances on young female journalists. And Old Oyster Eyes, Snoddie.

MacConnachie's moustache fluttered. "Reviewing tonight's bash, are you, phoney Tony?" he said. "Tony Masturbani's inside verdict on the Ninja Sub's big send-off: he came, he saw, he sneered - one star."

Tony composed a withering put-down - *Five-star face-fungus, fat-boy* - that he was too slow, too timid to say out loud. He grinned what he hoped was a devil-may-care grin, knowing he'd failed.

Chisholm stepped up to a non-existent tee, lashed an unseen golf ball. "Tiny Tony Big Words," he jeered, " 'The Ninja Sub's retirement party was searingly cogent' - no, 'cogently searing,' "

Bunker off, Tony thought but didn't say, blushing.

Time for the *Chronicle's* serial lecher, Grieve, to try his hand. "Missed any good stories in Italy lately?" he asked. Tony grinned and raised his glass, remembering how his old work mates had derided him as The Comedian ("The joke's always on Tony!"). If only his years of watching stand-up comedy had taught him how to bat hecklers away.

"Dudes, after all this time... a pressure to see you," was the best Tony could manage, his throat constricting, his voice weak.

"Soda water and lime, signorina?" Grieve said. "Hang on, Father Superior's on the lager! Tony Baloney's condescended to drowning himself in drink with us lower orders."

Snoddie oozed forward. "Good move, Moany Tosscardini becoming a photographer," he said. His sidekicks snickered and snorted. "Flapping snappers on the edge of everything, not at the centre like us wordsmiths.

"What's that song? If a picture paints a thousand words... three of your wee snaps and we're spared a four-mile-long Moany Tosscardini opening paragraph! 'What's Tony Baloney on about now? Dunno - one of his photos'll make more sense!'!"

Tony smiled, trying to share the joke, his face tight, aware how embarrassed he looked. Thank god no one at the *Chronicle* had ever found out moscardini was Italian for baby octopus - oh, the put-downs.

A sudden thought: what if Rachel was watching his discomfort. Not a good sign, still trying to look cool in her presence, he chided himself.

If he spoke now, he knew he'd sound high-pitched, defensive, adolescent. A tone of light sparring was beyond him. Against the usual way of things, it was McCrindle who rode to Tony's rescue.

"None of you lot have changed in 10 years, I see... still wearing the same crap clothes," he said, appearing at Tony's side. "Not that they fit now. Some folk say the newspaper game got small - I reckon you lot just got really fat."

MacConnachie, Chisholm, Grieve and Snoddie glanced at one another, shuffling their feet. Their turn to fail to look cool. They didn't move off, though. Tony remained in the firing squad's sights. Their four drink-emboldened faces blurred into a single sneer.

"We were just having a wee chat with our old mate Teeny-Tiny Mantovani," MacConnachie said. "Telling him not to leave his participles dangling."

Chisholm joined in. "Didn't see you at Bob Sturgeon's funeral,

Tony… can't think why - oh hang on, I can - why would you go to his funeral when he was never good enough for you when he was alive? None of us everyday reporters were ever good enough for you, smarty-boy, you made that plain."

Grieve was next: "We were just clueless hacks churning out words to fill holes - but *you, you* were an artist."

"A tortured artist - torturing the English language," snickered Snoddie.

He hoped he appeared less rattled than he felt, worrying again that Rachel would see him made small - immediately worrying more about why he should still be concerned with what she might think of him.

But at this point a genuine physical danger presented itself: Keenan, bony fists, elbows out barging past MacConnachie, Chisholm, Grieve and Snoddie, a spit-soaked barrage of angry accusations.

****

"You were too good for the News Desk, so you thought… stuck-up, better than us," Keenan said, menacing up close.

Tony studied Keenan's face, noticing how the one-time heart-throb reporter's looks had coarsened. Blue eyes clouded. Nose bulbous, purple-blue, covered in broken veins. Drink. The passage of 20 years.

"Not so much Paul Newman, more Paul Veryoldman," he chose not to say out loud.

"No routine dirty work for you," Keenan was saying. "Wouldn't stoop to filing six pars about roadworks on the Kingston Bridge. But what single clever-clever word of yours ever meant anything to the guy having a pint in the bar at Harroldwood Golf Club?"

McCrindle reappeared, staging another cavalry-to-the-rescue

act. "Harroldwood Golf Club?" he said. "Harrold-Wouldn't Golf Club for you, more like, you bunkered old bletherer."

"Shove your mashie niblick up your hole in one and be done with it."

Even Keenan had to laugh. He'd made a strategic blunder. "The man who showed up to a verbal knife fight with Glasgow's most middle-class golf club as his weapon," McCrindle muttered as Keenan backed off, forcing the kind of wry half-smile that Tony couldn't.

More partygoers had drifted off. He avoided scanning the room for any particular face. One particular face. If I don't look for her, I won't see her, he told himself.

She must have been among the early exits. Changed days in Glasgow: journalists off home from the pub by eight o'clock on a Friday.

The lights had gone out on the newspaper trade. Vic's clientele appeared defeated and shrunken. A decade of job losses. Waves of redundancies. Budgets slashed. Payrolls reduced. Horizons shrunk. Hope extinguished.

Most journalists under 40 had shipped out, taken safe local government public relations jobs, Tony knew: *paid to mollify folk with half-truths, unable to fool themselves they were doing anything else.*

Those few still employed in newspapers were over-worked, underpaid, insecure, cowed and bitter, shabbier than ever. No one in Vic's looked happy. Not even the man making his long-overdue escape, the retiree.

He realised there were no young *Chronicle* workers in the room tonight, no next generation to whom a wizened old-time journo might raise his battered trilby, bow, wink and hand on the symbols of a grand industrial tradition: a glass of Laphroaig, a blunt-nibbed pencil, a whisky-soaked notepad, every dog-eared page filled with illegible shorthand.

Vic's: a natural habitat for the older-but-no-wiser; a dead-end dump for the gloomier, the dimmed, the doomed.

"Thank God we escaped when we did," McCrindle said. "This business, what a state. If you're still doing your terrible glass half-full/ half-empty comedy routine, lemme tell ya, bub, the newspaper industry ain't worryin' 'bout no half-empty glass no more.

"Newspaper empty glass done gone and shattered, man. Lucky if it's a paper cup nowadays… with dust in it.

"Speaking of which, I'm getting me another drink, plus half a shandy for you. You need to slow down, Tony Must-have-a-Martini, you're past your maximum one-pint limit."

Tony hoped he didn't look as old and ground-down as everyone else in the room. He certainly felt drunker than they looked. However many pints in, he was feeling… unsteady… untethered. Blurred round the edges.

How proud he'd once been of his professional detachment as a newspaperman, his impartiality. Him the neutral observer, the unbiased outsider. A spectator on the sidelines. That was his role, wasn't it? Non-partisan. Dispassionate. Getting in close enough to look but holding himself apart, avoiding compromise.

But was that how he'd truly been? More likely, he thought, he'd pandered to his natural fearfulness. Too scared to get in close and commit. A craven bystander, a scurrying passer-by, a rootless drifter. A man reluctant to engage in anything. In everything. Job. Marriage. Dodging the dirty work.

He scanned the room, everything out of focus. Should have stuck to red wine. Eaten better beforehand. The place was sparse now, but it suddenly hit him that everyone had turned up for an event in someone else's honour. They'd made an effort to unite and generate some communal warmth in another person's name.

He wondered how many folk might think enough of him to do the same. None most likely. He imagined his own funeral. Tony Moscardini, eternal outsider. Now at peace. No doubt looking down on the attendees from on high, down his nose. No change there, then.

Crematorium empty, save for the undertaker. Maybe McCrindle. But hey, a meagre funeral turnout would only mean less hecklers. Then again, if an empty room is your legacy, has your life been a failure? Probably, he guessed.

McCrindle handed him another pint. The fourth? Fifth? He tuned back into the ebbing noise of old *Chronicle-ites* swilling round Vic's dowdy function room, swigged his lager and let his vision roam.

He saw only one person, couldn't help it: Rachel Ballantyne and only Rachel Ballantyne.

Everyone else in the room blurred into a part-dissolved background of pensioned-off beige, slow brown and inert grey. Sepia-tinged nit-pickers and out-of-focus old blowhards. Muted braying.

Rachel circled the ragged edges of the last dozen or so bunches of party attendees, floating from one to another, her head bobbing with a vital bird-like quiver as she laughed, her smile finding a ready welcome.

She was doing what he she did best, using what she had to get what she wanted. Working a crowd. Teasing out confidences. Or was she baiting a trap? Spinning her web.

She turned to face him, and there was no way he could stop staring back at her. Rachel was looking at him, and only him, and as she did so, she was opening and closing her right hand in the kind of stiff, awkward wave that a small child might give.

Tentative, innocent, charming. Greeting him in the way he'd never forget she used to.

In that instant, the image of Gabriella's business-like farewell wave yesterday in Colonia popped into his head. It cheered him, he didn't know why, even though it wasn't like Rachel's wave, the one he was looking at now.

Rachel's wave was disarming, enticing. He reminded himself it was doubtless intended to be. He told himself to be careful - and then of course he waved back in the same childlike fashion. She smiled. He smiled.

She crossed the wooden floor, pigeon-toed and shy-seeming, and then stood in front of him, a frank expression on her face. He stared into her brown eyes.

Did they still offer the same promise of excitement? Was his mouth hanging open? Was his tongue hanging out? So long as he wasn't drooling…

He swallowed, forced a grin. Keep it non-committal. Let her do the talking. Stay cool. Keep it zipped. "I'd been wondering whether you'd be here," he heard himself say.

"I could say I'd thought the same about you," Rachel replied, "but I'd probably be lying." She laughed, the dirty-joke chuckle he remembered. Matey. One of the lads. Unlady-like.

He felt light-headed. It was the drink, nothing more. He half-slumped, half-sat on the arm of the nearest bench to stop himself falling headfirst into his shared past with Rachel Ballantyne.

Friday night
Chapter 16

He tried getting comfortable on his low perch, the sofa's hard narrow arm, midway between sitting and standing. Torture. His buttocks ached. He strained to stay upright, bracing both feet against the floor, scrabbled for purchase.

Struggling to look nonchalant, he lifted his head. Rachel Ballantyne's chest filled his field of vision, no avoiding it, a metre from his face, close-up. Breasts.

Three shameful words burst into his lager-sodden head, rowdy adolescents jostling one another: Ample! Full! Prominent! A terrible punchline. He had an impulse to blurt the words out loud. No joke. Not funny. He was drunk. *Tipsy titterer Tony...*

Rachel was de-emphasising her shape, as she'd always done, disguising it with a buttoned-up white shirt and a masculine tweed waistcoat. But she was a woman. No question about it. A woman-shaped woman.

A woman with a woman's chest - a bust. A bosom. Ample, full and prominent - often stared at by leering men. He was not such a man. Much.

He raised his eyes higher, focusing on her hair. A gentleman, no matter how drunk, he told himself, never addresses himself to a lady's chest. Look at her hair. Safer. Much safer than her eyes.

Brown eyes. Avoid them, he told himself. Warm and inviting. Deep, unfathomable. Amused? Mocking? Dangerous whichever way. Eyes to get lost in. Eyes to drown in. Comfort and challenge in equal measure.

He reminded himself not to look down. But of course he did, lowering his eyes to her chest again, and in that drink-clouded instant his mind was lit up by three other terrible words.

Appalling words. In lightning-white letters, six-feet high. *Bounteous. Balconied. Breasts.*

Unspeakable words. Crass. Clumsy. Perilous, a reminder of his old closeness to her, once upon a time, long ago, when such words could be said as a stupid compliment, for a laugh.

He stared down at his shoes, levering himself upright, feeling the room pitch a little beneath his feet. And in that moment Tony and Rachel's long-lost shared past lurched back to life. Because across the room he heard McCrindle shouting a name that had once helped unite him with Rachel.

"Gerry McAvoy? Dead? *Gerry McAvoy?*" McCrindle was shouting at a high pitch, in obvious disbelief. "Dead drunk, drunk'n'dead - when they cremate him, they won't be able to put the fire out!"

Harsh. But fair. Compared to Gerry McAvoy, George McHattie was a teetotal beacon. Compared to Gerry McAvoy, Edward Penney had been the founder of the Temperance League.

Hearing Gerry McAvoy's name made Tony shudder, a memento of the worst of his bad times with Rachel. Ironic, given that Gerry McAvoy had been most journalists' good luck charm.

"As long as piss-head Gerry McAvoy still had a job, we all did," he heard McCrindle say across the room to loud laughter, before re-telling the legend of Gerry McAvoy.

What had made Gerry McAvoy a legend - a hoot, a hero - was his triumph, 20 years previously, as Reporter of the Year in the annual Scottish Press Association Awards. A prison riot had broken out, a guard taken hostage. Prominent among the rioters was a Glasgow gangland enforcer serving three life sentences for murder.

By phone from the prison governor's pillaged office, the gangland enforcer presented himself as a peacemaker, brokering a hostage-exchange deal with Scotland's best-selling tabloid, the *Daily Bugle*. The hostage would be released when the *Bugle* sent in a reporter to record and amplify the rioters' righteous grievances.

Which *Bugle* reporter was available for immediate dispatch to a dangerous prison siege? With no wife to complain if he became the gangland enforcer's fourth victim? The half-cut *Bugle* reporter slumped at his office desk at 10.30am pretending to read the papers: Gerry McAvoy.

McAvoy's Reporter of the Year award cited "selfless bravery in risking his life while pursuing his duty as a journalistic observer."

In reality, the story that had filled eight pages of the next day's *Bugle* was invented by its newsdesk. McAvoy had been equipped with a tape recorder, but hadn't turned it on. His drunken short hand was illegible. His memory a blank.

The prisoners' demands turned out to be a scrawled note from the gangland enforcer. "Better grub - stinken fish!" it read. "Ban chips. More lettis. Hand's off ma wife whiles am in here, McGinty ya bam."

The note went unpublished. No one saw it till months later: McAvoy had put it in his pocket and forgotten about it.

"And there we are," McCrindle said, delivering his punchline: "The best stories are the ones you never read in the papers - especially if they're about newspaper folk." The room rang with laughter, including Rachel's dirty-joke chuckle. Tony realised he still missed it.

His eyes met Rachel's. Because what they both remembered was the name of the runner-up in that year's News Reporter of the Year category: Rachel Ballantyne. And what they alone knew was that he had given her the story that had been good, but not good enough.

A story of showbiz egotism and last-minute demands for money, featuring a small-screen national treasure, adored by the Scottish public and hated by all her fellow actors.

Sure, the story lacked a prison riot, an illiterate gangland enforcer, a hostage, and a journalist too drunk to write his own name, so it was never going to annex the top Scottish press award. But it had still shone with enough celebrity pzazz and back-stage intrigue to improve his standing at the *Chronicle*. If he'd wanted it to.

But he hadn't. So he'd given it away to her.

Because at this stage he wanted to accelerate his career's descent. If he couldn't control anything else in his day-to-day working life, he could at least control his own rate of collapse. He would take perverse pleasure in seeing his story succeed elsewhere, ascending in the public eye as surely as his own status at the *Chronicle* waned.

Gifting Rachel the story would also cement his deepening friendship with her, too. A problematic friendship. Too close a friendship, they both knew. Him: older, with a wife. Her: younger, not looking to be a wife.

What was it he'd wanted from her? Friendship. No, more than that. He'd wanted a heat that his wife did not provide.

And eventually Rachel had offered it, freely and willingly, gifting herself to him. And what had happened? Nothing. Poised on the very brink of adultery, his guilt and shame had stopped him taking what she was willing to give.

But at least she got to be runner-up Reporter of the Year - in concrete terms, an ugly etched window pane glued to what looked like a glass potato plus a cheque for £200. He had consoled himself by devising imaginary headlines: Smart Woman Accepts Dumb Man's Prize Donation. Failing *Chronicle* Veteran Hands Gun To Potential Mistress, Shoots Self In Foot.

"This must be the night for blasts from the past," she said.

He sat down again on the sofa's uncomfortable arm, all at once feeling too woozy to stand. Here they both were again, after so many years. Close. But not face to face.

He reddened, super-heated by her cleavage. He forced himself to stand, ever so casual-seeming, he hoped, only to stumble a pace sideways.

So much for looking cool, unreadable - a man, not the middle-aged boy he'd been 20 years ago. He looked into her eyes, innocent yet knowing, still offering that familiar blend of maternal solace and daring frankness.

The room swirled around them, noise levels increasing despite the party entering its end phase. More laughter. Shouting.

He stood and tried to look cool. Strove to appear what he was. A mostly contented late-middle-aged bloke, he supposed, who was wary of starting a conversation with her for fear of re-starting… something.

He wasn't sure what that something was, but it worried him. Was he alarmed his old lust might re-ignite? Frightened, even.

Or was he more scared about an old heat *not* being re-kindled? Was he afraid that someone who'd once said she loved him would judge him lacking again - and he'd be rejected - again…

Was he scared he'd be angry with her, unleashing his hurt? Or maybe he feared being too drunk to speak. He felt himself slipping into an old habit from the bad old days: thinking too much, doing too little.

She spoke first. Measured. In control, although she'd been drinking, too, a glass of white wine in her hand, near enough that he could scent the wine's acidic heat on her breath.

"So here we are again," she said, "after all this time… Signor Moscardini."

He replied with what he hoped was a polite smile. Lips only, no teeth. Keeping it amiable. Non-committal. Nothing to be read into anything here, sister.

He couldn't think of a word to say. Not one. A foolish grin. Silence swooshed in his ears. A terrible impulse to blurt out something hideous, stupid. Bounteous balconied breasts.

She spoke again. "And you've relocated to Italy - the Moscardini ancestral homeland. Bella, bella, tarantella. Allegro, mi amico!" she said, laughing.

Typical of her to know things about his new life when he knew nothing about hers. Warning signs flashed in his head: *molto pericoloso, rallentare.*

He cleared his throat. "Yeah, Italy… a quiet little town - you have to make your own entertainment, not like Glasgow," he said.

"And you're a photographer," she said. "The ace lens-man. Not writing?"

"Vowed not to… pens… keyboards. I used to be a newspaperman, but I gave it up, like I gave up Glasgow - go out in the rain, fall apart."

A small smile crossed her face. "You should be writing," she said. "You were good at it. If you've got a talent, it's a sin not to use it. Write your memoirs. You always had a way with words - a certain facility. Persuasive."

He pondered what she meant. Persuasive. Him and his way with words. He kept smiling what he hoped was a civil smile, out-skirting any old cosiness.

"Things change, folk change, time goes by," he said, trying too hard to seem off-hand and unbothered by what she thought, annoyed he couldn't master his speech's drunken slur.

"Do Tony Moscardini's photographs sell?" she asked.

Safety in formal chat. Business, commerce. "They do OK," he said. "Online direct from me, a bit. Mostly via a gallery, in Glasgow. They've got the resources, the technology, the fine art paper... for the big prints. I stick to what I want to do - I'm just the snapper. Keeps me occupied."

He sensed himself relaxing, smiling more brightly, contravening his better judgement. She smiled back.

"Sunlit scenes of old Tuscany?" she asked. "Mediaeval churches? Sun on a vineyard? Ripening grapes hanging low and heavy?"

She grinned as she said the phrase. Could he hear a lingering purr, sense a vulpine leer, a smutty promise? His heart pounded faster. Just remember you're drunker than it's wise to be, he told himself.

"I photograph all sorts, a mix," he said, feeling hot, hoping sweat wasn't visible on his upper lip. "Tourist Italy's staples. Cute villages, centuries old. Stone-flagged winding streets, sunflowers in bloom, the clichés folk want. Escapism, the dream of Tuscany.

"Then again, the best-seller is what you could call photo-journalism... a modern image, not pretty - graffiti sprayed on a wall. Spotted it in a back street in Pisa, shabby, nowhere picturesque.

"Political protest, I thought at the time. Turned out to be lyrics by some Italian skinhead fascist punk band. '*Giornalisti terroristi* - Journalists terrorists.' Fair summary of the tabloids, maybe. Never saw it as a commercial winner.

"But folk keep buying Giornalisti Terroristi through the gallery - steady sales, handy pension boost. If it is fascist punks buying it, better my quality print on their wall than some tatty Mussolini calendar, I suppose.

"Or maybe I'm catering to clapped-out journos same as me, kidding ourselves we're still a threat to public order."

"Plenty of old giornalisti terroristi still lurking in Glasgow," she said, her smile seeming bigger, warmer. Was this the same look she'd given him years ago, frank and forward, a ready hint of more than friendship? *Hazard Ahead...* Or maybe he was just dangerously drunk.

An impulse flashed across his mind: tell her the joke he'd made yesterday as he was leaving Colonia to the old man suggesting Tony take photos of young women with no clothes on. *Young women don't want me with no clothes on taking their photos...*

He applied the brakes. Clamped his mouth shut. Say it out loud and he was the one responsible, no blaming it on the drink.

Out of nowhere, after all these years, he was ready to dredge up a casual reference to not having clothes on, ever-so-hilarious. He was poised to give in to an urge to open his stupid mouth and get cheeky and saucy and in closer, like the old days.

How had that stuff worked out for him back then, he asked himself, recalling the hurt, the pain. That first time, he hadn't known where getting close to Rachel Ballantyne would lead. He'd enjoyed being the subject of her attention, enjoyed watching her watching him.

But where had that led? He couldn't plead ignorance second time round.

"So what have you been up to?" he heard himself ask in a voice slowed by drink, clumsy, deceptive in off-hand intent, his mouth operating independent of common sense, running red lights, ignoring icebergs. "Still working on the papers?"

"Sunday Citizen. Somebody's got to keep churning out linings for the bottom of birdcages."

"Settled down… married, kids?"

He hoped she didn't notice him wince as he realised too late that he'd dived in with the big question straight away. Too eager. A giveaway. Right from the start, too personal, obvious.

Why had he asked her that? A frown darkened her face, an angry look he hadn't seen before.

"A daughter," she said quietly. "My husband… he was just what I needed when he turned up. He's good for me. He looks after me - he's not a journalist."

And he's not a journalist married to someone else, like I was, a guy who's only looking after himself, he thought.

"Time goes by," she said, "and it'll all come out in the wash… everything does, doesn't it? That's what happens."

It'll all come out in the wash. She had said it often back then. Her catchphrase. Her philosophy. An ever-ready excuse for helpless surrender to temptation.

It'll all come out in the wash. He'd adopted it, too. Hands up and give in, in other words. Anything for an easy life. Go with the flow. Sink to the bottom.

Live for the minute. Abdicate responsibility. Drown in your own desires. Forget everybody else. Ditch your marriage vows. Bin faithfulness. There's nothing either of us can do.

A nice wallow in selfishness. What harm could there be? Plenty.

It'll all come out in the wash. He had spent years failing to overturn her words of wisdom. It'll all come out in the wash? As if. How grubby he'd felt, mired for years in an old longing for Rachel Ballantyne.

Trapped in unwelcome floods of old romantic clichés concerning a time when he'd walked on air, skipped though clouds, swooning, mooning and being helpless in love.

A fated couple held within each other's orbit, revolving within the weighted magnetic force of planets and stars and sexual attraction, powerless to resist; powerless to break free. Let the chips fall where they may. There was nothing they could do about it, they'd told themselves.

He reminded himself that he knew better now. He recalled his guilt at focusing on another woman when he should have been focusing solely on his wife. How his wrongdoing had gnawed at his sense of who he was back then, making his stomach clench and ache, shrivelling his old certainties, preventing him from sleep.

Soon after that he'd felt the additional pain of Rachel's rejection, an instant withdrawal. His loss. His remorse. And that taunting phrase: it'll all come out in the wash.

And in truth it had. Although, in his case, his former way of life had come out shrunken beyond use. Nothing fit anymore. Everything was less colourful. So what on earth was he doing talking to this woman again now?

She muttered something he couldn't catch amid the retirement party hubbub, turned and walked away from him across the room, rejoining some other group of old *Chronicle* never-wases.

He hoped he didn't look the way he felt. Because he felt confused and annoyed with himself. And he was annoyed with himself because as he watched her retreat, he felt a little disappointed that she was walking away from him again.

****

McCrindle appeared with another pint and predictable words of McCrindle-esque consolation: "Get it down you, get it round about you, get it up you." Then he was back into the ruck.

He sipped and remembered how he and Rachel had started

off with one another. As colleagues. Friends. More than friends. Confidantes.

The *Chronicle* had been her first job as a newly-graduated journalism student, early 20s. Apprentice newshound. Capable. Quiet. Dependable.

From the start, there had been something singular about Rachel Ballantyne. She was approachable, unthreatening. A younger woman with the manner of a wiser, older owl. Dressed in a sensible, grown-up, middle-aged way. Nothing to set alarm bells ringing. Matronly you might say, if you chose to be unkind.

She'd been dressed in a work uniform of confined waistcoats, concealing jackets, unrevealing skirts. Brown. Tan. Beige. Tomboyish, small, dark, brooding, not a conventional beauty, easy to talk to...

"Are you Tony Moscardini?" a reedy old male voice was asking. A stooped, frail white-haired man stood and glared, repeating the question. He was sure he'd never seen him before. He looked about 80... so if the guy was however many years older than he'd once been, back then he might have been... 50? Maths not a strong point.

The angry old man repeated his question with greater insistence. "Are. You. Tony. Moscardini."

There was something about those milk-clouded blue eyes. As the man drew breath to ask again, scowling, Tony forced a smile and replied that he used to be Tony Moscardini - but he was all right now.

The man didn't see the joke. "You *are* Tony bloody Moscardini," he snorted, "and I'm Jim Thornton and don't say you've forgotten messing up my byline and making me look stupid - and let me tell you, you were a bad enough Fancy Dan features writer, but you were a worse sports sub."

Jim Thornton. As Tony watched the *Chronicle's* one-time chief sports reporter huff away back to his seat, he recalled his miserable month as a sports sub-editor.

A false start to Tony's *Chronicle* career, rectified by his swift banishment to the backwater of the features desk. The Jim Thornton byline stramash. He shuddered at the memory of it.

Jim Thornton: Football's Voice of Reason was the *Chronicle's* billing. Prickly Jim Thornton: Football's Unreasonable Voice, Tony would have said.

Years ago, the *Chronicle's* star soccer scribe had been covering some Scottish football team's big match somewhere in Europe. "Germany," Tony muttered aloud as the awful details came back.

A hectic midweek night, Tony working a late shift, 6pm till two in the morning, juggling unfathomable numbers from a range of sports he neither liked nor understood. A football cup on some far-off foreign field.

Ever-changing scores, goals, constant screeds of words describing grievous acts of sporting intrigue that he'd never grasped. And in among the football, unstoppable tides of other new sporting numbers, so many. Greyhound racing, golf, rugby.

First-edition deadlines looming, second editions needing amendment, endless updates - and the constant pressure of knowing that an angry football-maddened readership stood ready to glow red-hot over the minor mis-placing of one little goal, some stupid name, one extra-time shoot-out penalty statistic or red card total.

Aware of the threat posed by his total lack of football knowledge, he had been extra careful to avoid mangling the smallest detail of Thornton's report. He'd checked and re-checked players' names, team names, details of scores and scorers.

He'd ensured a portion of prose described each goal, furrowing his brow till his face ached. Everything where it should be. No errors.

But somehow his stressed-out younger self had amended pompous, prickly Jim Thornton's byline. It was inexplicable. So instead of Jim Thornton reporting live from Munich, Jim Thornton had apparently reported live from Frankfurt.

Not a huge error, but enough to embarrass pompous Jim Thornton the morning after the game. Arriving for breakfast in his hotel, which had remained all night in Munich where it was meant to be, he'd found himself transformed into a career-long object of ridicule among his football writer peers: Jim Thornton, the *Chronicle's* man 200 miles away from the action.

McCrindle re-appeared again. Another full pint glass was pressed into Tony's hand, replacing one he'd scarcely noticed draining. He saw Rachel talking to another group of aged retirees.

Talking to Rachel. When they'd begun talking to one another, all that time ago, she had got straight to the point - she was a fan of his work, almost shaking with admiration. He was flattered, couldn't fail to be.

It was a meeting of minds. It was raw lust. He was 42, she was 25. She quoted sections of his gig reviews, stuff she'd memorised as a teenage journalism studies undergraduate, not long before.

They had shared the knowledge of insiders. She understood the job they were in. His wife didn't.

Rachel knew the newspaper game, its hazards, the common pressures, the people, the frustrations, the annoyances, the occasional moments of elation. The two of them communicated in giggly workplace shorthand.

They began holding grave high-minded talks about their craft. As a kindly mentor might aid a star-struck young protégée. Paternal. Serious. Yet impassioned.

How journalism might function better if only its practitioners would look up from the grind and allow themselves the luxury of principles, scruples, ideals and - the two of them agreed - morals.

Morals? Ironic, he thought, as the pair had drifted closer. An old story. Well done for bringing a cliché to life, Mr Must-have-a-flingy.

Older married man, of the softer-hearted variety. Younger single woman, hard-headed. It was bound to happen. It would all come out in the wash…

She had a sympathetic way of listening; of posing deft questions and being a subtle co-conspirator.

She was skilled at teasing out confessions, winkling out secrets. She could insinuate herself into anyone's confidence - anyone with something to hide. "Everyone's got something to hide, Tony," she'd said more than once.

As a result, she had the most delicious gossip; the hottest, juiciest inside line on the most diverting scandals. Her ear was attuned to clandestine liaisons, the most unlikely pairings. Who was too close to who. In the media, high office, politics, the judiciary.

But especially at the *Chronicle*. Whereas he barely knew most of his colleagues' names, she knew everything about everyone including, he remembered, Keenan and the story of his shock wedding-day declaration of forbidden love.

On the morning of Keenan's wedding, he'd phoned a young woman on the *Chronicle's* features desk, Rachel had told Tony. The call was unexpected.

The young woman certainly hadn't expected to hear Keenan telling her she was the woman he wanted, not his bride-to-be. All she had to do was say the word and his marriage in four hours' time was off.

And all as a result of a clinch'n'grapple beneath the mistletoe at the *Chronicle's* alcohol-fuelled office Christmas party. Naturally, the young woman said no and Keenan's wife never discovered how close she'd come to being alone at the altar.

Tony, being naive, had said something about never knowing what terrible upset folk can cause in the name of love.

"It wasn't love, it was lust," Rachel had replied. "Sex drives some folk mad - you should never keep sex corked up."

She'd said it with a look on her face that he'd struggled to identify. Comic? Sarcastic? Suggestive?

Inviting in some way, he was sure. And so their friendship became a liaison. A dalliance. A shared secret. A workplace relationship conducted unknown to everyone else in the workplace, barely acknowledged by either of them, too.

Fevered chat in darkened corners. Covert smiles conveying harmful messages. Unhealthy. Unsafe. A voyage in deep, dark and risky waters.

Chapter 17

Her talent lay in inspiring other people to open up and tell all. Politicians. Officials. Men. It was rare, though, for her to divulge anything personal, shine a light on her emotions.

Yet she'd made a disarmingly frank admission back at the very start, two decades before, almost as soon as she and Tony had met, minutes into their first conversation. He'd never forgotten it.

The two of them had been discussing some male singer in some credible band they both rated, and she'd told him that the band's singer was definitely her type.

"I could look after him," she had said, almost purring, the phrase oozing from her with a smack of shiny-moist lips. And then a further declaration that showed the very heart of her. "I do like my sex," she said. He was entranced.

And as she had said this, such a small but forceful avowal, it seemed, stated so bluntly and so matter-of-factly, she'd been looking him straight in the eye. And he'd blushed, making her laugh aloud at his embarrassment over her honesty, her enthusiasm, her open declaration of her appetite.

Thus their two-way infatuation had begun. Passionate, but chaste to begin with beyond the occasional fleeting thrill when his hand brushed hers. When one party's resigned sigh of longing had coincided with the other's…

"Tony Moscardini!" Another voice derailed his train of thought. He was more prepared for it this time. "Not me," he said, "I just kinda look like him."

He regretted providing the conversational opening, because through it barged another *Chronicle* olde-timer. A guy who wouldn't shut up, Colin Legge, he recalled too late.

Off the bloke went on a convoluted non-stop yarn about some mutual former colleague, Billy Spence, another sub, mostly did the letters page, Tony must remember, he'd gone out with that Vic's barmaid, red head, Catholic, Bernadette something - O'Shaughnessy maybe, and what a turn-about that was for Billy Spence, him a Glasgow boy growing up on Orange walks, highlight of his summer - and hey, how could anyone have forgotten Billy's story about Bernadette, some sort of name like that, the love of his life that girl, Billy laughing when he said how she'd always open up - if you got what Billy meant - whenever Billy arrived at her place after a late shift, three in the morning with a jar of pickled winkles - winkles! - yeah, she needed a right good winkle, loved the old winkles, and Glasgow back then, early eighties, remember, only one or two all-night shops and if you missed the bloke who went round Vic's selling jars of the bloody things, big wicker basket on a chain round his neck, miss that guy and there's major effort involved in the after-hours procurement of a jar of winkles, and Bernadette had always shown Billy plenty of appreciation - and then suddenly she'd dumped him, poor Billy, Bryan Ferry haircut, 1982 it was, and Billy completely withdrew from the rest of them, his heart broken, damn shame, stuck in 1982 he was ever after, listening to headphones, same Bryan Ferry haircut ever after - and never a word to anybody again, retreated, not even speaking to the Ninja Sub, Billy Spencer withdrew, became another bloke gliding around saying nothing, Tony must remember everybody talking about it…

"I don't know what you're talking about," Tony said, halting Colin Legge in mid-speech, a hurt look on his face. Tony pointed towards a door. "Bogs," he said.

****

He was aware he was walking unsteadily across a floor that seemed to be moving under his feet. Someone overtook him, Colin Legge, an angry face, glaring back at Tony.

He took an age at the urinal, fumbling to re-fasten his trousers before walking slowly back to pick up his glass from a table he didn't recall putting it down on.

He stared at the glass. He looked across at Rachel. Him and her back then.

The complexity creeping up on them. Bigger. Overpowering. Excluding everything and everyone outwith Rachel.

They'd been eating together one lunchtime in a back-street bistro. Hiding away had become their custom, an unacknowledged habit. And then she'd said something out of the blue that alerted them to their shared deception.

"We're both in denial," she said.

He couldn't help himself. Mr Stand Up Comic. "You might say that," he said, "but I've never been anywhere near Egypt."

Rachel had laughed. He should have savoured the moment: the last time he'd made her laugh. Cheating's no breeding ground for comedy, or for happiness, he told himself.

Their relationship had deepened more quickly from this point, growing into a thing of mutual suffering and regret. Was it becoming somehow warped and sharpened into something dangerous through lack of physical expression, he'd sometimes wondered.

Especially after Rachel's next admission, suddenly deepening their pain even further - an unforeseen consequence of her frank enjoyment of sex, as a woman who saw no reason to disobey the sexual imperative, and all the less so if it came free of emotional complications.

Because Rachel had chosen to enjoy what should have been just another one-night stand: "A bit of a tussle, keeping it physical, a routine fuck," as she'd put it.

It had been with the *Chronicle's* self-styled office stud, a news reporter they'd both mocked with the nickname Romeo Standfirst.

"And a proper loverboy he turned out to be," she told Tony after her routine fuck, nothing to distinguish it from any other, exploded into a ruinous piece of newsroom lore, casting Rachel as its victim. Overnight.

Because the morning after, Romeo had boasted to his leering *Chronicle* buddies that he'd tumbled the funny-looking new bird with the big tits, thereby triggering the age-old gender divide, still alive as the twentieth century drew to a close, with a woman menaced by male double standards. Sex with one *Chronicle* workmate led to Rachel being pressured for sex by another, her newsdesk boss. The creep. The married creep.

Bossman Creep, she called him.

In return for sex, Bossman Creep promised Rachel she'd be assigned choice stories, every one a potential page-lead, guaranteed an eye-catching display in the *Chronicle*. Plus regular day-shifts.

And all she had to do was continue what she evidently enjoyed doing. But with him.

Tony had fumed and stormed when she'd told him. He'd looked angst-wrought, stricken, pain-wracked. He wrang his hands, raged to the heavens.

The injustice of her treatment. The wrongness of it. He made a fist and thumped the bistro's table.

"It'll all come out in the wash," she'd said, in that moment registering how he had turned her distress into an affront to him.

Odd then how his self-regarding assistance had served to foster closer contact between the two of them, intensifying a mutual lust which was denied outright expression, fostering shame and guilt.

He had cast himself as her avenging Sir Galahad, a role he knew he couldn't perform. She took refuge in a role she knew she could perform - helpless damsel in distress, wounded bird with a broken wing trying to be brave, downcast brown doe eyes blinking back tears - and which encouraged further male attention.

So many men. Her self-styled knight in shining armour, the two-timing Lothario husband. Romeo Standfirst. Bossman Creep. Other workmates. Guys she met at parties, in bars, on the street. She was ground down by it.

Submitting to Tony's ineffectual gallantry was easy, a question of lying back and letting it all come out in the wash. She had relaxed in his gaze, melted into his arms, grown distracted, gone weak at the knees, allowed her sleepy eyes to lose their focus. Fainting, capsized, sunk...

"Tony Moscardini, it's you, is it no'?" Another querulous voice interrupted Tony's thoughts as they spiralled round long-ago events. A third old-timer stood before him. A care-worn face, a shy smile, kindly-looking.

He half-smiled back, feeling himself sway under the effects of - how many lagers was it? He tried to think straight, played for time.

Who was this nice-seeming guy? What was it the old josser had just asked? His name. Wheel out the standard quip.

"Oh, I was maybe him once, but I'm OK now," he said, realising that he'd now denied himself three times in the past 10 minutes.

He forced a grin, hoping the old guy couldn't spot that he had no idea who he was. Another ex-workmate with a grudge, a score to settle? He grinned harder. No idea who the fellow was. Not a scooby.

McCrindle reappeared, handing over another lager. "You've got a drink problem," he crowed, moving off again, "your mouth's not big enough!"

Tony took the glass, sipped it. "Bob Paterson," the old man said. His manner was more frosty. Unsmiling now.

"Bob, nice to see you, yeah," he said too eagerly, with too much jollity as he battled to recollect a single thing about Bob Paterson, features sub. A man he'd chit-chatted with at the *Chronicle* most days for 20 years: story-lengths, word-counts, headlines, work stuff. He'd had some sort of nickname. Alliterative. Bouncy Bob?

"Not seen you in ages. I take it you're… still keeping busy? Bees! Still keeping the bees… breeding them! If that's what you call it, with bees. I suppose the bees do the breeding… leave them to it… don't get involved… don't get stung!

"All that honey… the hives… the worst thing about it, I suppose, Bob, about keeping bees - having to give them all names. How'd you remember? Thousands! Difficult. Telling them apart… bees…"

He felt the joke die on his lips.

"It's budgies," Bob said. He sighed, turned away and moved off.

"Catch you later," he said to Budgie Bob's back. Too late the correct farewell came to him: *don't get in a flap*.

Caged birds. Beating wings. Pounding hearts. He lost himself in history again… the time when he and Rachel had begun embracing, finding private spaces in which to surrender to one another, meeting in her flat rather than restaurants.

Well, it surely made sense to avoid uninformed scrutiny, base and potentially ruinous gossip. They kissed more frequently, more ardently.

They no longer needed to hide their feelings from one another, only the rest of the world. *Ms Mills, meet Mr Boon*. What they were doing was natural, and what was natural was surely good, wasn't it? Made the world go round.

Some sort of unspoken assurance grew between them that, as they scarcely had the strength or will to stand up in each other's presence any longer, such was the depth of their consensual suffering, they could begin reclining… increasingly on her living-room sofa. Which just happened to be on his route home.

And in truth they were dog-tired and oh, so depleted by their emotional entanglement. People who didn't have the grave misfortune to be them - such a perfectly love-lorn, lust-wearied duo - would scarcely guess their fatigue, their agonies. Could never fathom how they'd both grown dizzied, worn out, fevered, short of breath. And so they'd just lain down. For a rest. Natural.

The hellish stress and trauma of being friends and workmates who'd ever so innocently happened - against their wills, beyond their control - to find one another physically irresistible.

Why, they had been so consumed by the frightful months-long pressure of being attracted to one another that it was inevitable they should be reduced - against their will, of course - to lying in a more restful prone position and hugging and kissing one another. Much, much closer together.

And as one thing led organically to another, no fighting it, there had been once - and only once - a union on her bed, fully clothed and close to consummation… for less than a minute - before such intimacy was curtailed in an instant by his belated commitment to courtly purity and marital honour, causing his abrupt recoil from her as if he'd received an electric shock.

Chapter 18

How insulted must she have been by his prim and startled slide out from under? An abrupt sideways shimmy of rejection, the act of an 11-year-old schoolboy repulsed by his first biology lesson, his introduction to sex and its stark library of scientific terms for all that lurking female apparatus down there: vulva, labia majora, vagina, pudenda.

How ignorant and scared he must have looked, nowhere near grown up enough to bear the heavy, hungry rhythmic pressure with which she had in that moment been grinding down hard on him, pubic bone to pubic bone. She was a woman, an adult. He was a fool, a boy.

At the last minute, he'd developed a bogus sense of moral duty so he could maintain the illusion of being a faithful married man.

As he stood in Vic's, it began to dawn on him who he'd been 20 years before. Self-righteous, sanctimonious, self-deluding, self-serving.

He'd savoured Rachel's nearness, her availability, without making any commitment himself. He'd been a coward. A coward in thrall to social convention, gorging himself on the thrill of illicit love.

But not illicit sex. When it had been offered to him, he'd been an upright, lying-down, lying and cheating husband who had obeyed one law: thou shalt not commit adultery if it contains the risk of getting caught.

But while Rachel wasn't having sex with Tony, she was telling him about the other men she had been having sex with - as one friend to another, casually, in the spirit of sharing information, being upfront, no big deal.

She was having sex. With another workmate. With guys she met away from work. Not every guy she met, but guys she liked the look of. As she'd told him at the start: "I do like my sex."

It wasn't as though she was falling in love with these guys, in the way she had with him, she'd more than once assured him. She wasn't sharing her heart, her soul with any other man, just her body.

On loan. Just for sex, fulfilling a requirement, a basic need. Physical inter-action. Feeding a natural appetite.

"The only time you should worry," she told him in the last admission of hers that made him laugh out loud, "is if I start talking about my love-life as an itch that needs to be scratched - too much like admitting I've picked up a sexually-transmitted disease."

There was nothing he should fret about or grow jealous over - not that he had any right to grow jealous, he knew. Her sexual activity was her business, not his.

He was grown-up enough to handle her honesty, the facts. Sex: a mundane bodily function - unlike their higher connection, heart and soul, based on friendship, emotional frankness, kindred spirits. He would dismiss her sex life from his mind.

"I'm a big boy," he'd told her. Only he hadn't been.

Adolescent jealousy became a faithful attendant, his best pal. There for him round the clock. Chucking him under the chin. Digging him in the ribs. Matey, then intrusive, hectoring, mocking and unshakeable in the weeks after she'd dumped him.

To begin with, he could frame jealousy as just another of his comedy routines.

Jealousy as a slimming aid, robbing him of his taste for food - his personal weight-loss diet. He pictured the advertising campaign: raise a tempting morsel of food to your lips and have jealousy make it taste like dust - watch the pounds drop off, guaranteed near-instant effects!

It wasn't funny. Images of Rachel with other men taunted him as he'd tried and failed to sleep.

Fevered nightmares disturbed what little sleep he got. Part porn film. Part horror movie. Arousing. Disturbing. Exhausting.

A film he was unable to stop watching. Rachel silhouette'd in a blaze-red hellfire glow, naked and eager, grinding against other men.

His torment was amplified by the fact that while Rachel had been having sex with different men, he wasn't having sex with his wife.

This marital celibacy signified nothing unusual in itself. From the start, theirs was not a union of racing passion, the absence of intimacy never signalling the lack of a shared future.

But admitting Rachel to his heart had cast a shadow over his perceptions of Katharine, diminishing his wife's attractiveness, making her less desirable, less of a woman.

Each time he admired some fresh aspect of Rachel - the smell of her shampoo'd hair, the smoothness of her milk-white skin - he fancied he divined a new physical flaw in Katharine. His wife's calves were chubbier than Rachel's. Katharine's breasts could not rival Rachel's for fullness. His wife's eyes advanced less promise of sex.

So this is where innocent-seeming months of dreamy adolescent longing had led: fatal fault-finding. Love's extinction.

The brink of adultery, marital destruction, the gradual erasure of his wedding-day pledges. He stood revealed to himself as shallow, selfish, immoral.

As well as feeling edgy and drained back then, with grit-filled eyes and a head that was forever sore, he'd developed a constant nausea. Given his diseased morality, it was right he should feel sick.

Just as sickening was what he came to see as his lack of guts: he hadn't been man enough to commit actual adultery. Not brave enough to get stuck in there, act natural, go with the flow, keep it meaningless, keep it physical, get dirty.

His conscience was sullied with imagined stains. Washing's no use when there's nothing to come out, he'd told himself.

He'd tried hard not to keep an exact tally of Rachel's bedmates over those intense, jumbled-up final four months or so. Seven or eight different men, maybe.

None of whom, she'd assured him, could compare to him.

Indeed, didn't she once tell him that she'd been kissing some guy only to scare him off by bursting into tears. Because although he'd been right there, this guy, his arms round her, pressing himself into her, his lips mashed against hers, he hadn't been Tony.

She'd begun sobbing again, saying: "I'm unstable now - no one will marry me."

"I'd marry you," Tony had said, aware in saying it how ridiculous it sounded... knowing it was a lie.

It was after this that things between them had changed. He continued basking in the warmth of her attention while at the same time he half-realised it was growing cooler.

So long as being a part-time husband and none-of-the-way lover didn't disturb him too much, costing him his nice big house filled with books and CDs, everything was fine.

He was comfortable with his half-life as a middle-aged, middle-class married man conducting an affair. A run-of-the-mill sneak. A cheat. Lazy, complacent, spineless. A comfortable, self-satisfied coward.

These were the truths it had taken him 20 years to learn, he knew now, staring into the warm dregs of his fifth or sixth pint. It was only tonight, years after the fact, that he'd acknowledged them in full.

What he'd failed to recognise back then was his lack of usefulness to the people around him. To his wife. To many of his workmates, the ones he despised without real cause. Certainly to Rachel in her most pressing hour of need, fighting workplace manipulation by Bossman Creep.

He'd been all talk, sweet blandishments, verbal palliatives, no practical help.

In the end, Rachel herself had decided what needed to be done about Bossman Creep, and she'd simply done it. In public. With triumphant finality. In the very arena beneath their feet tonight. Downstairs in Vic's.

He looked down and felt dizzy as he did. How much of an idiot he must look right now, a tottering fool, staring at his shoes, lost in thought. Doing nothing.

Just like that night when Rachel's action had delighted everyone who'd been in Vic's to see it - Tony not being among them, of course. He'd been at his desk, spurning Vic's as ever.

She'd entered Glasgow newspaper legend by striding up, drink in hand, behind Bossman Creep as he stood at the bar, haw-hawing with his newsdesk cronies. She'd tapped him on the shoulder and as he turned, she'd tipped her full pint over his head.

She didn't say a word. No need. Red card, arsehole. Fuck yer patriarchal hegemony, pal. End of harassment. Every toper in Vic's laughing, cheering.

Bossman Creep's mates had never seen anything funnier. He'd tried to laugh along with the joke, but beer ran into his open mouth, making him cough and splutter, confirming him as a figure of fun.

He looked over at Rachel now. She had her back towards him, chatting to a beaming flock of rapt old *Chronicle* men. Same as ever.

He wondered how he'd managed to paint Rachel as the root of his woes 20 years ago. It was obvious now. His ills had all been his fault. He belched and continued staring blearily at her.

Typical he should be absent from the Bossman Creep showdown in Vic's. He'd not been present in his half-hearted marriage, either. Missing, too, from his half-cocked affair.

The perennial by-stander, a spectator, the inactive ingredient. Passive on the sidelines, forever detached, wringing his bloodless hands, contextualising for the sake of it like the jobbing arts critic he was.

Picturing himself with Rachel in *Brief Encounter*, that was the most he'd done. He'd often daydreamed they were the old film classic's tremulous lovers doing the conscience-stricken thing by not acting on their urges - avoiding surrender to sinful physicality.

Traditional British repression. Not even a toe dipped in unfettered ardour's teeming undercurrents. Caged desires. Self-lacerating love. Agonised abstinence.

It didn't matter that he hadn't seen the film all the way through, nor that Rachel - 17 years his junior - hadn't seen it at all. What mattered was that she was no delicate rose-tinted Celia Johnson and he was no virtuous Trevor Howard.

She was a modern-day woman whose sole regret had been carnal: "If only we'd got the sex out of the way at the start."

Sex. He had wanted it.

So one day, surprising himself, he'd decided to tell Katharine their marriage was over. He tried to convince himself he was being honest, doing the decent thing, open and honourable. How foolish he'd been.

The best time to dump your wife? Before she dumps you. Katharine got there first. She'd told him their marriage was over.

She was buying him out of their newer, grander, suburban semi-detached. He could move back into the type of one-bedroom flat their marriage had begun in.

Which should have been a result for him. Free to declare himself to Rachel. But when he did, later that same day, Rachel cut him short. She'd reached a decision.

He needn't leave his wife on her account because she'd found a more uncomplicated man. It had all come out in the wash.

She'd despatched him just as she'd despatched Bossman Creep, although without the theatre. Tony hadn't deserved the effort.

Sudden sounds of curses and shattering glass broke through the pub's regular chatter, startling him and silencing the room. Keenan and McCrindle were locked together on the dancefloor, each having grabbed the other's jacket lapels, shoving and pushing, red-faced and sweaty, animals.

****

"Why'd you step in when I was winning," McCrindle slurred, smoothing his jacket back into shape after Tony had manhandled him into a corner, shielded from Keenan.

"If I hadn't stepped in, you'd be playing marbles with your teeth," he said. McCrindle was squinting over Tony's shoulder, keeping his head low and trying to gauge whether his tough-guy waltz with Keenan was about to re-start.

Tony turned, snatching a quick look at Keenan, pinned in

the opposite corner by a scrum of *Chronicle* folk. He assured McCrindle that Keenan's chums had a good hold of him.

McCrindle was encouraged enough to form fists and raise them in what would have been a cocky boxer's stance if only he wasn't taking care to keep them below waist-height, so his opponent couldn't see.

"Ready to punch a dwarf or unzipping your trousers?" Tony said.

"Coppy pock!" McCrindle said quietly. "Two more minutes and I'd have had Keenan in the gutter while I farted in his face."

"You've missed out the bit where he would've killed you," said Tony.

"Did you see why it kicked off?" McCrindle asked. "I reckon I must've started it. I hope I started it… there's no way I can finish it." He began giggling, keeping his head down, avoiding giving Keenan an excuse to re-start things.

There was a sudden increase in angry babble from across the room. Tony turned as casually as he could, hoping he didn't look as alarmed as he felt.

Keenan was being led towards the door by old workmates, flicking a V-sign as he left. Tony hoped McCrindle couldn't see it. Thankfully, he'd slumped on to the nearest leather seat, lying on it behind a table.

"Take a shufti," he mumbled to Tony. "Any sign Keenan's coming over?"

"He's being led out," Tony said, glancing to make sure, spotting Rachel on the edge of the dancefloor, staring at him. As he puzzled over the exact expression on her face, she walked over to him, stopping close.

"I've a favour to ask - join us on a job tomorrow night, would you?" she said, giving him no time to reply. "I've a story. It might seem odd after 20 years… after how it ended between me and you.

"I'm still a working journalist - and you were a journalist, you know the routine - it's something a bit tricky. If you could help... for a couple of hours. It's hard to explain. Kind of undercover. You might even enjoy it.

"There's nobody else I can ask, there really isn't. I need some help. From a professional. A bloke. Seven o'clock tomorrow. Meet me outside this dump, outside Vic's, I know you won't want to go inside..."

She was hunched, her words framed with the same intense, sparrow-like quiver she'd employed two decades before.

He frowned, puzzling over what she'd said, and what he should reply. "Will it all come out in the wash?" he managed to say after a long pause.

"Eventually," she said after an even longer pause. "Everything does, I suppose."

And with that, for no reason that made sense - but knowing it had everything to do with having drunk too much - he knew he was going to agree to meet her. His thoughts tripped over one other like a glassy-eyed mob of drunks and he heard himself say yeah, no problem, outside Vic's, seven tomorrow.

He'd become intoxicated. The alcohol, obviously. Plus it seemed he still found something potent in Rachel Ballantyne, something head-turning - something that he still lacked.

What else explained why he'd suckered himself into feeling responsible for her again, manoeuvred by her ability to seem in need of assistance - by his willingness to let himself be manoeuvred.

She was still looking at him, he realised, her brown eyes seeming to grow more liquid and starting to sparkle. Shimmer. Dance. Extend the promise of... what? Comfort. A trial. Everything. Anything.

She turned, walking out with the rest of the crowd.

She'd been a danger to him once. But now he'd mastered his former flaws, hadn't he? He'd escaped. And he'd found a new woman, a constant woman - not a woman who advanced the constant promise of inconstancy.

But maybe Gabriella was his for the losing. Maybe she was about to tell him she saw him as the same old weak-kneed Tony he'd always been.

What truly mattered, though, was that Rachel no longer had him in her thrall. He'd freed himself. Or had he?

To demonstrate it, he only needed his freedom to be tested. It might never happen...

He began to feel sick. Too much lager. Or self-knowledge. Or self-loathing. Who could tell?

Saturday
Chapter 19

He awoke with an acid wash in his throat. Nausea. Too much beer. Heartburn. Worry in the pit of his stomach.

What did he have to worry about? The return of an old temptation, maybe. He pictured himself impaled on tabloid pages.

Exiled Scot's Drink And Sex Flirtation Shame. Rekindled Love Ritual Enflames Runaway Lens-Jockey. Hick From Italian Sticks Nixed By Sin-City Glasgow Minx.

Headline-writing, never his strong point. Too few words, the right ones elusive. No scope for nuance.

He sat up in bed. The room's horizontal plane tilted, making him feel sick. He groaned and laid his head back on the pillow.

If only he could blame McCrindle. He half-remembered them stumbling into a taxi, holding each other upright. What's the best thing for a hangover? Drinking heavily the night before with McCrindle.

He lay staring at the ceiling. He had only himself to blame for feeling so bad. About everything. Imagine agreeing to some ill-defined meeting with the woman he'd tormented himself over for years.

A reunion. A rendezvous, even. On a Glasgow Saturday night.

A night for coupled-up romance. A night for self-harm. Voluntary unsettlement.

He'd been drunk. He was stupid. He would get out of it. Invent a previous engagement. Feign illness.

But he didn't have Rachel's phone number. He'd have to stand her up. It would be cowardly. Adolescent. Wrong.

Had she bewitched him again? If she had, he'd let her. He'd bewitched himself, aided by drink. He couldn't blame her... it was his fault.

He'd been the guilty party back then, too, manipulating her, preying on her attraction to him. Not discouraging her attentions, revelling in them. As an older married man, he should have known better.

And last night, 20 years too late, he'd finally seen himself clearly for what he'd been: weak, selfish, self-pitying. He'd understood why he'd failed his wife and Rachel, too.

And he understood how he'd become a better man. So he would go and meet Rachel tonight. Because he was no longer a moth to a flame. There was no meaning to him seeing her, unless he let it have meaning.

He wasn't going to fall under her power. A power she'd given no sign she'd use anyway. Why would she? But why had she asked him? Why? He didn't know.

He just knew that nothing bad would happen to him in Glasgow tonight. Why should it? Glasgow was the past, with its random shocks and surprises.

Colonia in the present was where real life happened. Maybe it happened too slowly, a little too tediously. Slow and formal, repetitious and predictable.

But living a more manageable life was what had led to his becoming a photographer, a film-maker, an artist. It had led him

- for now anyway - to the attentions of a good woman. But ah, the thrill of a bad woman, the wrong woman.

He considered how many times over the past 20 years he'd wanted to hurt Rachel for the pain she'd inflicted. But he was no longer vengeful.

He also knew he couldn't hurt her now: she didn't care enough about him to feel it. He'd lost the power. We only hurt the ones who love us most…

He smiled at the thought of Gabriella's smile. At the thought of Gabriella. Sunshine. Warmth. Summer. Floral scents. Those buzzing bees. Her smile that last day in Colonia… when was it? Years ago. The day before last.

If Gabriella did end their relationship as soon as he got back, at least he could say that he, Hugh Antonio Moscardini - self-defeating ex-journalist, sit-down comedian and cinema parodist - had occasionally inspired Gabriella Sarti to smile at him in a way few men had seen.

He wished he was back in Colonia with her, with Ken and Prof. Making things happen. Making films. Living a new life.

He vowed that this day in Glasgow would be one in which he would do things. The right things. A creative day. Productive, a day of not anticipating, not fretting, not letting his imagination render him inactive. Of not looking back. A day of action.

Nevertheless, by wandering about and seeing Glasgow as it was nowadays, he risked seeing the city as it used to be, perhaps noticing what he'd been missing.

What did he miss about Glasgow? Nothing. No, that was incorrect. He missed buying music he hadn't heard before. Not one new CD bought during his two years in Italy.

There was no opportunity in Colonia, of course. Nearby Lucca had one record shop. It sold only brand-new vinyl at prices that made him curse. He'd bought mail-order CDs at first, soon finding that Italy's postal system didn't work. CDs went missing. Co-Op teabags were diverted. Porridge oats went astray.

He'd tried online music-streaming, finding new stuff by bands he already knew and liked. Finding newer bands who maybe sounded like the bands he already knew and liked. But streaming wasn't enough.

Turn the music on, turn it off. Leave it undigested. Never allowed to percolate, to capture mind and heart. Fleeting internet consumption. In one ear, out the other. It was wrong. He needed to study CD sleeves, register names. Guitarists, drummers, producers, engineers. Make the connections. Listen. Learn. Think. Feel.

He needed to be possessed by the music. So he had to purchase it. It was his duty. He was honour-bound to make full and proper payment to the musicians who made it.

He knew most of them needed his money. Hapless broken-down wretches, most musicians, less fiscally stable than the average journalist. How ruinous must that be?

As he began feeling less ill, he vowed to devote his day to Glasgow's most vaunted record shops, the city's cathedrals to sonic ambition. Its hallowed sepulchres for the terminally groovy. Its infirmaries tending all those diseased with the rhythm.

And in so doing he would similarly visit some of his old Glasgow haunts, musical or otherwise. His past no longer controlled or oppressed him. He could revisit it in safety, finding sustenance to steel him against whatever problems the future might pose.

Before he began his walking tour, there was a long voicemail message from Ken. The premiere was under control, despite expanding into a bigger event.

Tomorrow night's screening would open with a live performance by a quintet led by Davide Pastori. The rumpled musical wizard had worried the film-makers by taking three months to re-interpret and re-record the original three-minute Twistin' Gears *Bullitt* theme.

As Ken had often stated, it had taken the three men of MBM Studios the same time to capture the movie's whole footage.

Ken had also veto'd a last-minute notion to screen the original *Bullitt* chase sequence ahead of their new one: "It could only make our version look like it didn't cost a million dollars.

"Folk who haven't seen *Bullitt* can't fail to be impressed by our go at it," Ken's voicemail went on. "Folk who have seen *Bullitt* don't need reminding that ours isn't it."

When Tony first got up, sunshine was streaming through the hotel room curtains. By the time he reached the street, though, around mid-morning, Glasgow was clouded grey. Rain seemed likely. It wasn't hot. It wasn't cold.

The city's summertime self lolled defiantly before him, slouching at some untenable point between fresh and clammy, jaunty and consumptive, hot and loosening its collar while at the same time reaching runny-nosed for a hankie.

Gallus. Diseased. Glasgow in July. As much as you'd like to, you couldn't beat it with a stick.

His quest for recorded music met an instant impasse: commercial reality had wiped out 90% of Glasgow's record stores. All the big chain-store music shops had closed, replaced by temples to video gaming, fast food and disposable teenage fashion.

Most of the small independent music outlets had declined into nail bars and mobile phone accessory shops, or were abandoned and unoccupied, boarded-up and filth-spattered. He'd pictured his Glasgow return as a pilgrimage. It was shaping up to be a funeral.

Sodium Records was at least still in business. Its interior

was clean and neat. Too clean, too neat. No evidence of messy humanity. He felt uneasy.

The shop's polished pine album racks were too new, the sleeves they held stood too neatly ranked, un-browsed by eager hands. Four near-identical staff members stood at the shop counter, arms folded, curling lips in disdain, hard at work spitting out vicious putdowns, he could hear: assorted bands, most musical genres, the record-buying public.

From time to time, one salesperson might price-gun a record sleeve with listless disdain. None of the four could spare a second to look in his direction. *The Sardonic Shit Quartet.*

There was something familiar-looking about them. "By all mis-tunings necessary," he muttered under his breath.

They could have been members of any number of Glasgow bands circa 1980, all sharing a common manifesto: critical validation by the forces of hip, absolute rejection by anyone who valued musicianship or a song with a hummable melody.

He couldn't gauge how well the four sardonic shits had succeeded in either aim, but he had to admire how they'd retained their hair, unlike him. The too-black, too-dyed-to-be-true hair of the living dead cool. Better than being bald.

They'd likewise maintained their waxen junkie pallor, despite 30 years morphing from underfed black-clad teenagers into overweight black-clad middle-aged men.

The Sardonic Shit Quartet continued sneering about the rest of the world. He continued an inward critique of their poor retail skills. It was enjoyable: everyone insulting everyone else for the crime of not being each other. This was what he missed most about Glasgow.

Italian condescension was done much more subtly, without open relish. A roll of the eyes, a sigh, a tut. On top of that, how could you look down your nose at anyone in Colonia when everyone, even the most elderly, appeared so good, so fulfilled.

He grew more depressed the more closely he scanned Sodium's tidy interior. Mostly vinyl, all by new bands he'd never heard of.

He looked at the names and adjudged their inventors guilty of crimes against typography and linguistic good sense. BiFoLdn XyZ, Tarte, oscilloscope periscope, Trompetta di Morte, Rangoon Mongoose, Chimps With Forks, DJ Mmmfff Bmmff.

In his long-ago *Chronicle* rock critic days, he would have known them all. He'd either have anointed them - "Shrieking Pus Hound are the patellae of the winged honey-gathering insect" - or found them wanting: "The Fenomenal Phreedomme Band: not even household names in their own households - don't grant them living space in your head."

He exited Sodium Records confirmed as a clueless old-timer. He artfully muddled a few sleeves in the shop's adjoining Folk and Funk sections, taking care not to be spotted by the Sardonic Shit Quartet.

That would show them. Fenomenal Phreedomme!

****

Glasgow's only other city-centre record store was Faster Louder, his favourite, becalmed behind Queen Street railway station on a seedy, oddly sawn-off little thoroughfare, Grieve Street. He offered a thankful prayer to Glasgow's patron rock saint, the Blessed Alex Harvey, for letting it survive.

Grieve Street might once have thrived, but that had been 40 years earlier, before it was pedestrianised, blocked to traffic by a flight of stairs. He was shocked to see the litter-strewn steps colonised by homeless folk, some comatose in sleeping bags, the more alert begging amid a scum of polystyrene food cartons, empty cans, green shards of broken Buckfast bottles.

One whole side of Grieve Street's blasted scene of inner-city decay was in permanent shadow, darkened by the vast brick back wall of the millennial shopping mall on neighbouring Buchanan Street.

Grieve Street's short two-storey row of old shops grew as tenacious as any weed, a gaudy nuisance, a rebuke to chain-store might and city planners attempting to take Glasgow upmarket, bidding to turn shopping into a recreational pastime.

Next to Faster Louder's graffiti'd frontage, there was a military surplus clothing store with a window display given over to hunting knives and air pistols. Beyond that, a shabby tattoo parlour, two grease-scented fast-food shops, a taxi office. And more beggars.

When he walked into Faster Louder, it greeted him with a comforting smell of mildew, weed-smoke, perspiration, unwashed denim, crushed dreams - the homecoming scent of music.

The shop's linoleum floor was sticky, pock-marked and dirt-blackened. Its rough-hewn wooden bins held miles of second-hand vinyl LPs and CDs. He estimated several days could be spent flicking through those racks without seeing everything.

The store's owner was lifting a hinged flap in the counter and retreating through it to perch on a tall stool at Tony's approach. He was in his mid-to-late 50s, about Tony's age, a similar veteran of the post-punk indie era. Small feet in scuffed black winklepickers. Skinny black jeans.

A voluminous black Brooklyn Dodgers button-through baseball tunic held tight to Mr Faster Louder's broad mid-section, whereafter he tapered away to a tiny head displaying ice-cream wisps of white hair, his complexion sausage-roll grey; Buddy Holly specs, a snowy soul patch beneath his lower lip, evoking a rhomboidal long-lost nephew of Billy Connolly.

The shop's workforce - a slender omni-gendered youth leaning on the counter - sported an equally arresting look: head shaven at the sides, purple quiff, eyes shaded a delicate metallic blue that somehow didn't clash with his/ her/ their gingery moustache.

Mr Faster Louder favoured Tony with a glare of semi-recognition and began lambasting some absent staff-member for his manifold flaws.

His time-keeping, his lackadaisical approach to salesmanship - "I once heard him tell a customer we didn't have the new Springsteen when he was leaning his stupid see-nothing elbow on a pile of the damn things!" - and his peerless ability to mis-file things in the shop's back-room vaults.

This vehement and - to Tony's ears - amusing rant went on to include the absentee's over-large and spidery hand-writing and his ongoing failure to master the alphabet. "If it was left to him, our racks would have the world's biggest T section - every fucking band that ever gave themselves a fucking name starting with 'the' filed in there - the Beatles, the Doors, the god-damn Rolling Stones, the Fabulous Thunderbirds, the shitting Style Council - all in the one fucking T section… four cunting miles long and as wide as a fucking house - and you'd never be able to find a cock-sucking thing!"

Mr Faster Louder was multi-tasking, resolute in dispensing insults while also ignoring the shop's one other potential customer, a peculiar-looking man in stained double denim with a bony grinning face that was mostly yellowed teeth.

Worse still, the mal-toothed, skull-faced disregarded customer stank of urine - the reek bad enough to make Tony back-pedal into the shop's furthest corner, holding his breath.

The unfortunate man held a CD case in one hand and spoke loudly, insistently, grinning and repeating himself over and over again. "CDs, aye? Vinyl, aye? AC/DC, aye? Hawkwind, aye?

Motorhead, aye?"

He placed the CD case on the counter. Mr Faster Louder didn't move. He'd heard it all before.

The strange stinking, grinning man went off on what was plainly another recurring tangent. "When you buy a hi-fi, aye... is it the amp that's more important or the speakers, is it, aye?" he asked. "The amp, aye? The speakers, is it? The amp, aye? No' the speakers? Or what about the turntable, is it, aye?"

The omni-gendered youth offered a steady flow of patient but absent-minded interjections. "Well, Derek, that's one way of putting it," he/ she/ they murmured. "I guess it's down to personal preference, Derek... There's no hard and fast rule... It's how it sounds to the individual, I suppose."

It was almost but not quite a conversation. Tony had never realised record retail staff shared skills with mental health-care professionals. Neutralise and deflect. Pacify and absorb.

Once upon a time, he supposed, working in a record shop must have involved finding things out before anyone else, being in the know. Informing and guiding public taste; feeling superior to the common herd. Getting free stuff. But no more. Same as journalism.

Faster Louder was home to a community. Music lovers. A dying community. It explained the acrid stench of stale piss. Tony recoiled further.

By now, pungent Derek had reached that stage of his routine where he dipped into a pocket, brought out a photo and thrust it at the pan-gendered sales assistant.

"Aye, there's you, Derek - you and him, Mister Kilmister. Lemmy. Motorhead. Back in the day. Win some, lose some, all the same to us," he/ she/ they said.

"Me, aye," Derek said, spotting Tony now and turning to

him, holding out the photo. "Lemmy and me! Me and Lemmy! Motorhead, aye? Look! There's me! 1978! Me! I was 18! With Lemmy, aye? Lemmy! Motorhead, aye?"

He was trapped in Derek's eye-watering orbit, the photo pressed into his hands. "Lemmy and you, aye?" he heard himself say, studying the uncanny 40-year-old photo of an unchanged Derek, those same grinning dead-nag's teeth. Lemmy, three years dead, the eternal prickly pirate Nazi rocker. He held his breath and handed the photo back.

Mr Faster Louder had had enough. He picked up the CD case Derek had put on the counter and wagged it at him. "Are you sure you haven't got this AC/DC album already, Derek? I mean, I can't stop you buying it… but if you've got it already, we won't give you a refund."

Derek fumbled for some money, handed it over, claimed the CD and, to Tony's relief that he could start inhaling again, left.

The shop's door had barely thudded shut when Mr Faster Louder danced out from behind the counter with a canister of air freshener, spraying with urgency as though the life of everyone in the place depended on it.

"Christ, it couldn't smell worse if you stuck your fucking head up a fucking dead dog's arse," he announced.

As the stink abated, Mr Faster Louder at last trained his sights on Tony, correctly divining which musical sub-genres and bands he was interested in, expertly directing him to a cache of recent-release live radio broadcast albums ("These would've been called bootlegs years ago, when we were lads, but it's top-quality sound these days, official recordings, not just some bozo in the crowd with a cassette tape recorder") and an assortment of gems and rarities.

Tony busied himself in this CD treasure trove for over an hour, he supposed, soundtracked by albums by the B52s, Suicide and Television, plus Mr Faster Louder's spasmodic background commentary on the death-rattle of Britain's High Street record retail industry.

"Vinyl resurgence, my arse… CDs are dead, too," he half-listened to the shop-owner saying. "Nobody cares enough about music to pay for it anymore.

"Young folk just see it as stuff that takes up space. If I had anyplace better to go, I'd be off… find a job with a future. But I don't know how to do anything else - and I guess being in here is better than working for a living."

His eventual haul comprised LCD Sound System, the Black Keys, Nathaniel Rateliff and the Night Sweats, Sturgill Simpson, the Hold Steady, St Paul and The Broken Bones, the James Hunter Six, JD McPherson and best of all, CDs by Pucks he'd somehow missed.

Pucks. His all-time favourite purveyors of disaffected American post-punk indie rock. They would be the next stop on his ad hoc one-man Glasgow tour: the university in the city's West End, where he'd once interviewed the band before a gig.

Had it been 1990 or 1991? Almost 30 years before, definitely before his ears were submerged in a constant tinnitus fizz and whistle, a war wound from four decades of frontline gig-going.

By chance, that meeting was close to the venue where he'd last seen Pucks live on stage, an open-air show at Kelvingrove Bandstand, his final *Chronicle* review.

The summer before last, must have been. Two years ago already. 2014 or 2015. It was after he'd left the paper, the tickets gifted by the arts desk on condition he wrote 180 words.

He would conduct his expedition on foot, a tour of his own past, in the fearless missionary spirit of St Mungo, Glasgow's patron saint, the inspiration of the city's crest, depicting the bird that never flew, the tree that never grew, the bell that never rang, the fish that never swam.

Where was the joke in it? *St Tony! The adulterer who'd never screwed his mistress, only his marriage. The writer who no longer wrote. The comedian who never got a laugh. The professional observer who'd never truly seen.*

A Glasgow summer's day was in prospect. Overcast. Unripe. Not warm enough. Yet not too cold. Not raining, though. Not yet.

Chapter 20

After 30 minutes, he'd reached the seductive foothills of the city's verdant West End. A thick green overhead canopy of spreading trees. Glasgow University's Gothic spires. Old home territory.

Dreaming students sauntered on broad avenues. He'd arrived at his first landmark: Stitch's, the basement comedy club where his stand-up career had stood up and, within two minutes, dropped down dead.

He'd convinced himself he had to do it - for his credibility as a comedy critic. Could he keep decrying other folk if he was too scared to try? He'd surely seen enough comedy - the good, the bad - to know how to do it.

He chose a quiet Tuesday night, Stitch's regular open-mike spot, in a venue where people listened, were likely to be more tolerant.

He'd worked up a West End routine outing himself as a local, mocking his own smugness and social pretension: the poseur with a green carnation in his corduroy jacket's buttonhole.

He depicted himself sashaying about the West End's most aspirational street, Kelvinshaws Road, in tweed jodhpurs and a beret hand-woven from mung beans. Cut-price supermarket shopping concealed in upmarket supermarket carrier bags. Artisan breeks concealing shitened scants.

Dodging unicyclists and jugglers juggling houmus, edamame

beans, olives, copies of *Marxism Today*; other unicycles ridden by other jugglers - jugglers juggling unicycles. Ordering a stonebaked ptarmigan supper in a West End chip shop and being delighted to get change from a £50 note...

Prime self-satirising West End observational comedy material - plus a topical routine about Princess Margaret, deceased only days before.

Cutting-edge, and in bad taste, too.

The crowd would surely love it. How could he go wrong? The Moscardini laws of comedy. Go out and slag your physical flaws before anyone in the crowd does. Baldness, incipient paunch, spectacles, hangdog demeanour. Self-deprecate to accumulate.

Don't put on an act, you're not an actor. Be yourself. Downbeat. Conversational. Appear to know where you're going so folk feel comfortable joining you. Be likeable without being desperate. Remember to breathe.

He looked down the stone steps into Stitch's, remembering his airless night in hell. Dying is easy. Comedy is hard. Dying a death on stage is worse than actually dying, he'd learnt. When you're dead, the suffering ends.

Die on a stage and you're alive to a roomful of anger and contempt, pity and embarrassment. No laughs.

He recalled an old gag that every Glaswegian enjoyed: *where would we be without laughter?* Long pause. *Edinburgh!*

Or, he murmured to himself, in the audience at a Tony Moscardini gig.

All his clever jokes had come out at Stitch's sounding clever-clever, sausages from a machine. His words stumbled out: too fast, too slow, punchlines gulped and swallowed, not funny.

His reassuring scene-setting start? He won no friends in an opening minute that seemed to last an hour, during which time he was conscious of his flat drone and a river of cold sweat down his back.

The crowd sat soundless in the dark. A grudging snicker. Some restive shifting. A sigh. Chairs scraping as audience members fled. He knew what he should have said - "I know I'm rotten, but leave now and you'll have paid to miss the good stuff" - but he couldn't get the line out.

His panic became neediness. Another leaden West End observation stalled, failed to grow wings and refused to become joke-shaped. He decided to cut his misery short by going into the Princess Margaret routine.

"This week's news… Prince Margaret," he said. Two people snickered, assuming "Prince Margaret" was his punchline.

He was thrown. Small signs of amusement where he'd planned none. He suddenly felt exhausted, knowing he lacked the skill and confidence to take charge of his blunder, turn it around, make it funny.

"The funeral procession…" he heard himself say. "Princess Margaret's funeral procession… all round London. Her favourite places."

She'd died of lung cancer, having been a heavy smoker, so he'd reckoned there was groundbreaking, taboo-busting comedy if he recited a list of London place-names that were also cigarette brands.

"So the funeral cortege passed Mayfair… Marlboro Avenue." He'd paused, anticipating the room starting to fill with laughter.

No one laughed. "Park Drive." Pause. No laughter. "Pall Mall." Pause. A part-stifled groan.

"Then it passed the Swedish Embassy." Pause. Silence. "French Embassy, German Embassy." Silence. "In total, 20 Embassy." His big-pay-off. "Good grief," said a scornful voice in the darkness.

He'd walked off the stage. Not to the sound of his own footsteps, but to murmurs of relief, eager activity as the crowd rose to wash the foul taste of Tony Moscardini away with drinks from the bar.

If the secret of successful comedy is timing, he knew he should have been on stage at a time when there was no audience. Another funny line he'd managed not to say out loud on stage.

Standing outside Stitch's 15 years later, he vowed to thank Ken and Prof for the amiable scepticism and occasional chuckles with which they greeted all his seated stand-up attempts in Colonia.

He resumed walking further westwards, destination Kelvinshaws Road… *the* Kelvinshaws Road, as snobbier locals announced it: the West End's busiest promenade, a mile-long parade of small shops, cafes and restaurants, the swankier supermarkets.

Glasgow's sales-minded civic overseers, keen to boost tourism, had lately begun promoting *the* Kelvinshaws Road as Glasgow's answer to the Champs-Élysées, Oxford Street, Fifth Avenue, Rodeo Drive.

A retail destination of global renown, a byword for cosmopolitan fine dining… bohemian Kelvinshaws Road.

Kelvinshaws Road? Bohemian? He rated it as a high street of the sort found anywhere in Britain, albeit less shabby than most. Wider pavements, maybe, slightly fewer boarded-up shopfronts.

He'd latterly lived off Kelvinshaws Road, all too conscious that most Saturday nights it resembled garish Blackpool's downmarket seafront strip. Shrieking hen parties and growling stag nights drawn by the area's many bars.

Drunken gangs of women wearing baseball caps with outsized inflatable penises affixed, lurching and tottering on six-inch stilettos. Drunken grooms being egged on by drunken best men to show passers-by what they weren't wearing under their kilts.

Coach parties drawn in from the sticks. Rivers of urine running from shop doorways. Pools of vomit in cobbled side streets.

Bohemian wasn't a word that had applied to the place for 40

years, since the time he'd pitched up as a Glasgow University student, amid streets of once-grand demi-mansions split into shoddy, ill-maintained bedsits for callow undergraduate youths like him, alongside a residual crusting of sixties hippy free-thinkers and vanquished seventies radical Trots.

Kelvinshaws Road wasn't what it used to be, as folk had doubtless said since the day it was first named. Not that he'd ever been a fixture there, a genuine local. What was the one Kelvinshaws Road business he'd patronised on a regular basis?

Its Scots-Italian chip shop, Caffe Università. Handmade floor-to-ceiling wood panelling, ceramic-topped wrought-iron tables and rickety tip-up seats unimproved in the century since their construction by the cafe's founder.

That pioneer had been an impoverished ship's carpenter from Genoa, Tony knew, who had failed to find employment in the Clydeside yards (barred by his religion).

Hence membership of the *chipfaterati*. To use your time-served skills in a profession or fatten up Glaswegians for cash? He'd had no choice. *È stato sempre così...* 'twas ever thus for so many of Scotland's Italian incomers.

Little had changed about the varnished mahogany of Caffe Università's interior. He settled down to his usual order. Cappuccino, homemade minestrone, roll'n'Lorne sausage.

In other ways, Kelvinshaws Road was very different from how he remembered it, most obviously in the numbers of raggedy-looking homeless people begging on its pavement. Slumped on sheets of cardboard next to refuse bins, swathed in filthy blankets and blackened sleeping bags, grubby paper cups at their feet for stray coins, lost and beaten.

Where had all these broken people come from? Why had they ended up this way? Hate-filled homes? Vindictive Tory policy? Ill luck? Some hairline flaw in their nature suddenly cracked wide by circumstance? What was going to happen to them? Is there any solution to the problem? Does no one care?

He felt saddened, alarmed - more sharply so when he realised he should have visited Glasgow with his good camera.

Because the beggars' faces were the ones he should be photographing if he considered himself a truthful lensman, an artist even. Not fields of sunflowers, not pretty views - not the nourished faces of old people approaching the end of lives well-lived.

He should be documenting the young urban dispossessed, telling their wretched stories of life-long neglect, abuse, misery and pain. He should be recording faces that people turned away from; that they almost certainly wouldn't buy prints of.

These were the faces whose photographs would be pored over centuries hence as successive generations puzzled about how cruel and savage life must have been in the primitive days of the early twenty-first century.

But he knew he had no idea how to approach homeless folk to seek their permission, win their confidence - how to take their photographs without taking what little truly belonged to them, their defeated demeanour, their filthy appearance.

Without their licence, he was a thief, a judgemental voyeur, another oppressor of the downtrodden - someone offering them only an additional blow in their most desperate hour of need.

What must these people ask themselves as they bed down in filth night after night, he wondered, a version of his old journalism motto popping into his head: *what does the rest of the world know that it doesn't want us to know?*

Colonia had only one beggar, a much-pitied young woman. Much shunned, too. Lumpen, dirt-streaked, unkempt. The most unfortunate member of the town's most unfortunate and sole notorious family: a damaged-looking product of - so it was rumoured - incestuous in-breeding plus sindrome alcolica fetale, her mother's reckless drinking.

Colonia's beggar begged only during the summer months, when uninformed Glaswegians were plentiful, hanging around Conad's car park trying to appear helpful by returning shoppers' empty supermarket trolleys for them, thus helping herself to the Euro that she anticipated people might forget having deposited in the trolley's coin-tray.

If anyone objected, she'd make a grotesque sad face and rub her stomach in a feeble pantomime of hunger, or put her hands together in prayer and pretend to cry.

If she misjudged her audience and tried it on with a local, she'd be rewarded with angry curses, every Coloniesi knowing the beggar's family was assisted all year round by the church, via its parishioners' weekly donations; fed and clothed and housed in an old outlying church property.

Large-scale homelessness and begging were functions of every city, he figured. Escape to big-city free-living from small-town censure. But beware the downside.

In cities, nobody cares. They don't care what you do, who you are, how you look. You're free to express yourself in public any way you choose, in dress, thought or behaviour. You're likewise free to starve to death.

Dying on every street corner, side by side: an artist, a bum. The saviour of mankind next to a flea-ridden corpse. On the one hand, a cure. On the other, a disease.

****

He drank his coffee, ignored his conscience, day-dreamed about his next destination: the place where, decades earlier, he'd interviewed the band who at that time were the world's most-talked-about group - Pucks.

The venue for their gig had been Glasgow University's main student social centre, the QM: the Queen Margaret Union. It was closer to Kelvinshaws Road than he remembered so he arrived on its concrete steps sooner, feeling slightly surprised, dislocated.

He'd felt the same way during his Pucks interview, too - no, he'd felt more than surprise: he'd been alarmed, scared even.

Why? The band had arrived in Britain from Philadelphia three days earlier, finding themselves immersed in instant all-conquering fame, feted with unprecedented levels of critical acclaim and commercial success. To his astonishment, the band's frontman and chief songwriter was seething with anger about it.

Chuck Redd - aka Redd Charlie; real name Charles Michael White Simpson IV - was red-faced with rage. Incandescent. Shouting. Swearing. A volcano of discontent.

He decried the unstinting praise and adulation the band were being accorded by the British music media. He knew Pucks hadn't courted it and insisted they didn't warrant it.

Chuck ranted about the unearned adoration he was receiving from the band's audience each time he went anywhere in public, uncomfortable at being hailed by name by admiring fans ("I did not come over here to have strangers shout at me in the street!").

Tony and Chuck had been in the dressing room seated opposite one another at a low table, Tony's cassette tape recorder between them, the rest of the band variously lying half-asleep or pacing around drinking beer.

Chuck's disgust was all-too-evident on tape, the stocky and pugnacious singer-songwriter repeatedly thumping the table-top with his fist in an insistent show of dismay and irritation.

What was happening THUMP THUMP THUMP just wasn't

right THUD THUD THUD and Chuck was sure mad THUMP THUMP THUMP about it THUD THUD THUD and it wasn't what THUMP THUMP THUMP Chuck had signed up for THUD THUD THUD when Chuck had started Pucks.

As off-putting as those graceless thumping thuds had been close-up when Tony first heard them, they disturbed him more when he played the tape back: their loudness obscured all the fine detail of what Chuck had been saying.

He had turned up to praise Pucks' frontman for his musical talent; he'd lacked the bravery and insight to confront his bad behaviour. He had disappointed himself with his resultant *Chronicle* piece, a placatory profile of a man who, it was plain, was a monster. It had been a mess, a journalistic opportunity spurned.

He kept on walking. Pucks had at least been terrific on stage that evening. He reminisced about other bands he'd seen at the QM.

The Smiths early in 1984, a time when band and audience had been mutually in love, wooing each other with reciprocal sprays of flowers, gladioli bouquets arrowing back and forth all night between stage and crowd.

He recalled guitarist Johnny Marr observing the audience's reaction every bit as much as the crowd were watching him and the band. Marr had looked amused and delighted, unable to believe he was having such a wondrous effect on so many people yet at the same time sure that this nonsensical outbreak of mass joy was his absolute due.

Another Smiths memory followed. A painful one. Failures, embarrassments and misunderstandings linger longest, he knew. Barrowland later in 1984, when he'd bungled what could have been a minor scoop by mis-identifying the title of what Morrissey had announced as the Smiths' next single.

All he'd had to go on was his hearing of the song's lyrics, as

Morrissey trilled and yodelled them live. He cringed as he recalled how confident he'd been in urging *Chronicle* readers to look out for the prosaic-sounding "Humdrum Town" - the sole phrase he'd been able to make out in what proved to be called "William It Was Really Nothing".

He kept on walking, grateful it hadn't started to rain. He thought of other Glasgow venues and half-remembered gigs.

Countercultural Manhattan anti-heroes Nihilation in a small side-room at a big mainstream disco in the early 90s - late 80s? - on a drab midweek night.

The gig had been over and done by an unsuitably wholesome hour, 9pm, as Nihilation had failed to generate ticket pre-sales to match their status as pioneering minimalist electro-art-punk deities. Hence their relegation to an uncool early-evening slot.

Thirty years on, he chided himself for his self-appointment as an all-knowing arbiter of cultural taste. Maybe Nihilation hadn't ever been edgy and underground. There was definitely nothing avant garde about vocalist Arturo Hale's physical appearance that far-off night in Glasgow.

Tubby in late middle-age, Hale had sported a look that a blind Glasgow crone wouldn't have considered for a night at the bingo in 1974: an ill-fitting jumpsuit, belted and bunched at the waist, teamed with an acrylic wig so obvious it served only to draw speculation about how hairless its wearer must be.

During the show, sullen keyboards player Hector Vibe had lurked in the darkness, triggering pre-set sounds and rhythms but otherwise almost static, hiding behind trademark outsized sunglasses.

Halfway through the gig, everyone in the room had spotted Vibe suddenly grow animated, fumbling back and forth along a waist-high wall-ledge next to him, finally admitting defeat by lifting up his shades: he couldn't see his pint of lager.

Sad old men deluding themselves that they're young and cool, unaware that everyone else knows they're not. He knew he'd often been guilty of the very crime himself. Deluded trend-surfer. Old fool.

****

His next West End stop was upon him almost before he'd realised. Kelvingrove Bandstand. The reformed Pucks had played there in 2016, his final gig review.

He halted, took out his phone and Googled it, taking childish delight in defeating the *Chronicle's* pay-wall. He stood in Kelvin Way and scanned his review's intro.

"What you don't get from bulky, shaven-headed frontman Chuck Redd, his lived-in black suit giving him the air of some harassed mid-ranking supermarket manager, is showbiz concession. Not a word of condescending between-song patter or specious bonhomie for Monday night's wildly-enthused sell-out crowd. No 'Hello, Glasgow.' No song titles.

"What you do get from Redd and his three Pucks cohorts is way more valuable, of course: a reminder of the pithy and enduring perfection of their songs. Plangent melodies within a testy racket.

"Songs close to 30 years old now, but still uniquely intense and observant sub-three-minute-long blasts of rage and self-disgust that refuse to be contained within ye olde poppe musicke formatte of verse-chorus-verse, and which address topics far beyond the ken of Justin Bieber and his facile pop ilk."

Less well written than he'd hoped. So many big words. So many adjectives. Showy coinages. Hardly any adverbs, though, blessedly. He wondered whether the *Chronicle's* readers rued the day the flow of golden Moscardini prose had ceased. Aye, right.

His *Chronicle* overseers and workmates had all scorned his writing: its quality, its subject matter. Open dismissal. Endless sneers. None of them needed to read about stuff they'd never heard of, weirdo bands with weird-sounding names, playing weirdo noise: Nihilation, Pixies, the Smiths, Pucks, the Cramps, the Velvet Underground.

All the paper's news desk had ever wanted in terms of pop music coverage was star-struck tripe about celebrity names, preferably Scottish ones. Self-important Simple Minds. Pompous rumbling Runrig.

Anything else - electrical guitars and drums and shouting - was all an overnight teenage fad, a fleeting novelty unworthy of contextual analysis or wild enthusiasm.

For every Scottish daily newspaper, it was sufficient now and again that their pages should hail some emergent local band - however bad or indifferent - as surefire millionaire superstars-in-waiting, whereupon they'd disappear.

Likewise, all hit-makers visiting Scotland from America would be marvelled at, fawned over and/or prompted by some lazy *Chronicle* news reporter to assert their genetic possession of a Highland granny.

Further dubious stories might depict the band hiring kilts for their Scottish shows. Or planning a round of golf on the Old Course at St Andrews. The band would also be recorded as wishing to sample the finest Scotch malt whisky, inevitably mis-pronouncing the name of their favourite brand, to the wry amusement of the lazy *Chronicle* news reporter.

Condescending drivel. Three decades on, he felt himself well with rancorous anger. He'd managed to establish a music column in the paper despite workplace incomprehension and hostility, but had failed to persuade the *Chronicle* to take his kind of music seriously.

Back then, the *Chronicle* knew its readership, of course:

100,000 daily purchasers. Golf-playing actuaries, cardboard-box factory owners with tidy back gardens, Freemason accountants and conveyancing lawyers.

Every *Chronicle* reader was aged 55, male, residing in Glasgow's dead outer suburban promised lands (Jordanhill, Bearsden, Milngavie, Shawlands, Cathcart, Bishopbriggs), and none of them with a second to waste on adolescent pop nonsense.

He stopped walking for a moment and scanned the dove-grey sky, with its single depressing summertime promise: damp clothing. In the presence of whatever omnipotent deity it is who afflicts Glasgow with summer rain, he renewed his solemn pledge never to write another word.

He started walking again, turning the night before over in his head. Rachel's praise for his writing: *a certain facility with words.* There's nothing like a resounding endorsement, he thought, and that was nothing like one.

He should write a Glasgow newspaper memoir? Sure, he could jot it down in his own blood, easy… plenty of that available after he chewed his right arm off, use the stump for a nib… give him the same level of exquisite agony.

Decades spent typing and thinking, forming words into sentences, paragraphs, pages. He'd started out believing in the improving power of well-chosen words. He'd had faith in journalism as a means to educate, entertain, amuse, uplift and enlighten.

And he'd learnt that most folk wouldn't read anything that didn't confirm what they already thought. Too much effort.

Anything more taxing than a slogan or an insult or a joke? A whole newspaper article? Too long. In the online news era? Allow me to hawk up my own gobbet of brain-mucus, Mr Journalist.

Had he ever found fulfilment on the olde-tyme word-count chain gang? The odd moment, maybe. But day in, day out, for years, he'd seen his words mangled by pitchfork-wielding sub-editors.

Informative stories, assembled with painstaking care, reduced to two paragraphs. Gripping original articles about commendable Glasgow folk spiked, replaced by fluffy mince about that week's passing TV fancy.

Reasoned opinion pieces that had concluded before he'd expressed an opinion, halting abruptly mid-sentence two paragraphs ahead of their planned finale. He'd taken his words seriously - his labour in mining them, their final assembly - only to be accused of taking himself seriously.

He winced over the review of a stage play he'd phoned in to a bored-sounding *Chronicle* copy-taker late one night. His considered verdict had described the actor portraying the villain as having "a face with eyes like raisins in custard."

An arresting image. He'd been pleased with his labours. Less so the next day when it appeared in print as "a face with eyes like ravens in custard."

At least his detractors had been pleased. Further proof Moscarty-farty writes in riddles, the joke journalist. He'd had enough.

When it came to writing any more words on any topic, he hadn't surrendered, or given up, or ceased and desisted. He had implemented a conscious decision to withhold his services as a time-served nib-wielder. And he would continue to do so.

The past was safely gone. There was no future in looking back at it, at anything that could not be changed. The present was all. So why every so often did he torture himself by wallowing in his own history? Because he knew he was as much of an idiot as everyone else.

"Keep your eyes on the horizon and keep walking, dumbo," he counselled himself.

Chapter 21

His phone vibrated in his pocket. A missed call. Ken. Odd he should be in touch again so soon. Ken's first voicemail was brief and to the point: "We have a wee bit of a problem - ring me."

Before he could call Ken back, a swift follow-up voicemail made it plain that the wee bit of a problem had been joined by other not-so-wee and more problematic problems, resolving themselves into a large impending disaster.

Ken's new recorded message was very, very long, as well as increasingly despairing and curse-laden.

Things had begun to go wrong, Ken said, when he'd received a casual and at first routine-seeming phone call from a laidback-sounding *Daily Bugle* tabloid news reporter.

The reporter informed Ken that the paper had planned to cover *Bullitt da Colonia's* screen debut within the next couple of weeks as a wee Sunday arts feature... but they'd spoken to another Scots-Italian Colonia resident, Frank Wylie, a friend of its star, the late Larry McMillan, as well as his one-time fellow *Lochhead!* workmate, and they understood that Mr Wylie was a touch unhappy about the film going ahead.

So much so, in fact, that Mr Wylie was getting his brother - a retired Glasgow lawyer recently relocated to Colonia - to impose an injunction or some such Italian legal formality to stop the film being premiered tomorrow, if not stopped from ever being shown at all, because Mr Wylie's big complaint was that the film-makers hadn't had the decency to show him the film in advance - which wasn't true, Ken knew - and how did Ken feel about that?

The question had been asked with a deceptive casualness that only perturbed Ken a little to begin with, because hadn't he visited Frank Wylie's home earlier in the week and handed him a sodding memory stick with the film on it, and tutored him in how to use it, stopping short of slotting it into the old man's ancient desktop computer for him.

Ken's mild concern became panic, bafflement and alarm: their film was facing a needless last-minute threat to its existence. Finally, it took shape as annoyance - a low-level rage that Frank had somehow not bothered to look at the film that Ken had expressly given him.

And so, for once failing to temper that anger with his customary patient understanding, Ken had boiled into rage and told the bloody *Bugle's* disingenuous shit of a reporter, one Colin Scoular, more than he intended.

Much more than was prudent. Way more. Ken had told Colin Scoular something that was most unwise. That was about to explode into print as a bona fide tabloid bombshell. A catastrophe, in fact.

Because Ken had inadvertently revealed that Frank Wylie and Larry McMillan had long been a gay couple, as good as married, sharing a life together for close to 50 years in a stable loving relationship which predated their more prominent two-decades-long screen association as the stars of *Lochhead!*

Bent Coppers! TV 'Tecs Hide Real-Life Gay Drama! Tony groaned aloud, picturing the *Bugle's* headlines.

Larry and Frank's romantic union wasn't news to anyone who'd ever known them, certainly not in Glasgow TV or acting circles.

Nor in Colonia.

But it would certainly be news to *Daily Bugle* readers, who'd never suspected that *Lochhead!'s* bulky, lumbering and very manly-looking Detective Sergeant Sanderson, played by Frank Wylie, had been more than a dogged workplace assistant to his on-screen boss, the taciturn-but-intuitive, often irascible and equally hetero-seeming Detective Chief Inspector Lochhead.

Ken's confirmation of the pair's gay status - gossiped about for years on the *Bugle*'s news desk - had of course overjoyed Colin Scoular - "Colin bastard Scoular," according to Ken.

"The soft-soaping shit shot straight back for another innocuous wee telephone chit-chat with Frank, deploying that same reasonable-seeming tone of voice he'd used on me," he said.

Ken was thus startled anew when the reporter phoned again and told him - still using that quiet voice - that Mr Wylie was now even more horrified and furious about Ken's betrayal of his homosexual status, dreading that it would mean greater mockery of his late partner's name at a time when his life-long professional status was already menaced by his involvement in what was sure to be a terrible little home movie cobbled together by clueless amateurs.

Mr Wylie was thus definitely getting his brother to unleash the full weight and process of the Italian legal system to stop the film ever being shown anywhere.

Scoular took further delight in again asking Ken how he felt about that, no doubt savouring the same palpable squawks and quavers of angry terror that Tony could hear now in poor Ken's voicemail.

Ken's voice rose in key. Their wondrous film project had been stifled, stymied, strangulated, KO'd - and it was all stupid bloody Ken Moody's stupid bloody fault.

Indeed it was, but Tony couldn't blame him for becoming ensnared in a gauzy web of tabloid deception hand-woven by a practiced newsprint sleaze-hound.

They were all at fault. The three of them. Him, Ken, Prof.

Blinded by their pride in their own creativity. Convinced they were home-free, artists immune from everyday problems.

The very least that all three of them should have done was sit down with Frank Wylie and ensure he actually watched the film so he couldn't dwell on its non-existent flaws.

Ken's usual measured tone had returned when Tony phoned back. He'd calmed down in the hour or so since his original panicked call.

Tony asked Ken to get him Frank's number, along with Frank's lawyer brother's number, and then suggested what Ken should do next: deploy the ultimate diplomatic weapon, the master of conciliation.

"Send Prof round to see Frank," Tony said. "Immediately. And if you go round, too…"

Ken cut him short. "I've already seen Frank, and we'll both see him in the next half-hour," he said. "I went round straight after I left you the voicemail when I realised how much my gormless flapping mouth had upset Frank.

"He's accepted my apology, and I've convinced him our film won't harm Larry's reputation. When he sees it with us, he'll be fine. But if I ever meet the creep from the *Bugle*, he won't be fine."

The tide was turning. "Tell Frank how much Larry liked the unedited footage he saw," Tony told Ken. "Tell him what he said: '40 years and not a word worth saying.' "

But that hadn't been Frank's only worry about being outed by the *Daily Bugle*. "He thought folk in Colonia would be shocked finding out him and Larry were gay," said Ken.

"I told him folk in Colonia would only be shocked if they found out him and Larry *weren't* gay. Two veteran actors sharing the same house? Always dressed the same, like English country gents... tweed sports jackets, cords, shirt and tie.

"Folk in Colonia might've disapproved, I said, if they'd swished around together in yellow satin hot pants - no one likes mutton dressed as lamb, I told him. I made him laugh! Years studying at the Moscardini Comedy College have paid off." Tony could almost see the smile on Ken's face.

"But that's not Frank's only worry," Ken went on. "He's sure the tabloids will make *Lochhead!* look ridiculous - I didn't say lots of folk already think it is, and that's why they watch it.

"He's convinced sensational stories about two secret gay cops will sink the show's worldwide repeats. No more repeats means no more repeat fees. He's worried he won't get by on his pension."

Tony fell quiet. "Tell Frank I've still got Scottish newspaper contacts, so there'll be nothing nasty in the papers," he said.

"No muck-raking. Because there's no muck to rake. They've only got the facts. The shock revelation that two people loved one another? Big wow. Love's love, isn't it? Fifty years of love, that's heartwarming - not nasty.

"Straight, gay, it doesn't matter much anymore, does it? It's the 21st century, straight folk have gay relatives, friends, workmates - *Bugle* readers are no different. So the paper is insulting its audience if it makes fun of two gay guys... shooting itself in the foot."

An idea was shaping up. "When you think about it, *Lochhead!* only ever showed its two main characters' working lives.

"Two blokes together. Neither of them with a private life that we knew about - no boring sub-plots involving wives or girlfriends. No time wasted on anything apart from solving murders, that's why folk liked it.

"So there was no inference they were straight. Just two guys whose sole relationship was with each other… through their work, side by side, the killers they caught together.

"It was an all-male love story all along - for decades. A hit TV show about a couple of blokes. So the revelation that they were real-life lovers could win *Lochhead!* a new worldwide gay audience… the brave, groundbreaking 40-year-old gay cop show that didn't have to shout about how gay it was because *it just was!*

"Academics will pen theses about it. No one will ridicule it anymore." He could hear Ken cheering over the phone.

****

Frank's lawyer brother quickly cut Tony's call short because Frank's lawyer brother wanted it made plain that he had no intention of stopping any film premiere, mostly because there were no legal grounds he could see for doing it - not that he knew much about Italian law.

More to the point, Frank's lawyer brother was now retired after 40 years' toil as a lawyer in Scotland, and there was no way he was starting up again, wasting his time on something with the potential to turn into hard work.

There was one piece of non-legal advice he'd given Frank: he'd told his brother to get a grip on his gin consumption, especially his afternoon gin consumption, something he'd been doing too often in the months after Larry's death, and it was doing him him no good.

Tony thanked Frank's lawyer brother and breathed a big sigh of relief. The legal threat to their film had gone. Now all that remained was to be kind to a grieving widower. As all he had to do was be honest, it should be easy.

It was late afternoon in Colonia. Over the phone, he could tell that a woozy-sounding Frank had ignored his brother's advice on gin-drinking. Keep it positive, keep it simple, he told himself.

He assured Frank that he only needed to watch the film with Ken and Prof when they appeared on his doorstep, which would be soon, and he'd enjoy its 11 minutes. He'd be proud seeing Larry on screen at his best - Larry himself had thought so. He'd said it.

The *Bugle*'s story? Rubbish. A pile of old newspaper shenanigans. And old newspaper shenanigans was what he understood. He was a past master of old newspaper shenanigans.

"We'll give the papers fabulous exclusive photos of *Bullitt da Colonia* - Larry as our Steve McQueen, you'll see," he said, going on to reassure Frank they'd stymie any tabloid excesses by wheeling out yet more heavy artillery.

Tony hoped he could announce the manoeuvre with easy professional sovereignty, shrugging off the fresh weight of defeat that was crushing him. He forced jollity into his voice.

"Best of all," he said, "I'll write an article that does what needs doing, that gets the facts across - accurate, fair, dignified, sensitive... that shows how Larry helped us make a film that's a testament to his acting ability... and that's a monument to the love you shared, too."

"Thank you," said Frank. He sniffed, gulped and began crying.

Tony felt like weeping, too. The thought of all that typing. The need to write words again. So many damned words, sentences, paragraphs. The betrayal of his most sincere adult pledge - more heartfelt than his matrimonial vow...

Chapter 22

There were more calls to make. McCrindle first, growling hung-over curses as soon as he picked up the phone, but intrigued when Tony outlined the problem.

"You can sort out the *Bugle* in minutes, with your contacts," Tony said. "A trade-off - promise them a better, fuller version of the story within the next couple of days, scintillating prose, written by an insider, plus world-exclusive photos, so long as they hold off for now."

McCrindle agreed. There was a winsome young *Bugle* exec he'd once wined and dined. He'd give her a call, she was sure to melt... putty in his hands... *pussy in his hands...*

Tony cut him short, agreeing that McCrindle was - of course - every woman's ideal sex-partner but reminding him of a need to move with urgency. He ended their call, straight away spotting a new text message.

It was from Gabriella: *Ti amo.* She loved him. Now he felt like crying. With relief, with happiness.

Texts from Gabriella were rare. He could picture her angry denunciation of texting, mobile phones, all forms of stupid, time-wasting modern-day digital communication not many weeks earlier, as she'd stood part-dressed in his bedroom in the hazy afterglow of a pleasant afternoon.

Her contempt for those people who spent all day staring into their hands at little computer screens like teenage fools, tapping out nonsense words, had made her stamp her foot with such vigour that her breasts jiggled - something she'd grown even more comically annoyed about when he'd pointed it out, smiling at her, praising her for having something about which she was so passionately moved... no, *physically moved.*

Texts were a nuisance, a distraction, an irritant, plus - what else had Gabriella declared - they had no legal status, no validity: "They are without contractual worth - I am a notarised *immobiliare* and I do not ever say anything worth being said by stupid text message!"

His happiness evaporated. Gabriella's text message was most likely some kind of informal precursor to his being officially bulleted. A diplomatic softening up. A decoy - no, that made no sense. Gabriella was about directness in all things... in which case...

He phoned Ken again to tell him that he and Prof might be receiving conclusive extra assistance in talking Frank round. "Provided that I can be persuasive enough over the next few minutes, I'm going to get you an assistant - this is woman's work."

When he rang Gabriella, he ran into her standard telephone version of herself. Which meant she was more than a little off-putting. Telefonica Gabriella. Brisk, brusque, business-like.

He took a deep breath and told her he loved her, and he loved the fact that she'd embraced the reviled, hated medium of text messaging to tell him that she loved him.

In response, she made a throaty groan. Of annoyance? Irritation? A dismissive tut? Maybe a growl. Possibly a moan.

It was a sound which might signify aggression. Or that he'd tested her patience beyond all reasonable bounds. It could mean anything. It wasn't obviously good. Nor was it manifestly bad.

He ploughed on. He explained the film-sinking potential of a Frank-and-Larry gay-shocker TV-cop tabloid revelation and asked if she'd help by joining up with Ken and Prof that very minute.

Frank couldn't fail to be impressed if Gabriella were to reveal that she'd generously been Larry's on-screen stand-in, doing all the driving so that he hadn't been taxed by it.

There was a long silence. During which Tony felt like he might never draw breath again, to the verge of expiry. And then Gabriella agreed.

Another major problem out of the way. Nothing as troubling and strange and unforeseen could loom on his horizon within the next day or so, surely - could it?

He wondered whether the same sentiments had ever before been expressed with similar self-congratulation; a clear horizon and no evident threat of capsize… by the night-watchman aboard some smooth-sailing Atlantic cruise liner or other, say.

****

His meeting place with Rachel, outside Vic's, was 10 minutes on foot from his hotel, he estimated. An easy stroll, light drizzle, downhill all the way. He walked across George Square, pausing to eye the rain-dampened Glasgow piazza's display of public sculptures, surprised to recall facts he'd pillaged for one of his shameful late-career cut-and-paste *Chronicle* articles.

George Square's monuments, all you never needed to know: one queen, one prince (both on horseback). Three politicians, one chemist, one inventor, two military leaders, one novelist, two poets.

Or as Glasgow would choose to weigh the dozen statues'

accomplishments, enough for a football team - 11 outfield players plus a substitute, Glasgow Disunited.

He halted before the black-patinated bronze statue commemorating Scotland's most famous poet. You, me and Tam o'Shanter against the world, he said to himself and George Square's dandified representation of Robert Burns.

There was a longer pause as he struggled to recall any actual lines of poetry from his long-ago school-classroom exposure to Tam O'Shanter's epic form. There had been drunks and prancing witches, one of them wearing a tempting short chemise - a cutty sark.

Clearest of all, he remembered the long-suffering wife, who relished giving her man a good sherricking whenever he lurched home on Friday night with his pay-packet opened. *Gathering her brows like a gathering storm, nursing her wrath to keep it warm.*

Which woman in his life did that apply to? His ex-wife, for sure. He'd deserved her frequent brooding glances. More recently, there'd been the occasional lecture from Gabriella.

But he assured himself he was done with drink-addled Scottish journeys through history that only lead to trouble. Enough of Glasgow… enough of cautionary tales and past lives…

By the time he reached Vic's, it had stopped drizzling.

Barely a fortnight since the west of Scotland's longest day of the year, the midsummer solstice, when Glasgow's northern latitude meant it should be light till 11pm, maybe later, but tonight's early-evening sky was a dismal pewter grey.

He stood in the street, checking his watch. Blue-grey Glasgow hard-case pigeons pecked in the gutter at days' old bread rolls, rain-sodden to a stale off-white mush.

He thought of the ad slogan: We Built This City On Morton's Rolls. A Glasgow built on grey bread, grey skies. Grey streets.

Grey pigeons. Grey mush for breakfast, dinner and tea. Blackened statues. A restricted palette. Limited palates.

An old joke came to mind, the one about the world-weary Glasgow city-centre public-lavatory attendant, long disgusted by the unspeakable late-night goings-on folk routinely conducted in his porcelain kingdom, uttering a poignant lament: "See when somebody just comes in here for a shite… it's like a breath of fresh air."

He wondered whether he could work up a new routine on the same theme - some shtick about a mad knifeman running amok in grey Glasgow crowds, buckets of blood… *at least it was a welcome bit of colour.* Maybe not.

No chattering thrum reached him from Vic's. The place was dead on a Saturday. A taxi drew up. Rachel stepped out. She paced carefully towards him, four inches taller in grey suede platform shoes.

She narrowed her eyes, flickering a thin smile on and off. He nodded at Rachel's long black waxed cotton coat, extending below the knees and buttoned up to her neck. Prim, forbidding. "Battened down against the weather - I assume it's water-repellent… proofed against spillages," he said.

She looked back at him with a wariness that was puzzling, as though turning his throwaway remark over, divining a trap. Odder still was the long pause before she replied.

"Demure is always the word with me," she said at last.

"You're never dressed right for Glasgow in summer," he said, the words spilling out, rushed, too eager in avoiding a conversational lull. "Italians don't believe me when I explain Scottish weather. They think rain in summertime sounds great… refreshing when Italy's so parched.

"They don't get it when I tell them you'll be too warm and

then you'll be too cold in a Glasgow summer, almost at once. Outdoors, soaked in rain and chilled by a gale. Back inside, running with sweat. Clammy. Humid.

"Welcome to Steamy Windows City! Twelve months, one crap season. Summer's always summer in Italy. Sun. Hot. Dry. Blue skies for months. Then some time in August, late afternoon, up in the hills where I am, same time every day, a little monsoon - 20-minute downpour, then the rain's finished, more sunshine. Depend on it, regular as clockwork."

Her face remained blank. Further silence. He told himself to stop talking. Tony Meteorology: master of weather-focused small talk.

"Predictability's over-rated," she eventually said.

They stood and looked at one another. He couldn't help jibber-jabbering to fill the awkward silence, cursing his enthusiasm, sure he sounded keen, needy. "Anything to tell me about tonight's... news assignment? Whatever it is. Why you're not going alone."

She sighed. She pondered. He kept his mouth shut.

"It's a place I've been to a couple of times before," she said, "and always felt a bit, I don't know... I'm not being mysterious - a witness is handy, a second pair of eyes.

"An outside observer... to validate the experience, you might say. Nothing to worry about. Nothing too scary... nothing unpleasant. The opposite." She looked at her wrist watch. "Time to go."

Chapter 23

Rachel looked around for a taxi. The black cab she'd arrived in was still idling at the kerb. She scurried over and slid open the cab's door, climbing in and bunching herself in the furthermost corner of the taxi's back seat, turning away from him to stare out of the window.

It didn't stand out as the the warmest Saturday-night invitation he'd ever received. Even as he walked to the taxi and stepped in, closing the door behind him, he reminded himself that he didn't have to accompany her.

How soon can I leave, he asked himself. He took his corner of the back seat and eyed Vic's battered front door. No one entering. No one inside to make an exit. Dead. The taxi clattered into motion.

She said nothing. He said nothing. Around them, busy city-centre streets unspooled in a colourful swirl. Groups of young people exchanged greetings. Handshakes. Hugs. Kisses. Inside the taxi, the two of them stared in opposite directions.

As they neared the Clyde, the crowds thinned before vanishing. The taxi drove on along the empty waterfront in silence save for the occasional jolting thud as it crashed through a pot-hole, Tony speculating about the name of whatever abandoned post-industrial zone of blasted loss they were passing through.

Miles of forsaken quayside razed half a century earlier, abandoned rust-brown moorings and weeded sections of cobbled paving that were resistant to gentrification. A barren stretch of river that once upon a time you could almost walk across, stepping deck to deck from one tied-up vessel to the next.

Grand transatlantic liners berthed beside heavy-laden cargo boats, scores of them, mixed in with tramp steamers and tugboats, framed by dozens of cranes unloading sugar, cotton, tobacco. Dockside, dockers, derricks: all gone.

Glasgow: the port that misplaced its ships. The city that forgot it had a river. That turned its back on the Clyde and its wider link to the world.

He resumed his study of vacant lots overgrown with rampant purple buddleia, uneven with rubble. A hard-to-re-imagineer netherland of cracked pavements littered with cigarette packets, shards of shattered glass, fast-food wrappers, discarded drinks cans, sodden newsprint mulch. Bleak. Arid. Ugly.

Dockyard warehouses had stood there once upon a time, he guessed, but now there was only crumbled masonry, crushed and burnt-out oil drums, collapsed plywood fences, a holed and rusting skip. Shredded black bin-bags fluttered where they'd been caught on broken-down wire-mesh fencing.

In time, some bunch of council-approved Porsche-driving speculators might devise a bogus but urgent-sounding name for the place. Atlantic Front. Plantation Sound. KeyTech One.

But tonight it was a nameless scene of depression and loss, forsaken. Gutters choked, pooled with black mud. No pubs, no shops, no housing. No hope. No evidence of people, apart from the rubbish they flung. And now it had begun to rain, too, of course.

The taxi slowed. A faded, peeling poster on a huge weather-beaten billboard advertised some unrealised exercise in aspirational Clydeside residential loft-living.

They were nearing a run-down row of seven or eight buildings in a short dead-end side street. A partially-lit oasis of commercial activity.

There was a trade-only D-I-Y store. A place displaying bathroom fittings in its orange-lit windows. Van hire. Car rental. A soot-blackened church, its windows boarded-up, with a sign above its door offering architectural salvage, no longer in the business of saving souls.

The taxi stopped. Rachel reached for the taxi's door-handle. They were outside a low, oil-smudged building with a steel-shuttered frontage. Its large red neon sign read Speedy Tire & Muffler.

He couldn't help but read the sign out loud - three times - saying "Speedy Tire & Muffler?" in a more and more quizzical tone, baffled as to why a Glasgow back-street fast-fit car-repair centre would deploy two Americanisms in its title.

"We don't call them mufflers in this country, they're exhausts - and using the American spelling of tyre doesn't make this place any more glamorous," he said, aware his voice was sounding more and more shrill, rising to match his scorn and incredulity.

"And red neon lights? *Here?* Viva GlasVegas, my arse!"

He heard her tutting as she exited the taxi. "Tony Nitpickerini," she said from the pavement, a strained note in her voice, glaring back at him. "Pedantic as ever. Distracted by the detail, missing the bigger picture… it's not the garage we're going to, it's the place above it."

There was a sarcastic edge now, as if to puncture any notion he might have had about their old relationship somehow re-igniting. He realised he was relieved to hear it.

"I'll understand if you crap out early - you've got past form, I suppose," she said, leaving him to get the taxi fare as she headed for a shadowy arched doorway to the left of Speedy Tire & Muffler's shuttered ground-floor service bays.

He got out, paid the cab fare, and then paused, wondering why he hadn't stayed in the taxi and ordered it to drive off, avoiding this woman, sidestepping this place, this night, spurning this opportunity.

And an opportunity was what it was. Once a journalist, always a journalist: if you get the chance, have a nosey about.

****

He followed Rachel through the arch, climbing a short flight of concrete stairs. At the top, she buzzed an illuminated entry phone at a grubby-looking door.

He stooped to read the small handwritten sign taped next to the buzzer: Abasement. "Abasement?" he said. "But we're up stairs."

The door opened, illuminating Rachel in blue light. She turned her head to him.

"Whatever floor it's on," she said, "a sex dungeon is always a sex dungeon." The door opened, and she stepped over the threshold.

"A sex dungeon?" he said, hearing himself and knowing that his voice sounded squeaky and adolescent - fatuous, embarrassing, frightened. She halted in the doorway, turning towards him again.

"Yep," she said. "A sex dungeon, Tony - a first-floor sex dungeon. Overlook the solecism. Just this once."

"But... er... I'm not dressed for a sex dungeon," he said, regretting the attempt at stand-up the instant the words took form and confirmed him not as a comedian but as an idiot.

"You get *undressed* for a sex dungeon," she said in a voice harsh and cold, matching her blue-lit face, "and nobody'll be looking at you anyway. Not unless there's any gay men here who fancy pernickety bald old straights." She advanced along Abasement's hallway.

He felt himself boil with anger. There was an impulse to turn on his heel, march off into the night, retreat to safety. The next second, he was steeling himself and edging forward into the unnatural melancholy light of Abasement.

For who was he, he reminded himself, if he wasn't Tony Mustavanosey obeying the old urge to find stuff out, his need to know whatever it was that somebody else knew that somebody else wanted to prevent him knowing. That *they* didn't want him to know, whoever *they* were.

Ahead of him, he registered the parp of some meek, low-grade, low-volume pop tune having the guts noodled out of it by an offensively inoffensive saxophonist. He was looking into a large red-lit room filled with 40 or so people, he supposed. A get-together. A shindig. A party. An event. A gig. A gig for him to review.

The party-goers were mostly dancing together, swaying, talking, embracing or else half-reclining on sofas, drinks in hand, entwined, touching, kissing… and despite trying not to notice, he couldn't help but see they were wearing very little.

Underwear as outerwear. Bits of diaphanous black nylon. A slow-moving sea of leathery skin, stretch-marked and flabby. Hairy male backs, female cellulite.

No one young, or lithe and slender. Instead, he saw only overweight bodies. Old bodies. He was shocked. Repulsed. Horrified. Scared more than anything.

He tried to joke his way out of it: Tony Moscardini reporting live from the Glasgow Darby and Joan Sex Appreciation Society AGM. He failed. It wasn't funny. He feared being noticed, and dragged into whatever circus of old flesh that this was.

Worse still, if he let himself observe close enough for long enough, he might grow excited, aroused. He mustn't look. No one must see he still has clothes on.

Rachel had turned her back to him, watching the full crimson-lit spectacle. A woman of about 70 appeared from a door on his left, nodding to Rachel as she limped past her, hobbled by cruel red stilettos.

She wore little else: a black fishnet body-stocking with a convenient circular cut-out round her depilated groin. On her head, a red acrylic-fibre hairpiece.

The woman took his hand. She limped back up the hall, slowly leading him, stunned into polite compliance, towards the door she'd emerged from. He kept his gaze off the woman's imperfect body, feeling sorry for her.

He locked his eyes on the woman's hairpiece. It had slipped to a sad lop-sided angle. Should he tell her?

Wouldn't she want to be told so she could adjust it, prevent being embarrassed? Should he reach up and straighten it for her? No.

The woman who turned up at an orgy wearing a cock-eyed wig, he thought. Perfect.

He let himself be led through the door the woman had exited. A small room. Harsh fluorescent overhead light. Too bright. Painful.

He blinked, recoiling from the woman's over-illuminated skin, mottled with fake tan to a yellowy-brown. Clothing hung on hooks on the room's walls. A changing room. The woman extended a blue-veined hand towards the zip of his jeans.

"Ah, no - there's no need... it's OK," he said, a little too quickly. He guessed he was sounding too panicked to pass for a seasoned raunch-hound, a priapic freebooter, a man of the world.

He hoped the old woman wouldn't be offended, spotting his amateur group-depravity-participant status. The Sex Party Police would have him thrown down the stairs.

He forced a grin, backing away from her out into the hall. "Suit yourself, love, but it's £20 extra for keeping your clothes on," the woman said in the same matter-of-fact tone she'd use on grandchildren reluctant to eat Brussels sprouts. She extended the palm of her hand, Tony giving her the cash.

Keep it cerebral, he told himself. Focus on higher things. Keep it comic. What do you say when you bump into someone you know in a Glasgow perv club: come here often, pal?

He saw Rachel turn off the short hallway into another door, entering what was evidently a different changing room. Because seconds later, she re-emerged having not just changed her outfit, but transformed.

****

Rachel was minus her long black coat. She was wearing her shoes. And nothing else. Under her long black coat in the taxi she'd been naked, ready for the evening's activities. She'd been prepared.

Demure? Prim? He didn't think so. The naked Rachel - one side of her body blue-lit, the other side bathed in red - strode towards him into the main room.

It was imperative that he didn't look at her. That she couldn't accuse him of looking at her. He kept his head down, stared at the floor.

And of course as Rachel neared him, she stopped. "Like my new fuck-me pumps, do you, Tony?" she asked.

She lifted her right foot, extending it towards him, pointing her toe down. Dainty. He stared at the grey velvet shoe, her foot.

He kept his head down. "Do you like them, Tony?" she asked again. Her attention made his heart beat faster, made him blush, made him sweat.

"Write one of your clever reviews of my new fuck-me pumps," she taunted. "You do like them, don't you? You know you want to like them.

"Do you like anything else I'm not wearing? Nothing catch your eye?"

He felt humiliated, powerless, not knowing how to deflect her sneers, feeling himself redden with shame. He was cornered, trapped. He swallowed, gulped, unable to speak.

He focused on the shoes to the exclusion of everything else. His life depended on him looking at those shoes, he knew, and those shoes alone.

He stared at them with such intensity that remembering to breathe became an issue. Her shoes were the one safe thing in the room, he was certain of that. The only things to look at.

He wondered if his mouth was hanging open. Whether his tongue hanging out, dragging on the floor. Should he say it out loud, try and be the comedian: mind you don't trip over my tongue in your new fuck-me pumps.

He reminded himself he was a critic. What would he write? Something about a new Saturday-night Glasgow sports event - the undressage.

He made a sudden effort to look away from Rachel's shoes, away from her. He half-closed his eyes, looked up and became fascinated by the room's ancient cornice. He could see now it had been painted some delicate shade of pink.

He was sure there'd be a more upmarket name for it than pink. Overwrought Sex Dungeon Matt Genital Rose Blush. Dusk Depravity Damask.

He registered Rachel turning away from him, entering the flesh-baring scrum of the main room. In that moment, every head turned to her. Glittering eyes sought her approval, devoured her.

He congratulated himself on not looking at her as she walked away, suddenly realising he'd been holding his breath. He shrank back, hiding his own fully-clothed status behind a pillar in the entrance hall, blending in with his surroundings, his usual ploy, remaining unseen.

He studied the room, large and open, ignoring the half-naked forms inside it. Previously some sort of retail showroom, he supposed.

To his right, what were once floor-to-ceiling windows overlooking the street, he supposed, now painted out in a matt finish, some pale shade of reddish-pink. Muted Communal Orgasm Raspberry Coulis?

He was startled when the ceiling suddenly began moving above him - reflections in its mirrored surface. An orgy plainly wasn't an orgy without its participants seeing themselves.

Tony couldn't help but see double the number of hairy male backs and balding heads. Outnumbering the amount of dimpled female buttocks and pendulous breasts. Doubling his unease.

Could he spot himself up there among the hopeless men? There he was: the furtive onlooker, mouth open, penned in a corner, cowering. He tried not to look up. He tried not to look at any of it.

He did a rough head-count. Maybe 50 people in the room, two thirds of them men.

Some things he couldn't help seeing, much as he tried not to. All the men were upwards of his age, 60-plus, plump, most wearing black thongs several sizes too small - waistbands cutting into hairy bellies - accessorised here and there with heavy gold neck-chains, a gas mask, a black PVC ski mask.

One man wore black Lycra cycling shorts. Another's groin was emphasised by a bulbous nozzle protruding from the front of his shiny black skintight latex hot pants.

Every man was shod in Crocs. Practical, he supposed. Not sexy. Ursine male bodies slicked with coconut oil, the aroma competing with the smell of bleach.

The women were of a similar age. Dutiful wives, dragged here against their will? They all seemed to be enjoying themselves, smiling, jolly.

No woman wore Crocs. They'd made the effort, self-torturing in high heels, likewise strapped into stereotype sexy gear. Skimpy. See-through. Black. Nylon. Suspenders, stockings, basques, PVC peephole bras.

All of which, it was obvious, had served its purpose. To disguise blue and purple thread-veined thighs. To excite. Enflame. Engorge. To lubricate some late-night, late-life game of wiggle, jiggle, giggle, pout, wobble, teeter, grope, gobble, fondle.

A rolling maul of near-naked couples - or trios, possibly quadruples, he refused to look - occupied the room's large collection of leather sofas, engaging in every variant of sexual discourse, intercourse, outercourse… heads bobbed, rumps rolled, breasts and buttocks bounced, men and women thrust, rucked, shook.

****

He allotted himself the role of stock-taker. Quantity surveyor. Logistics overseer. Distanced. He studied the off-cut rubber matting in assorted sizes on the wooden floor. Deployed in spill-prone hazard zones, he guessed. Rugs problematic: fluid leakages inevitable, constant cleaning bills.

Low side tables stood against each wall, neatly stacked with foot-high piles of towels, dozens of them. Each corner of the room had a gaudy orange plastic laundry basket.

He imagined triumphant post-ejaculate men lobbing balled-up towels into the baskets as though scoring points. Signs might be helpful. Place Towel In Basket With Care Following Use. Or maybe the men expected the womenfolk to clean up after them.

He wondered whether he was the only male sex-dungeon orgy attendee ever to expend all his imaginative energy considering the venue's hygiene and cleansing arrangements?

He stared up at the ceiling and concentrated more fully on being offended by Abasement's intrusive background music. Defanged sub-jazz. Tired tunes softly strangled.

Underpinned by the stink of Domestos. A red-palled room full of lust-crazed oldsters bulging out of cheap wisps of man-made fibre.

And then, just as he began smiling to himself and relaxing into the absurdity of the night, he noticed Rachel. He couldn't help but look.

She had almost reached the room's centre, walking her shy pigeon-toed walk in a way that drew further attention to the sexual signal posted by her towering shoes, greeting assorted attendees, bestowing smiles, a mock curtsey to this one, a mouthed "Hello" to another.

Everyone else in the room had fallen still. There was a sense of expectancy.

Rachel was Abasement's youngest, slenderest female patron, and she was envied, admired, desired, adored, lusted over. Once it would have tortured him, but not now.

It was plain that this had never been a work assignment. She was a regular here. She was there by choice. For her own enjoyment. For everyone's. So why had she invited him along? To humiliate him? To mock him? It seemed unlikely after all these years.

Had it been important that she not enter Abasement alone? Had she needed to be accompanied by someone who was more than an acquaintance? Why him?

There was concerted movement at the room's centre. As he bid not to watch, Rachel was all at once surrounded by 20 or so people, mostly men. She was kissing and being kissed, caressing and caressed. She was enveloped, savoured, eaten alive by a dozen or more hungry mouths.

He witnessed the man in the black latex hot pants touch her side with a hand, and she twitched and shivered, quivered and gasped and moaned, her legs buckling in surrender.

She lay back, offering herself up, her arms extended as if immersing herself in a sea of flesh, floating, swimming, bathing in naked men.

She was lifted off her feet, her body held horizontal for a few moments before it relaxed and began to undulate, pulse, twist, feather. She was floating, she was flying until she sank beneath the wave of her devotees.

He closed his eyes, only for an urgent new sound to drown out the terrible saxophone music. The crowd were gasping out loud, groaning, moaning, grunting, making all the faked noises of a pornographic film in a staged tableau that made him feel sick.

He opened his eyes again, concentrating on the men on the ragged fringe of the orgy's surging ant-hill of participants. Their imperfect late-middle-aged bodies reminded Tony of his own.

Such a limited range of expressions on each man's sweat-shined, open-mouthed face: all the way from half-starved to 100% stupefied with nothing in between. He briefly sighted Rachel's face, an expression of enraptured victory as she accommodated her ravenous worshippers. Singly. Doubly. Multiply. Simultaneously.

He knew he was meant to stay and watch, as surely as he knew

Rachel enjoyed being watched. He guessed he was meant to feel jealous. He felt a moment's arousal, a tiny pang of envy at having not taken his chance at intimacy when it was on offer 20 years before.

But more strongly than that, he felt relief. Relief he wasn't one of the enslaved mob.

He felt glad, too, that he hadn't had anything alcoholic to drink, certain he would have retched and brought it all back up. Not the kind of emission of bodily fluids they encourage here.

There was an unexpected touch at his elbow, light but so startling that he flinched. The little old red-wigged woman he'd first met glared up at him.

She'd layered a transparent black dressing gown over her fishnet bodystocking. *Dress warm, missus, fend off those night-time chills, elderly folk need to be careful.* She sported a fierce no-nonsense scowl. Part-waitress in some greasy spoon, part-scrapyard Alsatian.

He maintained eye-contact with her to stop himself gawping at her low-hanging breasts. She was frowning. Her eyes narrowed with impatience. "Anything I can do for you?" she said at last, a wheezing rasp of annoyance in her voice.

"Er… no - thank you," he said.

He feared what the woman might say or do next. He was unsure what to say, keen to leave. Yet he also had a feeling that he'd not finished whatever task tonight had demanded of him, troubled by a notion that he was meant to wait for… something.

What, though? He had no idea. He kept his eyes on the old woman's eyes, conscious that she was growing more exasperated, her chest heaving, rising, falling, shaking…

"Thing is, bud," she said, sounding more asthmatic, "if you just keep hanging about on the edge… like a spare prick at more than one wedding… you'll need to fuck off."

"Point me at the exit and I'm straight through it," he said. The woman grew angry, raising her right arm and jabbing a thumb over her shoulder towards the door.

He nodded curtly. He might even have bowed. What he knew for a fact was that he was overturning a grand British tabloid newspaper tradition by making no excuses as he left a sex party.

He walked away from the ammonia reek, the soul-crushing musical soundtrack, the clichéd sexy outfits, the oppressive pink walls and the all-you-can't-eat buffet of quivering vintage flesh with his head held high, his eyes fixed on the far horizon.

There was no looking back. If he ever saw Rachel Ballantyne again, it would be too soon.

It was nine o'clock on a Saturday July evening in Glasgow, and as he reached the bottom of the stairs and set off to find a cab back to his hotel, he was delighted it wasn't raining.

For once the sun was shining. He had survived a visit to a sex club. He'd seen things he wished he hadn't. He'd undergone what he supposed he might one day be able to laugh about and call a sexorcism.

Because he no longer felt any physical attraction towards a woman he'd spent years longing for. Instead, he pitied her. And he felt relieved. If not outright victorious in the game of life, he was as yet undefeated.

Nothing lay ahead that could test him to such an extent that this night had. No future challenge that could be so grievous, so wounding.

Well, apart from the challenge he'd face when he got back to Colonia if Gabriella had decided he was history. That was a trial for tomorrow, though.

Sunday/ Domenica

Chapter 24

Tony awoke free of nightmare flotsam, calmed by the hotel corridor's reliable background thrum: its ice-making machine. No terror-stricken sense of drowning, trapped in frozen darkness, no sinking Titanic. Sunday, 6am. Perfect timing for the noon Pisa flight. He yawned and stretched.

An old joke tip-toe'd into his head: how'd you find yourself this morning, sir? *I just rolled back the sheets and there I was.*

The morning after his longest, strangest Glasgow Saturday night. Unique. Stark. Another old gag: *under my clothes, ladies and gentlemen, let me remind you that I am at all times totally naked.*

How did he find himself following his ascent to Abasement? Feeling confused. More confused than usual.

He'd let himself be distracted by an old forbidden excitement. Did that mean he was flawed, lacking? That he had the potential to be a cheat, a bad guy? If so, what kind of a potential bad guy?

He was the kind of bad guy who'd chosen to walk into temptation's path… but who'd resisted temptation when temptation had failed to present itself. That's the kind of bad guy he was. So not too bad a bad guy.

A potential good guy even. Although short of being an actual saint.

He'd committed no sin. He'd dodged deadly icebergs - and not crossed the line. Crossing the line, such a phrase. A movie-making flaw. A moral crime.

Using his comedy imagination, he re-fashioned the line. It became a tightrope, a high-wire he could teeter along congratulating himself on his balance, trying not to look down.

He stretched and yawned again, cleared his throat, got out of bed. Why had Rachel asked him to go out with her last night? He had no idea. Did it matter? Probably not. Maybe. Yes, but...

In time of puzzlement, he reassured himself, fall back on your oldest journalistic certainty. Invoke your first commandment: what do you know that the bad guys don't want you to know? What had he learnt that might bring succour to the downtrodden and pain the oppressor?

It would help if he knew who the bad guys were. He wasn't one of them, not completely, that seemed plain. But if he couldn't identify the bad guys, how could he identify the downtrodden, the oppressed? How to gauge what was succour to one and poison to the other.

Perhaps he was the oppressor and the downtrodden combined. Years before, he'd oppressed Rachel with his lust - a lust that had masqueraded as friendship.

Last night he'd avoided sexual involvement with her at a sex party, long having lusted after her. So he supposed he'd defeated the bad guy he used to be.

Had Rachel ever been his oppressor? Or had he let her keep him downtrodden? Such pointless questions. Questions only a fool would ask. What really mattered was not giving in to temptation.

He'd avoided surrender. He hadn't done wrong. He hadn't betrayed himself. He hadn't betrayed Gabriella. Did he still feel guilty? Yes. A little. Saturday night was not something he could share with anyone, not Gabriella, not Ken.

All that truly mattered was that he'd prevented next week's *Bugle* on Sunday publishing an article that would wound a grieving widower.

Tony had faith in McCrindle. As well as reservations about McCrindle. Because McCrindle had always done what suited McCrindle: taken what he wanted and moved on. Usually in the form of a laugh at someone else's expense.

He appeared in Tony's life from time to time when it suited him, when he had nowhere better to be. Now that he needed him, how much use was McCrindle likely to be?

He checked his phone. Five missed calls within the past hour from a number he didn't recognise, no voice-message. It could only be one person: Rachel Ballantyne.

Twenty years go, her persistence would have thrilled him. Now it annoyed him. He would not return her calls.

What did she have to tell him? Why did she think he might want to hear it?

There were no calls or texts from Gabriella. He hadn't expected any, but… He stepped into the shower cubicle.

By the time he'd washed away the taint of disappointment with which Glasgow too usually marked him and then dressed, there was a text from McCrindle.

"I can't silence the *Bugle*," it read. "My line of credit has expired - the story appears next Sunday. I'm no good to you. Sorry."

He winced. An old dread returned.

Sure, tonight's film premiere would go ahead. Folk might even claim to like it. Larry McMillan's screen farewell hailed as a triumph. And a week later, loud tabloid snickering would undo any benefit, and leave Frank Wylie as miserable as before.

He and his deceased partner would both be outed against their will, humiliated; their personal and professional reputations mocked in print.

Read all about it! Larry McMillan: the crap actor and closet queer who ended up in some daft old men's stupid wee film.

Get your scorn and titillation! Frank Wylie and Larry McMillan, their secret uncovered! Have a giggle at the shabby true story of *Lochhead!'s* bent coppers!

If Frank grew sad enough to start drinking more gin earlier each day, Tony would be responsible. Frank already had a broken heart. If he drank himself into an early grave, how bad would Tony feel?

He had to prevent the story from running. But how?

He didn't know any present-day Scottish tabloid journalists - well, he knew one. Well-connected, a ceaseless networker, cultivating her contacts and working her sources, one who knew every other journalist in Glasgow.

If anyone could effect a tabloid trade-off that pleased everyone, it was Rachel. But he wasn't going to beg a favour from her. Or maybe after last night, he was the one who held the upper hand. Blackmail - a way to stifle any story.

It would be a more suitable conclusion to the Ancient Ballad of Ballantyne and Moscardini, too. Public exposure of her starring role in Glasgow's seediest theatre of sex as payment for the pain he'd suffered thanks to her.

If only he still felt bitter about her. If only he was nursing an urge for vengeance, keeping his wrath warm. But he wasn't.

No one would learn about his trip to Abasement or about Rachel's star role. Well, maybe he'd tell Susan. No. No, he wouldn't...

The phone beside his bed rang. A familiar soft voice spoke from reception. Rachel asking him to meet her.

He considered ducking out through the hotel's back door. Courage, he told himself. Do the right thing.

As he stepped out from the lift into reception, she had her back to him, standing beside the hotel's revolving front door in last night's grey suede platform shoes, looking out into the street through a floor-to-ceiling window.

She still wore last night's long black coat, too, her hands in its pockets as she turned to face him, the coat fully buttoned. *Run into the street, son, if she moves a hand towards undoing any of them.*

He had his backpack, his hotel bill was paid - but if he ran off, his final newspaper task was left undone. There was no choice. He had to engage. Advance towards go.

Black coat, grey shoes. Colours to match the overcast skies outside. At least it wasn't raining… yet.

Should he mention last night, he wondered as he looked her over. Rachel Ballantyne: wearing not much more than her watch-me-being-fucked pumps. He was sure she hadn't come to express her dismay at his not having hung around for that.

If she did, he had his reasons ready. A pressing engagement elsewhere - atop the moral high ground, polishing his superiority with wire wool. True to form, he didn't say anything.

She turned. She glared at him, exasperated. Impatient. Angry. As though he was the one who'd violated social norms last night.

He wasn't sure how a woman who'd been the eager focus of a mid-sized Glasgow orgy would look the morning after, but it wasn't the way she looked now.

Shadows under her eyes, without looking especially tired. Or used…. used up. Anywhere near worn-out.

Her face was paler, but her skin was fresh and shiny, damp-looking, fresh scrubbed. Same as her hair, combed severely behind her ears. She was wearing lipstick, a restrained autumnal shade closer to brown than overt signal red. Humdrum Orgy Ochre, not Siren Scarlet Stereotype.

He said nothing, looked beyond her through the picture window, avoided being caught conducting scrutiny.

Their silence was becoming awkward. He resumed his study of her shoes. He'd thought he'd known who she was, but he hadn't. He didn't. Sassy shoes, their wearer unreadable.

She suddenly looked uncertain, frail, ready to burst into tears maybe, and then she snapped out of it, clenched her jaw, steeling herself, her face hardening, growing fierce.

Her words poured out in a rush, quiet and measured, nothing to alarm the hotel receptionist, but indignant and aggrieved, and she was asserting that she wasn't here now to justify last night or explain anything, or be judged, it was her life, something she enjoyed and she was in control of, that placed her at its centre, and she didn't care what he thought, there'd been nothing he could get offended about - she certainly hadn't planned to re-start anything with him if that was what he was thinking, not that there'd been anything to re-start with him, if she looked back at it even for a second… which she hadn't, and given his past history, his impulse to drift along, how could he possibly think… that she might… that he could dare presume… after all this time…

"You were convenient," she said at last, looking him in the eye.

"I'm a convenience - a public convenience," he said, wincing as he did so. The man who always had to try and be funny.

She glared at him. "You left the party early," she said, "and I don't know what you're going to do… I'm worried… worrying whether you'll do something… say something… talk to someone."

Now he became indignant. "I won't tell anybody about whatever last night was, give the game away - thanks for the accusation," he said. "I won't use last night against you, why would I? It's not my business.

"It's your concern. Not mine. There's one thing I'll say. You asked me to go with you. I did. Why I went, I don't know.

"But it's gone and forgotten. Right now for reasons that suit me, reasons that won't harm you, I want to do you a favour - so you'll do a favour for me.

"I want to give you a story - but only if you'll take it, if you don't mind. An exclusive, a big one. No strings attached.

"It's a free gift - and of course, yes, it benefits me. But it benefits you more. So everyone's a winner. And I'll never ask for anything else. Can I explain?"

There was another pause, shorter this time, before she nodded, looking suspicious. He carried on. "There's one thing you need to do to set this deal in motion, a little step I'll ask you to take - nothing difficult, nothing unpleasant. A negotiation you need to do, a wee newspaper trade-off - to make sure that you beat somebody else to the story.

"Because a guy at the *Bugle* on Sunday has got the story already, he's planning to publish next Sunday - Colin Scoular, you'll know him. You're Scottish journalism's No1 networker, he'll be easy to deal with.

"How many favours will he owe you already? Dozens. There'll be another story you can feed him later, no problem.

"My problem is that Colin Scoular will write the story in the standard nasty tabloid shotgun splatter way... and if he does that, it'll hurt somebody - not me - somebody who doesn't deserve to be hurt. So to prevent that, I'll give you the real story, in full.

"Quotes, exclusive photos, the whole lot. A good story. The best story. And I'll write it. You did tell me I can write, I should write - so I will. No work for you.

"When you get what I write, do what you like with it - prune the usual Moscardini hearts and flowers - but please don't go all shock-horror with it. There's no need. You'll see when you read it.

It could win you a Press Award, you never know."

"And this story is…?" asked Rachel. They sat down on the sofa, side by side, and he explained. Named names.

Donated the showbiz scoop of the dacade. Scottish television's longest-running world-famous cop show, its gay stars, the most famous of whom had kept his best screen performance till last.

He observed her shift into hawk-eyed professional mode. Keen, dispassionate, focused, noting all the angles.

"I'll email it to you tomorrow - all of it," he said. "For you, I'm breaking my most solemn pledge…" He detected her shift in her seat, edging away, watching him, frowning.

"My solemn pledge never to write another bloody word. I'll give you the raw material, it'll take you about 20 minutes to finish the job - add byline, light blue touch paper, stand back."

He dug inside his jacket's pockets, finding a business card to hand over. He'd had 10,000 of the things printed a week or so before his *Chronicle* exit, a time when he half-figured he might need to earn a living as a freelance journalist. He had at least 9,990-odd left.

The cards had proved useless for his photography business, one side featuring a monochrome snap of a vintage typewriter with a trilby next to it, a card reading "Press" tucked into its band.

On the reverse, his name, his contact details, his proud motto: Business Is My Trouble. At least that still held good, he supposed.

"If you email me back straight away, now, I'll take that as us shaking hands on this deal," he went on. Rachel took his card, took out her mobile phone, pecked the screen with her fingers. Moments later, his phone pinged. "Colin Scoular's sorted," her email read. He knew it.

He had taken care of business and deflected trouble. Had he won with kindness? Or because he was a pragmatic fixer keener on keeping *Bullitt da Colonia* taint-free than on protecting Larry's memory and Frank's happiness?

He didn't know. It didn't matter. He closed the book on other questions he would never ask. Why had Rachel wanted him there last night? Did she believe she retained a hold over him?

Had he betrayed a lingering interest in her? Was he meant to be an agonised spectator? Was he meant to join in?

His questions remained unasked because Rachel relaxed and began volunteering answers.

The real reason he'd been asked along, she said, was because it was something her husband enjoyed: seeing her arrive with another man but going home with him at the end of the night. Her husband was waiting outside now: "We're happy together - with our shared…"

"Pastime?" Tony suggested. "Everyone should have a hobby." As he said the words, he feared she might smile. He'd made her smile a lot back then. He didn't want a fresh pall of friendship to descend. She didn't smile. The relief.

He knew what he had to say to finish things between him and her, whatever they might have been. He'd worked it out. A one-liner. A joke that had a point, that he'd sharpened. A tiny dart of truth, tarted-up, made memorable.

He knew he should deliver it without showbiz sparkle, no risk of making her laugh. Yet he was the Comedian.

Throw-away delivery is best, he reminded himself. So he didn't look at Rachel. He didn't elaborate. He kept it simple. Timing. To confirm the end of it all, he stood and said: "No hard feelings from me." And walked out.

****

Getting Susan to answer her front door at 6.50am on a Sunday was less easy than she'd assured him it would be. He kept ringing the bell.

When she opened the door at last, her face was puffy with tiredness. She was wearing a track suit.

"If only you'd opened the door in your dressing gown," he said, "I could have done a joke about you having a door in your dressing gown - best you didn't give me the chance."

She forced a smile. "Don't forget the prescriptions," she said, pointing at the plastic bag on the hallway floor and retreating into the kitchen. "That fourpenny rag you won't buy is in there as well - as demanded by Glasgow scandal addicts."

The Grubber. He tutted and thanked her for her thoughtfulness.

"You've got time for a coffee," she said, disappearing into the kitchen, "so sit down... but don't hang about if you want to catch your plane and be back for the film premiere."

"There's three hours before the plane, I'll be fine," he said, seating himself on her sofa, "and if I go too soon, you'll miss my hot gossip."

He recalled an old movie effect, a blurry newspaper rotating in a swirl towards the cinema audience, slowing to reveal a sensational headline: Ageing Ex-Hack Stuns Former Sister-in-Law With Tell-All Nude Sex Dungeon Confession Shocker.

He spent a second wondering how to describe his peculiar Saturday night-out ("Went to a sex dungeon - up a flight of stairs. First floor sex dungeon! Only in Glasgow, eh? I got invited by an ex-kinda-girlfriend from years ago. Nothing happened... well, lots happened - it was a sex dungeon. But nothing that included me").

Bad idea. Instead, he explained the film premiere's latest problems: "Thought we'd have to call it off, all sorts of stuff inside the past 24 hours. A possible legal embargo. Then a potential tabloid gay sex scandal. I mean, as tabloid gay sex scandals go, it's not much of a tabloid gay sex scandal - "

Susan reappeared. "Stop saying tabloid gay sex scandal," she said. "Explain!"

When he'd finished, Susan was - possibly for the first time in her life - unable to speak. *"Lochhead!?"* she said at last. *"That Lochhead!? Him? Lochhead!?* A gay TV icon - made in Scotland? Since 1980?

"Wow. *Lochhead!* Up there in TV history. Beside *Cagney and Lacey, Starsky and Hutch* - I mean, it's still rubbish. But's it's groundbreaking gay rubbish... pioneering gay Scottish rubbish - it's *our* rubbish."

Having decided against telling Susan about his trip to a sex dungeon, he'd needed to mask the identity of the journalist ("An old workmate") who'd averted the tabloid threat to a grieving widower and to their film.

Susan had been especially pleased to learn that McCrindle had failed to do the same job ("What have I always said about that useless eejit"). Her final statement was unequivocal: "Go and catch that plane now, dumbo."

****

His first task on arrival in Pisa was composing a text message to tell Gabriella he was back. Easy. A few simple words. Barely a dozen of the darn things.

It hardly counted as writing, he told himself, the damnable occupation to which he'd return soon enough, tomorrow, trashing his principles to write the full story of *Bullitt da Colonia* and Larry McMillan's stately performance, the hidden true story of Larry and Frank and the unknown Scottish TV gay landmark, *Lochhead!*

So why was it taking him so long, seated in his idling Merc in Pisa airport's car park, wasting precious time peering at his mobile phone, pondering what precise interpretation might be put on whatever he was about to write.

"I'm back" was how he began. Obvious. But then he kept fighting the urge to add "Ti amo." And so he became trapped when he should be driving, forever looking at his watch, fretting, time-pressured, failing to assemble his tiny word-pile.

Because if he said he loved her, typed it, did such a teenage-style declaration make him look needy, oblivious, stupid? Did it make him look pitiful, thus confirming he was worthy of being given the news that it was all over between them.

Sure, Gabriella had texted the exact same phrase to him only the day before... but, well... in his experience, women could say one thing when what they meant was the exact opposite. Women, men, miscommunication between the genders - life's most enduring mystery... He urged himself to write.

He glanced at his watch for the thousandth time in the 20 minutes since his plane had touched down. It was 3.10pm, around an hour's drive to Colonia, film screening at 7.30pm.

Before that, a meeting with Frank to reassure him that Tony would handle the Scottish tabloid press on his behalf... assuming that his Colonia lieutenants had already calmed Frank down, but what if... what if...

He typed "Ti amo," but then added "my most beautiful blossoming *bocca di leone!*" which was plainly a preposterous comic flourish, a lightening touch: to compare his beloved to a snapdragon, the flower that the Italians styled the mouth of a lion.

But not such a preposterous declaration that it would undercut the seriousness, the essential truth of his avowal of love. Or so he hoped.

His finger hovered over the "send" arrow on his phone's screen… it was time to drive, drive with all speed, yet still he sat immobile…

One final addition. He appended "on the blessed soil of mother Italy" to his initial announcement of his return. Ridiculous! There. Press. Sent. Gabriella would at least be able to jettison him with a smile on her face, knowing he was a man of insufficient gravity for her long-term needs, a joker.

Chapter 25

He was still in the act of closing his apartment's front door behind him when his arm met unexpected resistance. Some force was pushing him off balance as he shrugged the laden backpack from his shoulder while also trying to avoid dropping his carrier bag of medications.

He stumbled a couple of paces. Gabriella stepped into the hallway, closing the door.

She's dumping me in person, he thought. Conducting the necessary process with due formality. In what he took as confirmation, she gave a curt nod, holding tight to the strap of the leather attaché case looped over her shoulder, as though about to oversee a property viewing.

Her smile seemed thin. Official.

"This won't take long because I know you'll be here only for a few minutes, that you must rush to Frank's house to meet Ken," she said, slightly breathless, perhaps apologetic, "so I am here to say that I will see you tonight properly at *il Sagre* - and that I have something else to tell you. Something important. News."

Lingering on his apartment's threshold, she looked down now, staring at the floor, one foot tracing the shape of its grubby old ceramic tiles with dainty precision.

"I will always hate these damned floor tiles," she said. "There is vintage old which looks good - and there is old, worn-out, fit for disposal. These tiles are old beyond purpose."

Just like me, he thought.

"Cracked. Ingrained with dirt. Awful. *Finito*. They must be replaced."

Don't spare me, he told himself. Once I'm consigned to the spoil-heap of romantic history, these grubby worn-out old honeycomb tiles are no longer your concern, Signorina Sarti. Same as grubby worn-out old me. *Sono finito.*

"I will change these tiles," she continued. "I will have them changed. There are many modern tiles to choose from. Better colours. A warmer feeling to the entrance area. Updated. More welcoming."

Professional small talk. She was sugar-coating his demise. She'd be feeling bad about binning him. He predicted her next statement, imagined her telling him he was a nice guy - he wasn't the problem, it was her.

She would mean it, too. This is what happens when you encourage a decent honest straightforward woman to fall in love with you: universal suffering.

What she actually said next was much less dramatic. "I can get the man from Barga Ceramica here on Tuesday, I think - he owes me a favour."

Here it comes, he thought: the big kiss-off, the short goodbye. She ceased inspecting his floor, looking up.

Her eyes grew large and locked on his. "I am pregnant," she said.

He became conscious of the tinnitus white-noise fizzing and whining in his ears, an industrial injury from decades of gig-going.

He was aware of little else, save that his mouth gaped open. He tried to be subtle in closing it.

Tried not to gulp so loud that she'd hear him. And failed. He drew air in through his nostrils and there was a terrible catarrhal snuffling whistle. His opened his mouth again.

No words emerged, only another noise - embarrassing, part-way between a cough, a sob and a stutter. A sound not unlike one of the Botti brothers' Bees trying and failing to fire up its puny engine.

He was relieved that she was looking down at the floor again, unaware of this gasping, choking, croaking old fish plucked from a river, floundering before her on the riverbank of human life, an ancient creature overwhelmed and overturned and beached by the flow of everyday nature; a primitive thing opening and closing its clueless fearful mouth, blinking blindly into the sunshine.

And in that moment when he realised he had no idea what to think or say about what she had just told him, he was surprised to hear himself begin speaking in a voice that sounded wise and calm. A voice that wasn't tense and stilted, shaking and ragged with the flood of emotions that he actually felt.

"News... truly, definitely this *is* news - good news - unexpected and surprising news... very good news, for me," he heard his better, truer self say.

"This is the best news I have ever heard, and I am very, very happy to hear it - but how I feel is of no importance, none at all.

"Because this news is about you, and how you feel about it, and if for you this news is not good news, or not the best news you've ever had, then please let me tell you..." the voice said, and he felt himself smile and relax as the voice truly became his, "that the only thing that matters is you. Right now. Do you feel well?

"You look well. Very well. You look beautiful. Are you OK?"

Gabriella continued to look down, her mood impossible to gauge. As he spoke, she'd carried on tracing the black-grouted margin of one of his flat's hated six-sided floor-tiles with her extended foot.

For a moment the new sage-sounding, calm-seeming Tony wavered, almost giving way to his less certain, more diffident old self, but then he regrouped and began reassuring her that if she had perhaps made a decision not to continue along the path she was on, that they were both on… whether she felt she should consult a medical expert… visit a hospital, a clinic… consider some procedure, if she has formed the opinion that such a procedure is best… the proper route… she absolutely must - because whatever her decision is, he will support her.

Because she is right, whatever decision she makes is the correct one. His speech petered out.

Gabriella still said nothing, head still down. Her shoulders shook. She stopped making a pattern on the tile with her toe. She walked the five paces across the hall to him, looked up at him - and he saw she was laughing. Laughing so much that tears ran down her face.

"You idiot," she said, hugging him, still laughing, taking his left hand in both of her hands and using the back of it to dab the tears from her cheeks, kissing his fingers - and then she was smiling up at him, taking a step back, inspecting him as if for the first time, much amused by what she saw.

"The only procedure that will proceed is the natural one," she said. "The usual one which takes nine months - or around seven and a half months in this case. The baby - your baby, my baby… our baby.

"There can be no better outcome to anything than a baby. Our baby is what we will have."

She tapped the middle of his chest with her finger. Held it there. Firm and decisive. "What will happen will happen," she said, "so long as we just let it. Before then, we have a movie premiere to attend - our baby's first film!"

And at the words "our baby" his eyes filled with tears. Joy. Hope. A lump caught in his throat.

"Now I am a father," he succeeded in saying after a struggle, hoping his voice wouldn't flute and break, undoing his new calm and capable status, "I suppose I should get used to being cried on."

Our baby's film - the film! He gave a start. "I need to go and check on Frank... I know you and Ken and Prof will have won him over already." She nodded. Of course she had. They all had.

"But I need to go in person to explain to him how I am going to tell his story in a newspaper... I'll meet you outside the *immobiliare*, 7 o'clock," he continued, "and don't forget to bring our baby."

****

When Tony arrived at Frank Wylie's little house, in a lane behind the duomo, it was Ken who greeted him. Frank was in the kitchen making cups of tea, allowing Ken to whisper that no injurious afternoon gin had been imbibed to bolster their host with either misplaced grievance or false confidence.

Just as importantly, four months after Larry's death, Frank had finally watched *Bullitt da Colonia*, supported by Ken, Prof and Gabriella.

"Dream audience," said Ken, "Floods of tears from the off - cathartic blubbing from all parties." His summary was perfectly timed, prompting a smile from Frank as he barged back into the living room, his giant street-fighter's fists holding a mug-laden tray.

"I'm glad you sat me down to watch your film... I'd been dreading it - and that's no' meant as an insult, by the way," Frank said, surprising Tony with how non-actorly and hard-ticket

Glaswegian his accent was.

"Larry looks fantastic, the film looks fantastic. Gripping from start to finish, a great wee movie - such a relief. Sorry I made a stupid fuss."

Frank looked embarrassed, shifting uneasily as he stood over the flimsy card-table on which he'd placed the tray, the smallness of the room emphasising his bulk.

Despite Frank being in his early seventies, he was still a muscular big guy, with the manner of a burly Glasgow workman. Tony felt extra sorry for him as he shuffled from foot to foot, an Oliver Hardy figure undone by his own foolishness.

"I was daft with all the lawyer stuff," Frank said. "I'm proud of Larry's work for you, and I know he was proud of it, too. He was grateful you were so kind to him those two or three days, considerate, helpful - you went out of your way to make it easy for him to do his best, and I thank you for it.

"Thing is, I was frightened folk would use the film to make fun of the two of us, a stick to beat me and Larry with… 'Yon two old bum-boys from that terrible *Lochhead!* show - no wonder it was always crap, Larry McMillan and Frank Wylie used up all their acting to kid us on they weren't boyfriends!' Folk like to think stuff like that.

"But the film's so good. I'm not one for being soft the way folk think actors are - but I can tell you, Larry was my personal action man Steve McQueen, and now everybody else'll have to agree when they see him driving a Bee, chasing yon Botti twins."

Frank smiled again, blushing, starting to laugh when Ken asked him to stop radiating such pride and happiness, it was making him and Tony feel sick, a bit jealous.

On top of that, Ken went on, Frank's retired lawyer brother had seen the film and he'd loved it, too, saying the only legal damned thing he'd ever sign his name to concerning *Bullitt da Colonia* would be some sort of affidavit having Frank, fool that he was, committed to a mental institution if he didn't do everything in his power to help promote the film and thus help more folk notice Larry's status as a real actor.

Frank had likewise become convinced that worldwide TV audiences for *Lochhead!* could only increase once more folk knew about the real-life love between its two male leads.

"Imagine it - a big lump like me, some kinda pin-up boy," said Frank. "At my age! Romeo Wylie - in the story of Romeo And Romeo!"

"Ach, if me and Larry's story can add something that increases folks' enjoyment of the show, it'll maybe stop folk looking down their noses at *Lochhead!*, stop them sniggering about it.

"We weren't doing Shakespeare, we knew that, but we always did the best we could. On top of that, it was a Glasgow show that helped two Glasgow boys make something of themselves, me and Larry.

"Neither of us came from theatre backgrounds - apart from the annual trip to the panto. No advantages. We came from nothing - Larry started out from less than nothing compared to me.

"Larry starts off as Lorenzo - Lorenzo Collodi, this camp wee Italian-sounding boy in Glasgow, picked on because he was different. Just him and his mother when his dad died, in the forties straight after the war.

"He told me he'd been bullied at school so he fought the bullies back, punched the worst bully, split his lip - and the bully's mum complains! Larry's mum gets called in to see the headmaster about her violent son.

"Larry's mum's Italian, of course, an immigrant, only in Scotland 10 years. When the headmaster hears her accent, the old bastard makes fun of it - he-a speak-a slow, makes Larry's mum's sound like a half-wit.

"Larry's sitting there, listening to this, a wee boy, the wee Eye-Tie sissy-boy they've called him, he's watching the headmaster make a fool of his mum so Larry stands up and shouts 'Don't you make fun of my mother!' and launches himself across the desk.

"His poor mum's mortified, she doesn't know what's going on - but she knows she has to grab a hold of Larry bloody quick and drag him off, take him home.

"New school for Lorenzo Collodi... he's expelled. Larry's mum skelped his arse. But nobody ever called him a wee Eye-Tie sissy-boy again.

"Larry said that was how his acting career started - make yourself bigger and braver than you are, be brave when you don't feel it or look it. Play at it well enough and you'll convince everybody.

"So I'll be out in front of everybody in Colonia tonight, standing up and introducing this great film starring Larry, the love of my life - and I'll say that out loud in my best Glasgow Italian.

"The two of us were years hiding things, denying who we were. It takes guts and bravery to admit you are who you are - I owe it to Larry to be as brave as he was and tell the truth.

"And I trust you, Tony, to write it all down, and not get it back to front. Put it in the papers - I trust you the same way Larry trusted you when he was doing your film."

Everything was working out the way it should.

Another thing remained for Tony to do: share the good news of his forthcoming fatherhood with Ken. He hadn't cleared the formal announcement with Gabriella, but it would be public knowledge soon enough - and Signor Moody was his closest Colonia chum, after all. She would hardly object to him telling Ken...

"I've got good news - the best news a guy can have," he said.

"Gabriella and I are going to be parents... she's pregnant. Me, a father! At my advanced age. Who would have - ..."

He halted mid-sentence, puzzled by an odd expression on Ken's face. Embarrassed. The man knew how to manufacture on-screen fiction but he couldn't pretend to look surprised by what Tony was telling him.

"You knew Gabriella was pregnant already, didn't you?" said Tony. "She told you before she told me? I suppose I could get annoyed, but..."

Ken blushed. "It wasn't just me," he said. "She told Prof as well... and his wife. And four old women from Lucca stood waiting for a bus outside the Co-Op... no more than half the residents of the Serchio valley in total - you know I'm joking, don't you?

"She told me first because she wanted to know the best way to tell you - she wasn't sure how you'd take it. She wasn't worried you'd run away...maybe she wanted you to run away. She was just... concerned. She wanted to find the right words.

" 'Tell him straight and he'll be delighted,' I said, 'although it'll be him struggling to find the right words - he'll stand there opening and closing his gormless mouth like a fresh-caught trout.' Dare to say different, you big galoot."

He smiled. No wonder Gabriella had laughed at him when she told him he was going to be a dad. Moscardini, baby octopus; gaping fish out of water.

Chapter 26

As Colonia's streets started softening as the evening sky darkened, so the level of animated chatter rose. A buzz and thrum of eager anticipation propelling festival-goers to *Il Sagra del Pesce e Patate*'s opening events. As Tony stood and waited outside Gabriella's office in Via Pascoli, he hoped every one of them was en route to Via Roma for the movie premiere.

He supposed he should worry about the audience reception to *Bullitt da Colonia*. They would either like it or they wouldn't. As a film auteur, he would accept it and move on.

He was a father now, so life offered more important considerations. As a father... speaking as a father... as a father myself... He turned the phrases over, trying them on for size and taking pleasure in their fit.

Gabriella emerged into the street in a cream-coloured linen floral summer dress that he was sure must be new, form-fitting and low-cut, the cream overlain with a bold pattern of red and yellow roses, large red buttons in a row all the way down the left-hand side.

The dress bared her shoulders. Wow, he thought. How tanned she was... how gorgeous, advancing towards him, smiling, full-lipped, dark and sultry, steering him down Via Pascoli with a light push on his upper arm and a pointed finger, imperious, unstoppable...

A real woman. A movie star. Giovanna Ralli in *40C Under the Sheets!*

They were walking towards the old oak, Gabriella stepping on the uneven street surface with care in very un-businesslike red espadrilles. Very attractive. Such very taut and shapely sun-bronzed legs. Ever more attractive.

He composed himself. He had less enticing everyday matters to address. A delicate topic to broach. His behaviour of late. Had she noticed he was somehow different? Less than present?

"If I've seemed odd over the past few weeks - odder than usual… if I've seemed preoccupied, looked worried… if I've played the funny guy more than usual, worse than usual - it was a defensive thing, a way of coping, I always have to try and be funny…"

"You do amuse me," she said gravely and without the slightest hint of a smile, "sometimes on purpose." Then she smiled. Almost laughed.

He explained his worries. He'd grown convinced she was going to ditch him either because she'd tired of him, or he wasn't good enough - she was definitely embarrassed about being seen with him in Colonia…

"When you wear your shorts and those teenage boy's trainers, like a Scotsman in summer, then yes, of course I am embarrassed to be seen with you on Colonia's streets - but that is your style," she said, shrugging and rolling her eyes, "and I will change it eventually, and turn you into a proper Italian man.

"Or maybe I won't… proper Italian men take themselves too seriously, they are in love with the way they look. They don't try to be funny, and no Italian man will ever… will ever…"

She laughed so much, she choked trying to finish her sentence: "No Italian man ever dressed up in clothes that made him look like a teenage clown."

Tony laughed, too, but stressed that while he might be a teenage clown, he had serious grown-up points to make and he hoped she listened to them.

He was many years older than Gabriella, he explained, and so he must warn her that before long he would become a venerable liability, a drain, a weight... withered with age, stooped and wrinkled - he would become a health-care burden. More like a grandfather than a father.

And she would obviously want him to help her raise their child, but children are things of which he has no knowledge, no prior experience - plus in only 10 years time, no sooner has she finished caring for a child than she will need to tend a man in his second childhood, entering his dotage, in terminal decline - and...

She gave him a severe and pitying look. "I will overlook the fact that you have no idea how old I am," she said, "which is possibly some kind of compliment - and I will confirm you are definitely an old man now - an *annoying old* man... but you are the least annoying old man I know.

"Better than that, you are a good old man. A kind old man, a man who is thoughtful about others - your friends, your neighbours, all the old Scottish *Coloniesi* who depend upon you - and I know you will share the work of raising our child."

"Because I will kill you if you don't. And as you die, you will thank me for it - for ending the suffering I will heap upon you if you fail to help me with the baby."

"But before all that, I have a confession. It concerns all the furniture in your apartment, the brownest, biggest and most ugly furniture anyone could ruin a home with. That you somehow put up with and overlooked.

"While you were away, I had it emptied and removed from Via di Mezzo, so if any of those terrible brown wooden boxes had some form of sentimental meaning for you... well, that's a shame because some of it has been given to a charity - a charity that punishes poor people by imposing ugly wardrobes on them. Teaches them to work hard at school so they don't become poor.

"And if I tell you that some of the biggest terrible furniture needed to be dismantled to get it out... well, that would be a lie. The big things that were an offence against good taste? Chopped up with axes... why are you laughing, Signor Moscardini?

"It was a serious and painful process that took four men two full days. They complained to me there were three trips each day, and skinned knuckles, blood spilt and strained backs, holes gouged in the plaster on the hall stairway that they had to repair. I will be repaying favours to them for years! On your behalf!

"Soon I will choose bright modern new furniture from the Ikea in Lucca. Because your apartment will need to be rented out, it will achieve a good monthly income as a tourist property, and no one would have been attracted to it with all its dead wood furniture - not even a Scotsman who dresses like a teenager."

Tony was puzzled, and tried to hide it. Not for the first time, he failed.

"Ah, the famous look on your face," she said, "like a trout caught in the Serchio, gaping and gasping on the river's bank until it can breathe no more."

Gabriella was in charge. Practical. Pragmatic. Certain. His possessions were leaving Colonia. Him, too. To go where?

Her full and wondrous lips were forming many words. He could hear them. Hypnotic lips. Enchanting sounds.

He was unsure exactly what much of it signified. All he knew was that she was providing succour and salvation, sensuality and... He told himself to snap out of it.

What was she actually telling him? Her accommodation has been reconfigured - one less room for paying *agriturismo* guests

- and soon he is to reside 200 metres or so higher up in the *Apennini*, out of Colonia.

In a place that made sleepy Colonia look like Manhattan - Faggio Basso. With her.

He heard her tell him this. He marvelled again. He guessed raising a child would keep him busy, occupied in mind and body. She continued telling him what was going to happen.

He need not move into his new room straight away, she was saying. He can begin by sharing her house, her room, although she suspects he snores, and this will keep the baby awake at night in the bedroom, not to mention keep her awake. But such small details will shape themselves into whatever might be their fated resolution at some stage in the future, no sense worrying about it today.

What is plain to her, and what truly matters in her opinion, is that he will not be able to walk back and forth cradling a crying baby in his arms in the middle of the night in Faggio Basso if he's living down in Colonia for the next few months... the next few years.

Because having raised one child without a father, she doesn't plan to do the same thing with the second. Genuine fatherhood is about being there for your child.

He hoped he wasn't standing with his mouth gaping open, as was the norm. She had outlined what was going to happen to him. He was moving in with her... he was being moved in by her.

He nodded. He smiled. He was becoming part of a new Sarti-Moscardini family, a dynasty with living local roots here in Toscana... He had a role, a part to play, a place, a path ahead.

All of this sank in at once, literally and instantly, with each step the pair of them took hand in hand along Via Pascoli's thousand-year-old pavement. He absorbed her words as he trod in the very same indentations formed in Colonia's ancient setts by the footfalls of residents long deceased.

Streets that had been worn down just a little by so many footsteps, year after year, century after century, as the living and the dead merged and persisted in shapes impressed into unyielding granite by the fleeting form of humanity - a miracle. Conquered by love's softness. He looked down at the street.

People had preceded him here, as he was now following them, in the same way that he in turn was preceding those yet to come. Their mark had been left, as his now would.

How many expectant fathers had walked this same street before him feeling the same emotions, pride and fear and joy and rejoicing and overwhelming love and a sense of having arrived home, he wondered.

Forebears. Ancestors. Successors. One generation after another. He understood now that his child had worked the miracle of enrolling him in human history's unending parade.

Late in his 56 years. He had shared his love with Gabriella to begin another life, which meant that as a parent he himself had no end. The triumph of procreation.

She had finished speaking. He smiled at her. She smiled at him. She continued holding his hand in hers. He looked into her eyes. She looked into his. They walked on towards the old oak through an empty Via Pascoli.

If ever Colonia creates the post of town philosopher, he thought, then he was a contender for the job. For now he is forever a part of Colonia. Some element of Hugh Antonio Moscardini will persist in walking the streets of Colonia for as long as there are people.

But he could not form these thoughts into speech. They were such big ideas, and so formless, they floated inside his mind and rendered him mute.

Instead, after a while, he began to prattle about the little things, the things that don't truly matter, but at least he could find words to voice them: his practical worries, his fears, his complaints.

Even as he said them, he was conscious of sounding petty and self-obsessed, unaware, complaining, irksome, like a persistent whining insect. How will Gabriella's brother and his wife react to him arriving to live beside them in Faggio Basso?

Badly for sure. Will they be angry with him? Hostile? Wary? Unwelcoming? Will they feel suspicious - a leech, a gold-digger?

And as for Gabriella's adult son, how will he view Tony? As a sudden belated interloper, a threat to be resented - any son would rightly be suspicious of a new male rival for his mother's affections, a paternal usurper, an old cuckoo pushing him out of the nest, stealing his mother's affections, reducing his inheritance.

She let go of his hand to fuss with some detail of her dress, falling behind him in the deserted street. There was a distant sound of music from their destination on the *centro storico's* eastern fringe, the festival movie crowd gathered in Via Roma.

He was glad no one else was in sight to judge him for inflicting his dreary complaints on Gabriella. He had to warn her against his many flaws.

When he arrives in Faggio Basso, he went on, she alone will become aware of his multiple failings.

She had fallen even further behind him, her voice sounding more distant, muted. "There are many natural splendours for you to photograph in Faggio Basso," she was saying, "things your eye can feast upon… which go unseen by most people."

An odd statement but doubtless true, he thought, surprised to hear it, slowing to let her catch up with him. He continued his litany of personal concerns - so tiresome, he was even boring himself - an elderly fool chuntering on.

Now at the last minute, he stated, he had a new worry, over whether the movie-making effort had been in vain. What if no one tonight appreciated *Bullitt da Colonia*, saw it as the home-movie folly of three deluded old men, its public display disappointing a whole town?

And that reminded him: after the film-making, he had lately begun awakening some mornings with pains in this knee or that, a sure sign he was past his peak, which had been years ago, and what else was sure to go wrong with him…

"Just don't have a heart attack," he heard her say in a low, soft, warm tone some way behind him. He turned, and she was standing in the most deeply-recessed doorway of any shop in Via Pascoli: Salumeria Tancredi.

His eye registered the delicatessen's century-old gold lettering above its shopfront, and as he processed that detail of the image now framed for him, he reproached himself - *Idiota!* - for his stupidity in focusing on such a thing when in that still and very perfect moment his eyes and every other sense should be arrested by something infinitely more remarkable.

Gabriella had framed herself in the shop doorway with her dress unbuttoned, drawn back from her shoulders, with her hands formed into fists on her hips. There she was before him: care-free, rapturous, glorious Gabriella, baring herself to him alone - naked.

She angled her head up and a little to one side, quizzical, like a scolding schoolmistress, the tiny suggestion of a sulky pout on her lips. A small smile, too.

It was a coy pose which seemed to confirm that the notion of coy was a ridiculous one in a love as strong and practical as theirs. Frank showgirl. Blushing bride. Teasing him a little; promising him everything.

He knew that he would remember her standing like this for him until his deathbed's last seconds.

For a fleeting moment he felt the old base male impulse, that crude imperative to judge, weigh, catalogue and evaluate a female form's fleshly components. As if women existed solely as a visual stimulus for their masculine onlooker. As if Gabriella's sole worth was as a gauge of his desire, an incitement to his pleasure.

Such nonsense. And he knew that he had at last found the only place he'd ever known he had to be, and that was on his knees before Gabriella. A supplicant. A worshipper. He walked back to her, his eyes locked on hers.

He knelt at her feet, placed his forehead on her stomach, his hands on her hips and kissed her navel, and he felt like crying, and at no time in his life had he ever been so happy.

Time passed. The world continued to turn. He could maintain this pose forever, although he was becoming conscious that some passer-by could yet chance upon them. He became aware of her growing restless and drawing circles with her fingers on his closely-shaven scalp.

"Don't have a heart attack, baldy," she ordered again, laughing and fending off his hands as he began caressing her abdomen ever lower, moving southwards...

She shrugged from his grasp and drew her skirt closed with a comic finality, smiling, saying *Allora* - time to go," back to being disciplined professional business owner Signora Sarti once again.

If he had been stunned by her announcement of her pregnancy, he was exhilarated, buoyed and - of course, what else, he was a man - aroused by this sudden frank public declaration of desire.

A heart attack? It was possible, he guessed. A man of his age, excited by a younger woman. Should he tell her it was more likely he'd explode in a fatal outbreak of priapism?

Or maybe this was another chance to try and be funny... He

groaned and rose to his feet slowly clutching his chest, staggering slightly.

Worry clouded Gabriella's face as she re-buttoned her dress tight across her body. He grinned before his supposed joke became too cruel.

"My comedy wears thin - your beauty never will," he said. She punched his upper arm.

"*Madama padrona di casa*," he murmured, embracing her again: "I am your tenant for as long as you want me. Shall we discuss terms?"

She drew back, giving him a sceptical look. "You've already made a down-payment on your new accommodation," she said, stroking her stomach, "one I can't refund."

****

They set off together holding hands. For everyone in Colonia to see. Everyone in the milling throng outside Bar Nasone, talking and gesticulating - being loud and expansive and Italian - in the warm evening air. The whole town, gathered around *il quercione*, shading themselves from the setting sun beneath the giant oak's still green leaves. All ages. All backgrounds.

He spotted the town's sole beggar, accompanied by two under-sized grime-streaked children. The beggar's siblings? Or, as some Coloniesi whispered, her incestuous offspring? Rumours: always malicious.

A stooped elderly woman, hobbled by arthritis, stepped from a nearby house carrying a tray bearing three soft-drinks cans and a plate of pizza slices. She offered them to the raggedy trio, smiling at the eagerness with which the food and drink were snatched, waving off thanks.

Too-sleepy Colonia was more enjoyable than overly-exciting Glasgow, he now knew. He realised, too, that the nearer he and Gabriella got to the crowd, the less time he had to tell her some things he could no longer prevent himself saying: the promise he'd broken in Glasgow.

He stopped walking and turned to face her, taking her hands in his.

He babbled, assuring her of his love; of his devotion as a father-to-be, his eagerness to master every paternal skill.

Obviously, he would teach their child everything that he had learnt in life, in as much as he'd learnt anything. Whatever wisdom he had accrued, he would pass on.

He would teach their child how to be a good person. How to reason. How to question, to share. He would be their child's educator in every respect - almost every respect.

"I'll teach our child to add up, subtract, read... but as for writing, I won't pass that skill on - I can't, typing is the route to misery, to madness itself." Gabriella was looking at him sternly but with kindness. A woman's look which tells a man he's a self-centred, self-dramatising idiot.

"When I left Glasgow, I left writing behind - I vowed never to write again," he went on. "And then I go back and I break my life's one pledge - I betray myself by having to write for a newspaper.

"Yes, it's in a good cause, about Larry and and Frank and the film... but... now let me reassure you, Signorina Sarti, that my single broken pledge about writing is the last promise I will ever fail to keep, because I'm making you another promise, one I shall never break, or bend or wriggle out of under any convenient circumstance. I vow I am yours forever."

"*Sa idiota*," Gabriella said.

He had prattled on, waving his arms, growing more effusive,

more Italian, more like every other man under the oak tree, more a part of the town's scenery. She smiled. Were there tears in her eyes?

She hugged him close, burying her head in his chest. He held her tight, enfolding her in his arms, looking down at the word baked in white paint on the tarmac at Via Roma's crossroads: *Rallentare* - Slow Down.

An urgent order, Tony thought each time he braked at the junction - instant action in safety's name - yet delivered via such a long, relaxed-looking four-syllable Italian word.

Less an imperative warning, more a sheet-music notation for pianists - *Rallentando:* a gradual reduction in tempo. *Rallentare.* You'd have crashed before you'd read it, Tony had always thought. So charming, so crazy. Only in Italy.

Life's path here might throw up unforeseen perils, but nothing bad enough to demand you move too quickly. Whatever was going to happen would happen anyway - no point making yourself look undignified or foolish by rushing in vain to avoid it.

He wondered whether Gabriella would think he was behaving like a fool, racing into a headlong vow of commitment that wouldn't last. If so, she'd have told him by now.

Even so, he hoped she wouldn't spot *Rallentare* written on the road at their feet. Possible danger ahead.

He had the strangest sudden sensation: time was standing still in Colonia and everyone on this spot occupied the one place in the universe where they were meant to be, where they could be nothing but the very best version of themselves, as imperfect as that might be.

Chapter 27

The sun faded. Tony felt himself flooded in forgiveness. He had been pardoned. He was embraced by a stable and companiable love.

He was holding hands with Gabriella in what hadn't been Pinocchio's birthplace. Nor had it been Romeo and Juliet's birthplace, nor any other fiction in any other fairytale romance.

But it was home to her clear-eyed love for him, and his for her. And somehow, too, it was a place ideal for creation, invention. How had Gabriella once described it? A perfectly-imperfect venue for fashioning nonsense for public entertainment.

Where unchangeable past and perfectly-imperfect present met and mingled, contributing to some unimaginable future. For better or worse, there was no controlling any of it.

Best not share such half-baked thoughts with Gabriella. She would declare them ridiculous. And she would not be incorrect. *Rallentare.*

Her warm hand in his, that was real, along with everyone around them. Faces swam into Tony's vision, resolved into people he knew.

Tony realised he knew almost every Colonia face. He could place them. Their stories were his. His, theirs.

There were the quiet folk whose humanity and generosity could not be contained within their homes, whose goodness flooded out into the street, who could not help but improve Colonia with their smiles, their well-tended flowers, their commitment to public tidiness.

There were the sour-faced souls who complained aloud about everyone, everything. Inconsiderate car-parkers alongside inveterate volunteers; Trojans, idlers, gamblers, saints, cheats, exemplars, tender ministrators.

Expansive optimists. The pursed-lipped and resentful. They all had a role. They belonged here. In the same way that Tony knew he did. It felt good to know he belonged, as flawed a mixture of good and bad as he was.

He saw Davide Pastori, neat in a blue velvet suit, for once not looking like he'd awoken two minutes previously in a rubbish dump, instead looking energised after having entertained the crowd for an hour with his quintet.

Sergio and Renzo Botti ambled by, nodding at Tony, smiling and looking calm. Neither twin was fighting the other - or not yet at least.

One marvel gave way to another. Dressed in civilian clothing, Gabriella's brother winked, going on to ball one of his meaty heavyweight prizefighter's fists, feinting this way and that before feigning a blow to Tony's chin.

Piero then slapped his new family member heartily on the back, wished him good luck and pretended with his right hand to twist the throttle of an invisible motorcycle on which he then roared away.

Next he spotted Ken and Prof, glasses of chianti in hand, looking flushed and exhilarated, further testament to what had united the town tonight beneath the impromptu bedsheet cinema screen set up on Bar Nasone's wrought-iron first-floor balcony.

Their world film premiere. Tension fluttered in his stomach. What if Colonia hated it? Ken and Prof were evidently unworried about the crowd's reaction, so…

And such a crowd. Unprecedented. Astounding. The whole town.

Old couples seated on benches, the women freed at last from everyday domestic slavery to join their men in public.

Younger folk lounged on the grass mound formed by the oak tree's roots. People had brought kitchen chairs. Whole families stood in conversation. Children played. Everything was a beautiful dream, but all of it real.

He stood and watched, a spectator like everyone else. He saw Frank ascend Bar Nasone's front-door verandah, beneath the balcony, to deliver his speech.

In his gruff Scots-hewn Italian, Frank spoke words of love and gratitude, thanking Colonia for having welcomed him and Larry, two more uncalled-for old men from Glasgow, prompting chuckles.

They had both loved the town. They had loved each other and were grateful that Colonia had never judged them for it.

Frank hoped Colonia would love seeing Larry in a work which spoke the international language of cinema. When Signors Moody, Bartolomei and Moscardini made their next film here, he hoped they had a role for him - although there was no way big Frank Wylie was squeezing inside a Bee.

Colonia laughed, applauded, fell hushed. In the darkening night, Bar Nasone's bedsheet projection screen became a rectangle of flickering illumination. Tony reminded himself the film was the festival's prelude, *antipasto* before *il primo*.

The menu's main dish was multi-generational ballroom dancing in the adjoining grounds of the football stadium, music again by the Davide Pastori Quintet. Early departures from the screening shouldn't worry him overmuch. Dancers needed to stake out their space on the floor.

Still, he felt it best to hang back on the crowd's rearmost margin, hidden, monitoring the audience's reaction more than watching the film. He held Gabriella's hand tighter. Stress was making him feel light-headed, distracted, about ready to float into the night sky, an untethered balloon.

Colonia fell silent, the crowd drawn to the screen's first movement, coming alive with colour. Every eye fixed on Larry's face, cool and magnificent, the driver at the wheel, sparking the action, evaluating his opposition: the Botti twins.

Sergio and Renzo were perennial figures of fun so of course their first appearance prompted a ripple of laughter. Tony tensed. This was not the best response to the opening seconds of a tense, dramatic car-chase sequence.

He fretted. He frowned. Was the film too slow? He saw it for the first time through others' eyes, sensing the crowd were unsure what was being asked of them, how they were supposed to react.

Such a relief when Davide Pastori's acoustic take on the *Twistin' Gears* theme provided the audience with direction. This was serious music for serious action. It was urgent, insistent. Watch carefully, it said.

The music might not possess the snarl of the big-screen original, but its home-spun jauntiness had an energy, forward momentum. The on-screen action gained an intensity to match it, picking up pace.

He studied the faces around him, turning as little as possible to avoid detection, torturing himself. Did Colonia's cinemagoers still appear perplexed? Could he discern an air of restlessness?

He wondered how many people watching *Bullitt da Colonia* were familiar with *Bullitt*, re-running in his head the debate he'd had with Ken and Prof: screening the original version first would have helped non-devotees engage with this new homage.

Then again, a million-dollar Hollywood studio epic, complete with orchestra, versus something by three hobbyists and their elderly cast? The real *Bullitt* could only ever have worked against them.

He continued to look at his fellow cinema-goers from the corner of an eye - they were concentrating on the screen. Every child sat open-mouthed, entranced. Gripped by the thrill of the chase. No one in the crowd was leaving early.

They liked it.

Time seemed dislocated. To him, it seemed each second flew past while also lasting an hour.

Finally, after 10 minutes and 43 seconds, the film reached its dust-shrouded, Bee-obliterating climax and there was such a roar, a deafening wall of applause and shouting. It was as if the audience were a single new-born creature with a single voice, formed from their enjoyment of *Bullitt da Colonia*.

When Gabriella had stopped hugging him - in public, a welcome development, most unforeseen - he began to register the smiling, clapping, eager crowd around him, although he could no longer pick out a single individual face.

Maybe this unity, this self-surrender, is what draws people to football, he mused. He'd never warmed to football like the rest of Glasgow. Never lost himself in anything.

What was that old saying - about a thing being more than the sum of its parts. He had joined in with the crowd tonight. A first. Perhaps he would start attending football games - but no football result could be this joyous.

But tonight's joy was surely fleeting. The crowd would always have cheered the film, even as they'd hated it - because they liked the folk who'd made it. It was politeness.

Everyone would be honest in saying what they truly thought about it - discreetly, formally - when they next met him in Zio Beppo. And that was fine - because everyone here tonight in Colonia was part of a family. Open. Honest. And family frankness was to be expected, to be encouraged.

What mattered was that somewhere, on some astral plane that he would love to believe existed, Lorenzo Collodi and Steve McQueen basked together in the spun-gold glow of their hair, sharing an aura of ineffable cool and calm.

Back in the here and now, just as the crowd's applause began to ebb, Davide Pastori marshalled his four sidekicks into a reprise of Twistin' Gears. Over there, the Botti twins stood together, alongside their two scarce-seen wives, all looking delighted.

He heard Sergio say *"Siamo stati una fonte d'ispirazione!"* to Renzo (it might have been the other way round, of course), and imagined the phrase subtitled in English for international consumption in some new monochrome film in which the Botti twins might star: "We have been an inspiration!"

Some Laurel and Hardy variant maybe, in which the pair would try - and fail in many hilarious ways - to carry a bulky parcel from one or other of their Bees up il duomo's long flight of stone steps, say. "We have been an inspiration!"

There were calls for someone to make a speech. He found himself ushered on to Bar Nasone's verandah by Ken and Prof. He heard himself thank the crowd, thank Larry for letting them show Colonia his brilliance. More cheers.

"Larry gave us a gift, and we have shared it," he said, prompting yet more cheers, cries of "Aye, aye!" mixed with "Si, si!".

Sure, he went on, the film's making had aroused - how to put it? - passions in Colonia. The crowd laughed, making him pause before he could ask them to agree that a little upset had proved worthwhile.

"Scots-Italian passion!" he continued. "United together, we turn tiny Bees into mighty Mustangs - we import San Francisco's streets to Toscana!" The oak tree's branches echoed with renewed cheering.

He stepped down and hugged Gabriella, half-whispering, half-purring in her ear, re-working the phrase she'd uttered so many months before during *Bullitt da Colonia's* making.

"The same tiny routine, the endless repetition of it, the satisfaction in doing it right, my secret stunt-driver stand-in Steve McQueen... so slow... let's enjoy doing the one damned little thing over and over again, mi amore," he murmured with comic heavy breathing, taking a punch to the ribs for his trouble.

Louder cheering and wolf-whistling reminded them they were being watched. A Scots-Italian voice shouted: "Get a room, you two - rent one from Sarti Immobiliare!"

Gabriella took a couple of paces back before drawing Tony in again and kissing him. Her face had reddened, but he'd never seen her looking so relaxed and happy.

Already, though, they were losing their audience, the crowd drifting off to the festival's first-night dance, following the siren lure of the Davide Pastori Quintet.

Old married couples would soon sway together on the dancefloor in the warm evening air *sotto le stelle*. Old men would dance with tiny squealing granddaughters, whirling them in the air. Wistful *nonnas* would grow minded of long-lost teenage dancing boys.

He smiled. Memories of the past. Anticipation of the future. Love. The things that make the world go round.

Up and down the town's streets, delighted children made revving-engine noises and fearlessly pursued one another in imaginary vehicles - some in humble Italian three-wheeler delivery vans, some in thunderous all-American muscle cars.

Carabiniere Piero had begun putting up police crime-scene tape, making a safe circuit for the child racers. Tony noticed the dour cop doing something he'd never seen him do before: he was looking happy - smiling in fact, baring big teeth, thick lips drawn back.

A smiling Carabiniere. Could any sight be more ominous? He would get used to it, he hoped, living in Faggio Basso.

Gabriella excused herself and went to speak to her staff. "I have news for them… affecting the business," she said.

"About our new family life, the future - remember I'm including you in it, so don't fuck up, maestro. And remember: we will not be living out a crazy car chase. Our new life will be a steady promenade."

As he watched her being swamped in her grinning workforce's hugs and shrieks, his old journalistic mantra flared up out of nowhere: what did he know now that once upon a time someone else might have preferred him not to know? That he himself might have avoided finding out?

What big secret had he found? What revelation?

It dawned on him: more by accident than diligent design he had created a new life - a new member of the human race… one who might easily - if he helped nurture that little person properly - make the world a better place after his aged father was gone. He would be taking part in a relay… handing on his adult knowledge to a new person, his child.

Prof and Ken approached, a glittery shine about their eyes, an unsteadiness to their walk. They had been drinking. Of course they had. The three of them embraced each other and jumped up and down in a madmens' dance that just avoided collapse.

Prof fixed Tony with a cross-eyed stare and grasped his hand. "At the same time that you have a new project... a fresh diversion... we... we... " he said, losing his train of thought.

Ken stepped in: "We have a new beginning, too!" He belched and fell silent.

"We start because we must," said Prof, growing ever more slurred. "We start therefore we are! Aren't we? Because we've decided Colonia needs a monument to its Scots-Italian forebears and their achievements in far-off lands.

"Maryhill, Ruchill, Govanhill - Partick in excelsis." He listed the names as if conducting a priestly rite before running out of steam, looking every bit as drunk as he truly was.

Ken took over. "Look to the hills of Toscana and see the potential..." he said, pointing upwards with such energetic vagueness into the stony peaks around Colonia that the effort sent him staggering sideways.

"A new landmark!" he went on, steadying himself. "A Scots-Italian tourist shrine, see it for miles!"

Prof composed himself. "This is thanks to you saying Larry's face should be carved into Mount Rushmore," he said.

Back came Ken: "We're going to do the same thing! Here! For our own folk! We've got mountains! The *Apennini Apuane*! We've got faces!

"Famous Scots... carved in granite, 18metres tall - the giants! Chic Murray, Billy Connolly, Francie'n'Josie - they count as one. And... Larry McMillan - *Lochhead!*"

Prof chipped in. "Wouldn't want to upset the locals, mind - we've done that once. Can't risk it again. Mustn't! The fuss! The stress! We'll carve Italy's greats an' all! Celentano!"

"Sophia Loren!"

"Totò!"

"The Botti Twins!"

Ken and Prof wheezed with laughter, a comedy double act. Batting words between them. Set-up, punchline. The feed. The lead. Which of them was which? It was hard to tell.

"Artistic vision, that's the thing," said Prof, "and depute the mechanics to your associates."

"Do you know any sculptors?"

"If Colonia's got the granite, Glasgow's got the chisel!"

"It's still in its planning stages, mind, because we've only been talking about it for... what? Fifteen minutes, after just the two bottles of the chianti, was it?"

"Another noble cause for us to waste our days with. We have proved we have the artistic vision, shown our ability to overcome all obstacles."

"We've made one film masterpiece - we don't need to make another. Do something different. What do you say?"

Before he could answer, the pair of them began laughing again, choking, coughing, bent double, clutching their knees. "Come on, let's away up the dancin'," Ken said, and away up the dancin' he and Prof went, arms round each other's shoulders, chuckling.

And as they tottered towards the football stadium, the two men's comedy partnership soared to fresh heights with the joyous chanting of assorted names, back and forth - a game of table tennis in words. Italian names, Scottish names. Scots-Italian names.

Some names were famous ones, sportsmen, artists, actors, writers, film-makers, musicians. Other names were familiar only to Ken and Prof.

Chip shop owners. Ice cream makers. Doctors. Lawyers. The Everyman Italian on the streets of the West of Scotland.

"Johnny Moscardini! Peter Capaldi! Armando Iannucci!"

"Eduardo Paolozzi! Richard Demarco! Aldo Tortolano!"

"Enrico Cocozza! Oscar Marzaroli! Tom Conti!"

"Lena Zavaroni! Carlo Biagi! Joe Beltrami!"

"Eilish Angiolini! Lou Macari! Paolo Nutini!"

As he watched them go, it crossed his mind to ask the duo if they'd be willing to create one more film re-enactment together in Colonia. Re-sink the *Titanic* in an Italian version of *A Night To Remember*, maybe. *Una Notte da Ricordare.*

It sounded better in Italian. They could film it properly. No basic cinema rules would be breached, no lines crossed. There must be some part of the Serchio deep enough. The Botti twins liked fishing - perhaps they had a boat.

With a little carpentry, some ice cubes, clever camera work, it was surely possible.

From nowhere, a malignant joke popped up, the notion of another film project, as menacing as an iceberg. What about re-shooting *Brief Encounter?* A modernised version.

A couple seated in a railway station cafeteria, each married to someone else. They're absorbed in their mobile phones, scrolling through online dating profiles. Each briefly alights on a photo of the other - and in that very instant they both dismiss the possibility of mutual romance with a flick of a finger.

No dialogue for him to write. A practical drawback, though, in that the nearest railway station, Castel di Colonia-Mologno, had only a bare platform - no cafe. So no new *Brief Encounter.*

He allowed himself a smile. Hugh Antonio Moscardini would not be revisiting past Glasgow failures, toying with illicit thrills, or mourning a doomed love.

He was going to be a parent, so he'd no longer have the time for such fiddle-faddle - plus his life now featured the only woman he wanted, with no room in it for another. Unless of course Gabriella were to deliver them a daughter.

He imagined himself in a home surrounded by women, all telling him what to do, pointing out his failings. He no longer needed to try and be funny. As a husband and a father, life would make him the punchline to its joke.

He felt good. He had been an old newspaperman. Now he was a new old papà.

He'd earned a living asking questions, expressing doubts. There was no longer any need. Now he understood. Why keep asking "Why?" when "Because" is always the answer.

Other titles available from Into Books...

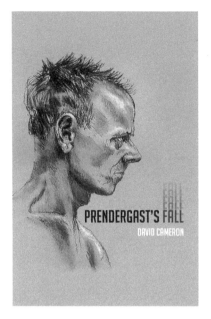

Prendergast's Fall by David Cameron

This is the story of a fall. It won't take a minute.

Businessman, son, husband, lover, father, Martin Prendergast stands high up on an office ledge. He falls – perhaps physically, perhaps only mentally as yet. As he falls, he sees from various surreally appearing vantage points (such as a cliff, a slippery pole, a ceiling) scenes from his life unfolding in reverse order, a chronology reported in a minority of near-death experiences (to quote his mother, 'he always did do everything arse-over-elbow')

The Girl, The Crow, The Writer And The Fighter by George Paterson

May Morgenstern has started a book she cannot afford to put down.

From the pre and post-war streets of bohemian Paris to the cool azure skies above the Mediterranean, 'The Girl, The Crow, The Writer and The Fighter' takes the reader on a visceral, labyrinthine trip with a notorious sexual anarchist, the most dangerous man on the planet and a young woman who finds herself drawn into their complex world of murder, carnality and duplicity.

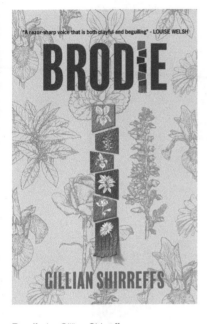

Brodie by Gillian Shirreffs

A 30-year journey of love, loss, and the perils of being an object in a human world.

Brodie is the irresistible story of six women whose lives intertwine over three decades, told by Brodie, the beloved object that connects them all.

On a spring day in 1988, Sandra Galbraith runs her long, curious fingers over a bookshelf tightly packed with the titles of her favourite writer, Muriel Spark. She's on a quest...

Westerwick by George Paterson

Magic is afoot...

When the country's most wanted man inexplicably hands himself into the police, decades after absconding from the state mental institute, a young, but damaged lawyer is called back from his recuperation to interview him. As Thomas Leven is drawn into the complex, preternatural mind of Westerwick born serial killer Angus John MacMillan, what appeared a perfunctory task quickly proves to be anything but.

Available at
www.intocreative.co.uk/shop
and all good bookshops

Photo: AJ Nugent

David Belcher lives in Glasgow and used to be 'in the papers'.

His writing has appeared in everything from the *Sunday Post* to *Marxism Today*, the *Glasgow Herald* to the *Dundee Evening Telegraph*, *Architects' Journal* to the *New Musical Express*, the *Radio Times* to the *Irish Weekly News*.

Over the last 30 years, he has DJ'd in assorted Glasgow clubs and bars that no longer exist. More regularly, he ran the monthly suburban vintage vinyl club nights Soul Bowl and Thank Funk It's Friday.